# Introduction to the Main Characters

**Serafina Jordan** is affectionately called "Sera" by her friends and family. A sensitive Sagittarius, she loves hard and because she loves so hard she falls even harder when that love is betrayed or taken away. Loyal and passionate, she longs to find a man who is capable of loving her with the same intensity in which she's willing to give her own heart...

**Ayzha Darwin**, Serafina's best friend, is trapped in a stale marriage. At the age of twenty she married Riley Darwin, a man fifteen years older. Eight years into her marriage, the novelty of having a younger wife has worn off and Riley has placed her back on the shelf like an old bowling ball that he dusts off and throws down the lane every once in a while. Starved for affection and thirsty for romance, it's just a matter of time before another man breaks down her defenses and feeds her exactly what she's been craving...

**Khalil Roberts** is an aspiring musician and music producer. The son of a famous Jazz saxophonist, Khalil has spent the bulk of his life taking advantage of the carnal perks his privileged lifestyle has afforded him. Hard partying and fast women were the norm until a serious discrepancy in his past caused him to look deep inside of himself and figure out what type of man he wanted to be. Spiritual, poetic, and sensitive, Khalil is the ideal man now because he's chosen to learn from the mistakes he made way back when...

**Dr. Jeremy Sanders** is a player his father can be proud of. However, instead of playing sports, Jeremy plays women and he always scores big. Love is not an option, not even when Sera, his girlfriend of two years walks out of his life, leaving him to ponder whether or not he's been thinking with the right head. Jeremy's thoughts will take you on a journey that reveals that no man is born a dog, but he can be trained to chase multiple cats...

"Ebony Farashuu's writing style adds a poetic flair to an intriguing storyline that will have you hooked from beginning to end."

**-Bestselling Author, Travis Hunter**

"The poetic soul of newcomer Ebony Farashuu shines through in Slow Burn. This passionate tale of love and betrayal reads like that of no other. You will want to have these characters over for Sunday dinner, because they feel like friends. I look forward to more to come from this refreshing new voice."

**- Gena L. Garrison, Author of 'Baring It All'**

"The characters of Slow Burn are people we recognize because they are us.... everyday people who are looking/searching for real love in a world where love is used to control and manipulate."

**- S.K. Poole, Avid Reader**

"I feel that Serafina sings the song of my life. This book represents real life, and real love."

- **Maya Azucena, National Performing Artist**

"So hot and so steamy. Slow Burn changed how I look at men and relationships."

**- Holly Lane, Founder of Zebra Lane**

"Slow Burn is the hottest book that I've read all year. The intriguing characters, twisted plot, and explosive ending allowed me to relate to each character. This is a must read!!!"

**- Carla Roberts, Marketing Manager**

"This book was absolutely fantastic. I HIGHLY recommend it to anyone looking for a good read about life, love, and relationships."

**- Kesha Mixon, Dentist**

# SLOW BURN

by Ebony Farashuu

Kobalt Books LLC
St. Louis / Philadelphia

Cover Design by Rob Viper
Book Edited by Sharia Kharif
Cover Photography by Cedric Mixon
Cover Models – Maya Azucena and LuQuantumLeap

Library of Congress Control Number: 2007923500


For information:
Kobalt Books
P.O. Box 1062,
Bala Cynwyd, PA 19004
Printed in the U.S.A
www.kobaltbooks.com


Published by Kobalt Books L.L.C.
An original publication of Kobalt Books L.L.C.

# DEDICATION

Mama Ruth: We didn't think you could handle my poetry...until you reminded us that you'd birthed 12 children and could probably teach us a few things! We miss and love you tremendously!

Daniel Webster Nash: Uncle Dan, remember the name game we used to play? Whenever I say or write my full name, I think of you and I smile! I know that you and Mama Ruth are waiting for us in heaven.

Spud, I'm so glad we got to say 'I love you' before you were taken from us. I think of you often.

# Slow Burn

I'm contemplating the theory of fornicating
Anticipating your touch, it's just too much
For my mind to discern
This slow burn...

Creeping, seeping never retreating as it travels up my calf
Rests briefly on my knee and continues it's ascent until it's
resting between my thighs
And I never imagined it could be like this.

You haven't even touched me and already
I feel those hurt me good tingles, the pain in my gut that mingles
With the memory of the last time and I sense it again
That... slow... burn...
That sensual churn
That ohhhh where did you learn
To do that?

It's more than sexual, It's borderline intellectual
As the heat rests in my core but still takes time to explore
My complex mind as my emotions pantomime
I'm boxed in.

My eyes are locked into yours
You've rocked me to my molten lava core
And I can do noting but sigh as it envelopes me.

I can do nothing but comply
As you beckon me
To step into the fire
Of my deepest desires
And embrace
This... Slow... Burn.

# Chapter 1

## Ayzha Nicole Darwin

I loved him too hard. Mind...body...soul...heart...lungs...I exhaled with every breath he took. I'm choking on that love...that hard, unyielding love...that blood in my tears kind of love. The kind of love that slowly eats away at you, until there is nothing left but a rotting carcass with a fist-sized stone where a beating heart once lived. Love is for fools; and I'm a fool in love with the way things used to be. I'm in love with the way he used to hold my hand for no reason other than to bring my palm to his nose and inhale the cherry almond scent of my Jergen's lotion. I'm in love with the way he used to speak to me...passionately, loudly, intimately, softly. He used to call my name, in such a way that I'd have gladly sold my soul if it meant witnessing my name birthed from between his lips and cradled in my ears just one more time.

I'm so in love with the way things used to be that my heart refuses to let go of the lingering hope that he could possibly love me that way again. He no longer calls my name. He speaks in monotones. No excitement, no passion, no anger or dismay...just emotionless, inaudible, monotones.

It was slowly killing me and as I sat in that chair, at that table, in that club, surrounded by heart palpitating bass and cigarette smoke I wanted to break a beer bottle on the table and slit my wrists, rather than listen to Stacie share yet another "Trevor sent me flowers," "Trevor took me to lunch," or "Trevor made wild love to me today" story.

But, sit there I did. I stared at my girlfriend over the rim of my third margarita, and managed what I hoped was a convincing smile before taking a small sip of the drink. I licked salt from my lips and sighed softly, recalling how, eight years earlier, my mother, rest her soul, had warned me about Riley. I was too young for marriage. I was too young for Riley. I was making a mistake. But I was twenty and thought I knew everything. Although Riley was fifteen years older than I, he related to me better than any man my age. So I told myself that Mama just didn't want to see me happy. Mama didn't understand. Mama wanted to control my life. Mama, rest her soul, was using Riley's age against him. Now, eight years, five miscarriages, three secretaries, and two psychiatrists later, I see that Mama was right.

"Where is Sera?" Stacie inquired about our best friend.

I managed to pull my thoughts from the past and focus on my present.

"Sera didn't feel like dancing tonight."

"Is she still depressed about Jeremy?"

"She just needed some time alone," I said between sips of my drink. "Anyway, I saw Jeremy when I walked in. So, it's just as well Sera stayed away tonight. You know how smooth he is."

"Excuse me ladies," a tall waitress with a skirt slit up to her neck interrupted our conversation and motioned toward the table behind ours.

"The gentleman at the next table would like to know what you're drinking."

I slowly turned my head and immediately recognized the easy smile of Tyree Mitchell. He was a bit overdressed for the club in his shiny black suit and even shinier shoes, but there was something about him that intrigued me.

"Damn, Ayzha, he's staring over here like he knows you," Stacie noticed.

"He doesn't know me." I turned away from Tyree's stare and rolled my eyes. "Anyway, he's looking at you, not me."

"No. He's definitely looking at you. Who is he?"

"He works with Aleesha."

"Your cousin?"

"Um hmmm," I mumbled absently.

"Do you want the drinks?" I'd honestly forgotten the waitress was standing there, until she asked.

"I'll have an apple martini and she'll have another margarita," Stacie answered before I had a chance to refuse.

"Stacie," I hissed, "that's not right. I don't need to be accepting drinks from that man."

"Why not?"

"I'm married."

Stacie chuckled softly and took a long satisfying drag of her cigarette. She slowly exhaled, and the smoke oozed from her mouth, creating a cancerous halo around her head.

"So what if you're married. There is nothing wrong with getting a little attention from another man, especially when you're not getting it at home."

"I do get it at home," I said a little too eagerly.

Stacie laughed loudly, "Why are you lying to my face, Ayzha?"

"I'm not lying."

"Girl, please." She took another puff of her cigarette and looked me square in the eye. "Not with all that dust falling from beneath your skirt every time you take a step. You need someone to polish up that coochie and make you feel like a woman again."

"You're nasty."

"But my coochie is well oiled and dust free."

"Bitch! Bitch! Bitch!" the left side of my brain screamed. "True! True! True!" the right side responded. I couldn't deny the rush I felt when I glanced at Tyree. His gaze was intent, forceful, unnerving and yet it excited me in a way that made me feel as if the small gold crucifix I wore around my neck was burning a brand into my chest. I told myself to breathe in, breathe out, look away, but his eyes called out to me, forcing me to look at him. The waitress placed a drink in front of me. As I sipped, I could feel the alcohol coursing through my veins, filling my head with a light, airy feeling. Tyree approached our table then, pulling out the chair beside me and straddling it. I couldn't stop the sweet smile that took over my lips.

"Thanks for the drink," I said, unable to tear my eyes away from his.

"Anytime, lady." He smiled.

Eyes as black as toxic smoke met my gaze. I appreciated the smooth darkness of his skin, the whiteness of his smile, his thin yet muscular build and manicured hands, the cut of his suit, the tongue that seductively licked his lips whenever our eyes connected. I was normally attracted to bald men, but there was something about his low cut Caesar that made me wonder how many cardboard cans of Royal Crown grease it took to make it that shiny.

Stacie coughed loudly.

"I'm sorry. It's Tyree, right?" I asked, as if I didn't already know.

"Yes. I'm Tyree," he answered.

"Tyree, this is Stacie."

"Nice to meet you, Tyree. Thanks for the drink." Stacie gently shook his hand and then winked at me.

To my dismay, Stacie grabbed her drink and excused herself from our table, leaving us alone.

"Why did you do that?" He asked.

"Do what?"

"Give her that 'please don't go' look."

"I didn't."

"You're afraid of me." Tyree caressed the back of my hand with his fingertips. The sudden contact sent a jolt of electricity through my body and I snatched my hand away from his challenge.

"Don't do that."

"Don't do what?" He questioned, "Don't touch you?"

"I don't like being touched."

"Then you haven't been touched by the right man."

A hundred thoughts ran through my tipsy mind but not one of those thoughts included my husband, Riley. Those margaritas were definitely in my blood because my imagination was beginning to take my body places that no sober, married woman would ever venture. I closed my eyes and bobbed my head as Tweet's voice filled the room. I needed to dance. Without a word to Tyree, I headed for the dance floor, and I didn't walk, I sort of glided out to the middle of the floor and started dancing amongst the other couples. My eyes were closed so I didn't actually see Tyree when he began dancing in front of me but I definitely felt his presence. Eyes still closed, I turned my back to him, swaying my hips provocatively, slowly winding my hands over my head as if I were belly dancing in a room filled with luxurious silk curtains and he was my sheik, admiring, lusting, wanting to touch but not daring to disturb my vibe.

I didn't jump when his hands encircled my waist. Tyree pulled me close. His chest practically melted into my back. I mentally reminded myself to thank Stacie for forcing me to wear this backless, black shirt and I thanked my mother for the long dark legs that flowed sexily from the short black skirt I was wearing. I opened my eyes and smiled.

Tyree's hands had left my waist and were now slowly sliding from my shoulders to my elbows to my hands, which he held as if he never wanted to let go. What could I have possibly been thinking when I wrapped his arms around me and squeezed tightly? Our hands were still connected so it was as if I was hugging myself too. This contact brought our bodies even closer and I could feel how much he wanted me, not only because there was something discreetly poking me in the back, but because I could feel the racing of his heart through his shirt.

"You look so sexy."

Tyree's mouth was so close to my ear that I half expected him to lick, kiss or bite it. He did neither until a slow song began to play. Tyree effortlessly twirled me around to face him, pulling me close. I slid an arm around his neck as one of his hands returned to my waist. Our left hands unconsciously found each other, and I sighed softly when our fingers intertwined.

This had to be the most natural feeling in the world, his body next to mine, his nose in my hair, his fingers gently playing with mine. Once again, I closed my eyes and let the music transport me to another place in time. The others in the room vanished as Tyree and I swayed together so slowly we may have actually been standing still on the dance floor.

"Open your eyes," he commanded.

I obeyed and found myself staring into eyes so deep I knew that every tangled emotion in my tortured body was being studied and memorized. I couldn't look away, didn't want to look away from him, didn't dare look away for fear that he'd disappear and leave me standing in the middle of the floor dancing alone. Once again, the song changed and we ended up standing together, staring at each other until one of us realized that it wasn't appropriate for us to be slow dancing to a club mix.

Realization coupled with guilt and instigated by desire forced me to pull myself out of the pool of vulnerability I was drowning in and breathe.

"I have to go," I walked away quickly, not bothering to see if he followed.

The front door seemed miles away as I manipulated my way through the crowd. There was no sign of Stacie, but I did happen to see Max Jordan, Sera's brother, staring disapprovingly at me. I felt guilty enough without having it confirmed by a third party, so I made a quick left and walked as far away from Max's gaze as I could. I had just reached the door, when Tyree blocked my path.

"Were you going to say goodbye?" He asked.

"Goodbye, Tyree. Thanks for the drink and the…dance," I said crisply.

"Let me walk you to your car."

"No."

"It's not safe."

"I'm a big girl," I told him.

"I would feel better if you didn't walk alone."

"Fine, whatever," I grumbled. I tried to sound indifferent, but in reality, hadn't exactly been looking forward to walking alone in the dark.

Tyree opened the door and a blast of cold air caused goose bumps to overrun my skin. We started to walk a little slower than I would have liked but at least I wasn't alone.

"You didn't wear a coat?" He asked.

"It's in the car."

"That's a good place for it," he chuckled.

"I know. That's what I get for trying to be cute."

"Trying?" He asked with an eyebrow raised.

I should have remained silent. I should have told Tyree goodnight and walked the rest of the way alone. I should have done these things but I didn't. I continued talking to him, telling him things about myself that he had no business knowing, that I had no business sharing. It was unusually cold outside yet we stood next to my car talking for about twenty minutes. I at least had the notion to put on my coat, but Tyree was still standing there in his suit.

"Well, Tyree, thanks for seeing me to my car. That was very gallant of you." I turned to open my car door but he grabbed me in a lingering hug. He didn't want me to leave. I didn't want to leave. We stood holding one another, until I gently pulled away.

"Aren't you cold?" I inquired.

"Kinda."

"Are you going to go to your car?"

"Not yet. I'm enjoying you." He flashed that smile at me again and my knees trembled.

"But I have to go."

"No you don't."

"Tyree, I have a husband at home."

"Then why are you standing here with me?"

My demeanor changed. I was suddenly defensive, arms folded across my chest, legs slightly apart, chin a little higher.

"Good question." I snatched my car door open, almost hitting my head in my haste to sit down in the driver's seat.

"Leaving so soon?"

I tried to close the door but his body was again in the way. Heat rushed to my cheeks. Anger and frustration threatened to take over my voice box and send piercing screams reverberating throughout the parking lot.

"You're angry." He observed.

"Tyree, move out of the way."

"That's right, Ayzha. Direct your anger toward me. That way you don't have to feel guilty for feeling the way you do."

"You don't know a damn thing about the way I feel!" I found myself face to face with Tyree again. Our faces were close enough to feel each other's warm breath battling the cold air.

"You are beautiful…and you're still here."

I backed away as far as I could. "You stay away from me."

"I can't. When I see something I want, I go after it with everything in me."

"My husband…"

"Your husband doesn't know you the way that I want to." Tyree leaned in and placed a gentle kiss on my cheek. "But I'll let you go home and pretend that everything is ok. I wouldn't want to stand between you and your denial."

"You don't know anything about my marriage."

"Baby, I know that if you were so eager to get back to your husband, you'd already be gone."

He left me there alone to contemplate what had just happened, why it had happened, and whether or not I was willing to let it happen again. The answers terrified me. I got into my car and turned the key in the ignition, dreading the ride home.

## Chapter 2

### <u>Serafina Danielle Jordan</u>

He once slid between my sheets smelling like cigarette smoke, vodka, and the wrong perfume. It wasn't enough that he'd missed dinner with my family again. He'd taken it five steps further by giving my time to another woman and then stumbling into my bed at an insane hour with her kisses still on his breath.

It changed me. It wasn't the first time he'd done it. It wasn't even the second or third time, and only God knew how many times he'd have done it again had that particular moment not changed me. Some view it as a positive change because he's no longer in my life, and although I never want to be the weak woman I was when I was with him...I sometimes dislike the resentful, distrustful woman I've become without him. I used to be such a sweet person. So sweet, that when I fell asleep after a long day, honey oozed from my mouth and covered my pillow instead of the pungent slobber that stained the sheets of ordinary women.

Ordinary. It's something I never wanted to be but somehow, with Jeremy, I was just another woman letting myself be played by a man who'd never even said 'I love you'. I was ordinary. I was naïve. I was ignorant. I was silly. I was, for lack of a better word, stupid. It's funny, cuz growing up, 'stupid', was a cuss word in our house. If I ever ran into the house screaming that someone had said the 's' word...my parents would have to figure out if the offender had said 'stupid' or 'shit'.

I almost chuckled at the memory. On at least three separate occasions, I'd been forced to pick out my own switch for calling my big brother, Maximus, the dreaded 's' word.

*"I don't have any stupid kids,"* my mother would say sternly.

I wonder if she'd still believe that if she knew the insane amount of bull I'd put up with before finally deciding to leave Jeremy alone. I closed my eyes momentarily, thankful for the most recent red light and leaned back in my seat as I waited for it to change. I wasn't worried about not being able to see it. I was pretty sure the people behind me would honk if I didn't move fast enough when it went back to green.

"Why aren't you smiling?"

I slowly opened my eyes and as I turned my head to the left I saw, out of the corner of my eye, a strange woman standing next to my driver's side window. Her sudden appearance startled me and I sat upright in my seat. She made a sudden move, as if she wanted to caress my face and I hurriedly raised the window before her grimy hands could touch me.

"I'm sorry, I don't have any money," I apologized as the window went up, shutting her out of my personal space.

She didn't leave, simply leaned her nasty self against my car and put her face so close to my window that I could see her breath gathering on the glass. I stared at her. I mean really *stared* at her trying to figure out why she was still standing there.

"Why aren't you smiling?" She asked again.

Why wasn't I smiling? Why wasn't I reveling in the dignity I'd stolen back from Jeremy when he wasn't looking? I wasn't lonely. I'd already gotten over the hurt and wasn't sad. I was just a little bitter and my bitterness wouldn't allow me to smile, especially not at the request of this tacky stranger. Just looking at her made my stomach hurt.

Her lips were huge and painted fire engine red, lined with a deep black pencil. Her face, caked with make-up, would put Bozo to shame. Her stained red dress was a little too snug for her overly voluptuous figure. She'd probably been beautiful once, but her age and questionable lifestyle had obviously helped speed up the hands of time. She leaned in even closer to my window and I cringed as she began drumming her raggedy red nails on the glass.

"Smile," she mouthed, drawing an invisible smile in the air with her pointer fingers. "I have something that you need."

"Please go away!" I mouthed back, slowly, so that she could grasp what I was saying.

I pointed to the other side of the street, but she just smiled at me with the most perfectly beautiful teeth I'd ever seen. I was stunned and momentarily speechless, as I marveled at the sight of such beauty amongst the rest of her grime. I almost smiled back, but because smiles often invited unwanted conversation, I chose to focus my attention on the stoplights.

She tapped softly. I turned up the volume on my stereo. She tapped louder. My speakers vibrated as I turned the stereo up another notch. She knocked. I sang along with James Blunt. As the words to "You're Beautiful" surrounded me, I desperately tried to cover my visitor's voice with my own.

"*You're beautiful,*" I sang

"Why aren't you smiling?"

"*You're beautiful,*" I sang louder.

"Why aren't you smiling?"

"*You're beautiful. It's true.*" My hands gripped the steering wheel so intensely that I began to tremble. My voice faltered, "*I saw your face in a crowded place and I don't know--*"

"Why aren't you smiling?"

"GO AWAY!" I screamed. I let go of the wheel and angrily

slammed both palms against the window.

She was gone.

I stared at my hands, not used to the violence her presence had instigated. It scared me because for a split second, I'd wished the window were open so that I could ram my fist down her throat and shred her vocal cords with my fingernails.

"What the hell is wrong with me?" I mumbled, nervously looking around for a glimpse of the strange woman. It was as if she'd evaporated. I almost questioned whether she'd actually been there, but the handprint on my window proved that she had.

The car behind me honked and I placed my hands back on the wheel, but couldn't take my foot off of the brake. Multiple horns sounded behind me as the light went from green to yellow then back to red. The car behind me swung out and passed me, running the red light.

"What the hell is wrong with you?" I heard the driver yell as he passed me.

"I'm the only one allowed to ask myself that question," I almost yelled back.

My cell phone rang, and in my haste to answer it, I accidentally dropped it between the passenger seat and middle console.

"Damn."

I reached over to dig it out and bumped my head on the gearshift.

"Shit!"

I rose up quickly, rubbing my forehead and making a mental note to add another dollar to my cuss jar. I cussed too damn much... another bad habit I'd picked up after my breakup with Jeremy.

"Make that two dollars," I mumbled.

The sound of multiple car horns suddenly filled the air...again. I was about to put my car into drive when I heard a small knock on my window. After my encounter with the strange woman, I was almost afraid to turn around, but when my peripheral vision focused, I couldn't keep myself from licking my lips to give them a little shine.

"Are you okay?"

He wore a black bandanna over his hair and the striking contrast against his deep caramel coated skin was hotter than the sunlight burning me through my windshield. He stared as if he expected some sort of response, but I couldn't seem to find my voice. He motioned for me to roll down my window, and like a good little girl, I nodded and did as told. I leaned back as this sexy piece of man reached into my car and turned on my hazard lights. He smelled like fresh sweat and jojoba oil. He withdrew his arm, and I wanted to grab it and pull him into my lap. He had dreadlocks and the moment I caught a glimpse one of those sandy locks snaking over his shoulder I had a sudden urge to go prostrate and praise his very existence.

"You're hurt." He reached out to touch me, and I winced slightly as his fingertips made contact with the small lump that had begun to form on my forehead.

"Oh…that. It's nothing," I said, finally able to speak. "I hit my head on the gearshift."

He gave me a puzzled look.

"There was this woman and she disappeared and then my cell phone rang and I was trying to answer it and--" I stopped myself before I ended up sounding crazy or stupid, "I'm ok." I managed what I hoped was a convincing smile.

"Are you sure?"

"Yeah." I waved him away with an absent flick of the hand. "I'm cool."

"Maybe you should pull into that parking lot." He jerked his head towards the Super Wal-Mart and as he did so, his beautiful locks bounced against his back. My eyes drank in the sight of him. He was tall and his muscular shoulders had no business being covered by the short sleeves of his black t-shirt.

"Uh-uh." I shook my head slowly, trying to release myself from the trance I'd fallen into the moment we'd made eye contact.

"Uh-uh?"

"I don't know you." Common sense gradually began to dismantle the damage caused by my carnal senses.

"I don't know you either, but I stopped to check on you."

"So?"

"So…I could have gotten run over but my concern for your well being pushed all thoughts for my own safety to the back of my mind. I risked my life for you. The least you could do is pull over into that crowded parking lot and talk to me." His logic was insane but he smiled as he spoke and ten thousand rainbows began with my eyes and ended on his lips.

"Okay," I heard myself say.

I watched this man walk back to his vintage black mustang, and point towards the parking lot as if I'd somehow forget where it was. I led the way, while my pot of gold followed close behind.

"This is crazy," I thought as I watched him park and get out of his car. "He's fine but he could be crazy. He could be a rapist or something. What if he has rope, duct tape, and knives in his trunk and he's just waiting for the opportunity to run into a woman stupid enough to let those hazel eyes overwhelm her?" As I had this little chat with myself, I tried to sneak a peek at myself in the mirror without looking too obvious. That lump on my forehead was starting to make me feel like The Elephant Man's love child.

I watched my rescuer walk toward me, and appreciated the way those black nylon shorts clung to his muscular thighs. There was no use trying not to imagine what kind of equipment he was packing between those muscles because my mind and eyes had already been there at least twice.

"He could be *cray-zeeee*." I sang softly to myself.

I left my motor running just in case I needed to run him over.

"Are you going to get out?" He asked me. I shook my head no. "Are you at least going to turn the motor off?"

"That's a negative."

"I'm not going to hurt you."

"How could I possibly know that?"

"Because I left all of my weapons in my car."

He squatted down beside my door until we were eye level. I stared and he laughed a deep throaty laugh that left me fighting the urge to laugh too. I could hear in the near distance somebody's child getting a good old-fashioned butt whooping. The sounds of footsteps and baskets seemed to pause as everyone tried to figure out where the racket was coming from.

"She's probably spanking that poor child for what he just did, what he did yesterday and what he'll probably do tomorrow," he chuckled as if remembering a similar beating he'd gotten in the past.

I laughed despite myself, "Don't ask for nothin', don't touch nothin', you ain't gettin' nothin'!"

"Oh, you know the *black mama golden rules?*"

"Oh, I am a *product* of the *black mama golden rules*! I'm a grown woman and sometimes, when I see that cheese in the can…I have flashbacks." I shivered mockingly.

"My mama refused to buy that for me too," he smiled.

"Did you buy some when you grew up?"

"It's disgusting," we agreed in unison.

We both cracked up, but my laughter stopped when he reached out to touch my forehead again. My body froze, as his fingers pushed my hair out of my face.

"Are you sure you're okay?"

"I told you, I'm fine." I shrugged self-consciously. "I look a mess."

"I don't know," he chuckled. "I think it's kinda sexy. It gives you that 'I'm cute but I ain't scared to fight a man' kind of look."

I laughed again.

"You have a nice laugh." He finger combed my bangs down

over the knot and smiled again.

I felt a small sense of loss when he stopped touching me and I placed my fingers where his had been.

"So, why are we here?" My voice softened. The hostility I wanted to hustle up just couldn't seem to get with the program.

"I don't know if I should tell you. You might think I'm crazy."

"Try me."

"Turn off your car."

"Why?"

"Just do it."

He stood up and backed away from my car door. I gave him a skeptical look but turned off the ignition, then stepped out of the car. I leaned against my door and stared at him. He kept his distance, and for that I was thankful.

"Okay, hero, tell me."

He took a deep breath, looked me square in the eyes and said, "God, told me I'd meet the love of my life today."

"And that concerns me because?"

"Because the moment I touched that knot on your forehead I knew you were the one."

Without a word, I got back into the car and started the ignition. I knew this fool was crazy.

"I'm not kidding," he yelled over the roar of my engine as I started to back out.

"You're crazy," I yelled back.

"Why did you pull over?"

I stopped, halfway in and out of my parking space. "I don't know," I said more to myself than to him. I put the car into park. "I don't know."

"Is this something that you would normally do?"

"No."

"Me neither." He told me.

I believed him. It was odd. I believed him and I barely knew him. I believed a stranger when I wouldn't normally believe anything that came out of a man's mouth. Maybe *I* was the crazy one. I didn't believe Jeremy when he told me he was sorry, but was actually listening to a strange man who'd just told me that God had told him to pull me over.

"When I saw you I knew that you were the one I've been waiting for." He cautiously approached the car. "You believe me. I can see it in your eyes. You don't want to but you do."

"Dude, you just told me that God spoke to you."

"You believe me."

"Yes, but I still think you're *cray-zeeee*," I sang.

"I'm crazy about this knotty headed woman I've just met."

"Okay, now you're gon' stop ragging on my forehead." I laughed.

His smile was so damn sexy, so calming, I could feel all of the frustration leaving my body. My phone rang again, and I ignored it.

"You're not married." It was a statement, rather than a question. Still, I shook my head. "Boyfriend?" I shook my head again. "Girlfriend?" He raised an eyebrow. I smiled and shook my head vigorously. "Crazy father with a shotgun?" He had me laughing again. "Will you take my number?" Before I could answer he'd already whipped a pen out of his pocket and scribbled his number on a scrap of paper. He then reached into the car, grabbed my hand, placed the paper in my palm and closed my fingers around it.

"You'd better not follow me home," I warned.

"I'm a good guy. Give me a chance." He said earnestly.

"Yeah, ok." I said, still unnerved at the effect this stranger had on me.

My hands shook, as he leaned into my window and placed a gentle kiss on my forehead. Then, without another word, he pulled away and walked back to his car. He waved as he drove away but the shock of his lips on my skin prevented me from waving back. I pulled out of the parking lot and got back onto the highway. I was halfway home when it dawned on me that I didn't even know the man's name. I looked down at the number I'd been clutching. Who was I supposed to ask for? God's homeboy?

I threw the number out of the window and stared straight ahead, gripping the steering wheel angrily. Tears of frustration stung my eyes as the shame and embarrassment over my own naiveté taunted me.

"Stupid," I sighed softly. "You almost fell for it."

I was alone in my car, not expecting anyone to answer…but in the back of my mind I thought I heard a small voice ask, "Why aren't you smiling?"

## Chapter 3

### <u>Ayzha Nicole Darwin</u>

I waited for him; fidgeted at the front door like an eager puppy anticipating her master's arrival, begging for a pat on the head or scratch behind the ear, begging for some small sign of acceptance. I'm not sure how I'd expected this night to progress. Had I expected Riley to hug me? To kiss me? To tell me that I was beautiful?

"You're blocking my path," he said dully, trying to maneuver his briefcase around my body as I stood in the doorway.

I took a few small steps backwards, leaving room for him to enter, but still stood there, waiting for him to respond to me. He didn't. He simply stared. He stared at me as if he were trying to figure out who I was and what the hell I was doing in his home. An awkward moment passed, before Riley gently pushed past me, placing his briefcase on the floor before walking into the guest bathroom. The door closed behind him with a gentleness so forced, it felt like the loudest of slams in my heart.

I slowly walked towards the bathroom and pressed my cheek against the door. Eyes closed, a soft sigh escaped my glossy lips as I heard the usual sounds a man makes in the bathroom. He was urinating loudly into the toilet and for a moment, I allowed myself the pleasure of a smile. There was a time, in the beginning, when he used to let me hold it for him. Somehow, I'd never manage to aim it right and he'd end up peeing all over the back of the toilet.

*"You'd be dangerous if you had one of your own," he used to laugh.*

*"I do have one of my own," I'd always reply, giving him a gentle shake. "It's just attached to you."*

The sound of the toilet flushing jolted me back to reality. I was listening to my husband pee from outside the bathroom door. Riley obviously didn't need me to hold his dick anymore.

Hope. It was all I had and in the spirit of misguided hope, I went into the kitchen and fixed him a plate fit for a king. Baked chicken, roasted red potatoes, fresh green beans, home made rolls, I'd prepared all of Riley's favorite foods. He used to tell me that I'd captured his heart with my cooking. . I seated myself at the dining room table, admiring the way the soft silk of my pale pink gown reflected the illuminating glow of the many scented candles scattered about the room. Hope kept me seated there, when it was obvious that he wasn't going to join me. Hope allowed me to ignore the ringing of his cell phone and the way he answered cheerfully when he usually let my calls go to voicemail. Hope was slowly killing me.

"Don't wait up. I need to make a run." Riley stood in the doorway ignoring the romantic scene spread before him.

"But, I made dinner," I said quietly.

"Yeah, smells good. Just put my plate in the fridge. I'll take it for lunch tomorrow."

He left. I sat. His car revved in the driveway. My heartbeat skidded to a painful stop. I stood then, slowly, deliberately, as if any sudden move would shatter the calmness of my demeanor. I walked around the room, blowing out candles and telling myself it didn't matter. I calmly cleaned up my mess, tossing the meal, plates, bowls, forks, glasses, everything into the garbage. The bottle of Moet, however, I spared the meal's fate, instead, cradling it like a baby as I carried it upstairs to our bedroom. I cleared the bed of rose petals in one exaggerated sweep of my free arm and sat on the edge, one fragile petal in one hand and the bottle of Champaign in the other.

A tear slid down my cheek but to wipe it away would have forced me to acknowledge the moment I gave into my weaknesses and allowed myself to cry over the emptiness I felt whenever Riley left me alone to do whatever it is he does when he leaves the house at night. I popped the cork and took several long unsatisfying swigs. The liquid coursed through my body, masking the pain, and replacing my cold frigidness with warm tingles. I laughed as tear number thirty-seven slid down my face, staining my gown. "He loves me not," I giggled as a lone petal slid from my hand and fluttered to the floor. "Happy anniversary, Ayzha."

## Chapter 4

### <u>Khalil Jamal Roberts</u>

I remember the moment I stopped chasing ass and started pursuing dreams that surpassed my previous identity as a spoiled rich kid with deep pockets and an endless supply of pussy.

*"Who the hell are you?" My father had suddenly asked after witnessing me walk yet another one night stand to a waiting cab in the wee hours of the morning.*

*His question had caught me off guard, and I'd paused a moment, knowing that a wrong answer would lead to the thing I feared most...my father's disappointment.*

*"I'm your son," I'd answered while trying to discreetly wipe from my cheek the lipstick of another nameless stranger. She'd missed my mouth as I'd turned my head away from her, no longer interested in her lips, face, or name.*

*"But who are you besides my son?" He'd asked, "Who are you besides the son of Karl Roberts"*

I didn't know. I'd always been Khalil Roberts, the son of the great Karl Roberts, the Sax Man, Saxophonist Extraordinaire, Multi-platinum Artist, selling out crowds while still finding the energy to run his own record label and develop the many properties he owned.

*"Who are you?"* The question haunted me, popped into my mind at the most inopportune times, and cheapened the thrill I used to get from saying the words and seeing what they did for me.

*"I'm Karl Roberts' son."*

*"The musician?"*

*"Yep, the one and only."*

*"Wanna fuck?"*

It was a script I'd followed so many times I didn't even know how to ad-lib. Being the Sax Man's son opened doors and legs that would have otherwise been closed if not for his name.

*"Who are you?"*

I was a man who could get any woman at any time in any place. I was a man who had three false paternity claims filed against him in as many years. I was a man who, two years ago, sat in his father's office, holding the results of an HIV test I'd been so afraid to open that my father had to snatch it from me and yell to me that my results were negative...this time

*"What are you going to do with the rest of your life?"*

He'd asked the question. I'd given the answer.

*"I want to be the man you and Mama raised me to be."*

Mama. Sweet, beautiful, Mama. Gone before her time, a victim of breast cancer. I could trace my whorish ways back to the day she died ten years ago. One of her best friends' daughters had decided to cheer me up in the only way she knew how. *"Sixteen, sad, and sexy,"* she'd whispered into my ear as I pounded my frustrations away. How much easier it had been to screw and screw over rather than love and risk having that love stripped away. Breaking hearts had been easier and far less traumatic than sharing mine.

*"Why did you stop writing? She so loved your words."*

*"Because I wanted to punish her for leaving me."*

*"What? Are you trying to piss her off so bad that she comes storming down from heaven to slap a knot in your ass?"*

If only she could. The absurdity of his words forced me to realize the lunacy of my intentions and the ridiculousness of the lifestyle I'd chosen to live. It was at that moment that I made a vow to never again waste my time, my life, or my seed.

*"Who are you?"*

I am Khalil Roberts, son of Karl and Amanda Roberts, brother to all but lover to none but the words that fill my notebooks and the sheet music that litters my piano on any given day.

I work, overseeing the development of my father's latest venture in our hometown, creating an exclusive community in the warehouse district. I create, writing lyrics and melodies for the artists on my father's label, producing tracks and collaborating behind the scenes with my band, *Interlude.* I abstain, unwilling to create soul ties that unravel the moment I flush the condom down the toilet.

I want to love someone with the same intensity that drives my music. I want to be loved in a way that allows me to just be who I am... Khalil, the man my parents raised me to be.

\*\*\*

"Are you gay?"

Her plum-tinted weave settled around her face in crisp ringlets. I allowed myself to tug gently on one of her curls to see if they felt as stiff as they looked.

"What?" I asked, an amused grin on my face.

"Are...you...gay?" She said the words slowly, as if I were in kindergarten, and I marveled at this woman's audacity, invading my space in V.I.P., then accusing me of being less than a man because I wasn't turned on by her over-stressed availability.

"Well, sistah," I said, leaning back into the plush red sofa, "that depends on what you mean by 'gay'. If you wonder if I'm happy, content with who I am, and loving life to the fullest then yes, I guess you could say that. But, if you're asking if I'm a homosexual then the answer is no."

I didn't need to tell her how far from gay I actually was because I'd always thought that any man who had to prove his manhood had obvious issues with his identity.

She leaned in closer, causing me to sink even deeper into the couch. "Then what's wrong? Don't you find me attractive?"

"You're very pretty but I don't even know your name and you're practically sitting in my lap. What's your name?"

"Ingrid."

"Ingrid, I don't want to waste your time." I gently removed her hand from my thigh before it could make the tell-tale climb to my zipper. "I'm not looking for a companion tonight. I'm working."

"Come on, Khalil...you've gotta play sometime. You can't work all night."

"You know my name." I commented.

"Of course I know your name. You produced that joint for Jasmine...the one they keep playing on the radio. That's a hot track."

And so it starts: lips parting, legs opening, voices expressing rehearsed praise in hopes that I'll take them home and decide to keep them around after I've used everything they've given me based on my credentials. It's a temptation I've learned to resist.

\*\*\*

"Today you will meet the love of your life."

I looked up from my notebook and allowed my eyes to quickly dart around the room, taking note of particular corners and doorways.

"Did you say something, man?" I asked Spencer, one of my band mates as he gathered his sheet music and placed it in his bag.

"No, I didn't say anything."

"Are you sure?"

"Dude, I didn't say anything."

"I could have sworn I heard..." I stopped talking and shrugged it off, "I must be hearing things."

"Man you need to get back on your meds," Spencer laughed. "Speaking of which, what was up with that little hottie pushing up on you last night? One minute she was in your lap and the next minute she was all up in my face, pissed off cuz you wouldn't give her the time of day."

"Who? Ingrid?" I asked as if I didn't already know.

"Yeah, fool, Ingrid."

"Too easy."

"Oh, I forgot. You're saving up all of your nuts for Mrs. Right."

"That's right." I chuckled.

"How long has it been?"

"Two years." I played a few chords on the piano before breaking into a familiar melody.

"Two years?" Spencer grabbed his nuts and doubled over as if he were in excruciating pain. "Nigga, my pipe would have burst by now! I gotta release at least twice daily."

"So did you take Ingrid home with you?" I asked, ignoring his usual routine concerning my celibacy.

"I had to! You broke her heart. I wanted her to understand that all men aren't dogs!"

I cracked up laughing, giving Spencer daps despite myself. It was no longer the life for me but I wasn't about to fault him for taking advantage of whatever was thrown his way.

"You need to stop screwing my rejects and practice that new song. You sounded a little rusty today."

"Touché." Spencer walked past me on his way out of the studio. "I'll see you tomorrow, man. Try to get some ass between now and then. It will lighten your mood."

I threw a small plastic bust of Mozart at his head but it crashed into the door as he hurriedly closed it behind him. I could hear him laughing as he walked down the stairs. I was just about to close the lid on the piano when I heard it again.

"Today you will meet the love of your life."

"Spencer that shit ain't funny!" I turned around but there was no one there.

I was alone in my studio. The voice had to be a figment of my imagination. I hadn't said it, and I knew that my piano hadn't suddenly developed a brain. I paused, deducing the probability of me, being of sound mind, actually hearing an imaginary voice more than once within a span of five minutes.

"Maybe it's God," I mused.

It should have sounded insane, but the moment the words were out of my mouth, they became real to me. Without giving the slightest thought to my destination, I locked up and strolled down to my vintage black Mustang convertible. I didn't know where I was headed but for some odd reason, I knew that whatever path I chose would lead to love.

I found that love in the form of a woman sitting at a green light holding up traffic for no apparent reason. She was breathtaking. Sandy hair pulled back into a tight bun, bangs hiding what looked like a fresh bruise on her forehead, I couldn't help reaching out to touch her satiny skin.

I put the Roberts charm on her, and she skeptically followed me to a Wal-Mart parking lot where I actually got her to smile and laugh the most beautiful laugh I've ever heard. I felt comfortable enough to tell her what had been whispered to me that day. For some reason it never dawned on me that she would believe me to be insane until she actually spoke the words.

"You're crazy!"

"Maybe she's *not* the one," was a thought that entered then left my mind with lightening speed. She *had* to be the one. I'd never felt so... so... determined in my life. I'd felt an instant connection with her. The static between us was so electric that I half expected to see sparks floating around and exploding above our heads.

She felt it too. I could tell because, although she was sitting in her car with the motor running, she was still there...and she wasn't frowning. I didn't know her name but I knew that I loved her. Yes, I said it...Love. Cupid had to have been sitting on top of that Wal-Mart with a bow and an infrared light because I felt the tip of the arrow pierce my heart the moment I touched her.

She was definitely *the one* and if someone were to ask me why or how I came to that conclusion, I wouldn't have had an answer. I just *knew*. I just knew.

## Chapter 5

### <u>Ayzha Nicole Darwin</u>

Thunder is the sound that lightening makes. I saw him leaning towards me smiling his electric smile, and heard his voice telling me all of the things I thought I wanted to hear. The low rumblings made me shiver. His cautious touch sent a jolt of raw energy through my body.

"So, when can I see you again?"

It reminded me of an old Babyface song. I loved the acoustic guitar on that track; and as I sat inside of Tyree's car watching storm clouds slowly descend upon the park where we'd chosen to meet discreetly, that song played over and over in my mind.

I wasn't doing anything wrong. We talked. I didn't touch him, not even when he placed his hand over mine and gave it a gentle squeeze. I didn't squeeze back so I was pretty sure it couldn't be called holding hands.

"You shouldn't be seeing me now," I said glancing over at him.

His dark eyes flashed with amusement and a satisfied smirk eased itself over his face.

"I do believe the lady is still afraid."

"Of you? Whatever." I dismissed his assessment of my emotions with a wave of my hand.

"I want to kiss you." He said it so simply he may as well have been telling me that he liked the color blue.

"What makes you think that I want to kiss you?"

"You're here." Tyree fingered the lace at the hem of my pink skirt.

He had no right to touch my skirt, had no right to squeeze my exposed knee, but I did nothing to stop him, just took a controlled breath and stared at his hand stroking my leg so familiarly.

"I'm leaving," I said evenly.

"Now, you know you're not leaving until I get my kiss."

"Then I guess we'll be stuck here for a very long time."

"Would that be so bad?" Now, he was tracing lazy circles on my bare arm, "Stuck here with me in the middle of a storm?"

I didn't answer. I reached for the door handle. He reached for my hand. I froze.

"I have to get back. I'll be late." I almost sounded as if I were begging.

"I know. The sooner I get my kiss the sooner you can leave."

I took another deep breath, and then another, and then another. Panic was beginning to sink in but I couldn't allow him to see the affect he was having on me. I should never have agreed to this. I knew that it was wrong. What had possessed me to agree to meet up with Tyree in such an intimate, confined space? Words like neglect, disregard, and despair popped into my head. Loneliness, frustration, stupidity... Oh just get it over with.

I leaned in and just as I was about to kiss him, Tyree shook his head and quickly exited the car. Dumbfounded, I watched as he walked around to the passenger side and opened the door for me. His strong hands grabbed mine, pulling me from the confines of his black Lexus. We were standing too close to one another. I couldn't look at him. Sensing my embarrassment, Tyree turned me around, hugged me from behind, and planted the lightest of kisses on the left side of my neck.

"You look beautiful today."

"Don't say that," I whispered.

"Why not? It's the truth." Tyree rested his chin on my shoulder.

I saw a flash of lightening. One Mississippi...two Mississippi...three Mississippi, thunder gently rolled in the distance. A significant amount of tension left my body and I began to relax in his embrace. Wobbly, my knees became. Rapidly, my heart beat. I felt as if I would slide right out of his arms and fold up like a chair after a tent revival.

"You'd better go."

"Yes."

He opened my car door and I quickly got in. My hands were shaking so badly I damn near poked myself in the eye trying to put my shades on. The sun wasn't shining anymore.

"Thanks for lunch." I allowed myself to look at him. I almost hated myself for liking what I saw.

"Anytime, Lady." He replied.

I drove away slowly, gently fingering the sensitive spot on my neck Tyree had chosen to kiss. I dared to close my eyes at the stop sign. I could still feel the gentle pressure of his lips on my skin. Suddenly, my situation was very clear. I had just had lunch, in a park, in a car, with someone who was definitely not the man I'd pledged my life to in a church full of friends and family eight years ago. My skin began to itch and I nervously raked my fingernails up and down my arm.

I had just had lunch with another man and instead of feeling guilty I felt...rejuvenated. I giggled anxiously. My body began to tremble, but the nervous itch was gone, replaced by a tingling sensation I wasn't accustomed to feeling. I spotted his car slowly approaching from behind me, and a smile overtook my mocha-glossed lips. Ohhhhhh....I'm in so much trouble.

## Chapter 6

### <u>Serafina Danielle Jordan</u>

I couldn't stop thinking about him. You know, HIM, the guy who claims to talk to The Almighty. My journal was filled with poetic images of him, and I could still feel that man's luscious lips on my forehead. The knot on my head had healed within days, but the knot forming in my heart seemed to grow larger each day. Twelve days, to be exact. I was literally pining over a man I'd met briefly in a damn parking lot. He was a stranger. A dangerous stranger. A deranged lunatic who heard voices. They had a name for that, and that name was schizophrenia. He was crazy and what else did I really know about him besides that? Okay so he was fine, and he obviously worked out, and I thought I'd heard Marvin Gaye playing in his car as he'd driven away.

He had rough hands. Man hands. The kind of hands that could work the hell out of a piece of lumber or an instrument, or some type of home improvement project, or a woman's body, my body. Lord, his hands had been rough but his touch had been so gentle. I had to shake my head at the memory. This deranged lunatic of a man with the rough yet gentle hands and a possible love of Marvin Gaye had taken over my mind and ruined me for any other man. I could barely function without his voice breaking into my thoughts, or his smile, or that beautiful hair, or those lips…

If this man really was crazy then he wasn't alone because it takes one to know one and I must have been certifiable, letting some stranger manipulate my brain cells like this. Despite these ridiculous feelings, I was once again alone in a candlelit bathroom, slowly disrobing as my shadow danced in the flickering firelight. The scent of peaches, honey, and burnt matches wafted around the room as I surveyed my work. Candles adorned everything from the counters to the commode.

As my panties slid to the floor, I shivered, imagining what it must feel like to be tickled by his dreadlocks. What would it feel like to lay on a goose down comforter and let him drag his hair down my naked back, over my thighs and legs until I trembled? The very thought excited me as I slowly descended into a tub filled with foamy bubbles and water so hot that I couldn't tell the steam from the smoke in the room. My skin felt tight and tingly the moment I settled in and I closed my eyes, savoring the relaxing scents.

Yes Lawd, I had yummy thoughts of caramel skin and full lips weaving in and out of my brain, oozing through my pores, causing me to shiver again, despite the heat of the tub. I saw his face through closed eyelids. He had a name that I didn't really care to know, at least that is what I kept telling myself. "God's homeboy" or "Black Jesus", hallelujah and good lawd! He had me wanting to let him hold praise and worship in my temple.

My fantasies of him were too good to be true which made it easier to lose myself in my imagination. Since he was out of reach and I didn't need a man in my life anyway, I was more than happy to settle for thoughts of him, the jets of my whirlpool bath, and my slender fingers all over and inside of me. Oh what a splendid feeling it would be, if I could just get there without once thinking about the torture that I was putting myself through by allowing his image to fill my mind as I climbed higher and higher, gasping for air because the air is quite thin when you reach the peak but comes rushing back to you as you fall. Fall I did, trembling, sweating, and practically drowning in a tub full of bubbles and my own release. I had, once again, managed to partially satisfy the cravings triggered every time he crossed my mind. I smiled, wondering if he ever thought of me as he showered in the evening after a long workout. Did he ever wish that the soap gliding over his naked body were, instead, my soft fingertips?

My eyes flew open and I returned to reality. Candlelight bathed my body as I pulled my knees to my chest, and hugged my legs tightly.

"You're a friggin' mess." I whispered to myself.

In my fantasy, I'd just been thoroughly loved by God's homeboy. In reality, I was kind of pathetic. I'd just masturbated in a tub full of bubbles, surrounded by candles like some kind of Voodoo goddess. It was stupid for me to think about him and touch myself, but I did it all the time.

"Hell, who needs a man when you have jets in the tub? I told myself. "The jets don't lie, baby. The jets don't lie."

I stood up and reached for my terrycloth robe, but the bathroom door flew open before I could even slide it around my shoulders. I screamed in terror until I realized that it was just Jeremy, the fool who was supposed to have returned the keys to my apartment three weeks ago.

"Have you lost your damn mind?" My voice reached new octaves as I angrily tied my robe while trying to step out of the tub without busting my ass. "What the hell are you doing here?"

"I just came for the rest of my stuff. I didn't mean to scare you." He surveyed the room and slowly walked towards me. "Your robe is getting wet."

I was tempted to hold up my middle finger but opted to just say the words instead.

"Baby, let me help you before you break your neck." He sighed and held out his hand. Out of mere necessity, I grasped it, allowing him to assist me. The wet ends of my robe slapped my legs, and I fought to keep the darn thing from flying open in front of him.

"So where's my stuff?" He asked, looking me up and down with a familiar look in his eyes.

"Don't even," I growled. "I should have put your shit in the dumpster but I was nice enough to put it in a trash bag and keep it in the hall closet for you. And why are you just now coming to get it? I asked you to bring my keys three weeks ago!"

"I was giving you time to change your mind."

"Giving me time to...I know you didn't." I started to laugh and a slow smile spread across his face. I immediately stopped my laughter when I realized that I was amusing him. "Let go of me." I hadn't realized he was still holding my hand until I started to suddenly feel uncomfortable with him.

"Sera, I miss you." He pulled me closer.

"Oh, please."

"Come on, baby doll," he coaxed in the tone that used to have me eating out the palm of his hand.

"Jeremy, just get your shit and get out." I snatched my hand out of his.

"I'll get it after."

"After what?"

"After I try to change your mind." His hands toyed with the sash on my robe. "Come on, Sera, just let me hold you one more time. Let me show you how much you mean to me."

One more time had gotten me in trouble with Jeremy several times in the past. I wasn't about to let myself fall into that trap, no matter how much my body still tingled from my earlier escapades.

"You have got to be the most triflin' man I've ever dealt with," I told him. I pulled my robe tighter against my body and snatched the sash from his hands.

"What the hell?" Jeremy backed away slightly. "What happened to you? What's up with all this cussin' and talking about throwing my shit in the dumpster? When did I become just another sorry ass brotha to you?"

"You've always been just another sorry ass brotha," I said flippantly. "I was just too stupid to know it then."

"Were you always this bitchy?" Jeremy threw his hands up in frustration.

"You made me this way, Jeremy. Get your shit and get the fuck out of my house before I call--!"

He grabbed me and before I could stop him, his hands were inside of my robe and his mouth was on mine, forcing an involuntary reaction from my body that was just too much for my mind to handle.

My head said *no*; but my body, sick of its own touch, was boldly disobeying. I struggled to take control of a situation that had the potential to slam me right back into a place where I knew I no longer wanted to be. This is what he does to me. He hurts me. Then, just when I think I'm over him, he comes over, starts an argument, then kisses me and pushes inside of me until I admit that I can't live without him.

"I don't want this anymore." I pulled away from him and tried to close my robe.

"Yes you do, Sera."

"I don't!" I slapped him, hard across the face. "I don't want you anymore. I've changed and it takes more than a kiss and a screw to make up for what you did to me!"

The look in his eyes caused me to back away from him. He let go of my robe, but didn't stop walking towards me until I was backed into the sink with nowhere to go.

"Get away from me."

I raised my hand to slap him again but he caught it, squeezing just enough to let me know that he was stronger than I was.

"Baby, you'd better be glad I'm not *exactly* like my father." With those words he released me and walked away, leaving me standing alone, shivering and clutching my wet robe around me like a shield.

A few moments later I heard the noisy sound of my key as it clanged against the kitchen table. I walked out of the bathroom just in time to see the front door closing behind him. He didn't look back, and for the first time in two years, I didn't run forward to stop him. I had nothing left for Jeremy Sanders. I wasn't sure if I had anything left for *any* man.

## Chapter 7

### <u>Ayzha Nicole Darwin</u>

Riley didn't even look up from his paperwork when I walked into his study. He didn't have time for poetry readings. Couldn't I see that he was working hard to keep a roof over my head and designer clothes on my back? It was funny. He said it as if I didn't have a job at all. I managed a small boutique in an affluent shopping district but in Riley's eyes it was just a cute little hobby.

"Oh, come on, Riley. It will be just like old times." I placed one hip on the edge of his desk and stared at the top of his head as he worked. His hair was thinning, but he was still just as sexy as he was when we met. I reached out to touch his hair. "If you want I could just stay here with you." I slid into his lap and wrapped my arms around his neck. "Remember when we bought this desk?"

He smiled. "Is that what you want, Ayzha? Do you want me to toss all of my papers on the floor and throw you on top of this desk?" There was something menacing about the way he said it, as if the christening of his desk was something to be ashamed of.

It was an emotion I was learning to live with. Shame.

I bit the inside of my lip and shook my head. "I just want you to love me, Riley. It's all I've ever wanted." I tightened my grip on him, silently praying that he'd please just hold me the way I longed to be held. "When did you stop loving me?" My eyes pleaded with him but he couldn't even meet my gaze.

"You won't even try." The monotone I'd become accustomed to returned to his voice. "You won't even try," he said again. This time he grabbed my hands and forced me to let go of him. "You're selfish and needy, and sometimes I can't stand the sight of you."

"What about the other times?" I asked desperately. He didn't want me to hold him but he hadn't pushed me off of his lap. That had to be a sign that he at least wanted me close to him.

"You won't even try," he repeated.

"I did try!" My voice broke as I fingered my jade necklace, twisting so tightly that I thought it would either break or choke me.

"Taking birth-control pills isn't trying, Ayzha. You don't want to have my baby!"

"How can you say that? After all that I've been through, after all of those miscarriages! I stopped taking my birth control last year. I wanted to surprise you, but you hardly even touch me anymore." I raised myself from my husband's lap and stood next to his chair. "I was pregnant six months ago, Riley."

"You were pregnant and didn't tell me?"

"I didn't want to tell you until I was further along but when I lost that baby just like all the others… I kept it a secret because I didn't want to see that look in your eyes. I didn't want you to look at me the way you're looking at me now."

Once again Riley had managed to shame me with just one look. Once again I begged forgiveness for something I had no power over. This was not what I'd imagined when Riley and I exchanged our vows. He was supposed to love me unconditionally. He was supposed to love me no matter what I could or couldn't do for him. He was supposed to love me as much, if not more than I loved him. He was supposed to comfort, not condemn me for something that broke my heart just as much as it broke his. I should have been able to run to Riley in my time of need but as usual, I found myself wanting to run away from his accusing stare and nonchalant tone.

"Why did you even marry me?"

He didn't answer the question, merely countered with a question of his own, "What did you do after you lost my baby?"

"I went back on the pill."

"So there's really no point to you staying home and trying to seduce me on my desk now, is there?" He looked me up and down before picking up his paperwork and reading as if I weren't even in the room.

"Why did you marry me?" I asked again, knowing full well what he was going to say.

"You were pregnant, remember?"

"Why are you so cruel?"

"Why are you still standing here?" His eyes remained focused on the papers he held in his hands.

"Riley-"

"Ayzha, just go away."

His papers began to tremble and my lip began to quiver, but I'd promised myself never to let him see me cry again. So I contained my tears until I reached my car. There, I allowed myself to breakdown in a way that would have both pleased and annoyed Riley.

Once upon a time, he'd loved me. He had often talked of starting a family with me but our fifteen-year age difference made him uncomfortable, made his family uncomfortable, made my friends and family uncomfortable. When I became pregnant with Riley's child, he proposed without hesitation. My pregnancy gave him a legitimate reason to settle down with me without having to deal with his friends' "cradle robbing" jokes. When I miscarried, I'd been devastated but Riley seemed to take it even harder. The moment the doctor released my body to him,

Riley worked on getting me pregnant again. I failed him again, in my fourth month.

Lighthearted conversations were eventually replaced by strained hellos and goodbyes. Lovemaking lost the passion and morphed into baby-making sessions that eventually disappeared altogether. After the fifth and most devastating miscarriage, I began taking birth control, and my marriage began its final descent into hell. Riley was now forty-three years old and his young wife with the unstable womb had proven to be the worst mistake of his life. I should never have told him about the sixth baby.

Tears blurred my vision, and I hastily wiped my eyes as I drove to the club. My cell phone rang, and when the familiar voice came over the line, my sadness and frustration began to mount.

"Hey, Lady." I could almost see Tyree smiling into the phone. "What are you doing?"

"Nothing." I tried to mask the leftover tears in my voice with soft, inappropriate laughter.

"You okay?"

"Of course."

"Where's your husband?"

"He had work to do," I said simply.

"And you are?"

"On my way to the club."

"So what if I told you to drive past the club and come to my house?" Tyree's voice was tempting.

"Tyree, I can't." I explained for the hundredth time. "When are you going to stop calling me?"

"I don't know, when are you going to stop accepting my calls?" He laughed. "Come on, I haven't seen you in three weeks," he referred to our lone lunch date. I'd felt so guilty over my lack of guilt that I'd been too afraid to see him again. "Maybe I'll come see you perform. Looks like it's the only way I'll ever see you again."

"No."

"No? You sound like you could use a friend."

"I don't need any new friends, Tyree." I forced myself to say the words when all I wanted was a masculine shoulder to lean on.

"That's what your mouth says." His chuckle mocked everything that I believed in.

"Bye, Tyree." I hung up, praying that Tyree wouldn't show up, hoping that he would.

When I got to the club, I bypassed the line and walked straight up to the doorman who smiled and unlocked the velvet rope, allowing me to enter. It's good to be best friend's with the owner's sister, I thought as

I spotted Sera's brother, Max, standing at the bar. Max is a six-foot- four, reddish brown brotha with closely cropped, brown hair with just a hint of natural red tint to it. His presence was massive, all two hundred and fifty pounds of it and I smiled when I caught his eye, which lately, always seemed to be on me.

"Well hello, sexy." Max walked over and hugged me tightly before leading me to our usual V.I.P. table. "Are you going to grace my stage tonight?" Before I could answer, he peered closely at me and asked, "What did he do?"

"Max, it doesn't matter. I don't want to bring that nonsense in here with me. I just want to have a drink, relax, and forget about Riley tonight."

"Yeah, like I saw you forgetting about him a few weeks ago. Who was that clown?"

"Nobody," I said dismissively.

"He's no good for you."

"Max, quit playing big brother," I laughed.

"I'm far from playing big brother with you." Max looked down at me, and I felt my palms begin to sweat. "I care, Ayzha, that's all. I don't like seeing you hurt or taken advantage of."

"I'll be ok. Guess what?"

"What?"

"Your little sister is performing tonight."

I hated to do it; but I had to get Max out of my business, even if it meant selling Sera out to her big brother. True to form, Max's eyes narrowed slightly. I could just imagine the over-protective gears in his mind beginning to spin. If I knew Max Jordan, he was trying to figure out a way to keep any and every man in the club away from his baby sister. As the owner, Max had the authority to throw out any man he saw as a threat to his sister. He'd done it on more than one occasion, much to Sera's chagrin.

"What the hell is he doing here?" Max mumbled.

I followed Max's intent stare and spotted Jeremy Sanders walking through the door of the club. Max excused himself, approaching Jeremy with the quickness and agility of a black panther. I couldn't hear what was said, but from the way Jeremy backed away, I could tell that Max was warning him to keep his distance from Sera. It was more than a shame. I studied the man who'd broken my best friend's heart and shook my head. How could someone that damn fine be so scandalous? Jeremy was so chocolate that a woman could satisfy a PMS craving just by looking at him. Tall, bald, and educated, the man was a resident at one of the best hospitals in town, but he was such a dog that I was surprised his mom didn't have registration papers on him through the American Kennel Club.

Jeremy slowly walked past me, "Hi, Ayzha."

"Jeremy," I said with as much disdain as I could muster.

He kept walking. I sat nursing the drink Max had sent over to my table. I glanced at my watch, hating that Stacie and Sera were late as usual. I turned down numerous offers to dance, but promised at least one slow dance to Max. He was safe. Although I'd often fantasized about him romantically, Max never made a pass at me, choosing to treat me as a sister instead. Pity.

"Who are you thinking about?" Stacie slid into the seat next to mine and I began laughing, explaining that I'd actually been thinking about Max, not Tyree, as she had suspected.

"Aww man, I thought you were going to tell me that you'd kissed Tyree or something naughty," she sighed.

I pushed my troubles to the back of my mind, reminding myself that Stacie was more of a playful instigator than the type of friend who helped you analyze your problems.

"Nope. Sorry to disappoint you," I told her. "I haven't seen him."

"But you still talk to him," she prodded.

I shrugged.

"You might as well see him."

"Stacie stop it. You know I can't."

"Well hell, at least kiss him and then tell me how it is. Trevor is out of town and I need to live vicariously through someone."

This chick never ceased to amaze me. Instead of telling me how wrong it was for me to even speak to Tyree, Stacie was actually encouraging me to commit adultery with him. I shook my head in annoyance. She was my girl, but sometimes I wanted to choke her. I held up my left hand, showing her my wedding ring.

"And where is Mr. Darwin tonight? Working?"

"Fuck you, Stacie," I snarled.

"See, there's your problem right there," Stacie snarled back.

"Stacie what is wrong with you? Why are you trying to get me to cheat on my husband? You're supposed to be telling me to chill out."

"Because Riley doesn't deserve you, and I'm sick of the way he breaks you down. You need to be swept off of your feet. Plus, Tyree is cute as hell and he looks like he has a big--"

"There's Sera," I interrupted before she could even finish that statement. The last thing I needed to be thinking about was what Tyree was packing between his legs.

Sera looked breathtaking, as usual, but like always, didn't seem aware of it. I marveled at her beautiful skin. It glowed as if she'd just bathed in a tub of sunshine. She seemed a little down, so I decided to try to lighten her mood.

"Aww…look at her, Stacie," I said sweetly. "Little Sera is still thinking about Mr. Wal-Mart."

"Alas, I am," she said dramatically. "I'll probably never see him again." Her demeanor changed. "Not that I want to. He's probably crazy and I've had my fill of crazy."

"What if you did see him?" I asked. "What if he walked over to this table right now."

"I'd kiss those pretty lips." Sera completely forgot that she'd had her fill of crazy. She said it so sensually that I suspected she'd already kissed him a zillion times in her dreams. I knew Sera well enough to know that she wasn't a spur of the moment kind of chick. This stranger had really made an impression on her.

"Lawd! Speaking of pretty lips…" Stacie discreetly pointed toward the door, and we all watched as Tyree slowly walked towards our table.

My breath caught in my throat. I lost all mental capacity, when he stood before me staring so intently that I couldn't look away, even if I wanted to. Had I prayed for him to go away? Or had I prayed for him to come? I couldn't remember.

"Hello, Ladies." He spoke to all of us, but never took his eyes off of me.

Sera and Stacie looked him up and down. Stacie gave me an indiscreet thumbs-up, while Sera just smiled. Her eyes were reserved, sizing Tyree up and scanning his guts for the slightest trace of unworthiness. I looked at her. She shook her head vigorously, warning me away, but it was too late. Tyree had already taken the empty seat next to mine. He slid his hand in mine underneath the table and held it tightly, as if he were daring me to pull away. The gesture was effortless, but the sensation was almost too much, as his thumb gently massaged my palm. I was just about to give in to the urge to lean into Tyree, when Max showed up at our table.

"The poetry is about to start," he said crisply, focusing all of his attention on me. Like a naughty child, I reluctantly let go of Tyree's hand and stood up, following Max and Sera as they made their way backstage.

"What are you doing?" Max grabbed my arm and pulled me aside.

"What?" I asked innocently.

"Ayzha you're playing a very dangerous game, and you need to be careful."

"I'm not doing anything with him."

"Yet," Max stressed.  "You forget that I was a bit of a womanizer in my day, Ayzha. You've got that look in your eyes, baby. You're unhappy at home.  You feel neglected, and this man is all up in your face like "Captain save a Ho", telling you any and everything to get you to spread your legs for him."

"Max, be quiet."

"Me shutting up won't change the truth."

"Tyree is different," I insisted.

"Ayzha, let me enlighten you for just a moment." Max leaned in close.  "There is only one thing a single man wants from a married woman. Live it. Learn it. Believe it. Lord knows I've had my share."

He walked away, as I silently seethed.  I could feel the blood rising to the top of my head  I glanced over at our table and saw Tyree and Stacie staring in my direction.  Stacie shrugged her shoulders as if to ask what Max and I had talked about.  I rolled my eyes and shook my head.  Tyree smiled.  That was all I needed.  I wanted desperately to believe that Tyree was different, that he was just a new friend trying to help me through a difficult time.

I wasn't about to let Max and Sera's uppity attitudes ruin my temporary high.  Max introduced me, and I walked out to the center of the stage as if it belonged to me, surveying the crowd briefly before reciting the first poem that came to mind.

*We toasted with red wine*
*Now our legs are intertwined*
*Causing friction*
*A direct contradiction*
*To the way this evening was supposed to end.*
*But once I tasted your kiss*
*I couldn't resist*
*Wrapping my legs around your waist and pulling you*
*Into my abyss.*
*Sheer bliss*
*As we stumble*
*Tumble*
*Onto a bed of roses*
*As the moonlight exposes*
*Naked flesh*
*Frolicking in the land of the forbidden.*
*Your serpent*
*Finds the end of my rainbow*
*Causing*

*Friction*
*Causing*
*Heat*
*Causing*
*Fire.*

The room erupted with applause as I finished, and I smiled, nodding my appreciation to the crowd before exiting the stage. A hard body brushed against mine, as I watched Sera perform. I didn't have to turn around to know that Tyree was standing behind me.

"I want to be alone with you," he whispered, his mouth dangerously close to my ear.

"I can't."

"Yes you can. I just want to talk. Come sit in the car with me for a minute," he coaxed.

I thought about the last time I'd sat in his car, and shook my head 'no', even though every fiber within me was screaming 'yes'.

"You sounded good up there." He placed his hands on my shoulders and began to gently massage them.

I was too lost in his touch to answer; when he gently nudged me forward, I led him to the front door as if I'd never told him no. We walked past our table and Stacie smirked as she watched me leaving the club with Tyree. The parking lot was noisy and crowded, the overflow that didn't make it into the club mingled as they waited in line. There was activity all around us but I didn't worry about being seen. I wasn't doing anything bad and if I were, Tyree's windows were heavily tinted. We sat in his car, not touching, not speaking, just sitting. All of my stage bravado left me as I sat there, afraid to even look at him. It wasn't too late to leave. It was merely a matter of opening the door, getting out, and going home, but lust kept me glued to my seat.

"Ayzha."

He called out to me and I turned towards him. His lips brushed mine, lightly, lingeringly, promising something wonderful. I wanted to punch him. I wanted to run. I wanted more.

"Don't do that."

"What? This?"

He placed his fingers beneath my chin and kissed me so brazenly it left me tongue-tied. I was unprepared and afraid of what he was doing to me. I was afraid to stop him. I was afraid to let him continue. I was terrified of the desire building up in my loins. I finally harnessed enough strength to pull away from him. Tyree leaned back in his seat with a satisfied grin on his face.

"Mad?" He asked as if he actually cared.

"Yes," I answered weakly. "Tyree we can't do this. I can't do this. We have to stop before this goes any further than it already has."

"We both know that we're not going to stop. So why are you wasting your breath talking about it, Ayzha? If you didn't want to be here...you wouldn't be here."

He slid his hand behind my head, making it impossible for me to pull away from him again. This kiss was longer, stronger, and more passionate than I could ever remember being kissed. I slid my arms around his neck and savored the sensation of a man's lips pressed against mine for longer than two seconds of faked affection.

"This is so wrong," I whispered.

"Then tell me to stop."

"Stop," I said weakly, not really wanting to, but knowing that I was supposed to be putting up some type of moral fight.

He stopped, staring at me so intently I had to look away. I could hear Max's voice in the back of my mind telling me there's only one thing Tyree could possibly want from me. Still, Tyree made me feel as if I were the most important woman in his life. Part of me suspected he was probably playing me like a game of spades, but in the back of my mind I wondered...could it be? Could he be? It sounded so good. It felt so good. He was telling me things I no longer heard at home. The more Tyree told me, the less I desired to hear those words from my husband. Common sense told me that Tyree was using my situation against me. He knew my struggle. He knew how unhappy I was. He was using my problems with Riley as a means to get closer to me.

I was letting him get away with it. Why was I letting him get way with it? Why did the sound of his voice thrill me so? Why did I ask him to stop kissing me and now, five minutes later, he was kissing me again and I wasn't even trying to fight it? I want him, no matter what his motives are because right now, I just need for someone to notice that I'm a desirable woman who deserves to be cuddled and made to feel loved. I needed to feel a man's arms around me. I needed to hear sweet nothings and impossible promises whispered into my ear. I needed to feel at home somewhere because my home was no longer where my heart was.

## Chapter 8

### <u>Serafina Danielle Jordan</u>

I approached the microphone with the caution of a child crossing the street alone for the very first time. I looked to the left and right, all the while taking baby-steps because I was truly afraid of what lay ahead. The smoke filled room was dimly lit, but I could still see their eyes. Even with my own eyes closed I could see them staring at me. Fear and apprehension made me want to run from the stage. Terror kept me rooted to the floor, unable to move. A spotlight hit me with the intensity of halogen headlights on a Mack truck, and I stood trembling like a deer in the middle of the road.

The room grew quiet as I stood there. It was too quiet. The eyes were beginning to grow impatient and a low murmur began to envelop the room. To hell with this. I took a step backwards in an attempt to leave the stage, but a sudden gravitational pull took control of my body and pulled me forward. My head turned slightly to the left and I knew, before I laid eyes on him, that he was standing there.

I saw nothing but his eyes, his face, his long locks sitting on his shoulders, and I focused on him, feeling a little braver when he flashed me an encouraging smile. My icy fear melted under his gaze, leaving in its place a boldness that caused me to suddenly grab the microphone stand. I caressed it the way I'd caressed him in my dreams. Lovingly, teasingly, I slid my fingers up and down the metal shaft, pulling the microphone close enough to taste.

I began to speak. My voice was soft and soothing, yet strong enough to carry the heavy words that were falling from my mocha-lined lips. I could hear it. I could feel it. I felt it so much that I decided to recite a special poem.

> *"If I penetrate your lips with my tongue*
> *Do you suppose I'd make you cum…*
> *…Pletely lose your mind as my*
> *Fingers travel up and down your thighs*
> *Would your soldier rise and salute me?*
> *Your commander in chief*
> *Between these here sheets?*
> *Allow this scenario to enter your mind*
> *For one moment forget about the bump and the grind*
> *And instead*
> *Concentrate on the sweet sticky taste*
> *Of my lips on your lips*

*No, the ones between my hips*
*And then the ones on my face*
*So that I can also partake*
*In that soul sistah flava that you love to saver.*
*Make haste my brother*
*This is your only chance you may not get another*
*Opportunity to experience the vision*
*That I've so cleverly positioned*
*In that prison that you call your mind*
*Unwind...with me*
*Let me take you to the top*
*Or better yet*
*Let me climb up there*
*And sit on the tip*
*Until anticipation has you thrusting your hips*
*Trying to burrow deeper into that warm place*
*That I simply refer to as heaven on earth inside of me*
*Inside of me*
*Inside of me*
*Oh don't you wanna be inside of me?*
*Is it vivid yet?*
*That picture I've painted for you*
*The canvas is still wet*
*Better make your move before it dries*
*And I disappear like the moon on the verge of sunrise.*

I stroked the microphone stand the entire time, never once losing eye contact with him, as I recited words that sounded so much better actually flowing from my lips than they did just staring back at me from a flat sheet of paper. Out of the corner of my eye, I could see the open mouthed stares of the men in the audience. They had listened to my words with the wide-eyed enthusiasm of little boys who'd just seen their first pair of naked breasts.

I smiled happily, as the room burst forth with applause. Shouts of "Go on sistah," and "Hell yeah", could be heard all around the room as they asked for more. I took a little bow and got the hell off of the stage, shocked at myself for reciting that poem. There were people, mostly men, clamoring to meet me as I left the stage, but I couldn't stop moving. I was on a mission. I had to find him.

"Hey!" A firm hand gripped my arm and I looked up in surprise.

"What the hell was that?" Obviously, my big brother wasn't at all happy with my performance. I looked around nervously, trying to catch a glimpse of my mystery man, but my brother's voice in my ear was threatening to ruin my exhilarated mood.

"Not now, Max."

"Yes, now!" He practically dragged me to his office and slammed the door behind him. "How could you get up in front of all of those people and talk so dirty?"

"I wasn't talking dirty!"

"Do you know how many men had the gall to tell me what they wanted to do with you?" Oh, he was really mad.

"They probably didn't know that I was your sister." I suppressed a giggle, not daring to laugh in the face of the big brother who'd been my champion for as long as I could remember. "Max, in case you haven't noticed, I'm a grown woman." I slowly twirled in front of him.

"Are you drunk?"

"Are you?"

"Sera!"

"Max, I'm a grown ass woman. You can't censor me."

"I can keep your grown ass off my stage. This is my club and you are my sister. I won't have you up there again. I know what goes through a man's mind when he hears a beautiful woman recite a poem the way you did tonight."

"You think I look beautiful?"

He looked me in the eye and sighed softly, "Sera, I just don't want you to get hurt. What if one of those fools followed you home or something?"

"What if you stopped treating me like a five year old?" I kissed his cheek and gave him a big hug. "I love you, but you tend to overreact."

"Was I overreacting when I warned you about Jeremy? Ever since you two broke up you have been a totally different woman."

"Well did you like it better when I was with Jeremy?" I asked angrily.

"You know that I didn't."

"Then what do you want from me?"

"I want my little sister back!" He put his hands on my shoulders and shook me gently.

"She's gone, Max, and I don't want her to ever come back."

I walked out of his office, leaving him calling after me. Slightly dejected, I left the club, not even bothering to cover my head when a gentle rain began to fall. I slowly made my way to my car, not noticing the black Mustang parked next to me, until I heard footsteps behind me.

"Did you write that for me?"

I smiled as his voice caressed my ears. I didn't have to turn around to know who spoke, but I wanted to see his face again. He stood about ten feet away from me, holding a large black umbrella. I walked toward him and he met me halfway, shielding me from the rain. Neither of us spoke. Somehow, words were not really needed. His unforgettable smell filled my nostrils and swirled around my head. Not even a summer rain could have penetrated the warmth that filled my body the moment I laid eyes on him. The conversation with my brother immediately vanished from my mind.

"So... have you had anymore conversations with God?"

He chuckled softly, "You thought I was crazy."

"I still do."

"Do you?"

I looked over at him and nodded with a smile on my face. "Cray-zeeee," I whispered.

"Is that why you didn't call?" He asked me.

"Well, that's one reason."

"And the other?"

"I didn't know your name."

"Anything else?"

"I hate men," I told him. "I mean I really hate men."

He looked down at me with a curious smile on his face.

"I thought you said you didn't have a girlfriend."

"I don't." I punched him playfully on the arm.

"So you hate me?"

"Yep." I stared up at him.

"How much do you hate me?"

"I hate you so much that I spend all of my time thinking about you." It was the truth.

"Then I hate you too, Serafina," he said softly. The sound of my name on his lips sent delicious chills throughout my body. "What does it mean?"

"What does what mean?" I couldn't stop staring into his eyes.

"Your name." He stared right back into mine.

I moved a little closer to him. He slid his free arm around my shoulders and for the first time in a long time I felt safe.

"Burning passion."

"It suits you." He reached out to touch me, and I didn't discourage him. His fingertips grazed my forehead, sliding a wet strand of hair away from my skin. "I see your head is better."

"Shut-up."

His kiss was unexpected, but a part of me knew that it was coming, wanted it to come. He pulled me closer and I wanted to sink into the folds of his shirt. I wanted to savor the taste of his lips, now covered in my lipstick, now smeared from his kiss. He took my breath away and gave me room to breathe at the same time.

"Hey," I whispered between kisses, "Homeboy of God."

He started laughing into my mouth. I tried to compose myself but couldn't help laughing too.

"Homeboy of God?"

"Well, I don't know your name. It's either call you 'that lunatic' or 'God's homeboy'." The rain had stopped, leaving the air thick with humidity.

"It's hot," he whispered.

"Yes."

He held out his hand. "Hi, I'm Khalil."

"Khalil," I said, liking the way it rolled off of my tongue. "Nice to meet you, Khalil."

"Would you like to go for a drive?"

"Are you going to kidnap me?"

"Yes."

It was exactly what I wanted to hear.

He walked me to his car and I didn't look back, as he helped me climb into the passenger side. The leather seat molded to my thighs as if I'd always been there. Khalil let the top down and the hot July air caressed my exposed flesh, leaving me moist wherever I was touched. I must have looked a mess. My hair was sticking out in numerous places, a victim of the wind and humidity as I rode shotgun in his Mustang.

The heat just wouldn't allow me to sit in a ladylike fashion as Khalil and I got better acquainted. Instead, my sundress was hiked up to my thighs, legs open as I tried to take advantage of the air conditioner that I'd turned on when Khalil wasn't looking. A blast of cold air traveled up my legs, and I leaned back in my seat with my eyes closed. I'd started to sweat in my secret place and the dampness mixed with the ice-cold air sent shivers throughout my overheated body.

The car slowed to a stop and I kept my eyes closed as the top descended over our heads, blocking out the bright orange moon that had trailed us on our outing. The music changed as Khalil pushed the random button on his stereo and the sounds of R. Kelly filled the tiny space. The cool air began to circulate throughout the car, and I shifted lazily in my seat as the breeze soothed me. His hand on my knee demanded my attention. His expression made me feel sexy, and I couldn't help smiling when his tongue spoke the words reflected in his eyes. He slid his hand further up my leg, letting it rest at the top of my thigh. I tried not to notice how my dress had bunched around my hips.

"I look a mess," I commented self-consciously despite his earlier compliments.

"You look sexy." His hand left my thigh and smoothed the humidity stricken hair away from my face. "You're the most beautiful woman I've ever seen," he whispered between kisses. "I don't think you could ever look a mess to me."

I looked around. We were parked in front of an old warehouse. I looked over at him questioningly.

"No, I am not going to take you in there and dismember you," he laughed. "I live here. My father owns this place. He's renovating it. In about six months, the first three floors will be six condos. We already have buyers for at least three of them."

"And what about the three top floors."

"Those are mine."

"All of it?"

"Yep. Wanna see?"

"Yes."

Neither of us made a move to leave the car. We were rooted in place. The song stopped and I asked him to play it again. It was a nice, slow tune that spoke of the greatest sex ever experienced. The bass felt as if it were pumping through my heart. Khalil kissed me again and I pulled away the moment his lips touched mine. Something was different.

"I love you," I heard him say. The admission seemed to shock him more than it shocked me, and I put my finger to his lips.

"Khalil, don't say that," I whispered into the darkness. "Don't ever say that."

I didn't need those words. All I needed was his body close to mine. I didn't want him to pretend or say things that he might later regret.

"You must hear this," he told me. "I know it sounds crazy to you. Hell, it sounds crazy to me too, but I've loved you from the moment I laid eyes on you." He cupped my face in his hands and said the words again. I'd heard the same words from many men, but there was something about that moment, that instant that made me want to run for my life. I'd spent too much time hardening my heart to allow a stranger to just walk in and take a sledgehammer to my emotional walls.

"I would never hurt you. I mean that, Serafina."

"I don't want you to love me."

"I love you," he said again. "Even if I never see you again, even if you tell me to take you back to your car right now. I know that I will see you again. This was meant to be."

"Take me back to my car right now."

"Ok." He put the car into gear, and I put my hand over his.

"Don't." With my hand still over his, he shifted back into park. "Khalil, you're driving me--"

"Crazy?" He finished for me. "Girl, how do you think I feel? I don't even know you, but I can't get you off of my mind. I'm not asking you to love me. I'm just asking you to believe in me. Believe in me until I give you a reason not to. Whoever did this to you…whoever hurt you so bad that you've decided that it's easier to just hate men…I'm not that man."

"That's the problem. I do believe in you." I whispered into the darkness.

"Look at me," Khalil gently demanded. He put his hand under my chin and turned my face towards his. "I want you. I'm not going to lie and say that I don't, but this has to feel right to both of us."

He could have been a pied piper the way that his voice drew me in, pulling my face close to his until our lips were barely touching. He played that song again, the one about the good sex, then proceeded to feast upon my mouth like a ravenous lion, biting, sucking, and licking, as if he never wanted to stop tasting me. A deep chill overtook my body, as he caressed my knee with his fingertips, slowly creeping up my thigh like a naughty spider. He held his hand between my thighs. His fingers lingered so close that I could feel them just enough to want their journey to resume. The locks holding my legs closed mysteriously disappeared as an unblocked pathway opened for him to continue in the direction in which he'd been headed. He pushed the straps of my sundress past my shoulders, replacing them with kisses that threatened to set my delicate skin on fire. He unclasped my strapless bra, exposing my breasts, and my hands instinctively rose to cover them.

"Khalil, someone might see," I exclaimed, shock and arousal dripping from my voice. I hurriedly looked around, trying to make sure that there were no peeping toms lingering around the building. We seemed to be the only people there.

Khalil silenced my weak protests with a deep kiss, swallowed my moans as his fingers caressed my moist center through my panties. His mouth was on mine, while his left hand wreaked havoc on the clitoris that I thought was just a myth. His right hand fondled my breasts, caressing until my nipples hardened to the point of cracking.

"Let me know when you want me to stop," he teased. His hand slid inside of my panties, and I gasped in pleasure as his fingers slid in and out, making erotic circles deep inside of me.

I didn't answer. I couldn't answer, not with the hot liquid feeling that was causing my insides to pulse and swell around his fingers. My eyes opened wide in surprise, for I'd never felt anything so painfully exquisite in my life. Scalding passion spilled forth from places that I never knew existed, drenching my underwear and bathing his hand in my sexual perfume. His mouth muffled my screams as a plethora of orgasmic spasms racked my body. Tears coursed down my cheeks. Khalil was taking my body places I never knew I was capable of going.

He put his mouth close to my ear and told me that it could be so much better, and I watched in fascination as he licked the fingers that had just been inside of me. He offered his lips and I accepted, for the first time, tasting the sweet sticky essence that was mine and I was neither ashamed nor disgusted. I was hungry for more.

"Khalil," I whispered, wanting nothing more than to have him touch me again.

He shook his head, "upstairs."

"Oh hell no," I said boldly, "here."

I slid my hand down his torso and unbuckled his belt. He stared at me intently; as I slid my hand inside of his jeans and claimed what I knew belonged to only me. I stroked him as if he were a kitten, and his purr made me feel powerful. Just ten minutes earlier I'd been prudishly covering my breasts, afraid that someone would happen along while Khalil and I were engaged in our risky foreplay. Now, I was straddling him, as he slid his seat back as far as it would go. I didn't care about anything but feeling him, loving him the way that I'd dreamt for so long.

He was fully exposed, and I could feel his hardness poking at me through my wet panties. I started to grind against him, not wanting to let go of the tingling sensation that seemed to be controlling my every move. Khalil slid his hand between my legs and pulled at my panties until I felt and heard the wet material being ripped away from my damp skin. There were no physical barriers between us and it would only take a slight move on his or my part to connect us, yet, he held me tightly in place, not allowing me to move an inch.

I struggled against him, trying to sink onto him, but Khalil just chuckled and kept his grip on my hips, teasing me with his tip until I begged for release. He let go and I slid my body over his, taking all of him in one swift motion. The car's dark interior filled with the sounds of carnal pleasure. Any passerby could glance at the steady rocking and figure out exactly what was going on beyond the tinted windows; but we were oblivious to that fact. I was only aware of him inside of me, touching me, kissing me, stroking me in ways that I had never been stroked before. He grabbed my hips, propelling me towards him so hard and fast that I felt as if my pelvis would shatter from the intensity of his thrusts. I was in pain. It was a sensual aching, the confusing pain of being suspended somewhere between sweet torture and ecstasy. The anticipation was on the verge of unbearable until I suddenly wrapped my arms around his bucket seat, holding on for stability as I slid over into the realm of rapture, crying out from the sheer joy of it.

He called my name over and over as he trembled beneath me,

and I buried his head between my breasts as he filled my body with his sticky essence. We stayed that way for a while, still connected, breathing heavily, each holding on as if letting go would somehow spoil the moment.

"I could live inside of you forever," Khalil whispered. He gently nuzzled my neck, and I laughed giddily.

"I can't believe I just did that." I probably should have been ashamed, or at least embarrassed but I couldn't even fake it. I was more surprised than anything. "We just met."

"Yeah, but technically, we've been on each other's minds for at least three weeks," he rationalized. "That has to count for something."

"Nice try," I mumbled, burying my face in his neck and inhaling his cologne. "I'm not normally this easy."

"I know," he replied softly.

"There's something about you." I sighed contentedly.

He kissed me and I smiled against his lips.

"Can I ask you a question?" I asked suddenly." I probably should have asked this before I left the club with you."

"What's that?" he asked.

"What's your last name?"

\*\*\*

I was basking in the afterglow of an exquisite lovemaking session. Khalil had stroked and kissed parts of my body that, once neglected, were now singing a song of praise. My thighs whispered words to my mind that made my cheeks flush with pleasure, thanking him for awakening feelings I'd long since given up on ever experiencing. My lips had been kissed so thoroughly they tingled with a hunger that can only be described as primal, meaning first, meaning he was the only man to make my body scream louder than my voice. I felt absolutely poetic.

Sitting up on one elbow, I watched as he walked naked across the room and flung open the curtains. The moon cloaked his marvelous body in fantastic rays of iridescent light that made him practically glow. The dark sky presented a spectacular view of twinkling stars. I wondered what he was thinking as he stood there. The air conditioning system kicked on, invading the silence with a dull hum that threatened to lull me back to sleep.

My eyes slowly closed. My body totally relaxed. My mind slipped in and out of reality as sleep overcame me. I heard music somewhere in the distance, soft piano playing, then singing, sweet melodious sounds that brought tears to my eyes. I felt as if I was bobbing in and out of a dream, drowning in the river of love that was Khalil. I wanted to sink to the bottom of his depths, to drink of him, be cleansed from him, lose myself inside of him.

He was calling my name or was he singing my name? I slowly opened my eyes. The curtains were closed. A single candle illuminated the room; and for the first time, I noticed a baby grand piano in the middle of his large bedroom. Had that been there when we'd stumbled in last night? I'd been so wrapped up in him that I hadn't noticed anything but the king-sized bed. The song he sang was a song filled with love. Every now and then, he would stop playing and start scribbling on a notepad, and then the singing and playing would resume.

The room smelled of peaches, jasmine, lovemaking and his cologne mingling with my perfume. It was the sweetest smell in the world. My eyes, once blinded by undeserving love were now open wide. I could see his love. My ears heard sounds beyond the piano, beyond his voice, beyond the constant whir of his central air system, beyond the rustling of the slippery satin sheets as I wrapped them around my naked body.

"*He is yours. Love him. Support him. Claim him as he has claimed you,*" a voice whispered into my right ear. Yet there was no one by my side. "*He is yours.*" The voice sounded familiar, but I couldn't place who it belonged to. I didn't know or understand half of the things going on in my life, but somehow I knew that I could trust that voice. I knew that I could trust Khalil.

"He is mine," I repeated in my mind. Satin sheets rustled again, as I slid out of bed and walked towards the piano. "You are mine, Khalil Roberts," I announced, straddling the piano bench. He lifted his hand from the piano, silencing the keys.

"If I am yours, then claim me as I have claimed you." He slowly turned to face me, but I could no longer focus on his face. His words, they were the same words whispered into my ear only moments earlier. I shivered. This was all too damn freaky. How could he possibly know what was in my mind?

"You're trembling," he observed.

"I'm overwhelmed."

"You're overwhelmed?"

"I'm scared."

"Of me?"

"Of everything. Of you, myself, my feelings…"

"I'm scared too."

"Why are you scared?"

"Because I've fallen in love with--"

"A stranger," I finished for him. "I feel things…familiar things. Things that tell me I'm in love, and I have this conflict inside of me."

"You feel it too?"

"I don't want to feel it," I whispered.

"But you do."

"I do." I admitted. "This is deranged. We just met but I truly feel like we know each other somehow."

"But how?" He was staring intently, and I stared back. His hand slid over mine.

"When I saw you that day, I knew that you were the one. I felt it in my heart. I felt it in my soul. I thought about you all the time and told all of my friends about you."

"Did they think you were as silly as my friends did?" I asked.

"They had words far worse than 'silly' for me." He answered with a smile. "I didn't care what they said, Serafina. I refused to give up on you. When I saw you on that stage, looking more beautiful than I remembered, I damn near lost my mind. I felt like we were soul mates. I know that sounds corny but I don't know any other way to describe it. It was like there was an angel on my shoulder telling me that what I've been looking for was within my reach. I had to grab you before the moment disappeared."

His grasp on my hand tightened, and my heart fluttered under his intense gaze. Things were too perfect, too damn romantic. This was the part of the book where I usually slammed the pages shut and flung it across the room because that kind of junk never happened to real people. I was petrified.

"What are you thinking?" he asked me.

"I feel like we should have been together all along. I think I loved you before we met. I mean, not exactly you but the thought of someone like you...the promise of you. Now you're here and I'm so afraid that I'll open my eyes and find out that this is just a dream."

Khalil gently placed his hand on my cheek and I closed my eyes as involuntary tears began to form. He told me to open my eyes but I couldn't. If I opened my closed lids, a river of salt water would run down my cheeks and flood his piano.

"Serafina, you are the song in my heart. I want to try to see where this thing leads us," he whispered. "Why fight destiny?"

He spoke to me so poetically but it wasn't an act. He was sincere and his sincerity made me want to damn the world and follow wherever he led me.

"You really are real." I opened my eyes and Khalil kissed my tears away before they even had a chance to fall.

"Yes," he said softly, "and so are you. So was last night, and so was three weeks ago when you threw my number out of the window." I smiled. Khalil spoke to me as if he were reading my mind. "Baby, how will we know how this will turn out, if we don't give it a chance? Woman,

I love you, and as crazy as it sounds…I've been waiting for you since the day I was born."

"You make it sound so easy," I murmured.

"It can be as easy as we make it."

"What will people think?"

"Do you love me?" He asked. "Do you feel as sick in the stomach as I do?"

"Yes," I answered with no hesitation.

"Then to hell with what anyone else thinks." He inched his face closer to mine, "Be mine, Serafina. Be my woman, my lover, my friend, my sister, my everything, just be mine."

"Tell me that you love me again." I needed to hear it again. I wanted to hear it a million times because each time he said it my heart would jump and I loved the way that his words were making me feel. I felt special. I felt loved. I'd heard the words before but I'd never felt them penetrating my soul the way they were at that moment.

"I love you," Khalil restated, kissing me in a manner that reiterated the seriousness of his words. He said it over and over again. He kissed me over and over again. And I, not totally knowing if I was in my right mind, decided to ignore my bitter mind and instead listen to the heart that told me that it was okay to dive into Khalil with no fear of drowning.

## Chapter 9

### <u>Khalil Jamal Roberts</u>

*"Who are you?"*

I'm a man in love, and I know that this is not happenstance. This isn't just some random emotion fueled by my imagination or the celibacy I sentenced myself to so long ago. Everything happened so fast, yet the pace felt so slow. It was as if each stroke, each kiss, each caress held years of vital information that passed between us through the miracle of osmosis. I know her as I've never known another. I love her in a way I never imagined possible. I love her so much that I want to write a letter of complaint to the makers of my thesaurus because their synonyms for love just don't adequately describe the euphoria I feel.

*"Who am I?"*

I'm Khalil Roberts and the woman sleeping so soundly beside me is the truth I've been seeking. She is the answer to the questions plaguing my soul. She is my heart.

\*\*\*

A sliver of sunlight invaded my bedroom and I blinked a few times in an attempt to get my eyes accustomed to the darkness of the room. I wondered what time it was, at least recognizing that the sun had finally relieved the moon of its' duties. Serafina stirred and I hugged her closer to me. I buried my face in her neck and snuggled as close as I could without melting into her. Inhaling Serafina's scent was like breathing in the essence of life and I didn't want to let go of the blissful sensation of having her wrapped in my arms.

Soreness overran my body. Love sore, car sore, bed sore, floor sore, we'd finally fallen asleep underneath my piano. I awoke her with kisses and teasing caresses, speaking poetic words of love that filled my heart and spilled forth from my mouth into her ears. Once again, I told her that she was the song in my heart. To my surprise, she answered with a poem of her own, her sleepy voice filled with passion.

"Khalil, sincere friend, your name stands alone strongly. I love to say your name, to scream your name, to whisper your name pleasures my tongue. If I am the song in your heart then surely you conduct the symphony that plays every time I look at you, every time I say your name. Khalil."

I rewarded her words in trade, and Serafina's symphony played for me alone. Violins serenaded my soul until I thought I'd weep. Later, as I bathed my sweat from her body in a sunken bubble bath, I knew. I just knew…

## Chapter 10

### Serafina Danielle Jordan

It was the first Monday afternoon of the rest of my life, and I sang along with Jill Scott as she crooned about the effects her man's love had on her.

"I feel ya, Jill. I feel ya!" I slapped the steering to the beat of the music, as I drove home from work. I hadn't been home in three days, opting to spend the entire weekend holed up with Khalil in his spacious condo. Thank goodness I'd forgotten to take my dry cleaning out of my car on Friday. I'd worn Khalil's shirts and socks all weekend, and while panties hadn't really been necessary, I kept some in my gym bag just in case.

The phone was ringing when I got to my apartment. One look at the caller ID told me that Ayzha, who hadn't seen or heard from me since our Friday night clubbing, was calling to cuss me out. I grabbed my cordless and got an earful of profanity before I could even say "hello". I kept smiling and waited for her to get it out of her system.

"Anything else?" I inquired when she finally stopped to take a breath.

"Slut," she said evenly, determined to get the last word. "You could have at least called to let me know where you were."

"Ayzha, I'm sorry. I got caught up and I wasn't thinking straight."

"Call Stacie on three-way," she huffed.

Her end of the phone was silent. I sighed softly, not quite sure how I could possibly explain my weekend to her. I did as I was told and dialed Stacie on three-way. After Stacie finished cussing me out, I clicked Ayzha in.

"Girls," I started then stopped, at a loss for words. They had a point. I could have at least called to let them know that I was safe.

"So where were you?" Ayzha inquired.

"Why did you call me a slut? Where do you think I was?"

"I saw Jeremy at the club after you performed. He went off looking for you," Ayzha huffed.

"Yeah, and naturally we put two and two together," Stacie chimed in. "Sera, how could you?"

"You 'fidiots' thought that I was with Jeremy?" I started laughing.

"Yes," they answered in unison.

"What's a 'fidiot'?" Ayzha wanted to know.

"Oh, you know…an 'effin' idiot," I said nonchalantly. "I can't believe yall thought I was with Jeremy. Hell, I never even saw him."

"Then where were you?" Ayzha demanded, "and I don't appreciate being called an 'effin' idiot."

"Well, remember when you asked me what I'd do if I saw him again?" I asked coyly.

"Saw who again?"

"You know...the guy I met."

"You saw him at the club? Sera tell me you didn't do what I think you did."

I didn't bother answering because I'd done exactly what she thought.

"You tramp! You've been with him all weekend? Sera that is so unlike you! I can't believe you slept with him! You don't even know him!" Ayzha was so shocked that she was practically stuttering.

"Forget that! How was it?" Stacie wanted to know.

"I can't describe it," I wistfully.

"You're a writer. Of course you can describe it," Stacie probed.

"Okay. Then none of your damn business," I said slowly. I walked into the bathroom and grabbed a bag of cotton balls and my Dollar Store fingernail polish remover. I plopped down on my bed and began the tedious task of removing salon toe polish with sub par acetone.

"Damn, this junk won't come off," I proclaimed, interrupting whatever Ayzha was saying at the moment.

"What are you doing?" She asked.

"Girl, trying to take this polish off."

"I told you to quit using that dime store shit."

"Shut up. Anyway, I saw you all hugged up with Tyree. What's up with that?"

"Yeah, Ayzha, what's up with that?" Stacie teased.

"Unlike some sluts I know, I didn't sleep with anyone this weekend," Ayzha said evenly.

"Yeah, not even your husband," Stacie coughed.

"Stacie, I'll be glad when Trevor gets back from Korea so you can get out of my business and get back to your own."

"Well, hell, I have to live vicariously through somebody," Stacie laughed. "So you say you didn't sleep with Tyree?"

"Did you kiss him?" I asked.

"Yes, but that's all." Ayzha acted like we were the FBI instead of her best friends.

"That's how it starts. First you kiss. Then you touch. Next thing you know, your panties are on the floor," I laughed, too happy with my situation to chastise Ayzha for trying to find this warm fuzzy feeling... even if it was with someone other than her husband.

My other line beeped, and I told the girls to hold on.

"Oops...I bet that's Max. When I couldn't find you, I called him," Ayzha admitted slowly. "He called the police, but they said he couldn't report you as missing for twenty-four hours."

"Damn, Ayzha. Hold on," I clicked over. Sure enough, big brother was beside himself with worry about poor little helpless me. Damn. The last thing I needed was for Max to find out that I'd spent the weekend with a man he didn't know. I'm sure one of his friends saw me leave with Khalil. It was just a matter of time before he found out.

"Sera, where the hell have you been?" Max yelled into the phone. I wanted to scream at him too, but decided to just stay as calm as possible while still telling him to stay out of my business.

"Max, calm down. I'm ok!"

"Where the hell were you?" He asked again, practically screaming into the receiver.

"Does it matter? I didn't mean to worry you, but you don't need to know my every move."

"Sera--"

I cut him off, "Max, it's really none of your business."

"None of my damn business? Girl, you left your car in my parking lot all night! I called the damn police!"

"You didn't call Mama and Daddy did you?" I asked nervously.

"No. I didn't want them to feel as sick as I did! Somebody said they saw you leave in a black Mustang. The cops told me that you'd probably met up with someone and gone somewhere to be alone with them."

"They were right. I picked up my car Saturday morning."

"Yeah. The fellas really got a kick outta that. You know I have friends on the force. Now, they're clowning me for trying to report you missing when you were obviously just creepin'."

"Look...I'm sorry if you were embarrassed, but you brought it on yourself."

"What's his name?" Max ignored my last statement and continued his prying.

"Max, I don't want to talk to you right now."

"I don't care. You're my little sister, and I have a right to know what you're doing with your time."

"No, you don't."

"Who is he?" He demanded.

"Okay, big brother," I said, not even attempting to mask the irritation in my voice. "His name is Khalil."

"Is he a tall brotha with dreads?"

"Yes. Do you know him or something?" I asked, wondering if

there was anyone in town that Max didn't know.

"I've seen him around. He's a musician, and he's pretty tight with one of my friends. You remember Spencer Meeks, don't you?"

"The bass player?"

"Yeah, him. So are you going to try and tell me that you spent the weekend holding hands with this dude?"

"I'm a grown woman."

"You don't even know him!"

"I know enough. How many women have you slept with the night you met them?"

"And I'm not with any of those hoes now! Am I, Sera?" He countered.

"Are you calling me a ho?" I stopped scrubbing my toenails and grabbed the phone with both hands. I didn't give a damn who Max *thought* he was. I wasn't going to tolerate his smart-ass mouth too much longer.

"I'm not calling you a ho. I'm just telling you that he's probably calling you a ho."

"He wouldn't do that," I argued.

"Sera, men like Khalil are always on the prowl."

"Men like Khalil?"

"Yeah, men like him. Don't you know who his father is? Karl Roberts, The Sax Man. Daddy has all of his albums. He probably didn't tell you because he doesn't plan on seeing you again."

"It didn't come up, and it doesn't matter, Max. This is none of your business! I don't need your blessing or your damn approval."

"You need to watch your mouth. You forget who you're talking to," he chastised. "Hold on, Sissy". Max clicked over, and a few seconds later I heard the ringing of another telephone. I couldn't believe it. Max had actually three-way called somebody. I was about to hang up when curiosity got the better of me.

"Sera, you there?" Max asked. "Don't say anything, okay?"

"Whatever," I muttered. A male voice picked up the other line and I sat there in shock when I realized that Max had called Spencer.

"What's up man?" Max asked in his usual homeboy way.

"Hey, Max, what's going on?" Spencer replied.

"Same ol' thang. Hey man, what's up with your friend Khalil? I got a friend over here who wants to holla at him."

"Man, I ain't introducing that cat to any more females."

"Why? What's up with him?"

"He's too damn particular. I used to hook him up all the time, but he always found a way to either end the date early or not show up at all. I mean, he's my boy and all, but if you ask me, that fool is crazy.

Number one, he's twenty-seven years old and he's celibate," Spencer told him.

"CELIBATE?" Max almost shouted.

"Yeah man. The brothas in the band clown his ass all the time for passing up perfectly good pussy, and believe me, plenty of ladies are throwing it."

"What the hell? Why celibacy?" Max sounded more than a little surprised.

"I don't know. Some punk shit about waiting for the love of his life," Spencer told Max.

"Why does it have to be 'punk shit'?" I interrupted the flow of their conversation.

"Who is this?" Spencer asked.

"Man, that's my sister," Max told him.

"Fine ass Sera? You trying to get with Khalil?"

"Why does it have to be punk shit?" I asked again, ignoring his question.

"Girl, you know what I mean." Spencer started laughing, "I'm just sayin' it would be different if he was a virgin or something. A couple of years ago, ol' boy just stopped fuckin' cold turkey. Talkin' bout the next woman he made love to would be his future wife or some mess like that." Spencer gave me a moment to absorb the information he'd just flooded my ears with. "I mean he's one of the good guys. That's no lie. I'd definitely introduce him to my sister if I had one. I'd introduce him to you, but you'd just get your feelings hurt."

"Why do you say that?"

"Because he's hung up on this chick he met in a damn Wal-Mart parking lot. Can you believe that? He swears that she was sent from heaven, and when Khalil has his heart set on something he doesn't stop until he gets it. He talks about her all the damn time. He's written songs about her, poems... Shit, if he ever finds her again, that girl better watch out cuz he's got two years of pressure built up in his--"

"Hey! Watch your mouth around my sister man," Max interrupted, but I was too busy laughing. Max bid Spencer a hasty goodbye, then sat in silence, a very rare occurrence with him.

"So this is who you spent the weekend with? Some man you met in a parking lot?" He asked finally.

"Uh huh."

"Well, I need to meet him."

"Didn't you just hear what Spencer said?" I sighed.

"I need to see for myself. You know that. I trust Spencer's judgment, but you're still my sister, not his."

"Whatever, Max." I hung up, no longer in the mood for

conversation with my brother. The phone immediately rang. Oops! I'd forgotten about Ayzha and Stacie on the other line.

"I'm sorry," I said as I got back on the line with them. "I can't believe yall held so long, I would have hung up in my face!"

"Girl please, we're trying to hear about your weekend. Does your mystery man have a real name?" Stacie said excitedly.

"Khalil," I sang.

"So was it Max on the other line?" Ayzha asked.

"Yes!" I answered, proceeding to give them a run-down of the conversation. I told them what Spencer said about Khalil.

"I know this sounds crazy, but I feel like I've known him my entire life. It's like he was put on this earth specifically for me, like…"

"Soul mates?" Ayzha finished.

"You think I'm crazy, don't you?"

"Well, hell yeah," I could just see her rolling her eyes. "Girl we're all crazy. I told you that you were going to find him again. Didn't I? What made you sleep with him so fast? I ain't mad atcha, but damn! That is not like you at all."

I knew that this was out of the ordinary but in my heart, I also knew that Khalil and I shared something that went far beyond pretty words and sexual chemistry. What we shared was something so spiritual that every moment with him was like prayer. There were no feelings of shame or remorse. No embarrassment, no 'how in the hell did I get here' self-examination type of questions, no 'oh-my-god-we-just-met-he's-gonna–think-I'm-a–slut paranoia', only prayer.

I once saw a movie called "The Price Of Kissing' with that sexy Leon guy, you know, the one who played Robyn's man in "Waiting To Exhale? No, not Bubba from "Forrest Gump", the other one…. you with me now? Okay, anyway. In this movie Leon is sexing this girl down and she tells him that there's something different about the way they made love that night. She said that he was always pushing and pushing as if he were searching for something. So he naturally wanted to know how she would describe it because he'd felt something different too. That's when she said it. She said that instead of pushing and pulling they were floating…they were like prayer. Now I didn't understand what the hell this chick in the movie was talking about but it was so beautiful that I'd stored the scene in my romantic memory bank. Now I knew what she was talking about but not enough to explain it to anyone else. I guess that type of prayer is something that can't be explained, only felt. Well, I felt it, I mean really felt it but I couldn't find the words to explain it to them.

"NO," I finally said. "Hell no."

"What?" They asked in unison.

"You'll think I'm deranged."

"Dammit, we already think you're deranged.  Tell us!" Stacie demanded.

"I love him," I whispered.

"You think you love him," Ayzha told me.

"No, really, I'm in love with him, Ayzha.  What I think is that I've probably loved him all my life."

"That's deep," Stacie sighed.  "I guess I need to stop hounding Ayzha and live through you.  You're the only one of us actually getting some."

"Don't be living through me cuz I ain't sharing details.  It would just make you feel sorry for yourself," I told her.

"Damn, that good?"

"I'm still having flashbacks," I sighed.  "Anyway, I really want you guys to meet him."

"When?" They asked.

"He's coming over later.  You should come over and get to know him.  That way, when I start dissing y'all to spend time with him you'll know why."

"Heffa, we'll be over around seven," Ayzha giggled.

"What are you going to tell Mister?" I asked casually.

"Not a damn thang," she said flippantly.

"He won't wonder?" Stacie asked her.

"Girl, he doesn't care what I do.  I'll see you in a few."

Ayzha's end of the line went dead.  She was obviously finished talking about Riley.  I just hoped she wasn't careless enough to get caught up with Tyree, but I could only tell her so many times.

"Maybe I shouldn't encourage her," Stacie said quietly.

"You really shouldn't.  She needs to leave Riley, not cheat on him.  He's liable to 'go Ike Turner on her,' if he finds out."

"Yeah," Stacie said thoughtfully, "girl, I'll see you in a few.  I'm glad you found him." she hung up.

I looked across the room and winked at my reflection in the mirror.  My reflection winked back, and I dared anyone to try to wipe the smile from my face.  Enough worrying about other folks' problems.  Serafina's got a man of her own now.

## Chapter 11

### Jeremy Trent Sanders
### REFLECTIONS OF A PLAYA

Her smile is lingering in my mind, clinging to my memory banks like a leech, sucking the very life out of me. I can't stop thinking about her and the memories are threatening to drive me insane. Somewhere between waking up and eating cold cereal for breakfast, I decided that a nice jog around my apartment complex would clear my mind. Ya know, help clear up some of that junk I've stored in there and get organized. Perhaps a good sweat will help to wash her kisses from my soul. Now, I haven't been jogging in about a month so I have to climb underneath my bed to find my good running shoes and since dust is not my friend I find myself sneezing multiple times, blessing myself as each gust of spit drenches my hands as I feel around for my left sneaker. It's dark as hell and I'm on the verge of saying 'to hell with jogging' when my hands make contact with something soft and silky. My fingers instinctively grasp the item and as I slide from underneath the bed, I close my eyes, not really wanting to see what I've found. In my mind I already know. My fingertips caress the fabric as sweet memories of silky panties sliding down cinnamon legs followed by soft sighs of bliss cause me to shudder as a sudden tightness grasps my loins.

For two months I've denied wanting her, blaming her lingering memory on my transition from whorish boyfriend to whorish single guy with no woman to answer to. Don't get me wrong. I'm enjoying the single life, and I'm not about to admit to myself or anyone else that the life I lead now is basically the same life I led while I was with Sera. I'm not about to acknowledge that the only difference is I no longer have to lie about it. Sera was never my one and only and yet, she was my one and only. She was the only one I wanted to come home to after a night of partying. Oh, how I loved clubbing and screwing, showering and climbing into bed to snuggle with my sweet, little teddy bear. No, Sera was never really my only woman. She was just the one I chose to call girlfriend.

But I don't want to think about that right now. I want to focus on the good times, the sweetness of her smile, the way she used to wake me up in the morning with butterfly kisses on my cheeks. I'm smiling now as I remember how she'd bring me breakfast in bed and feed me French toast. I've been craving that French toast for two months, but my attempts to recreate her recipe have only proven that I need to buy more frozen dinners. Plus, making a mess of my kitchen had forced me to think about the last time I'd seen her.

She'd stood in front of the refrigerator, after making me one last breakfast, and casually told me it was over between us. She was tired of being walked on, tired of being cheated on, tired of feeling like less than a woman because I didn't know how to love her the way that she deserved. She was sick of my shit, sick of my attitude, and sick of me putting her down. She was sick of me. She'd left me sitting at my breakfast bar with syrup stuck to my napkin as I cleaned my mouth and nonchalantly listened to what she had to say. The conversation wasn't new to me. Every few months Sera would watch Oprah or read some junk by Iyanla Vanzant and decide that she didn't need me in her life.

I'd usually give her a week or two to calm down, before kissing some sense back into her cute little head. Sera was my girl. I wasn't going to let her go, but I wasn't going to let her get the upper hand in our relationship either. I needed her on standby, just in case I truly decided to settle down. She was my sweet baby, my teddy bear, and the one I called on when I needed to escape the complexities of life. She never asked anything from me; only gave of herself...mind, body and soul.

She treated me like a king, and it was with that pig-headed attitude that I listened to her tell me how horrible I was to her, and how she deserved so much more. I hadn't even bothered to pause in eating. Number one, I had this speech memorized. Number two, the girl made damn good French toast and I wasn't about to let her spoil my breakfast.

Perhaps, if I'd paid more attention, I could have avoided the hollow feeling I'm dealing with now. Perhaps, if I'd bothered looking into her eyes, I'd have realized that this time she was for real. Perhaps, if I'd listened to the tone of her voice, I'd have realized that there was something different about this speech. There was something different about this situation. Sera, usually weepy and emotional at times like this, had been standing in front of me with no trace of tears in her brown eyes. No tremors shook her voice as she spoke to me. There was no nervous wringing of the hands. She'd been calm, collected, and sure of herself.

I hadn't paid attention to those details. Instead, I'd let her walk out of the door. I hadn't even bothered to say goodbye. I'd sat there, silently eating my breakfast, not realizing that I was about to lose the best thing that ever happened to me.

I didn't have time to worry about her. I was trying to finish up my residency at St. Michael's Hospital, and it was better that I didn't have to spend so much time sneaking around and worrying about hurting Sera's feelings. Hell, I needed to do more studying anyway. A girlfriend was good for distracting a man from his studies. So, the week after Sera left, I picked up where I'd left off. I saw patients, studied, and looked for some new stuff to get into. In my eyes, the only thing better than diving into coochie is diving into *new* coochie so you'll have to pardon my bluntness.  Speaking of which, Sheila, my next-door neighbor, has always been willing to accommodate; and I'd enjoyed more than my fair share of late night quickies with Allison, that shapely RN who worked the graveyard shift on the geriatric floor.  Since I had everything figured out in my mind, I didn't bother calling Sera.  I didn't think I needed to.  I always figured she'd call me up to see how I was doing, or pretend that she'd left something at my house as an excuse to hear my voice.  My plan had been to: wait for her call, engage her in a flirty conversation, tell her that I missed her, tell her that "I apologize" because I never use the word 'sorry'.  It's a word I refuse to use to describe myself.  I've heard that word used enough against my daddy.  I'll be damned if I allowed it to be used against me.

So, anyway, my plan had been to "apologize" to the girl, ask her to come over for a talk, and give it to her so good that she'd forget that she was sick of my shit.  She never called, and I didn't want her to think that I was actually missing her.  So I let three weeks pass, before using the key she'd asked me to return but I'd conveniently "misplaced".

Imagine my frown as I'd stood outside her bathroom door listening to her moaning and groaning, wondering who the hell she was entertaining.  Now, imagine my glee when I opened the door and found her alone, surrounded by candles, trying to give herself the pleasure that she could only receive from me.  I'd thought that I could join her in that bubble bath, but it was not going to happen.  Instead, she'd left me hanging with nothing but memories and a painful erection.  I return to the present, momentarily, as I breathe deeply, inhaling the scent of stale sex on silk panties. I feel like a junkie sniffing paint between fixes.

"Fuck it." I say this loudly, even though there's no one around to hear my declaration of independence from Sera's grasp on my mind. "Fuck Sera."

But I can't fuck Sera, and it's driving me crazy.

"Of all the available coochie in the world you're pissed off because you can't have Sera?" I ask myself.

Of course, there is no one here to answer me so I just lay there on my back with a pair of white panties lying on my face like an obscene veil. The scent of her Donna Karan perfume overtakes me, as I inhale again.  Memories of Sera come rushing back.  She's sitting on my bed, spraying perfume everywhere she likes to be kissed.  Unconsciously, my hand slides down my torso, slowly stroking my hardness.  Her face looms above me like a blurry vision, and I feel as if I could reach out and caress her smooth face.  Suddenly, her sweet voice fills my head.  I hear the words she whispered right before she walked out of my life.

"One day you're going to wish you'd treated me better."

"Maybe one day, but not today," I think before quoting one of Sera's favorite phrases, "and this too shall pass."

\*\*\*

"Goodnight, Allison." I smile as I walk past her. She doesn't answer right away, making a point of kissing her husband, showing him that above all, he is the most important thing in her life. It's only after she properly greets Earl that she acknowledges my greeting.

"It's morning," she reminds me with a hearty laugh. "Working graveyards is starting to affect your brain." She motions towards me. "Earl, you remember Jeremy, don't you?"

"Oh yeah, Dr. J. You're the one who stitched me up a few months ago, after that little motorcycle mishap."

*Women never cease to amaze me. I'm in awe of her cuz had it been me, I'd have taken the long way to my car just to avoid seeing her. I'd have never had the nerve to introduce her to Sera. I extend my hand, the one that was entangled in his wife's hair about an hour ago and accept Earl's firm grip. I feel kinda sorry for the brotha because it's obvious that he'll do anything for Allison. If one man's trash is another man's treasure, then Earl has hit the jackpot. I smile at Earl as he smiles at his treasure, and bid them both goodnight...or morning...or whatever the hell it is. The graveyard shift is starting to affect my brain.* My BMW isn't parked very far from where they're standing so I can't help but sneak a glance at them as I climb into the passenger seat.*

"I can't believe she's kissing him."

I shake my head in disbelief as I watch her kiss him with the same cherry lips that she kissed me with earlier. Well not actually kissed *me* per say, but lower, on the southern tip. Never the lips. No woman who'd let me screw her in a broom closet on her break is worthy of a lip kiss...especially if she'd actually be bold enough to kiss her husband with another man's dick on her breath. Yuck.

Disgusting, but funny. A wise man named Ice Cube once said, *"why don't he suck my dick and just cut out the middleman?"* I laugh loudly as I turn the key in the ignition, revving the engine a few times as I imagine a bunch of my unwanted kids sliding down Allison's throat. "Out of control," I chuckle and peel out of the parking lot, honking twice at Allison and Earl as he opens the car door for her. What a gentleman.

I'm hungry as hell and the subject of food brings to mind French toast which in turn brings to mind Sera so of course I'm wondering why in the hell she hasn't at least called me in over two months. Surely she hasn't found someone else. I don't mean to toot my own horn, but the girl was crazy about me. There's no way in hell she could possibly be over me so soon. Now, why I can't just bring myself to admit that I miss her eludes me, but I can think of at least a dozen reasons why she is probably missing me.

On a whim, I call her name, and my blue tooth phone instantly dials her number. Yeah, I've still got her on speed dial. Ya know…just in case.

"Hello." Damn she sounds sexy.

"Hey." My voice sounds too harsh.

"Jeremy?"

"Yeah, who else would it be?" I ask flippantly. I must sound like a total asshole but it's too late to turn back now.

"It's seven-thirty in the morning."

"But you're up, right?"

"Yeah," she says, as if her next line should be "*Duh…*"

"What are you doing?" I ask nonchalantly.

"Well, let's see… it's seven-thirty on a Thursday morning. What do you think I'm doing?" She answers huffily.

Well, damn! No need to get salty. She almost sounds like she doesn't want to talk to me, which is pretty unbelievable. I don't let it stop me from trying to continue the conversation though. She's trippin'. She almost had a brotha on the verge of an apology but her attitude is about to halt the process on *that* notion.

"On your way to work?" I ask. Stupid. Stupid. Stupid.

"Uh, yeah."

"Why don't you take off? I can bring the supplies, and you can cook breakfast. It will be like old times."

"Are you for real? Jeremy, I have to go." Sera almost sounds as if she wants to laugh.

"Well, what are you doing after work?"

"Why?"

"I want to see you."

"Well, I don't want to see you."

CLICK. Just like that, she hangs up, leaving me looking like a damn fool with a dial tone in my ear. Hell no! I'm not about to go out like that. So, I call her back.

"I'm on my way over," I tell her.

"I won't be here."

"Then, I'll just meet you at your job."

"I'll call the police," Sera threatens.

We both know that this is a lie. She's angry and I'm angry with her for being angry with me.

"Jeremy, what do you want?" Her voice is hushed, slightly faint.

"I want to see you."

"No."

"Why?" I articulate when my heart is silently begging "please".

"We're not even together.  We broke up two months ago, remember?"

"No.  You left," I remind her.

"Is there a point to this?"  Her question cuts through my heart like a Ginsu knife.  Suddenly, the player in me has been reduced to a puppy begging for a pat on the head and a scratch on the belly.  I really do want to apologize.  I want to beg for her forgiveness. I want to tell her how much I've regretted letting her walk away.  I want to tell her all of these things and more but the player in me fights back and says,

"Girl, when are you gonna stop playing this game and admit that you miss me?"  I don't even bother calling her back, after I hear the second dial tone.

## Chapter 12

### Ayzha Nicole Darwin

I feel his touch, even before his hands are on my skin. His kisses always take me by surprise, whether I see his lips coming or not. I'm never quite prepared to see him. The excitement I feel in anticipation of gazing upon him is always replaced by somberness when he actually comes into view. I can't allow him to catch sight of how happy he makes me so instead, I act nonchalant when what I really want to do is run towards him, arms outstretched, sundress whipping around my legs and blowing sexily in the wind as I clutch a bunch of daisies in my left hand, just like in the movies. I want him to pick me up and twirl me around as he kisses me with such intense passion, we can't help sinking to the ground and making love in the field of wildflowers that have overrun my mind. I want him to want me with the same fervor in which I want him, but somehow, when we come together, I can only show indifference.

He often asks why I'm always looking away from him. When this question arises, I normally make a point of looking him square in the eye for about three seconds, before reverting back to my old habit of staring off into space as we speak. Of course, the fault lies in him. Who gave this man permission to have eyes so dark, so deep, that staring into them makes me weaker than a shot of vodka in a gallon of water? I'm afraid of the weakness. I'm afraid of the words that fight to leave my lips when he stares at me. I'm afraid of what he sees when he studies me so closely. It's almost as if he's staring directly into my heart and dissecting my emotions one by one.

This relationship is slowly going nowhere, yet I can't seem to walk away from him. I've tried a few times; but the moment I hear his voice, that damnable weakness begins coursing through my veins, filling my heart with a thick essence that literally makes my heart cramp, pain shooting through my chest and wrapping around my ribcage. Of course, the only cure for this sudden tightness is to see him, touch him, taste him, bury my face in his neck and smell him. Once I've done so, I feel unsatisfied for I actually needed more of him.

More than the physical, I need for his heart to overflow, causing his tongue to spill forth the words I need to hear in order to make it through the rest of my day. I need for him to say, "I love you. I need you," and "I want you with me always." Instead, I get, "I miss you. I want you. I want to make love to you." It's not the same. One can live for days with only water to sustain you, but eventually you need some meat and potatoes to accompany that drink. I love hearing his pretty words, but I need more if I'm to survive the complexities of this...

relationship? Friendship? Lust affair? I don't even know what to call this thing we have.

Is he my friend? Is he my man? If so, when did we cross that line? Perhaps, we were never really friends. That would definitely explain how easily we transitioned from meeting for an innocent lunch to holding hands and kissing with the intensity of lovers.

I haven't spoken to him in seven days. The first day, I called his cell phone three times. The second day, I left a voice mail telling him to call me when he got a chance. By the fourth day, I had basically washed my hands of him, refusing to try contacting him again. My pride couldn't allow him to see how much he was missed. My heart couldn't allow him to slide without knowing that I was thinking of him. Two days ago, I wrote an angry email detailing my feelings and the pain I felt from being ignored for so long. I was just about to hit "send," when it dawned on me that we've never actually gone so long without seeing or speaking with one another.    Perhaps he was going through something I couldn't understand.

I deleted the email and sent an internet greeting, just to tell him that when he was ready to speak, I'd be there to listen. I received a response within two hours, thanking me for the card and assuring me he'd speak with me about his problems as soon as he could. I'm still waiting. I miss him, but I'm waiting patiently, knowing I need this time away from him to get my head together and decide whether this risk is worth taking. Once again, I consider leaving him alone. The phone rings. I answer. It's him.

"Hey you," I say softly, wondering if he can tell how happy I am to hear his voice at last.

"Hey, Lady."

"How are you?" I ask.

"Confused."

"About?"

"Us." he tells me.

"Is there an us?"

"I don't know. I have a bad habit of wanting what I can't have."

I close my eyes and try to control my emotions as I listen to him speak. His voice is slowly lulling me into a trance, and I'm fighting to stay awake.

"I want you but I can't have you," he tells me, "and most of the time, I feel like I can't tell you what's really on my mind."

"You can tell me anything," I assure him.

"Surely you already know what I'm trying to say."

"I only know what you tell me," I respond in anticipation of what he could possibly be trying to tell me.

"I'm think I'm falling in love with you."

"Oh Tyree." It comes out sounding like, Ohhhhh Tyreeeeee.

"I've wanted to hear you say that for a long time," he chuckles.

"Say what?"

"Ohhhhhh Tyree..."

I start giggling, despite the tense situation, but stop as quickly as I started. "I don't know what to say. I mean, I know what to say but...I can't say it."

"I know it's crazy for me to feel this way about you but I can't help myself. I told you. You're irresistible, Shorty...I just don't want to get hurt."

"I don't want to get hurt either," I tell him. "This is hard for me. You have nothing to lose. I have everything to lose."

"I do have something to lose. I could lose you, and I don't want that to happen."

"What are we going to do?"

"I don't know. What do you want to do?"

"I know what needs to be done, but I can't bring myself to do it." I mask the pain in my heart by lowering my voice an octave.

"Are you trying to walk away from me?"

"What else can I do? The last thing I want to do is hurt you, and I definitely don't want to hurt myself. I don't know what to do, Tyree. I only know that we can't keep going on like this."

"Don't walk away from me just yet, Shorty." He says it softly, almost pleading, and I begin to melt again.

I really do care about him. I can admit it to myself, but I don't want to tell him how I feel, even though he's just poured his heart out to me. After three months of sneaking around with him, I still haven't gotten around to sleeping with him. He hasn't even pressed me for sex, which leads me to believe he has someone hiding in the shadows. I've asked him and he always denies it, but somehow, I can't believe he'd wait that long for me.

"Tyree, I don't want to walk away but I have to. I have a lot of decisions to make about my life, and I can't base those decisions on the way I feel about you."

"I need you."

"I need you too, but I'm really torn up right now. I want to leave Riley, but I need to know that I can make it on my own. I can't run away from him, directly into your arms."

"So we should just be friends? Is that what you're trying to say?"

"Yes, before this goes too far."

Each word hurts. My eyes sting with unshed tears, but I can't allow him to sense any weakness in me. There is silence on his end and then the line goes dead. I sit there for a while, holding the phone, praying for the strength not to call him back. It's better this way. It has to be.

*** 

My dear cousin Aleesha sat eyeing me curiously. At first, I ignored her. After about ten minutes of her staring holes into me, I decided to ask what was on her mind. I could barely hear her over the commotion in our favorite BBQ joint, so when she mentioned Tyree's name, I honestly didn't know what the hell she was talking about.

"Have you talked to Tyree?" She asked a little louder this time.

"Tyree? Why would I talk to him?" I picked up my menu and began studying it as if I didn't eat at Big Daddy's BBQ every other week.

Aleesha placed her hand on my menu and gently lowered it to the table. The look on her face told me she wasn't playing, but I wasn't about to spill my guts that easily. Aside from Sera and Stacie, Tyree was the only one who knew anything about this situation. I knew he wasn't discussing it with my cousin.

"Are you ready to order?" I asked her. "Cuz, I need to get my hands on a Ghetto Potato." A "ghetto potato" was a loaded baked potato with smoked bologna and chicken. I figured it would take an hour on the treadmill to keep this potato from going directly to my thighs, but it was definitely worth the effort.

"Whatever, Ayzha, order me a chicken potato, okay?"

Aleesha doesn't eat meat but she will scarf up some chicken and fish with the quickness! I tried following her lead once, but cow was calling my name. About a week into my new diet, I went to The Outback and ordered the biggest steak they had! But anyway, back to the present and the BBQ I was about to eat, I went to the counter and ordered the food, taking my sweet time getting back to our table.

I sat down gingerly and smiled at Aleesha, hating the way she was looking at me with that knowing gaze. We made small talk as we waited for our meals to be delivered.

Aleesha told me about the trifling people in her office who were constantly in her business. I filled her in on the latest fashions I'd ordered for the boutique, and about the man I'd caught trying on ladies underwear in the dressing room. We cracked up laughing at each other's stories and by the time our food arrived we were ravenous.

"Girl, Tyree is so crazy," Aleesha said suddenly. She put a spoonful of food into her mouth so I had to wait for her to chew and swallow before she finished. "He asked me out on a date. Now that fool knows I'm married!"

I suddenly lost the ability to swallow. My food stuck in my throat like a horse pill going down sideways. I didn't laugh with her. I couldn't say anything. It must have shown on my face because Aleesha leaned in close, "So it's true."

"What?" I was startled.

"Does it bother you that Tyree asked me out?"

"Why would it bother me?" I finally managed to swallow my food. I ate slowly to avoid further conversation, but Aleesha pressed on.

"Because you've been seeing him. And before you fix your lips to lie, let me tell you that I saw you with him at the park a few days ago, and you looked more than a little too friendly."

"You didn't see us."

"Girl, please. I was out there scoping out shelters for the company picnic. Imagine my shock when I saw your car parked next to his."

"Aleesha, It's not what you think," I lied.

"Cut the crap, Ayzha. I saw you kiss him goodbye."

'Stunned' didn't even begin to describe the way I felt at that moment. What could I say? Hell, what could anyone say? I'd been busted and there was nothing I could say or do to change it, so I just shook my head and concentrated on my potato. My appetite was definitely gone.

"He asked you out?" I asked, my voice sounding very small.

"No, I just wanted to see what you would say." She sighed, "Why him, Ayzha? Of all people, how could you get hooked up with Tyree?" She asked disgusted, "How long has this been going on?"

"I don't know, a little over three months," I admitted.

"Have you slept with him?"

"No."

"Three months, Ayzha?"

"Aleesha, I promise, I haven't. Besides, you don't have to worry about that. It's over. I told him we should just be friends."

"You and Tyree just friends?" Now it was Aleesha's turn to shake her head. "Not with the way you reacted when you thought he'd flirted with me. You obviously have feelings for him."

"I'll get over it."

"I sincerely hope so cuz I'm telling you, sweetie, Tyree is only concerned about himself."

"He's not like that."

"Believe me. I've been where you are. There is only one thing that a single man wants from a married woman…and it ain't her heart." Aleesha said matter-of-factly.

I'd heard this statement before, and it hurt just as deeply coming from Aleesha as it did coming from Max, but I shrugged it off. I wasn't trying to hear anything bad about Tyree. He loved me. At least he said he did, and I didn't want to believe he could say so without really meaning it.

"Well don't worry. The only thing he got was my heart. I kept my thong on," I laughed but my heart was cramping. I literally had to put my hand over my chest to soothe the pain. "I don't want to talk about this anymore, okay?"

"Can I just ask one more question?"

"You might as well," I mumbled.

"Do you love Riley?"

"Riley?"

"Your husband."

"Oh, him. I don't know anymore."

"That's not good enough, ya know?" Aleesha frowned.

"I know." What I didn't know was what to do.

## Chapter 13

### Khalil Jamal Roberts

I sat on the edge of my desk. A large Harlem Ali original provided an eclectic background as I discussed my father's latest project with Belinda Bryant, a local television personality. I had to admit that two years ago, when my father entrusted me with what he'd called his "most important project to date," I'd been afraid of failing, disappointing him, and creating chaos instead of fulfilling his vision.

"This is a beautiful building," Belinda said for the umpteenth time, her eyes conveying the pride I felt in my heart.

It *was* a beautiful building, and I'd overseen every detail from the bricks lining the walkways to the large vase in the middle of the lobby. The basement housed a state-of-the-art gym, complete with a basketball court and Olympic-sized heated pool. The first floor contained a luxurious lobby and an art gallery, while the second floor was made up of four separate condominiums, each boasting a 1,500 square-foot floor plan.

"The third floor," I explained as Belinda and her cameraman followed me out of the office and into my private elevator, "was supposed to also be four separate apartments, but when we started construction, we had a buyer who wanted to purchase the entire floor for his brother and himself."

"The whole floor?"

"Yep. Two separate condominiums, each a little over 3,000 square-feet," I said with pride. "It was purchased by Harlem Ali. You saw his work in my office as well as in the gallery downstairs."

I inserted a special card key, and the elevator made its ascent to the fourth floor, my home. A gift from my father and a token of the pride he'd taken in watching me mature, the top three floors of the building belonged to me. I took pride in the spacious layout decorated in earth tones, but took even more pride in in seeing my mother's picture hanging over the living-room fireplace, watching over me with a permanent smile on her face.

After walking Belinda and her cameraman back down to the lobby, I immediately grabbed my keys and headed out in search of my lady. It was time to celebrate.

\*\*\*

A dozen long stemmed red roses, a spur of the moment purchase, lay cradled in my arms. As I stepped off of the elevator into the spacious offices of SHANI Magazine, all conversation seemed to stop.

"Looking for someone?" A tall sistah in a form-fitting pantsuit asked. Her words seemed helpful enough, but her eyes were sizing me up, as if she were trying to decide if she could fit me into her purse. "You look familiar, have we met?"

Actually, I vaguely remembered meeting her at a listening party a few years earlier, but it wasn't even worth bringing up. I was a different man then. Thankfully, I didn't remember doing anything with her that could have made this moment any more awkward than it had to be.

"No, I don't believe we have," I smiled. "Actually, I'm looking for Serafina Jordan."

"Sera?" She gazed longingly at the roses, her tone slightly changing, as recognition briefly soured her features.

"Khalil Roberts, I remember now. We met at a party a few years ago, but you probably don't even remember me. I'm Tamika Marshall, one of the contributing writers," she continued as if I hadn't asked her where Serafina was.

"Tamika Marshall, I'm sorry I didn't remember." I extended my free hand, which she grasped gently, tickling my palm with her fingertips before reluctantly letting go.

"So… who are you in the studio with now?"

"Actually, I'm taking a little break, and I don't have much time. If you can just point me in the right direction, I can find Serafina," I told her, hoping that I didn't sound too rude.

She narrowed her eyes at me, gave me another once over, and pointed one long red nail as if she were casually showing me where the nearest bathroom was. It didn't matter. Once my eyes zeroed in on the location, my conversation with her was over.

There she was, my baby, conservatively sexy in a sleeveless, black mock turtleneck with matching black slacks. . Her hair was pulled away from her face in a tight bun, but one or two strands had managed to escape. Simple gold hoops dangled from her ears, and the dark framed glasses she wore over her perfect 20/20 vision were slightly orange tinted. Damn she looked good, too good to be working as a receptionist. She needed to be standing on somebody's stage reciting poetry or singing in that sweet voice of hers. Better yet, she needed to be back at my place, laid up on the couch with me, trying to distract me from watching Sports Center.

It isn't the way she looks that gets my blood pumping. It's the way she looks at me when she catches me staring at her. Her eyes light up like Christmas, and her smile invites my heart into a place I used to read about in fairy tales. She was talking to Jennifer Collins, a woman I've met at several benefit concerts and awards dinners. When Miss Collins saw me standing there with an arm full of roses, she smiled broadly, and approached me with open arms.

"Khalil! What are you doing here? I want to say, 'you shouldn't have,' but something tells me that you didn't." She winked before giving me a loud kiss on the cheek, "How's your daddy?"

"He's in Paris, this week," I told her, "and he's still single." I'd always thought Miss Collins was a good match for my father, but he didn't seem interested in falling in love.

"So am I. Tell him to call me." She winked again, knowing full well that he wasn't going to call...not for that reason, anyway. Amused, Serafina watched our interaction. I smiled.

"Hey you."

"Hey yourself," she answered in her usual way, head cocked to the side, smiling sexily.

Miss Collins stared at me for a moment, and looked over at Serafina, and smirked knowingly, "This looks serious."

"We're just friends," Serafina said hastily, grabbing her purse and facing Miss Collins. "I'm going to go to lunch now. Do you need anything while I'm out?"

"No. Go. Have fun. See you in a while." Miss Collins winked at me again before going back into her office. Sera stared at the roses in my hands and sighed, her eyes speaking a silent apology.

"Friends?" I asked softly.

"I'm just not used to all of this."

"All of what?"

"People being in my business. People wanting to know things about me." She took one of the roses and held it to her nose, closing her eyes as she inhaled. I wasn't used to it either, but for totally different reasons. I wasn't used to being involved with a woman who didn't actively seek out the publicity a relationship with me brought. I was used to dealing with women who didn't hide from the cameras, but sought them out.

"Girl, you'd better claim your man." I chuckled, "Cuz I've definitely claimed you."

I wanted to kiss her badly, but it wasn't proper office behavior so I grabbed her by the hand, and led her toward the elevator. On the way, we were stopped several times by co-workers wanting an introduction. Serafina's smile remained, but I could tell that she was silently fuming. She looked at me as if to ask, "Is this what I'm going to be dealing with?" and I gave her a look that I hoped told her that no matter how many women crossed my path, I only had eyes for her.

"Check your back pocket," she said once we were finally alone in the elevator. I reached into my pocket and retrieved two business cards left by the boldest of the group. Serafina gave me that questioning look again. This time I spoke rather than trying to communicate silently.

"Never let them see how much it bothers you, baby. They'll just keep trying to push your buttons. Besides, I only see you."

She smiled and I couldn't help leaning down for a nice lingering kiss. Something told me she wasn't going to make it back from lunch.

## Chapter 14

### <u>Jeremy Trent Sanders</u>

*"Where are you going?" My mother's pleas broke into the stillness of the night, a desperate cry for help. "Jeremy, how could you do this to me? To our son?"*

*"This ain't the life for me, Georgia." Jeremy Sanders Sr. threw his last pair of socks into the leather duffel bag mama and I bought him for Father's Day. We'd picked it out together, so daddy would think about us every time he went out of town on business. They didn't know their only son was hiding in the shadows, watching, afraid to leave my own doorway but unwilling to climb back into bed where I belonged. I was ten years old. I should have been used to my parent's constant bickering. Daddy didn't want mama to work but he wasn't paying the bills. He kept coming in with lipstick on his collar. Some disrespectful broad had called the house looking for him.*

*"After ten years you've decided that this isn't the life for you? After all I've put up with? All of the whoring around and the gambling you do? You gambled away JJ's college fund, and you don't even care. Don't you even care that your son wants to be a doctor?"*

*"A doctor?" Daddy spat viciously. "That little nigga ain't never gon' be shit! Always following you around the house like a damn sissy. All I asked for was a strong son and what did you give me? A fuckin' mama's boy! Boy might as well get used to the fact he ain't going to college! Not with my money! Hell, I got me another little boy across town! Five years old, and he's already givin' the girls hell! Maybe I should pour all of my fathering into a son that's guaranteed to carry on the family name."*

*Daddy had another son half my age? A son he didn't hate as much as he hated me? What was his name? Who was his mama? Was she as pretty as my mama? Did she bake banana nut bread every Sunday morning and take him to church?*

*I didn't know tears were coursing down my young cheeks until my father walked past me, duffel bag in hand and said, "Never let them see you cry, son. Crying is for sissies."*

He always introduces me as his son, "The Doctor". It doesn't matter that he gambled away my college fund. It doesn't matter that he was never around. He takes credit for every major accomplishment in my life, as if he purposely set the plan in motion when he'd forgotten to pull out of my mother and spit his seed on the sheets the way he usually did.

Of course, I don't say it. I'm too busy smiling in his face, happy to be in his favor after so many years of trying to prove that I was worthy of being his son. I *am* my father's son. But unlike my pops, I'm a rolling stone that crushes women without leaving pebbles all over the place. That man has spilled more seed than a farmer, and he only produces sons, well, until recently. His crop is so varied that, if we took a family picture, you'd think we represented The Rainbow Coalition. The man is a global pimp, impregnating women of all races and origins. His jimmy is into celebration, not discrimination.

"*Nigga, all pussy is pink*," he'd told Jacob and me on more than one occasion.

The phrase runs through my head, the moment I spot Pops at a stop light with a young blonde at his side.

"Is that Pops?" Jacob, my brother from another mother while Pops was still married to *my* mother, took off his Prada shades and did a double take.

"Yep…but that ain't Michelle," I laughed, referring to the latest wife who thought she had what it took to keep Pops at home. A sweet girl, she reminded me of my mama, but was twenty-five, the same age as Jacob.

"Damn, that's dirty." Jacob put his shades back on.

"That's Pops," I replied, while honking my horn and trying to get his attention.

"You're pitiful," Jacob told me. "Why are you always up in that fool's face?"

"That fool is your daddy."

"Yeah, how could I forget? He tells everybody he sees."

"He's proud of you. Not every father can say that his son is a wide receiver for the Dallas Cowboys." I told him.

"Yeah, well, he wasn't too keen on being my father or yours until we made something of ourselves. Our mothers were the best things to happen to that man, and look what he did to them," Jacob reminded me. "That muthafucka is out with another woman, Jeremy. Michelle just had a baby."

"That's none of our business," I sighed.

"Jerica is barely six weeks old."

"Jacob you act like this shit is new!" I damn near yelled. "Since when did you give a damn how Pops treated any woman besides our mothers?"

Despite the circumstances of his birth, Jacob and I were close. We were closer to each other than to any of our other brothers because our mothers were adult enough to get to know each other and make sure that Jacob and I spent time together. Five years younger than me, Jacob looked up to his big brother. We'd made a solemn vow to take care of one another. One of the first things he did, when he got his signing bonus three years ago, was to pay off my student loans and finance my remaining years of medical school.

"My mother used to cry all the time, and I hated Pops for that shit," Jacob said, "but you know what I hate the most? I woke up this morning, looked in the mirror, and guess what I saw? I saw Pops all over me. He's all over my face, and he's all over my ways."

"Yeah, well we look so much alike I'm getting ass thrown at me like crazy," I told him. It was true. Jacob and I looked just like our father. No one would ever guess that we had different mothers. I'd been mistaken for Jacob more than once, and it usually worked in my favor.

"Well it makes me sick," Jacob told me. "I've turned out to be just like that bastard. You've seen it, Jeremy. Bitches are all up in my face, throwing the ass at me or anyone they think can get them close to me. I have a paternity suit against me right now, and I know damn well I ain't never fucked that bitch."

"Then you have nothing to worry about."

"Yes I do. When I finally do meet the woman I want to spend my life with…if she's decent… If she's someone like mama, she's not going to give me the time of day."

"Man, will you cheer up? You're going too damn deep for me." I started laughing. I finally gave up on getting Pops' attention, and focused on driving. I'd just picked Jacob up from the airport, and we were headed to his mom's house.

"I haven't begun to get deep, Jeremy," Jacob sighed.

He didn't know how to swallow the bitterness the way I did. Yeah, it had pissed me off to see my mama cry, to see him raise his hand to her, to hear him call me a sissified mama's boy; but I'd proven him wrong. I was a man now. I was a far cry from the little boy he used to look at with disgust. I can still remember his sporadic visits.

On the rare occasion that he would drop by to see if I was still breathing, his first question to me would always be, *"How many girlfriends you got, boy?"* Not, *"How's school?"* or *"How have you been? Do you need anything? How about some child support?"* Always, *"How many girlfriends you got, boy?"*

At first I would tell him the truth, none. After a few lectures on what it meant to be a man, and how he didn't want his son growing up to be a fag, I'd started lying. One visit I would have one girlfriend. The next visit, I'd have two or three until one day, when I grew into myself, those imaginary girlfriends became real.

He was proud of me, or so he said, but he never made it to any of my school functions. He forgot my high school graduation. He forgot my college graduation. He forgot my Medical School graduation, but he never forgot to introduce me as his son, "The Doctor".

"I swear to God, if any man ever treats Jerica the way this muthafucka…or the way you or I treat women… I'll kill his ass."

"Jacob, she's a baby. We don't have to worry about any men in her life for a long time." I shook my head.

"We have to worry about what she sees growing up. We need to worry about her growing up thinking this shit is just a fact of life that she has to deal with," Jacob continued. "We have to think about her growing up without a father the way that we did."

"Dammit, Jacob, what the hell has gotten into you?" I asked him. "Seriously, do I need to pull over?"

"Man, just drive," he said angrily.

I glanced over at him, wondering what had him so on edge.

"Talk to me."

He was silent, but I knew that if I just waited, he'd eventually open up and start talking. He always did. Jamie Foxx's new song started playing on the radio, and I sneaked glances at my brother's profile, as I hummed along with the music.

"Stop looking at me," Jacob sighed. "You know how Pops is always bragging about his super sperm only making boys?"

"Yeah, what about it."

"Jerica might not be his."

"Of course she's his. She looks just like him," I laughed.

"So do I," He said just loud enough for me to hear.

"So do I, and?" I retorted. "You must be on crack. Ain't no way in hell Pops can deny that little girl. She just came along and put a halt to his streak."

Jacob switched off the radio and leaned back in his seat.

"He hits her, ya know?" he said quietly.

"Who, Michelle? Hell naw."

"He hit your mother. He hit my mother. Why don't you think he's hit Michelle?" Jacob asked.

I didn't answer.

"I went over there, one day, and the front door was wide open. Michelle was sitting at the kitchen table crying. Jeremy, there were bruises all up and down her arms. Do you remember when we swore never to raise our hand to a woman?"

"I remember."

"Have you kept that promise? Because I know that I have and sometimes it's hard, but I have never, ever hit a woman." Jacob was intense. He was too damn intense. I knew that he was on the verge of a revelation, and I wasn't sure if I wanted to know what it was.

"I may be a dog but I'm no abuser," I assured him.

"Well your Pops, the one you're always trying to please... That fool doesn't know how to keep his hands to himself; and if Michelle doesn't leave him, I'm taking Jerica," he announced as if it were the easiest thing in the world.

"Take Jerica?" I pulled over, parked, and turned on my hazard lights. "Start talking."

Jacob took a deep breath, looked me square in the eye and asked, "Do you remember when Michelle left Pops, a while back?"

"Yeah."

"That was the day I found her with all of those bruises. Man, all I could think about was my mama with bruises on her, crying over that raggedy bastard. I packed Michelle's shit, and took her back to Dallas with me."

"You what?"

Time stood still. Two brothers faced one another but this time, instead of looking me in the eye the way he always did, Jacob looked away.

"Oh my God," I whispered disbelievingly.

"We never meant for it to happen. Man, Michelle is a good woman, and Pops treats her like shit...just like he did with our mothers."

"How many times?"

"Just once," Jacob confessed, "just once, and we both regretted it. She went home the next week, and a few months later, found out she was pregnant."

"So..." my voice trailed off. I felt like Miss Celie in *The Color Purple* after finding out that pa wasn't pa and her children weren't her brother and sister. "Jerica could be your daughter?"

"That's why I'm here. I need you to do a DNA test for me. You have access to that kind of thing right?"

"Yeah but--"

"Jeremy, I need your help," he pleaded.

"What if she's yours?" I had to ask.

"If she's mine, I'm going to ask Michelle to move to Dallas."

"And if she isn't?"

"I'm going to ask Michelle to move to Dallas." He looked at me again, "She deserves better."

"Damn," I whispered. "Nigga, that's yo daddy! Michelle is his wife! Have you even though about this? What it could do to your life? What it could do to *my* life? To Pops? To your career? What about your mama?"

"Mama told me to follow my heart, and that she would stand behind me, no matter what."

"That's yo daddy!"

"You're my brother, and we're closer than we've ever been to that man. I ain't trying to justify it, but what's done is done, Jeremy. We were wrong. Hell, I was wrong, but I love Michelle and I don't care about the consequences." Jacob's eyes began to water, which scared the hell out of me. I hadn't seen him cry since we were little boys.

Pops always said that crying was for sissies; but as I held my baby brother, I wondered if somehow, in this case, Pops could be wrong. I didn't know, and for the moment didn't care. Jacob was hurting, and right or wrong, he was my brother. I didn't condone what he'd done, nor did I understand, but I loved him too much to leave his side.

## Chapter 15

### Ayzha Nicole Darwin

He used to kiss me good morning and love me goodnight, and call me in between to let me know how much he missed me. We used to talk. We used to know each other. I don't know him anymore, and I feel like he doesn't really want to know me.

"Can we talk?" I asked Riley as he read the newspaper at the dinner table, totally ignoring the buttery croissants I'd placed in front of him.

"I'm busy." He turned the page and cracked up laughing at something he'd just read in the comics.

"Riley, we really need to talk."

"No, what you need to do is let me enjoy the paper and stop bothering me. This is the only time I have to relax, and I just want to enjoy it in peace."

And just like that, he was gone from the table, faster than I could say, "fuck you". At first, I just stood there in stunned silence, not really wanting to believe Riley could just dismiss me when I was trying so hard to make things right in our marriage. He'd basically told me to "shut-up" as if we had intimate conversations every day. I couldn't even remember when Riley last asked about my day, or mumbled anything other than "fine" when I asked about his. My first impulse was to cry, but I was too pissed to let the tears fall. Instead, I stormed into the den and snatched the paper from his hands.

"Why won't you talk to me?"

"Ayzha, now is not the time!"

"Then tell me the right time, so you can pencil me in! Am I the only one who sees this marriage crumbling around us?"

"If you hate it so much, why don't you leave? Why do you keep trying to hold on to a man who obviously doesn't want your barren ass?"

I started to shake. That was cruel, even for Riley.

"Ayzha, I didn't mean that."

Of course he did. It was more than my taking the pill. It was the fact that I couldn't carry a child. I could try until my womb fell out, but it would never suffice. I'd always known how he felt, but hearing him say it just doubled the pain. No matter what I did for him, it would never be enough. In his eyes, I had failed him. He stood up and approached me, but I didn't want his touch. Could he possibly think that he could wipe the hurt away with a simple touch? I turned around and walked out of the den. Riley followed.

"Ayzha, stop. I didn't mean it the way it sounded."

"But you meant it!" I opened the front door, but he slammed it closed, blocking it with his muscular frame. "Why won't you just let me go?" I asked, unable to stop the tears. "Is this my punishment? Am I supposed to live the rest of my life in agony because I can't give you the only thing you married me for?"

"Ayzha--"

"I hate you, Riley Darwin."

My words must have cut into him because he wordlessly moved away from the door and walked away, leaving me standing alone. With no hesitation, I walked out, closing the door quietly behind me.

Once in the car, I had no idea where I was going. I couldn't go back inside of that house, not this time, so I pulled out and just started driving. I wanted to call Sera, but really didn't feel like hearing the bliss Khalil had permanently etched into her voice. Stacie was out of town on business, and Aleesha was celebrating her anniversary. I picked up my cell phone and dialed a number I hadn't called in a while. I'd deleted the number from my phone, but couldn't delete it from my memory.

Tyree answered, as if he didn't know who was calling.

"Hey," I said softly.

"Is this my *friend?*" He exclaimed. "You know, the friend I haven't seen in over a month?"

"You know who this is." I ignored his sarcastic reference to our so-called friendship, and adjusted my earpiece so I could hear him better. "What are you doing?"

"Ohhh, just laying here staring at my ceiling fan. I've been doing a lot of thinking."

"About?"

"It's not worth mentioning. My feelings are irrelevant. You're trying to work things out with him. I don't want to get hurt any more than I already have." He sounded pretty pitiful, and since I was depressed enough for the both of us, I decided to end the conversation.

"Bye, Tyree." I hung up, wiping tears from my eyes, as I drove in the darkness. My phone rang immediately and I knew who it was without looking at the caller ID. "Yeah," I answered, trying to sound steady.

"Are you okay?" Tyree questioned.

"I'm fine."

"It's almost ten and you're calling me from your car. Where are you going?"

"I don't know."

"What did he do?"

"I don't want to talk about it."

"Why did you call me?"

"I don't know."

"Are you crying?"

"I don't cry, Tyree. Crying is a sign of weakness, and I'm a strong black woman."

"Well, why don't you bring your strong, black self over here. We can not talk about what Riley did, and then you can not cry on my shoulder?"

"Why don't you kiss my little black butt?" I didn't really feel like laughing, but Tyree always managed to make me chuckle, no matter what mood I was in.

"You won't let me," he snickered.

"Hush."

"Come over," he whispered.

"Nope."

"Why?"

"Because I don't want you to see me cry," I sniffled.

"What if I promise not to look at you?"

"You're silly, ya know?"

"You like it."

"Whatever, my friend, how do I get to your house?"

I told Tyree where I was and he guided me along the highway, not hanging up the phone until I was pulling into his driveway. He opened the door, before I could knock, pulling me into his arms, and holding me for what seemed like an eternity.

Of course, his affection made me weep. He was doing for me what my husband should have done a long time ago. He led me over to his couch, and pulled me down beside him, my back against his chest, his arms around my waist. I closed my eyes and told him what had happened with Riley, starting at the very beginning. I told him about my shotgun wedding, and how Riley had only married me because I'd been pregnant. Tyree listened attentively, wiping tears when they appeared, and hugging me closer when he felt my need for physical support.

"If you were my wife, I never would have let you walk out of that door without you knowing how much I love you. You'd never have reason to doubt my feelings. That selfish bastard doesn't deserve you, Shorty."

"I don't know what to do."

"Yes you do. You leave."

"And go where, Tyree? I can't just leave him."

"What's keeping you there? Do you feel like you owe him something because you can't give him a kid?"

"I took a vow."

"And how does snuggling up with me fit into your sacred vows?"

"We're friends."

"You don't believe that any more than I do," he mumbled. His mouth was barely touching my ear, and I was beginning to feel a little more relaxed than I should.

"Damn! He'd have to be a fool not to want you. You're everything. You're beautiful, intelligent, and talented. You need a man who can appreciate every part of you."

I almost didn't notice when his tongue began licking my ear lobe. My eyes closed as I instinctively snuggled closer to him. One of his hands slid underneath my shirt and I could feel his fingers gently tracing the outline of my bra. The other hand was on my face, gently turning it towards his. Tyree's lips descended over mine with all of the passion missing from my life and while my mind was telling me that we were supposed to be friends, my body was desperately craving his touch. He rolled over on top of me and I could feel myself slowly sinking into his couch.

He broke the kiss long enough to look into my eyes. My bra was unfastened, my pants had somehow come undone, and his hand was resting on my bare stomach, which quivered uncontrollably. At that very instant, lying on that couch half-dressed and looking into his eyes, I knew. I loved this man. . I was in love with him and if I let him make love to me I'd never survive when he decided he was through with me. I couldn't take a chance on being hurt anymore that I already was.

"We should stop." I was so conscious of his hands that I could barely get the words out. "I shouldn't be here with you."

"You shouldn't be anywhere but here." He loosened my belt and began kissing my belly. "I just want to lick you. I just want to make you cum."

"No."

"Why?"

"Because, it won't stop there."

"I can stop there. Once you cum three or four times you'll be too tired for anything else anyway," he boasted.

"You don't know me," I smiled. "It's been a while, and I can guarantee I won't be able to stop there. Anyway, I can't have one without the other. I'll want it all, and that's impossible."

"It's very possible."

"Look Tyree, I don't want to get attached to you."

He lifted himself off of me and sat on the opposite end of the couch. "That hurts."

"I didn't mean it the way it sounded," I apologized.

"Then what did you mean?"

"I meant that I don't want to become more attached to you than I already am. Are you still considering that job in Baltimore?" His silence was my confirmation. "See, you're talking about leaving, Tyree. I don't want to start something that we can't finish."

"You're scared," he accused.

"I'm terrified. I have all of these feelings, and I don't know how to handle them. I'm too passionate, and I love too much. People like me hurt too deeply, and I don't know if I can handle any more pain in my life."

"You're talking about the possibility of being hurt. I hurt right now. I hurt every time I think about you. You have someone to fall back on. I sit here every night alone, all by myself. Girl, don't you know my heart aches, every time I have to watch you walk away from me?" He said hoarsely.

"You think that I can't get hurt because I'm married. Who the hell do I have to fall back on? Don't you even understand what's going on in my life? I go home everyday and beg attention from a man who could care less. I don't even know if I love him anymore. Do you know how hard it is for me to live like this? Dammit, I care about you, Tyree. I care way too much," I confessed.

"Come here." He held out his hand and I folded my arms across my chest. "Please?" He asked softly and all resistance left me. I crawled across the couch until I was straddling him. I loomed above him and stared down at him for a while.

"You okay?" he questioned.

"I'm fine."

"Yes, you are." He smiled and I smiled back. More magic words that deserved more kisses.

We stayed like that for the next fifteen minutes, kissing, hugging, him touching, me moving his hands until frustration set in. He stood up and walked around the room, not saying anything to me. I stood and headed towards the door, feeling like an unsure virgin on the verge of getting her cherry popped. I didn't want to leave, but I knew I couldn't stay in a room filled with sexual tension, unless I was ready to give him what he wanted. He talked a good game, but would he still want me after I gave in? I opened the front door, but he closed it before I could step outside. It was the second time today that a man had tried to keep me from leaving. This time I was relieved.

"I don't want you to go, Ayzha." He locked the door and held my hand. I couldn't bring myself to look at him, but the sound of my name on his lips made me shiver. It was so rare that he ever said my name. I was "Sexy," "Lady," or "Shorty," sometimes "baby," but I was hardly ever "Ayzha". I often wondered if he never called me by name because he didn't want to get me mixed up with the other women he swore weren't in his life. He wanted me to believe that I was the most special person in his universe. He wanted me to believe that I was the only woman he was involved with, and I wanted desperately to believe it too. Tyree turned me around to face him, but I refused to look into his eyes. I refused to become lost in the lies I wanted so desperately to believe were true.

"Ayzha," he said again, this time with more passion. "Ayzha, please don't walk away from me."

"You know, you hardly ever call me by my name," I whispered.

"What?"

"Say my name again."

"Ayzha," he whispered, tilting my chin until I was forced to either look him dead in his eyes or close mine. "Ayzha."

My eyes opened, and lies became truth as his lips found mine. I found myself with my back against his front door, his body so close I felt like I was being molded into the wood. My arms slid around his neck. His hands slid everywhere, unbuttoning my blouse until it gaped open, revealing my chocolate brown bra. He kissed and licked my cleavage with gentleness I hadn't felt in years. I took a deep, ragged breath as I felt one of his hands caressing me through my jeans until I was a wet gasping mess.

"I missed you," he mumbled. My jeans slid to the floor, and I kicked off my sandals so he could pull them off completely. My panties lay at my feet, a damp ball of cotton, and I felt helpless as his tongue licked me in places that hadn't been touched in a very long time. I could feel my back sliding against the door, down, down, down until I was sitting spread eagle in his foyer with his face, still between my legs, feasting on me as if I were a seven layer cake and he wanted to taste each layer separately.

As promised, the first orgasm was exquisite, the second earth shattering, and the fourth exhausting; but I couldn't stop there. I needed more than just his tongue. I needed to have him inside of me, filling places that had been empty for far too long. There was no time to go into his bedroom. He wanted me right there, and I wasn't complaining. My back slid to the floor.

His clothes were shed so fast I couldn't remember him taking them off, but there we were, moist, naked, sliding over each other like snakes in the Garden of Eden. Tears slid down my face, as he entered me so deeply I felt as if he were penetrating my very soul. Each thrust brought a tearful cry to my lips; he kissed me deeply, muting my cries to soft whimpers, keeping the words in my heart from flooding his mouth. Afterwards, he lay sprawled atop me, kissing the damp hair at my temples. My freshly done hair-do was now just a mess of tangled curls with sweat-straightened ends. Anyone looking at me had to know I'd just been made love to, thoroughly and completely.

"Stay with me tonight," Tyree insisted. "He hasn't even called. He probably doesn't even care that you're with another man. He can't love you. Not the way I want to."

He'd said it again. Love. I looked into his eyes and believed him. I kissed his lips and believed him. I kissed his ear and whispered words I'd probably regret later.

"Tyree?" It was said with more than a hint of tears in my voice for the truth of my situation hurt like a festering wound. "What just happened?"

"Love just happened, baby. Can't you feel it?" Tyree murmured close to my ear.

"I can't stop shaking." He held me closer. I couldn't stop crying. He kissed my tears. I couldn't stop the words from slipping from my tongue, "I love you." He kissed me, and I could feel him smiling against my lips.

"Are you going to stay with me tonight? Or do I have to watch you walk away again?"

"Eventually, I will have to walk away, Tyree."

"But not tonight." He pulled away from me and I felt a deep sense of loss as my body reluctantly released him. Grasping my hands firmly, Tyree stood up, pulling me with him. He led me to his bedroom, where I slept in his arms until sunlight awakened me to a new day and a new reality.

## Chapter 16

### Jeremy Trent Sanders

Calling her to my apartment was the first mistake. Two o'clock in the morning, and I can't sleep. Dick in hand, I called Allison and told her that it would be in her best interest to wake up and come over. Earl was out of town, and it wasn't like she had anyone else to do. She'd shown up at two-thirty, wearing tight jeans, a lingerie top, and shiny lip-gloss. She'd never been to my place, but I didn't have time to give her a tour. I'd called her over for a specific reason that didn't include formalities. I put it on her, two feet away from the front door because there was no time to go into my bedroom. I needed to cum real fast and get her out of my house, so that I could get some sleep.

Afterwards, she went to the bathroom, to "freshen up". After about fifteen minutes, I went looking for her. She was in my bed, buck naked, waiting on me to hook her up again. I should have told her to get dressed and get out, but of course my other head was doing all the thinking for me. So I slid beneath the sheets with her, and we connected in a way we'd never connected before. I kissed her, I mean really kissed her for the first time. Before, there had been the customary pre-foreplay smooches that quickly led to sex, but this was one of those movie kisses that made the hairs stand up on the back of your neck. This was one of those kisses that made you want to take your time and savor the moment.

I closed my eyes and just like that, I was transported to another life. In this life, Sera was lying in my arms, receiving all the pleasure I could possibly give her. If I kept my eyes closed, and my mind open, I heard Sera's voice softly calling my name. I felt her hands gripping my shoulders, her lips grazing my neck, her nails clawing at my back. And then, out of nowhere, I heard my voice calling her name. Which would have been wonderful if it weren't for the fact that it was Allison, not Sera, grinding beneath me.

Allison was livid. She acted a damn fool, punching my shoulders, and kicking. It was almost laughable. Almost, because I was worried that she'd try and pull some ghetto mess like breaking a brotha's hard earned belongings. So I politely grabbed her arms and put her legs in an old fashioned scissors hold until she decided to calm down.

"Calm the hell down."

"Calm down?" She asked incredulously. "You just called me by some other bitch's name."

"My bad." I let go of her.

"What?"

"Look Allison, I don't know what you thought you'd accomplish by coming over here and climbing into my bed, but I've already accomplished what I called your ass over here for." The words sounded harsh, even to my own ears, but they had to be said. Allison was under the impression that these little lunch break, broom closet, on the roof quickies would eventually lead to something more lasting.   Allison was failing to consider the fact that she was married. I told her as much.

"That never mattered to you before."

"It doesn't matter to me now, but it should at least matter to you. Earl seems like a pretty good guy." I told her.

"Well, that didn't stop you from fucking his wife. Did it?"

"I'm a man, baby. You threw the pussy, and I caught it. Don't try to make this into more than it is." Her eyes watered and mine rolled. The last thing I needed was a naked, married woman crying in my bed.

"I left him," she whispered.

"You left him? You left him for what? For this?"

"I thought--"

"You thought wrong." I cut her off, before she could even complete the thought.   Allison pulled the sheet close, hiding her nakedness as if she was suddenly ashamed. For a brief moment, I felt sorry for her.

"What kind of man are you?" She asked tearfully.

I'm my father's son.   Once again I thought about one of the main reasons I ran so many women at once.  I thought about the one question Pops would ask every time he saw me...

*"How many girlfriends you got, boy?"*

*Not, how's school? Or how have you been? Do you need anything? How about some child support, but...*

*"How many girlfriends you got, boy?"*

I snatched my mind out of the past and stared down at Allison. "I hope you didn't tell him about us. I don't need that kind of drama."

With those words, I left the room, giving her the privacy she needed to get dressed and get the hell out of my house.

## Chapter 17

### <u>Serafina Danielle Jordan</u>

*Our bodies move to an orchestrated groove. Abstract notes caught in our throats. Sweat mingling, follicles tingling, toes curling, minds swirling, whirling, in a rhythm unexplained. Detained, restrained, but never complained. Like a guitar, plucked. Thoroughly fucked, licked and sucked. Mind blown like Coltrane's saxophone, as our moans distinctly crescendo.*

Every moment with Khalil feels like a poem waiting to be written. Every kiss feels like the first kiss. Every time he touches me, I feel like a virgin on a bed or rose petals. It's so new, yet so familiar. He has my nose open so wide that I smell him before he even enters the room. I know he's there before he speaks. We connect like puzzle pieces; I don't know where he ends and I begin. There is no him. There is no me. There is just us.

He's all up in me. He's deep inside of my body. He's deep inside of my mind. He's so deep inside of me that I wouldn't be surprised if we actually morphed into some kind of hermaphroditic creature. I'm lost in him, but I know exactly where I am. This probably doesn't make a lick of sense to anyone but me so to put it in layman's terms, I'm in love. I'm in love and more than that I *feel* love. I wake up in the morning feeling loved, I go to sleep at night feeling loved. If love were an apple martini I'd be drunk as hell because I drink it in all day, every day.

I can't imagine two loves like mine but I feel it every single time he looks at me. Isn't it funny? We often spend eternities loving people and being left to wonder what it feels like to be loved like that. I don't have to wonder any more. I *know.*

"You're a million miles away from me." Khalil placed a kiss on the back of my neck, and I closed my eyes, fighting the sudden urge to stretch and purr like a kitty cat.

"I'm right here."

"Your body is right here." One of his hands slid over my leg, "but your mind is in outer space."

"If I'm in space, I must be on Pluto cuz I'm freezing. Hold me," I whispered. I immediately warmed up, when he slid his arms around my naked waist, drawing me closer to the heat of his body. Khalil pressed a button on his remote, and Jill Scott's soulful voice filled the room, tempting me to sing along as his love rained down on me.

I hated this part. Lying with him, knowing I needed to get up and start my day, but not wanting to leave his side. I even didn't want to take a shower before I left his place because I wanted to smell him on me just a little longer. Whenever I showered, I felt like I was washing him away. I felt like I was losing something. It made me want to find him over and over again, until his scent became my scent. That way, I could smell him all the time.

But of course, I knew that I couldn't lay around in our lovely little funk forever, so I jumped out of bed and ran into the bathroom before he could grab me again. In the privacy of his bathroom, I stared at my reflection, scrutinizing my every feature: the full lips, sandy hair, brown eyes, and cinnamon skin once plagued by acne. If I looked closely enough, I could still see tiny scars. I was still a bit self-conscious about my appearance.

"What are you doing?" Khalil asked.

The sound of his voice made me jump. I backed away from the mirror and looked at him.

"What do you see when you look at me?" The fact that two of my gorgeous co-workers had slipped him their numbers was still bothering me a little.

"Hmm…" he mumbled walking toward me. He stood behind me in front of the mirror and admired the picture we made. "Close your eyes." He commanded and I obeyed. "I want you to look at yourself through my eyes." One of his hands grasped mine. "Your fingers are so long and gentle, I'm surprised you don't play the piano." He slowly ran his fingertips up the length of my arm. "Your skin is smoother than satin and softer than velvet. If I could sprinkle you over a piece of bread, I'd have cinnamon toast for breakfast, lunch, and dinner." I giggled and Khalil shushed me with a gentle kiss.

"Your legs are long and beautiful. Whenever I look at them I want to kiss them from here," I felt his tongue on my ankle and nearly jumped out of my skin. His tongue traveled up the entire length of my trembling left leg until he reached my inner thigh. "To here," he finished with a wicked chuckle. Khalil buried his nose in my secret crevice, inhaled slowly, and grasped my behind with both hands. "Damn, I love the smell of you," he confessed, "the smell, the taste, the texture. I love the way you tremble when I put my finger right here." Oh, my damn, I was about to fall because he was sliding his fingers inside of me one by one and licking my flavor from each. I couldn't take it anymore. I grabbed him by his hair and pulled him up towards me, but he refused to kiss me.

Instead he put his mouth on my ear and whispered, "Not yet. I'm not done, and if you open your eyes I'll stop." I didn't want him to ever stop, so I kept my eyes closed tight and my legs parted, as his hands played hide and go seek with my southern region. "Hmmm, where was I? Oh yeah, I need to taste you again."

His mouth found my spot again, licking, sucking, and nibbling until I could barely stand. The glass shower door was right behind us and I thought we'd crash right through it, we hit it so hard, but at least it gave me stability and kept me from falling to the floor with my passionate convulsions. I whispered his name but he put a sticky finger to my lips, quieting my voice and sharing his feast with me. His mouth was at my ear again, breathing heavily, whispering, "Maybe I can have any woman in the world, maybe I can't. All I know is that I have everything I'll ever want or need in you."

He positioned himself behind me again, with his arms around my waist, biting my neck and cupping my breasts in his palms. "Feel how perfectly they fit in my hands?"

"Khalil--"

"Shhh...tell me what you see."

"My eyes are closed."

"What do you see?"

"I see you inside of me."

My words had a double meaning. I literally saw him inside of me. Inside of my body, inside of my heart.

Khalil recognized both meanings and before I knew it I was being lifted, physically and mentally. My ass was on the spacious sink, my head was flying through the clouds, my long legs were wrapped around his waist, burying him inside and he penetrated me much deeper than he could ever imagine. He was filling me up, so much that it almost hurt but it was a good pain and I wanted more of it. He knew this and pulled out until only the tip remained within me, teasing my inner walls.

"Write me a poem," he mumbled, slowing to a complete stop.

"Don't stop."

"Write me a poem." He grabbed a handful of my hair and gently pulled my head backward, kissing the hollow of my throat, "I'll stop if you don't."

"Is it wrong of me to fantasize about tasting my sweetness as it drips from your talented lips once you arise from 'tween my thighs? Or better yet, once you've made it wet, I'll guide you in and let you ride, and once you're done I'll lick you dry."

"Oh shit," he mumbled, while thrusting deep within me. "Keep going."

I continued, saying whatever came to mind; "The lady on your arm would never attempt to express these thoughts. Her mind is exempt from the raunchy words that may be said by the insatiable whore who inhabits your bed. You love to be seen with a beauty queen with painted lips and acrylic tips. A bittersweet voice that would never think to utter in the language of the prostitute who stands near the gutter." I paused and he gripped me tighter, pulling the words out of me. "And yet, we are one and the same."

By this time, my legs were on his shoulders, and he was hitting it so good that I was forced to bite my lip to keep from screaming. He was sexing me like the whore in my poem, and I loved every dirty minute of it. We ended up on the floor, baptizing the rug in our juices, and as he collapsed on top of me, I locked my legs around his waist because I didn't want him to leave my body just yet.

"What do you see?" He whispered breathlessly.

"I see you inside of me."

"What do you feel?"

"I feel you inside of me."

"What do you want?"

"I want you to stay inside of me."

"Always." He kissed me gently and buried his face in my shoulder. "I love you. I love everything about you Serafina."

"I love you too," I whispered back.

"Still going home?"

"If I stay here, I'll never leave."

"Would that be so bad?" There's a deeper meaning in the question, and I realize he is not just asking me to stay the weekend. "This is a pretty big place, Serafina. It's way too big for one man."

"Well you should have thought about that before you moved in here," I joked.

"Well, it never seemed too big until the first night I brought you here. When I walked you to your car and had to come back here alone, it just felt crazy. I was actually lonely. I'd never felt lonely here, before."

"Khalil, what do you want me to do?" I asked him.

"I don't know."

"You don't know?"

"Ok, I know I can't just ask you to just move in here and play house with me." He said.

"Right."

"Serafina, I know we've only been together for a few months, but it just feels like forever. Ya know?" Khalil traced the curve of my jaw with the end of one of his dreadlocks.

"That tickles." .

"Then let me stop because I'm being serious right now," he chuckled, rolling away slightly. We lay on the floor, looking up at the vaulted ceiling. "I guess I'm saying that I just miss you a lot when you're not here, and I want to keep you all to myself."

"Stingy," I accused.

"Just a little," Khalil admitted. "Anyway, you'd better get in the shower. Aren't you meeting Ayzha here in minute?"

"I could call and tell her not to come."

"Uh uh, don't let good "D" come between you and your best friend."

"Good "D"? What makes you think it's so good?"

"Oh Khalil, don't stop, don't stop…" he mimicked in a high-pitched voice.

"I fake it."

"Do you fake all that shivering and shaking too?" He looked over at me and raised an eyebrow.

I tried to nod with a straight face, but couldn't help laughing. I could never fake anything with Khalil.

"I'm getting in the shower to wash your stank off of me." I left Khalil lying on the floor and jumped into the shower, fully expecting him to join me. When he didn't, I called out, "What are you doing?"

"I'm writing your poem down," he yelled back.

I rubbed shower gel into my loofah and smiled. I'd written at least ten poems in the heat of passion, and Khalil always remembered every word. He never failed to present me with a neat, handwritten copy to place in my journal. These were Khalil's poems, and he loved to listen to me read them as he reminisced about the way they came to be. I loved to read them and marvel at the way his touch could literally pull words from my mind.

"I think I have some music in mind for that one." He said sliding into the shower with me. He took the loofah from my hands and started scrubbing my back. "That is, if you're interested in recording it for my CD."

Here we go again. Khalil wanted me to sing a few songs with his band, and recite poetry using his music as a background. He'd already shared some of my work with the members of his band. They were excited about it, but I couldn't imagine performing those poems after what happened the last time I performed at Max's club. If I put that stuff out on CD for all to hear, Max would have a seizure! Plus, I had a feeling my daddy still thought I was a virgin. I didn't want to break his heart by talking to strangers the way I'd just talked to Khalil.

"You know, there is such a thing as living for yourself," Khalil reminded me. "What's the point in having this gift if you don't want to share it?"

"I don't want to talk about it, Khalil."

"Well, I do." He handed me the loofah and motioned for me to wash his back. "It would be different if you didn't want to do it, but you're letting what other people think determine your actions."

"It's not just other people. Boy, my Daddy would die if I showed up on a record talking and singing like a slut puppy." It came out harder than I'd intended, but he was beginning to piss me off. I stopped scrubbing his back, and threw the loofah at him.

"Let's not fight, Serafina."

"We're not fighting."

"Yes, but you're raising your voice and throwing stuff at me. I'd rather not go there this morning."

"Then stop bugging me about the CD. I'm not going to do it!"

"Fine."

We finished showering in silence, neither one of us attempting to leave the spray of water because we couldn't stand to be away from one another, not even in anger.

The doorbell rang as I was putting on my makeup, and Khalil let Ayzha in. She walked into the bathroom, a bundle of energy, and checked her hair. Something was up with her, but I didn't feel like trying to drag it out of her. I made a mental note to discuss it with her later.

"Smells like sex in here," she mumbled.

"It must be you because I just washed mine off," I retorted. I struck a match and lit a cherry-scented candle.

"Now it smells like sex and cherries." Her laughter hurt my ears. "What's wrong with you?" She asked, when I couldn't mask my annoyance with her giddiness.

I told her about my argument with Khalil, and of course, in true Ayzha fashion, the heffa sided with him.

"What do I always tell you about your talent?"

"You're gonna lose it if you don't use it," I mumbled.

"Sera, your mama knows more about you than you think. Do you think she'd ever ask you to stifle your talent because your subject matter might embarrass her?"

"Psychiatric Ayzha strikes again," I said sarcastically. "You should have your own action figure."

"It's a gift. I don't own it," she winked.

"Oh whatever." I tried not to laugh at her. "And anyway, you know those nosey broads at her church would flip their wigs if they heard my stuff."

"Well, knowing your mama, she'd probably ask them what the hell they were doing listening to it in the first place!"

I couldn't help laughing at that because it was true. I think I got my sarcasm from my mama. I blotted my lipstick and led Ayzha back into the bedroom.

"Soooo, this is Khalil's den of sin." Ayzha looked around the spacious room. "This bedroom makes like three of mine. This man must have a lot of dollars."

"He's blessed."

I hadn't noticed how huge Khalil's place was, until the morning after our first night together. We'd only been concerned about getting to the bedroom that night. I chuckled at the memory, thinking about what Khalil had said about being lonely without me in this big place.

"Khalil I love this place," Ayzha said as we walked downstairs to join him in the living room. "It must be nice to have all of this space."

"It's nice, when I have someone here to keep me company," Khalil said staring at me.

"Alrighty then, I'm going to go get a soda or something." Ayzha made her way into the kitchen, obviously trying to give Khalil and me a little time alone.

"Khalil--"

"Serafina--"

He held out his hand, and I grasped it, slowly walking towards him until we were holding each other, swaying to a groove that played in our heads. He sniffed my hair and exhaled slowly, sliding his hand up and down my back.

"I'm sorry about earlier."

"No, baby, I'm sorry. I shouldn't keep pressuring you to do something that you're not comfortable with. I guess I just want to show you off." He gave me a small peck on the lips.

"You know what would be funny?" I heard Ayzha say.

"I didn't see you there," I said.

"I know," she laughed. "I just had an epiphany."

"Please share," Khalil said.

"I think that Sera should record some of her poetry for you, use a fake name, and play it at Max's club."

"Are you insane?" I asked.

"Please. That would be so damn funny. Can you imagine? You could sing some of the lyrics and recite the rest. Girl, he would never know."

"He knows my voice."

"Do you really think he would pay that close attention? I mean, Khalil can just give it to the DJ. Max wouldn't know the difference."

"That's just evil. Clever, but evil," I told her.

"That's brilliant." Khalil gave Ayzha a high five, and I stared at them both in disbelief.

"Come on. Where is your sense of adventure? It's not like you'll be performing it onstage," Ayzha said. "By the time Max find's out it's you, the song will be a big hit, and he'll be able to say that it all started in his club."

"It could work," I mused.

"Hell yeah it could work!" Khalil grinned down at me. "The only thing holding you back was your family finding out. Right?"

"Yeah."

"So…"

"Okay, okay." I held up my hand in surrender. "I'll do it."

"Now you need a name," Ayzha told me. "Khalil, she needs a name."

"Well," Khalil said thoughtfully, "you're my sexy little poetess."

"Poetess," I repeated. "It's simple."

"…Yet sexy," Ayzha added. "I like it."

"Good, then it's settled." Khalil was grinning like a little boy, and I pinched his dimpled cheek. "You ladies better go now, before I take my sexy poetess back to bed."

"Oh hell no! I need my girl, today." Ayzha grabbed my hand and pulled me towards the door. Once we were in the elevator, she stared at me with the most blissful smile I'd ever seen. It reminded me that I needed to talk to her about the way she'd been acting earlier.

"Ayzha, what's up?" I asked, not knowing if I really wanted to know.

"Nothing, I'm just happy."

"I hate to sound…dreary…but 'happy' is not a word I usually use to describe you. Something dramatic must have happened in the past few days to make you shine like this."

"Oh Sera, you're so silly." She slapped my arm playfully and I took a step backwards because whatever demon had taken over her body was liable to throw up or do an *Exorcist* head spin.

"What the hell? Did ol' Riley get him some Viagra or something?" I was kinda joking, but Ayzha was acting like someone who'd just had some great sex after a dry spell.

"Girl, can you imagine Riley's stupid ass taking some pill just to please little ol' me?" She started laughing uncontrollably and I, not seeing the humor pushed the stop button on the elevator, trapping us between floors.

"What have you done?" I asked slowly. She wouldn't stop laughing, and I was tempted to slap her into silence. "Ayzha, what the hell did you do?" There was a name lingering in the back of my mind, but I didn't want to say it out loud. Ayzha had sworn she was going to leave Tyree alone, until she decided what she was going to do about her marriage. I hadn't told her about the conversation I'd had with her cousin, Aleesha. If Ayzha knew the things I learned from Aleesha…

With a small prayer in my heart, I asked her again, "Girl, what's gotten into you?"

"Sera, I'm in love." She said it so wistfully, I could have easily been happy for her, had I not felt uneasy about the man I hoped she wasn't involved with.

"Oh, Ayzha, tell me it's not Tyree."

"Of course it's Tyree, silly. Who else would I give the good stuff to? I'm getting my shit together, and in a few months it will be bye-bye, Riley."

"Are you crazy? Didn't Aleesha warn you about Tyree? Didn't I tell you to leave him alone?"

"Tyree is a different man when he's with me, and one day Aleesha will realize it. Don't you tell her!" She was suddenly very defensive, and I was quite taken aback. She almost reminded me of myself when I was dating Jeremy. It scared me.

"Ayzha, please be careful."

"Girl," she hugged me fiercely, "I haven't been this happy in a long time. Just love me, okay?"

"All I can do is love you, Ayzha." I whispered. And pray. For Ayzha's sake, I prayed that Tyree wasn't the man Aleesha had described.

## Chapter 18

### Khalil Jamal Roberts

*"If I penetrate your lips with my tongue do you suppose that I can make you cum...pletely lose your mind as I...run my fingers up and down your thighs? Would your soldier rise and salute me, your commander in chief between these here sheets."*

It's the poem she recited the night I found her again, standing on that stage with the lights shining down on her silky skin, accenting the glittery lotion she'd been wearing. I should have known how hard it would be for me to handle seeing all eyes on her beauty, all ears in tune with her voice, hands wanting to touch her, feel her the way I do when we're alone.

*What the hell have I done?*

She was singing in that sexy and mesmerizing voice of hers. Her eyes were closed. One of her hands massaged the back of her neck while the other hand kept perfect time on her thigh, gently tapping with her French manicured fingers. She licked her lips and began reciting her poem, slowly, sensually, as if she were kissing each word. The members of my band, *Interlude*, were so into her that their instruments seemed to be playing on autopilot. The pitch, the key, the timing, everything was perfect. To hit a wrong note or miss a cue would mean interrupting my girl's flow. No one wanted to do that. Interrupting her during one of her poems was like sex with no orgasm. No one wanted to stop playing, until she was finished.

I was having second thoughts. I shouldn't have pressed so hard. I shouldn't have tried to guilt her into recording for me. I should have let her stay in the background where she was most comfortable, but no. I had to show her off. I had to push her out in front of the world as if to say 'Look what I've got! All for me and none for you!' She didn't want to be shared, but she'd gotten over her fears, and recorded for me. Now that she'd accomplished such a miraculous feat, I wasn't sure if *I* was ready to share *her*.

"Shit," Spencer mumbled, as we played the track a little later. Serafina had already gone downstairs to start dinner.

"What?" I asked.

"Damn! I can't believe that's Max's baby sister flowing like that." Spencer shook his head, "I mean, I didn't even know she did poetry until I saw her at the club that night." He cut his eyes at me slyly, "I guess that's the night yall hooked up, huh?"

"Yes." I ran my hands through my locs and sighed loudly, frustration overtaking my every move.

"This girl should have joined the band a long time ago," Spencer continued.

"She's not joining the band," I said shortly.

"Did she write this?"

"Yeah," I mumbled, trying hard to tone down the agitation in my voice.

"Get the hell out!" Spencer turned the volume up and started snapping his fingers. "She wrote this?"

"We did this joint in one take. That's what I'm tripping off of," Monty, the saxophonist, added. "Man your girl is something else. No disrespect man, but when she was singing, I was so turned on, I was scared to fuck up." I gave Monty a guarded look, and he rolled his eyes skyward and started whistling.

*He's fired!*

"I know! I didn't want to interrupt her," Chico, the drummer, laughed at my uneasiness over Monty's remarks.

*Verbal warning.*

Spencer, noticing my change in attitude, tried to be the voice of reason. "Khalil, if she's going to be jammin' with us, you're gonna have to get used to her being looked at. We have nothing but respect for Sera, but man, if we ever performed this in public, you know damn well that muthafuckas are going to flock to her like bees to honey."

"She's not performing with us. She's not recording with us again. As a matter of fact, I'm destroying the masters for this whole session." I'd had enough.

I didn't want to hear anyone talking about Serafina this way, but I knew that they were right. There was something about her voice mingling with those words that made a brotha stand at attention. Now, I understood how Max had to have felt, seeing his sister onstage teasing every man in the room with that sexy shape and those provocative words. I'd been one of the men enthralled that night. I'd been one of the men thinking about how many ways I could love her, but it had been different. She wasn't mine yet. When did I become so possessive?

"Let me get this straight." Spencer stood up, blocking me from leaving the control room. "We just spent all this time arranging the perfect song and you're just going to trash it, as if that perfection never happened? You mean to tell me that after all the Keith Sweat begging and the "please baby, pleases" it took to get that girl in this studio..." He threw up his hands, "Nigga, are you crazy?"

I *was* crazy. This was crazy. Spencer was right. I couldn't keep Serafina in a box, play with her whenever I felt like it, and then hide her away when other people came around. She had to share me, every time I walked out of the door. I had to be willing to do the same.

"You're right," I finally admitted.

"You're damn right I'm right," Spencer laughed. "Now quit trippin' and play that shit back again."

I played the track again, and allowed myself to enjoy the perfection, rather than anticipate what some man I didn't even know would think if and when he ever heard or saw her perform. Hell, Serafina still wasn't sure if she even wanted her name on it.

"Now we are all in agreement, Serafina doesn't want anyone to know it's her yet. So, what goes on in the studio…"

"…Stays in the studio," we all finished together.

"Tell me again why she's keeping this quiet?"

"Because her brother is crazy." The smirk on Spencer's face was priceless. "How are y'all getting along?"

"I think he's gotten used to me. He knows I'm not going to hurt Serafina. It just took some time for us to get to know each other. We didn't exactly start off on the right foot," I chuckled.

"What happens when we have to perform this? You know this track has the potential to blow the hell up. I can't see anyone performing this but Sera."

"We'll cross that bridge when we get to it," I assured them, "but right now, my baby is downstairs cooking us dinner, and if we don't eat she'll be pissed off."

I didn't have to worry about the guys not eating. Serafina was a great cook. Whenever I took her to a restaurant, she tried to figure out what was in her entrée. Within the week, she'd prepare something so similar you'd swear the chef shared his secret recipe. Tonight it was red beans and rice, beer-battered fried catfish fillets, and home made hushpuppies.

The talk during dinner was light hearted and funny. Spencer kept teasing Serafina about some phone call he'd received. I asked her about it, when everyone had gone home. She told me about the three-way call Max had made to Spencer; after he found out she'd spent that first weekend with me. Sooo…Max had been checking up on me. Spencer hadn't told me about that phone call, but I wasn't really worried about it. I am an only child, but I can imagine what kind of big brother I would have been.

"You did good up there," I told her as we cleaned the kitchen together. "I can't wait to get that song in the clubs. I gave the lyrics to a radio executive and he says that we can get away with playing it on Midnight Madness." Midnight Madness was like love dedication hour. Only mellow, slow jams were played between midnight and four a.m. and with our risqué lyrics, the late show was our only option unless we released a prime time version of the song.

"Nope. I don't want to change one word," she assured me. "If they can't play it during the day, then so be it. I wouldn't really want any little kids listening to it, anyway. There are way too many fast girls out there as it is."

I started cracking up. "You're starting to sound just like Max."

"Ohhh, don't cuss at me like that." A dishtowel came flying out of nowhere, landing on top of my head. "Speaking of my brother... He was talking about getting together this weekend."

"Dinner?"

"Yep."

"Where?"

"I think he was going to cook."

"Serafina."

"You have to admit, he is getting better. That salad he made the last time was pretty good."

"Yeah, but that's only because salad doesn't require the act of actually cooking." I frowned at the memory, "I was starving when we left. Remember? We had to stop at *TGIF* and get a burger on the way home?"

I must love her because when she tilts her head and looks at me that way, I can't say "no" to her. My head shook in amusement. I'd said, "yes" without actually saying anything. There was nothing, absolutely nothing I wouldn't do to please her...even if it meant eating Max's truck stop cooking, and she knew it. Looking at her now, walking around my kitchen as if she owns it, makes me think about what it would be like to have her with me all the time. Going to sleep next to her every night, waking up with her in my arms every morning, parking my car next to hers, seeing her books lined up on the bookcase next to mine, her clothes touching mine in the closet.

The promise of her had been whispered to me in a dream, and I'd awakened to find Serafina sitting in the car next to mine. I was to meet my wife that day. I believed it with all of my heart then, just as I believe it now.

Serafina and I have been together for about four months now, but I feel as if I've known her for my entire life, so perfect is our bond. I've been so accustomed to having her by my side. I can't remember what life was like before she stepped in. I know everything there is to know about her. I've memorized even the little things that would seem insignificant to those on the outside. For instance, I know that she loves standing in the rain with her arms outstretched, as if she could embrace the world. Sometimes I watch her from a distance, afraid to touch her because I don't want her to lose the look of peace on her face, not even to smile at me. So deep is my love that sometimes I feel like crying because there aren't enough words in my vocabulary to define what she means to me, not enough adjectives in my thesaurus to describe the joy she brings me. If I die prematurely, I pray I be reincarnated as rain; so that I may bathe her in my love as she stretches her arms to the heavens.

Love. Thy name drips from my lips like nectar, sticky sweet, and abundantly rare. It's all around us, yet so few people are blessed enough to relish love's addictive flavor. So many believe they've found it, only to be recoiled by the bitter taste of deception. This is no trickery. This passion I've found is perfection multiplied by infinity. I am in love.

I hold her just a little longer, as we stand next to her car. She's leaving again, driving across town to her apartment, leaving me alone to pine for her. I want to ask her to stay with me forever but I don't and it's with great reluctance that I softly close her car door and watch her drive away.

I want to marry her. I want to take her hand in mine and give her my mother's ring. I want to say, "I do" in front of our friends and family. I have much to ponder, as I lie alone in a bed that could easily sleep the two of us...plus one or two babies comfortably. I want to bury my seed deep within her womb, and wait nine months to see what we've created together. I thought of Serafina's smile on my man-child's precious face, my dimples on a little girl's cheeks, our love surrounding the fruit of our harvest, growing together as our children grow before us. Are there enough tears in my eyes to rinse away any reservations she may have about our relationship or where it's headed? I just want to be to her, all that she is to me.

　　　***

My father, just returning from his European tour, made my place his first stop from the airport. I hadn't seen him in months. Of course I'd talked to him on the phone, but I hadn't told him very much about Serafina. My father hadn't yet liked a girl I'd brought home. So, I hadn't wanted to hear any negative comments about my relationship. He'd heard from Grandmamma that I was in love, and wanted to see for himself. I was right in the middle of writing a song for Serafina, when he rang the bell. When I told him what I was doing, he grabbed the saxophone he never left home without, and added his own style of smooth jazz.

"She's beautiful. Her presence in my life has been like that elixir my mama used to give me when I had a sore throat. She's soothing, coating the rough edges of my life with a love so powerful that it sometimes makes me tremble. One look...one touch...the sound of her voice…the sight of her. The smell of her sends me flying off into never-never land. I can never leave the place inside of her that I call my haven. She is my everything. She is my Serafina."

My father stared at me from across the room, but didn't stop the groove. He softly played his sax in rhythm with my piano. My words surprised him. He told me as much, as we both backed away from our instruments and walked into the kitchen to share a couple of brews. We sat together at the breakfast bar, shoulders touching, both sipping slowly, waiting for the other to speak.

"Serafina, huh?" He asked calmly.

"Yeah," I answered, unable to suppress the smile that appeared whenever I spoke her name.

"I guess I don't have to ask whether she's black or white."

"Have you ever had to ask?"

"Nope. Met her in a Wal-Mart parking lot, huh?"

"Yeah."

"You've got a lot of your mama in you." He peered at me over the rim of his beer mug. "You know she picked me up in the frozen food section."

"That's not how she told it."

"Oh yeah?"

"Yeah. She said that you followed her around the grocery store asking for cooking advice."

"I was a bachelor."

"And," I continued, "she finally led you to the frozen food section, and told you to forget about cooking and just buy frozen dinners."

"She always did have a smart ass mouth." He smiled at the memory, and I could tell that he was replaying the scene in slow motion. "I miss her everyday."

"Me too." We were silent again, both basking in the special memories of a woman who loved us as fiercely as she fought her losing battle with cancer. A silent tear slid down my father's cheek, and I watched as it spilled into his beer with a gentle ripple.

"You wanna give her your mama's ring?" He asked suddenly.

"Yeah, Daddy."

"She's the one?"

"She's the one."

"I see it in your eyes."

"I'm sorry I didn't tell you about her."

"I haven't always been the most accepting man, when it comes to the women in your life, but I've never seen you like this. Khalil, I am proud of the man you've become. A couple of years ago, I wasn't too sure about you or where you'd end up, but you've truly surpassed my every expectation." He grabbed two handfuls of my dreads and pulled me close until our foreheads were touching. "Whatever you do, don't let her go. When you find a love that makes your heart sing, you have to take care of it. You have to cherish every moment you have together, as if it might be your last."

He spoke from experience; and as we sat there, foreheads touching, eyes locked, I was five years old again and he was the biggest, baddest, hippest, coolest daddy in the world. I was his only seed, and he always made sure I knew how wanted and loved I was. I was his main man, his little sidekick. Now, at twenty-eight, I was still his main man; and he was mine.

"You're alright with me," he told me.

"I'm glad."

"So what does she look like?" He released his grip on my hair, and gently head-butted me, before turning back to his beer.

"She's about five-six, cinnamon skin--"

"Red gal, huh?"

"Depends on the light," I chuckled. "In the moon light her skin glows like a mocha halo. In the sun she looks like a cinnamon stick. I just want to dip her in a mug of hot cocoa and swirl her around."

"You sure you ain't just pussy whipped?"

I laughed. He laughed. I pulled my wallet out of my back pocket and showed him a picture of my love. Her sandy hair was braided up into a messy ponytail. I'd taken the picture myself, right after I'd made good and thorough love to her, sweating out her fresh-from-the-beautician's chair hair-do. She was beautiful, no matter what, even with her makeup long gone and lipstick kissed off.

"She is a beauty," he chuckled. "You're right. She does have a glow to her. Sorta like a little angel."

"Afterglow," I said, closing my wallet. My father and I could discuss anything.

"You wrappin' it up?"

"We've both been tested," I assured him.

"That's good, but what about babies? Are you ready for one of those?"

"She's on the pill."

"Okay. I'd hate to see that cute little nose spread wide with pregnancy before you're ready, that's all."

"Don't worry. We have all the time in the world for that."

"Yeah," he said slowly. "So when do I get to meet her? I don't go back into the studio for another three months."

"Three months? You're taking a vacation? When did you make

that decision?"

"Just now," he smiled, but didn't tell me why. He didn't have to. One look from him and I already knew.

"I love you too, old man." I finished my beer, and left Daddy alone with his thoughts.

## Chapter 19

### Jeremy Trent Sanders

Jerica is not my sister. The lab results are staring me in the face; but I'm still in denial, unwilling to pick up my phone and call Jacob to tell him the news. As I sit on a gurney in an unused exam room, I can do nothing but sigh loudly every few minutes. The lab results are only a formality. Jacob has already set his plan into motion. Apparently, Michelle plans on leaving with Jacob, the moment the results are revealed... no matter what they say.

"Do you hate me?" She'd asked, as I'd scraped the inside of her cheek with a sterile swab.

"I hate what you did," I said, trying to ignore the old bruise partially hidden by her turtleneck. Her big brown eyes were lifeless, as if she were looking right through me. She looked like she was just floating through life, a ghost of her former, sassy self.

I looked down at the baby in her arms, and imagined a man putting his hands on her the way my father did her mother. An unexplainable rage settled in the pit of my stomach. I loved Jerica. It was a strange emotion, one I thought I'd reserved strictly for my mother... one I didn't think I was capable of lavishing upon any other female. I'd come close once, but there was no point in dwelling on Sera and what could have been.

"Jeremy, I'm sorry," Michelle whispered tearfully. "I never meant...I never planned on this...I was confused and I felt unloved and I didn't have anyone to turn to. Everyone else saw it but they ignored it. Even my own mother wouldn't help me. She told me that I deserved it for marrying a man so much older than me. She threw it up in my face. Jacob was the only one who cared about me."

"Did you ever love Pops?" It was a stupid question. Michelle's parents had disowned her, the moment she announced that she was marrying Pops. He was her Prince Charming. She'd loved him enough to forsake her family and blindly follow him into the fairytale he'd laid out for her. It wasn't her fault that he'd turned into a troll, the moment he carried her over the threshold and under his bridge.

It wasn't Mama's fault. It wasn't Jacob's mother's fault. It wasn't Jerica's fault. It wasn't Michelle's fault. Hell, it wasn't even Jacob's fault. He'd seen, in Michelle, the vulnerability and sweetness of his mother, of my mother. He'd seen those genuine qualities that steal your heart and make you want to protect...make you want to kill anyone who disrespects her.

As I sit here now, swinging my legs on a gurney, face in my hands, lab results in my left pocket, cell phone in my right pocket, I am suddenly ashamed of the man that I've worked so hard to perfect. I look up at the mirror across the room and I am ashamed of my reflection. I'm pissed off at my father's bald head, at his eyes, his lips, his black womanizing soul. I don't know what to do. All my life, I've strived to be the son he always wanted me to be; but at this moment, I'm not sure if I want to be the man I've turned out to be.

"Dr. Sanders there's someone here to see you." Her tone is formal, colder than the white linoleum floor. I don't even bother looking at Allison. There's no point. At this moment, her icy stare is more than I can stand. I see Jacob's running shoes approach, slowly crossing the floor where I can't seem to pull my gaze. I feel like I'm participating in a rerun of the Maury Pauvich show... *"Jacob, in the case regarding seven-week old Jerica Trishelle Sanders..."*

"You are the father," I say, without looking up at him.

"I guess I didn't get the super-sperm gene." His stale attempt at humor falls flat.

"Jacob what are we going to do?" I ask. "Seriously, what are we going to do? Pops is crazy. He'll kill Michelle. He might even try to kill you, to save face."

"It's not your problem, Jeremy. I'll handle it."

"It *is* my problem." I finally look at him, wondering if he can see the bewilderment ravaging my brain. "Anything affecting you affects me. Has Michelle ever called the police on Pops?"

"Several times."

"You know how this is going to look? The media will have a field day with this. They're going to say he beat her ass because she was fucking around with you. People will turn their backs on you, and show him all of the sympathy."

Jacob holds up his hands. "It doesn't matter what they think. I won't leave them there. I'm going to get them, and that's final."

I close my eyes. My head is pounding but I will the pain away. "Hang around. I get off in about thirty minutes. I'll go with you."

"Jeremy, you don't have to do that."

"Yes, I do."

"This could mess up your whole relationship with Pops," he warns.

"That relationship was messed up a long time ago," I sigh, "I was just too damn blind to see it then."

"Are you sure?"

"I love you, dawg. You're my brother."

"He was your father first."

"He was never really my father," I say with finality. "I've always had your back. I'm not going to stop now."

I mean it. Jacob needs me, and I'm going to be right there. This will forever change my relationship with Pops, but when I think about it…there was never really much of a relationship there, anyway. Just a grown man seeking approval, like that ten year-old boy who cried the night he walked out. It's time for me to re-evaluate what it means to be a man.

*\*\**

A high-pitched scream invaded the tranquility of the morning, startling birds into flight, and causing a baby to cry. It motivated two brothers to stand still, listening to the wind, listening to the baby cry, listening to another scream, and then another. Then, we were running up the driveway, bursting through the door without bothering to see if it could possibly be unlocked.

There he stood, sweat dripping from his brow, clothes disheveled, dried blood on the back of the hand that seemed suspended in air and ready to strike at any time. Jacob was on him, before he could hit her again, throwing him into the wall and pummeling him with a fury I never knew Jacob possessed. Pops fought him back, punch for punch, as if Jacob were a stranger attacking him and not his own son. The sound of glass breaking reverberated throughout the room, amidst Michelle's screams and Jerica's terrified cries. I found an opening, and jumped between Jacob and Pops, hoping one of them wouldn't punch me by accident.

"Boy, this is none of your business!" Pops yelled angrily.

"It is my business!" Jacob yelled back. "Look at her! Look at what you did to her, you sorry son of a bitch!" He lunged at Pops again, and I stood between them, one hand on his chest and the other against my father's.

"This ends here!" I yelled, looking back and forth between the two of them. "Michelle, get in the car."

"Bitch, you move and I'll kill you," Pops spat venomously.

"Baby, he ain't gon' do shit," Jacob said, staring into the eyes of our father. "Take the baby, and get in the car." He pulled his keys out of his jeans pocket, and gently tossed them in her direction. They landed near her feet with a loud jangle.

"Baby?" Pops looked from Michelle to Jacob, recognition flickering behind his angry eyes. "Ain't this a bitch? You been fuckin' my wife, nigga? Is that what this is about? You done came in here behind me, and ate my leftovers?" He glared at Michelle. "You trying to make a fool of me? Bitch, I'll kill you."

Michelle stood there, trembling with baby Jerica cradled in her arms, blood dripping from her nose and landing on the baby she'd been holding, unable to protect herself as Pops had gone off on her I wondered if he'd ever jumped my mother as she held me, unable to defend herself because she didn't want to drop me.   Michelle had been begging, when we'd burst through the door.  It was the same way my mother used to beg.  It was the same way Jacob had heard his mother beg for mercy from the man who claimed to love her.  I could hear sirens in the distance, and wondered if the neighbors had had enough of looking the other way. Had one of them called the police, to stop my father from killing Michelle?  The sirens came closer but kept going.  I didn't know how to feel as the sound faded out and became a faint memory.

"Michelle," I said softly, "go get in the car.  We won't let him hurt you."

"We?"  Pops asked me, "We?  Y'all are in this shit together? You gon' stand here and help this little bastard?  What?  Are you messin' around with her too?"

Michelle held the baby against her chest, and slowly squatted, scooping Jacob's keys up with her free hand.  "That's it," I thought.  "You can do it.  Just turn around and walk out the door."  She kept eye contact with Jacob, as if she were drawing all of her strength from him.  She trusted him to protect her, and I could tell by the look in her eyes that she was terrified of putting that much trust into another man.  I recognized that look.  I'd seen it before.  Michelle backed away, slowly moving towards the door, dodging broken glass and overturned furniture.  She was halfway to the door when he said the one thing that used to bring me to tears as a boy. It was the one thing that kept my mother locked in a relationship that could have killed her, had it gone on any longer.

"You ain't shit, Michelle.  You weren't shit when I met you, and you ain't never gon' be shit!  Look at yourself!"

I reacted, before I had a chance to think of the consequences. All of the rage I'd felt as a little boy suddenly resurfaced and swelled inside of my fist.  I hit him so hard that he stumbled and fell backwards into the wall.  I wrapped my hands around his neck.

"I couldn't save my Mama from you, Pops, but I'm not a little boy anymore."

"I always knew you were a punk," he said hoarsely, struggling against the grasp I had on his neck.  I wanted to crush his windpipe.  I wanted to choke him until he died.  At that moment, I hated him for everything that he was and everything in him that I saw reflected in myself.  I squeezed tighter.

"Jeremy!"  Jacob put his hand on my arm.  "Jeremy, stop, you'll kill him."

"I want to." I didn't even recognize my own voice.

"He's not worth it." Jacob stood close to me, whispering in my ear, "I know you want to kill him for everything he ever did to us, for what he did to our mothers, for what he did to Michelle. I want to kill him too, but the consequences aren't worth it, dawg. It's not worth it. Let him go."

It was so cliché. I'd heard it hundreds of times in movies and television shows. "He's not worth it." There was really no other way to say it. He wasn't worth it. I thought of losing my medical career, of losing my life, of losing the opportunity to watch Jerica grow up, of never having an opportunity to have children of my own, of forcing my mother to visit me in prison... I slowly released the pressure I had on Pop's neck, and let Jacob walk me away from him.

"Let's go." Jacob put his arm around Michelle's shoulders.

"You muthafuckas are dead to me!" Pops yelled hoarsely. "You hear me? Dead! You want that bitch, you can have her; but that baby stays here."

"No!" Michelle cried brokenly. Jacob pulled her closer, wiping the dried blood from her face with the bottom of his shirt, whispering something that I couldn't hear. I knew that he was sharing the news that I was about to give my father.

"She's not yours," I said simply, pulling a copy of Jacob's paternity test results out of my pocket and tossing it down at his feet.

"She's *my* daughter," Jacob said evenly, "and if I ever see you near Michelle or Jerica again..." He let the consequence hang in the air, but there was no mistaking how serious he was.

Pops picked up the paper with shaky hands and silently read the results. Then, he looked up at us, as if we were strangers. He tore the paper into tiny pieces, and let them flutter to the floor. Just like that, any chance for a genuine and meaningful relationship with our accidental father lay on the floor, torn and shredded like confetti at a tickertape parade. There was nothing left to do but walk away and leave him standing in the middle of the mess he'd made of his life.

## Chapter 20

### Serafina Danielle Jordan

The smell of burnt hair and oil sheen filled the bathroom I sat in a chair I'd dragged into the confined space as Ayzha stood over me with a curling iron in her hair.

"He called me a while back talkin' 'bout he wanna see me," I said, slightly agitated. Ayzha accidentally burned me with her curlers, and I jumped.

"Ooh, I'm sorry. What did he want?"

"I don't know. He told me I needed to stop actin' like I didn't miss him."

"What did you say?"

"I hung up in his damn face," I sighed. "Bastard," I added as an after thought. "Now, he's started calling again. I don't understand."

"He must have really pissed you off cuz you sound ghetto as hell right about now," Ayzha scolded.

"I'm not mad. I just don't understand why he would call me now, after we've been apart for so long. The punk didn't even look up, when I left him. He just sat there, eating and staring into space like I was giving him the damn weather report."

"I told you he was a dog," she snickered She handed me a mirror so that I could look at what she'd done with the back of my hair. "What do you think?"

"You should open a salon."

"I'm too busy keeping the books at To The Max."

Ayzha had recently quit her job at the boutique, much to Riley's dismay, and started working full time at Max's club. This gave her more reasons to be away from home. It also gave her opportunities to hook up with Tyree, whenever he wasn't either "too busy" or "away on business". Her relationship with Tyree was beginning to look a lot like her relationship with Riley, only with more sex. You can't tell Ayzha a damn thing though, so I'd long ago stopped commenting on her relationship with Tyree.

"So what do you think Khalil and Max are doing?"

"Well, Max wanted Khalil to play at the club tonight. So they're probably going over the set. I love Wednesday nights. Next to Friday, it's the most money-making night of the week."

"Even more than Saturday?"

"Girl, yes. You know the older crowd spends more money than the young folks. Plus, the live jazz and free BBQ have those old men spending all of their paper."

Ayzha definitely had a head for promotion, and had turned To The Max into the hottest club in town. It was open five days a week, and making tons of money. Khalil and his band, *Interlude*, were playing tonight, and I couldn't wait to see him perform.

I'd dressed carefully, in the dress that Khalil had left on my bed next to a bouquet of roses. It was black, form fitting, with a high neck, and spaghetti straps that zigzagged across my back. The dress was so long, if it weren't for my three inch heels and the slit that teasingly ended mid thigh, it would literally trail the floor.

"You look like a supermodel. Khalil has good taste."

"He does, doesn't he?" I twirled around in the mirror and watched my dress twirl with me, exposing my right leg with every move I made. "This is scandalous," I whispered.

"You're going to make me look bad," Ayzha mumbled, adjusting the strapless Wonder Bra beneath her burnt orange top. She looked like a regal queen, and I couldn't imagine anyone making her look bad. With her smooth chocolate skin, bright eyes, and perfect shape, she'd always been the standout beauty wherever she went. She tossed her shiny black hair and smiled, making sure that she didn't have any plum lipstick on her teeth.

"Shut up," I said, draping a scarf around her shoulders. "If I were as beautiful as you--"

"If you thought that you were half a beautiful as you actually are, you'd be conceited." She gave my cheek a dainty air kiss, and grabbed my hand, pulling me to the front door before I could self-consciously view myself in the mirror again.

    \*\*\*

The club was packed, when we got there; but we had our usual VIP table reserved. So, I wasn't worried about getting a seat. Max met us at the door. As he led us to our table, I was surprised to see our parents as well as Khalil's grandmother sitting there, all dressed up, chatting with Aleesha and Stacie.

"Daddy? Mama? Grandmamma?" I was flustered, partly because I was shocked and partly because I felt naked standing in front of them in that slinky black dress.

"You look wonderful, baby," my mother said, kissing my cheek as I sat down next to her. "Khalil invited us all out to hear him perform." Daddy hadn't said anything yet because he was still staring at me in that dress.

"You look cold, baby girl," he finally said, draping his blazer around my shoulders.

"Oh, quit acting like an old man. The girl looks beautiful!" Grandmamma said winking at me. "If I could have gotten away with that back in the day..." Her voice trailed off a bit, "but I was one of those fast girls."

The whole table burst out laughing, and probably would have gone on forever, had the house lights not dimmed. I watched with pride as Khalil sat down at the piano, draped in iridescent lights. He was wearing the white linen shirt and loose fitting white pants we'd picked out together, and his sandy locs were shiny, thanks to the herbal oil I'd rubbed into them the night before. He started to speak, and I felt a shiver of excitement spread throughout my body, just as it had when I'd first heard his voice.

"Good evening, ladies and gentlemen. Before I begin, I'd like to bring a special guest to the stage." He began to play softly, and the crowd gasped as the mesmerizing sounds of a lone saxophone began to accompany the sexy rhythm Khalil played on the piano.

"Ladies and gentlemen, my father, the best sax player in the whole damn world, Karl Roberts." My mouth must have been hanging wide open because my mother gently patted my chin. I had no idea I'd be meeting Khalil's father tonight. I was totally unprepared. Actually, I was petrified. What if his father didn't approve? What if I wasn't pretty enough? Rich enough, educated enough? Or worse, what if he thought that I was just a gold digger?

"Right now, we'd like to perform a song that we wrote together." Mr. Robert's voice cut into my paranoia, and I stared at the stage, this time making sure that my mouth was closed. "A few weeks ago, my son told me that he was in love. So, we got together and had a little father-son jam session. This is what we came up with..."

*"She's beautiful. Her presence in my life is like that elixir my mama used to give me when I had a sore throat. She's soothing, coating the rough edges of my life with a love so powerful that it sometimes makes me tremble. One look, one touch, the sound of her voice, the sight of her, the smell of her sends me flying off into never-never land. I can never leave the place inside of her that I call my haven. She is my everything. She is my Serafina."*

His eyes were closed as he played the piano, but I could feel the power of his love, through the words he spoke. Goose bumps invaded my flesh, despite my fathers blazer draped across my shoulders. I saw no one else, heard no one else. For as he spoke, there was only Khalil on that stage, and I was the only person in the audience.

*"Without her my life is but a mere story, waiting to be told. A movie with no sequel...a pen with no ink. A hearth with no fire...a flask with no drink. But with her...with her my life is a never-ending story and I can't wait to turn the next page. I want nothing more than to spend the rest of my life creating new chapters with*

*her, for our love is a story that could never be told with words alone. I want to be with her for eternity, but I'll settle for a lifetime if she'll have me."*

The tears in his voice coursed down my cheeks, but I didn't want to wipe them away. If I moved, even to correct my blurred vision, I may have missed something. So I sat there, still as a tree, while his words caressed me like a cool breeze, tickling my face, making me smile and cry at the same time.

I was so entranced by his words that I didn't even realize the piano had stopped. There was only the saxophone, as Khalil slowly descended from the stage like an angel. He stood in front of me, and as I gazed up at him, the fear in his eyes somehow reassured me that this was not just a beautiful dream. Khalil slowly dropped to his knees, and took my left hand in his. I stared deep into his eyes, reassuring him that I wasn't going to vanish. He pulled a ring out of his pocket, a simple one-carat diamond solitaire on a white gold band. I thought I'd faint, but somehow kept my hand steady, as he teased my fingertip with the precious metal.

"This engagement ring belonged to my mother. Before she died, she made me promise that I would put this ring on the finger of the woman that I would love forever. God led me to you, Serafina. I want to spend the rest of my life with you, as your friend, your lover, and your husband. Will you marry me?"

I looked over at my daddy, but the look on his face told me that he'd already given this union his blessing. He put his arm around my mother's shoulders and winked at me. Max appeared out of nowhere, standing behind our parents, and smiling broadly at me, finally approving of my choice. Aleesha, Stacie, and Ayzha dabbed at their eyes, in an attempt to save their eyeliner, but each failed miserably. My heart soared.

"I love you," I said, turning back to Khalil.

"Is that a yes?" He asked, raising an eyebrow.

"Oh yes."

He slid his mother's ring on my finger, and for a moment, I swore I saw a familiar woman in a loud red dress winking and smiling at me from the crowd. She kinda looked like the chick who'd harassed me at the stoplight a long time ago, but she disappeared, as quickly as she'd appeared. Khalil kissed me, and that strange woman was the last thing on my mind. Applause broke out around us, as we embraced. I glanced over at Ayzha who just laughed. She'd finally mastered the art of keeping a secret.

The rest of Khalil's band took the stage, livening up the teary-eyed women in the crowd with an upbeat ballad. Khalil's father took this opportunity to grasp my hand and admire the ring he'd given his late wife so many years ago.

"My wife would have loved you," he told me. He kissed me on the forehead, and walked away, obviously affected by the moment. I stared after him, in awe of this great man who had just accepted me into his family, with no questions asked.

***

Later, as we snuggled together in Khalil's warm bed, I couldn't help remembering the first time we'd lain together. Two people who barely knew each other had become one that night. I held up my left hand, and watched in fascination, as the ring twinkled in the candlelight.

"I think I'll go build a fire," Khalil told me.

"NO!" I said, a little too quickly, "Don't leave me."

"I'll be back in a minute," he chuckled, sliding out of bed and throwing on his boxers. There were no more logs in the bedroom, so he had to walk out onto the balcony to get more.

I felt totally alone, and it was at that moment I realized the desperation in which I'd asked him to stay. I hadn't meant 'don't leave the bed'. I'd meant 'don't leave me', literally. Don't leave me alone without your love because I don't know what I'd do if I didn't have you in my life. Don't shake me awake because I want to keep living in this dream world forever. I grabbed his pillow and hugged it close, inhaling the sweet scent of his hair oil and Allure cologne.

My thoughts were interrupted abruptly, as the room was suddenly bathed in firelight. I watched, in awe, as he slowly walked around the room blowing out candles.

"It's time to write another chapter." He slid underneath the sheets with me, and I smiled with the realization that he'd shed his boxers, in the process.

"Khalil, are you sure about this?" I asked between kisses,

"Don't get shy on me now."

"No, I mean…" I held his face away from me and stared him in the eyes. "Are you sure? About…this?"

"I know that I love you, Serafina. I know that this is meant to be, and when you doubt yourself, you doubt me." He rolled over, pulling me on top of him. Now it was his turn to cup my face in his hands and stare up at me.

"Baby, don't ever doubt me. I'll never hurt you. I'll never leave you. I just want to marry you and make beautiful music and beautiful babies and beautiful memories with my Nubian queen." He kissed me slowly, "And yes, I'm sure about this."

## Chapter 21

### Ayzha Nicole Darwin

"So, what's up with you and Tyson?" Max handed me a glass of ginger ale, and sat down on the edge of my desk.

"His name is Tyree," I said without looking up. I was going over the plans for next week's activities and making sure everything was settled with the entertainment. Once again, I was working late, but I didn't mind. Riley was away for the third time this month, and Tyree was out celebrating a friend's birthday.

There were times when I really needed to talk to Tyree, but he seemed to only be available when it suited him. I found myself longing for him constantly, sometimes to the point of anger; but the moment I heard his voice, the anger and loneliness would disappear and I'd say, "Hey you," as if I'd just spoken to him yesterday.

"You know you deserve better. Don't you?" Max took my pen and studied the slightly chewed tip, "I'm going to start charging you for these."

"I know. I never used to do that. It's just suddenly I feel the need to chew."

"How are things at home?"

"The same," I replied. But were they really the same? Before Riley left, he'd actually asked me if there was anything I wanted him to bring me back from New York. I'd been so shocked that I'd just shaken my head "no". Was he making a feeble attempt at reconciliation? Or was he just being nice because he didn't want me to divorce him and take half of his belongings? He needn't have worried about that. If he ever found out about Tyree, he could leave me with nothing but the clothes on my back.

Serafina's engagement had me doing a lot of thinking about my future. After several months of sneaking around with Tyree, I had yet to leave Riley. I was afraid of what would become of me, if I struck out on my own. This didn't make Tyree happy, but didn't exactly make him angry either. Actually, he seemed content with messing around behind Riley's back. He hadn't mentioned my leaving my marriage behind, since the first night I'd slept in his arms. While that made me a little uneasy, I was so addicted to the way I felt whenever we were together that I was sickly satisfied with just being available whenever he needed to see me.

If Aleesha suspected anything, she didn't mention it; Sera and Stacie had long ago decided to stop giving me advice, when it came to Tyree. Either I was too stupid or too stubborn, just too sprung on the way Tyree was putting it on me. Whatever the case, I felt trapped between a man who didn't appear to want me, and another who wanted me passionately, but somehow managed to disappear, whenever I needed regular conversation.

I looked up to find Max studying me closely. He asked if I was okay, and I told him yes. However, the moment I stood up, my legs felt so shaky I was immediately forced to sit. Max placed a steadying arm on my shoulder and a hand on my forehead.

"Max, I'm fine. I'm just coming down with a cold or something."

"Well, colds don't make you dizzy."

"Maybe I have the flu," I joked, standing again. The dizziness had passed. "See, I'm fine. I probably just stood up too fast."

Max walked me to my car, but before he closed the door, he leaned down and whispered to me, "I meant what I said earlier. You deserve better than what you're getting out of life." His words haunted me all the way home.

## Chapter 22

## <u>Jeremy Trent Sanders</u>

She's licking her lips seductively as we dance. My dick is telling me to take this girl home and give her one of "Dr. Jeremy's Special Injections: Guaranteed to Have Her Begging for the Next Fix," but the very things that are making my friend stand at attention are making my mind recoil in horror. Her lips are large and inviting, blackberry gloss shining brightly enough to guide a plane onto a dark runway. Her hair is styled in what appears to be thousands of teeny-tiny braids. I think the proper name for them is micro. I run my fingers through them, and she sighs, which bugs me because it wasn't a sexual move. Hell, I was just wondering how long it took to do her hair, and who the hell was gonna take it down when her new growth becomes unbearable.

Don't get me wrong, Shakina's look is totally slammin', but I am truly amazed by the lengths a woman will go through just to look good. Shit, just give me a pair of clippers and a bar of soap, and I'm basically set. This girl has obviously put a ton of effort into her appearance, and it's definitely working for her. It's just not working for me.

"Watch out now," I say, as she dances closer, pressing her secrets against my answers. I can't control my disobedient body parts, and her smile tells me that she doesn't mind.

"Jeremy, how many ways can I throw it at you?" She purrs into my ear.

I know exactly what she's talking about, but the player in me wants to hear her say it. I need to hear the words, to boost my ego. Of course, she falls right into it.

"What exactly are you throwing?" I ask.

"You know," Shakina whispers, getting shy all of a sudden, as if she's afraid to say it.

"I can't read your mind," I tell her. "If you're throwing something, you have to tell me exactly what it is. Ya know? So, a brotha can be on the lookout." I came to the club to take my mind off of my troubles and find someone to go home with, but I'm suddenly turned off by the ease in which I can just slide in and out of this woman's bed, no questions asked.

*"I knew you were a punk."* Almost a year later, and I can still hear Pops' voice ringing in my ears. Even with my hands wrapped around his neck, he'd had the audacity to challenge my manhood.

Is that why I'm still messing around? Conquer and destroy,

cloak and dagger, I have so many games running inside of my head I'm starting to get them mixed up. Women say they want a good man, but the moment I dare not show any sexual interest in them, they're quick to label me a punk. Maybe that's why I have to screw the hell out of them…to prove that I'm a man. Of course, the moment I pull out of that woman, I'm out of her life, and instead of labeling me a punk, I'm given a new title…*dog*.

Jacob had been true to his word. He'd married Michelle, as soon as he could. Even with the pressure of being an NFL star, he manages to remain faithful to her and to the family they've created. Their situation had caused quite a scandal, but eventually, with the help of Pops' proud silence, and an appearance on "Oprah", Jacob was suddenly seen as a knight in shining armor. He'd ended up listed as one of *People's* "Most Beautiful People". Ain't that some shit?

I have to smile, as Jerica's chubby little face pops into my mind. I wonder if I could ever be as smitten with a grown woman as I am with my pudgy, little niece. A name immediately surfaces, but I wish it away. There's no point. "LIG," my brother often says, when I need to get over some drama or event and simply move on. Let It Go. Let it go. Let it go.

"So what's up, Jeremy?" Shakina's voice invades my thoughts. "You haven't touched me in months. Are we gonna do this, or what?"

It would be so easy. It could be so easy. It's too damn easy to jerk my head towards the club entrance, and have this woman follow me through the crowd. As we move along, I don't even have to glance behind me. I know she's there, trying to get her hands on some part of me, so that she doesn't lose me in the sea of people trying to get to the dance floor.

I'm about to pass the bar when I see her. Then I see him, standing next to her at the bar, deep in conversation. I stop so suddenly that Shakina crashes into me clumsily, almost knocking me off of my feet.

"What is it?" Shakina asks, following my gaze.

"Go wait for me outside," I say, not even bothering to hear her reply.

I shake her hand off of my arm, and slowly walk towards the bar, not quite knowing what I'm going to say, or why I'm even contemplating speaking to the two people in this world who I know hate me with a passion unparalleled.

Their conversation stops suddenly, as I approach. She's curious. He's scowling behind his smile.

"Well, if it isn't Dr. Sanders, long time no see. Are you enjoying yourself, tonight?" He greets me pleasantly. At this moment, in front of all these people, Max is the successful club owner; and I'm just another customer to him. Behind closed doors, he's Sera's big brother; and I know that he wants to kick my ass.

"Yeah, the place is jumpin'," I tell him. We don't shake hands.

"How are you?" I ask Ayzha, Sera's best friend.

"I'm fine, and you?" She narrows her eyes, openly scrutinizing me, "Can we help you with something?"

"I was just wondering how Sera is doing," I say nonchalantly.

"She's fine," Max answers, but I look to Ayzha for validation.

"Is she?"

"Why wouldn't she be?" Max stares me down, like a bull looking at a red flag.

I ignore his sarcasm, take a deep breath, and swallow a small piece of my pride, not wanting to believe I was about to share with them something I didn't even want to share with myself.

"Just tell her I said hello, and that I miss her." I say it quickly, and turn on my heel, in an attempt to escape, but Max's response freezes me in my tracks.

"She's getting married."

I falter. Married? To whom? I take a deep breath, and turn around to face Max again.

"Who is he?"

"Let it go, man. She's a few weeks from her wedding day. It's too late for you to start trying to kiss her ass, now," Max tells me with a guarded smile. "Stay away from my sister."

I feel like a fool, but can't seem to move my legs. I'm rooted to the floor, like a pesky weed in need of a good yank. Somehow, I manage to take a few cautious steps, but as I slowly walk away from their smug faces, I am unable to focus. My head is pounding, as images of Sera wrapped in the arms of a faceless man chase me to my car. She's engaged. I say this aloud a few times, but it still doesn't sink in. I have to see it for myself, hear it from her sweet lips. I have to see her eyes, when she tells me that she's going to spend the rest of her life with another man.

Shakina is sitting on the hood of my car, but stands as I approach. She wraps her arms around me, and attempts to kiss me, but I'm no longer interested in what she has to offer.

"I'm sorry," I mumble, gently pushing her away, while quickly getting into my car.

"Jeremy!" She yells, as I begin to back out. I pretend not to hear her. I pretend not to see her tantrum, or the shoe that suddenly comes flying in the direction of my car. I drive to Sera's apartment, half hoping to find her man there, so that I can give him a good beat down; but common sense tells me that I have no right to interfere in her life.

The clock strikes one-thirty a.m., as my car rounds the corner, and her balcony comes into view. Who did I think I was, showing up unannounced at this hour? I didn't dare call her because I knew that she would probably hang up on me. I only have a couple of options. I can A) walk up to her door and knock, or B) drive away before I get my feelings hurt. My mind tells me that I should go with plan B, but of course, my ignorant heart won't listen. My heart leads me up the stairs to her door, and forces me to knock, before giving my mind a chance to argue its point.

"I knew you'd forget something!"

The door swings open, and she stops mid-sentence, when she realizes that the man she sees on her doorstep is not the man she expected. "What are you doing here?" She's wearing an outfit that I've never seen, and it's obvious that she hasn't been home for very long. Her hair is in a series of complicated French braids, accented with wooden beads. She looks like a goddess. My first impulse is to finger one of her pretty beads, but she shakes her head and asks her question again.

"What are you doing here?" It's a simple question, deserving a simple answer.

"I wanted to see you." My voice sounds lighter, like it belongs to someone ten miles away. I resist the urge to touch her again, and opt to stuff my hands into the pockets of my suede jacket.

"Why?" Okay, this doesn't have such a simple answer.

"I miss you." I'm standing in front of her, throwing a small bit of my pride to the wind, and she's staring at me as if I'm a door-to-door salesman who just interrupted her dinner.

"I can't believe you," she finally says, moving to slam the door; but I haven't come this far to leave without telling her what's on my mind. I push my way in, a pretty bad move on my part, but I'm desperate for her to listen to me. For the first time, she looks at me defiantly, as if I can no longer hurt her.

"Just let me talk to you, and then I promise to leave." I'm begging now, staying close to the door to show her that I won't come near her unless she wants me to. "Sera, please give me five minutes. Five minutes of your life is not going to make or break you." I know that she can't stand the sight of me, but there is a slight hint of curiosity in her eyes, as I slowly close and lean against the door.

"Are you happy?" I ask.

"Yes," she answers simply, without the unnecessary embellishment that most women use when they want their exes to know how wonderful their lives are without him.

"Do you love him?"

"Yes."

I close my eyes. I'm not sure if I'm ready for her to see how she is affecting me. I lower my head, open my eyes again, and focus on her brown leather boots.

"I saw Ayzha and Max tonight." I have to clear my throat in order to continue, "I guess congratulations are in order."

"Don't say it if you don't mean it."

I don't say it. Instead, I force myself to take one last look at her face. She is staring openly at me, and I take a small step toward her. She doesn't meet me halfway, but doesn't back away either. Once again, I reach out to touch her cheek. This time she doesn't shrug me off. Her skin is just as silky as I remember.

"What did you want to say to me?" She asks softly. "What's so important that it couldn't wait until a decent hour?" I choose not to answer that question. My heart is finally listening to my mind. It's time for me to leave, before I say or do something stupid.

"I'm glad that you found someone who makes you happy," I manage to say. But, before my brain can stop it, my heart speaks, "I just wish it could have been me."

"It could have been."

"And now?"

"And now, I've found the man I should have been with all along…and it isn't you, Jeremy."

So, she's finally brought herself to speak my name. Too bad it's not in the context I would have imagined. I turn and walk away, without another word. I simply open the door, walk out, and close it behind me. My head hangs low, as I walk those stairs for the last time.

"*One day you're going to wish you'd treated me better.*" Her sweet voice echoes in my ears, as the memory of her parting words ring desperately true. The master of the player's game has just crapped out.

## Chapter 23

### Serafina Danielle Jordan

I paced back and forth in front of the dressing room's full-length mirror, and tried to stay calm as nervous tears threatened to ruin the make-up job Stacie had given me two hours ago. No one dared speak to me, as I dialed Khalil's cell phone number for the umpteenth time. The voice mailbox was full. Frustrated, I slammed the phone down, and walked over to the window.

Khalil was running late. He was never late. He was never late. He was never, ever late. Why was he so late? And how could he pick today of all days? Today was special. We'd been dreaming about this since we met. How could he do this to me?

Suddenly, a lone figure stepped out from behind the trees in the distance. I closed my eyes, not wanting to believe what I was seeing. It was the woman in red who'd harassed me so long ago, trying to force a smile out of me. I had not seen her, since the night Khalil and I were engaged; but there she was in all her glory, dirty red dress and hellish make-up. I took a shaky step backward and bumped into Ayzha, my matron of honor.

"Sera, what is it." Ayzha grabbed my hand, and pulled me towards her.

"She's here," my voice trembled.

"Who?"

I pointed out the window but Ayzha swore that nobody was there. I looked again, but she was gone. I turned away from the window, and looked around the small room. Everyone had gone out into the hall. I looked over at Ayzha, nervously, suspiciously, but I didn't have time to ask her the question lingering in my mind. A strong, firm hand squeezed my bare shoulder, and I didn't need to look at his face. I knew who it was. I slowly placed my hand over my father's, and held my breath. No, I didn't want to sit down. I wanted to stand up. No, I didn't want to look at him. Ayzha tried to pull her hand from my grasp, but I couldn't let go.

"Daddy please, just tell me what you have to say," I whispered.

He didn't know what to say or how to say it and when I saw my mother walking through the door I demanded to know where Khalil was and what excuse he'd come up with. She just grabbed me and hugged me. She was messing up my hair but every time I tried to pull away, she wouldn't, or couldn't, let me go. She was speaking directly into my ear but her voice sounded miles away as she told me that Khalil wasn't coming.

"Oh my God, I can't breathe." I couldn't speak the words; only grab my throat in panic. I couldn't breathe. I couldn't see. I couldn't think. I couldn't even cry. I could only run as fast as I could, down the hallway and out the door with the train of my wedding dress trailing behind me. A sharp pain grabbed me as I stumbled, turning my ankle in my ivory heels, but I couldn't afford to stop running. I needed to get to a car, any car.

"Slow down, child."

The woman in red stepped out of the shadows and stood in front of me, blocking my way. I couldn't scream. I turned to run the other way, and collided into my father. I tried to point the woman out, but she'd disappeared again. Daddy must have scared her off. He tried to hug me but I snatched away from him, trying hard not to see the pain in his eyes. The limo pulled up, and I climbed in, refusing to sit next to anyone. I didn't want to hear what they had to say. I didn't want to be touched. I didn't want to be held, and I didn't want anyone to talk to me.

Khalil's grandmother was hysterical, but I couldn't cry. Behind closed lids, my eyes burned; but I refused to let a single tear fall. Crying was a sign that something was wrong, and I desperately wanted to believe that as long as I kept the pain inside, everything was going to be okay. The moment I broke down would be the moment I screwed up and admitted that things were seriously bad. So, instead of crying, I sat with eyes closed, facing the window, my gloved hands folded neatly in my lap. I didn't even notice that the train of my dress had been trapped in the car door, resting on the pavement, and gathering oil and dirt as we sped all the way to the hospital.

\*\*\*

I sit next to Khalil's bed wearing gloves that, once white, are now streaked with black mascara, mocha lipstick, dust, and the oil free makeup I'd been wearing when I arrived. My hair hangs down to my shoulders, with tangles where the curls used to be. My wedding dress, once ivory and starched to perfection, is now just a dirty wrinkled mess.

I haven't eaten in days but I have no appetite. I have not showered, nor have I changed clothes. I haven't even given myself the luxury of crying. I have not left Khalil's side. I refuse to leave him alone, and so I've remained with him, stubborn and dry eyed for five days.

For five days, I've kissed lips that won't respond, and squeezed hands that can't squeeze back. I call his name, and when he doesn't answer, I just keep talking to him as if he had. Every time I lay my head down at his side and close my eyes, memories of the last time I spoke with him flood my mind. I've been closing my eyes a lot.

Six days earlier...

*The telephone rang at about 3 a.m., and I reached out to grab it before it could wake anyone. Ayzha, who was sleeping beside me, stirred slightly, mumbled something incoherent, and fell back into a deep sleep. Aleesha and Stacie were stretched out at the other end of the bed and if anybody made the slightest move they'd end up kicking someone. It was a good thing I'd splurged on a King sized bed when I first moved out on my own. The double bed I used to sleep in at my parent's house would never have held the four of us.*

*I didn't need to look at the caller ID to know who was calling. I'd felt him call my name, before the phone even had a chance to ring.*

*"Khalil," I whispered, instead of saying hello.*

*"Where are the girls?"*

*"Asleep."*

*"Drunk?"*

*"Slightly," I laughed, "but they'll be okay by four. Don't worry."*

*"So tell me again, why they felt the need to spend the night."*

*"To make sure the groom didn't try sneaking a peek at the bride."*

*"Or vice versa," he added.*

*"Or vice versa," I agreed.*

*"Did I wake you?"*

*"No, I can't sleep," I admitted.*

*"Nervous?"*

*"No, I just can't wait to see you."*

*I could hear his smile through the telephone lines. "Go outside and stand on your balcony."*

*I didn't question him. I carefully slid out of the bed, making sure not disturb my drunken babysitters, as I did so. I walked down the hallway to the living room, and told Khalil all about my bachelorette party. He told me all about the stripper who had tried to give him one last fling as a single man. I feigned jealousy, and asked him if he'd been tempted.*

*"Well, shorty was kinda fine." I pictured him stroking his new beard as he said so, and I burst out laughing. "Are you on the balcony yet?"*

*"I'm opening the door now." I unlocked the sliding door, and quietly slid it open. As I stepped out into the warm September air, I could smell the hickory that one of my neighbors had used in his barbecue grill. "I'm outside."*

*"Me too."*

*"What are you doing outside?"*

*"Staring up at the most beautiful moon I've ever seen."*

I looked up at the same moon, and silently agreed. It was a big, beautiful orange moon that seemed to light up the entire sky. I could hear Erykah Badu playing in the background, and knew that he was missing me the same way I was missing him.

*"The night I found you again, a moon just like this one watched over us, as we made love in my car,"* he reminisced.

*"Hmm...I remember that well."* I exhaled slowly, as the memory sent a shiver throughout my body. *"So what makes this the most beautiful moon?"* I asked.

*"Well, this is the last moon that I'll ever gaze at with Serafina Jordan."* The truth in his words shot right through me, sending tingles from my scalp to my fingertips. I leaned on the railing and smiled, anticipating the next time I'd see him.

*"I wish you were here right now."*

*"What would you do with me?"* He asked.

*"I'd curl your toes,"* I answered seductively

*"Sounds intriguing. How do you plan on doing that?"*

*"I don't know. I guess you'll just have to wait for Serafina Roberts to show you."*

He liked the way my name sounded combined with his, and asked me to say it again and again. We talked about our future. We reminisced about our past, and the nostalgia created a small lump in my throat. We kissed through the phone and hugged in our minds until our orange moon disappeared and we watched the sun come up together.

*"This is my last sunrise with Serafina Jordan,"* he whispered...

Those were the last words I remembered him speaking to me. I longed to get that moment back. I longed to be on my balcony again, watching the sunrise with Khalil, while he whispered words of love in my ear. Now, because of a drunk driver who hadn't had the decency to live and answer for his crime, Khalil lay in a hospital bed, slowly drowning in a deep sleep that threatened to keep him forever.

Khalil's father and grandmother also kept vigil at his bedside, watching over him in shifts. I was too distraught to realize that they were also watching over me. I was too wrapped up in Khalil to realize that my mother sat with me everyday, silently praying in the background. No one could convince me that I needed to rest. No one could coax me out of my wedding dress. No one could penetrate the Teflon wall I'd built around Khalil and myself.

"Serafina." I stared across the bed at Khalil's father as he said my name. "The doctor gave Khalil forty-eight hours to wake up. It's been five days."

"He'll wake up, he's just tired."

"Serafina--"

"He's tired!" I snapped. "He's been through a lot. You'd be tired too, if you had a broken leg."

"It's more than a broken leg."

"He's tired," I insisted. "Please stop talking. I don't want to talk about this anymore."

"That's my boy lying there. He's my inspiration, baby, my only seed." There were tears rolling down his face. "I love him more than anything in this world, but we have to prepare ourselves for the reality of this situation."

"Don't say it."

"Serafina, he's in a coma."

"I'm not listening, Karl."

He walked around the bed, and squatted down next to my chair, the same way Khalil had squatted down in front of me the first day we met. Khalil looked a lot like his father.

"You have to go home and get some rest. You need to take care of yourself. You can't help my son, if you're sick."

"I can't leave him."

"You have to. We are all worried about you. You're his fiancée, but I'm his father, and I can have you banned from this room if you don't start taking care of yourself!"

"Karl--"

"I want you to go home and change--"

"No!"

"...clothes, Serafina," he finished as if he had not been interrupted. "You have to take off this wedding dress."

He looked past me, and I turned to see who or what he was looking at. Max was standing behind me. The pressure of his hands on my shoulders scared me.

"You don't understand," I whispered hoarsely. "None of you understands." Khalil's father stood and walked out of the room, leaving me alone with my brother.

"It's just you and me, Sissy," he whispered softly. "You don't want to hear this, but Khalil is in a coma. The crucial point in his recovery passed three days ago. You know that I love Khalil like a brother, but I can't help him right now. I can help you, baby girl, if you'll just let me." I tried to shake my head, but he grabbed my face, holding it still in his hands. "Sera, you're a mess. Khalil may never wake up. Do you hear me? He may never wake up, but if he did, would you honestly want him to see you like this? It's time for you to go home with Mama and Daddy. Or you can come home with me, and let me take care of you."

"I'm staying."

"Sera! You can't help Khalil right now! You're making yourself sick, and I'm not going to stand by and watch you kill yourself. You're no good to anyone right now!" The room was silent, except for the steady beeps that let me know that Khalil's heart was still beating. I listened closely for any irregularities, but there were none.

"Max, if I take this dress off, Khalil will be lost to me forever. If I leave this room, I'll be gone when he needs me the most." As I spoke, tears began to roll down my cheeks and fall onto my satin dress, leaving dirty splotches in their wake. "As long as I'm here, in this dress, I know he'll wake up, and we can still get married."

"Oh Sissy, I can't stand to see you going through this." Max pulled me close, holding me tightly, as I finally allowed all of the pain and frustration of the past five days to spill forth. My cries sounded loud to my ears. It was as if I were in the Grand Canyon and my tears were echoing around me. Max tried to stand me up, but my legs were weak. Lack of food and rest combined with the stress of the situation had finally taken their toll on my body. I'd just been too stubborn to allow it. I didn't argue as my big brother, my champion scooped me up in his arms and carried me out of the room. At that point, I had only enough strength to cry, which is what I did with my arms wrapped tightly around his neck and my face buried in the shoulder that had caught many a tear in my lifetime. Like the hero he'd always been to me, Max carried me right out of that hospital, and took me home.

## Chapter 24

### Jeremy Trent Sanders

She's thinner than I remember. Her hair is pulled back into a ponytail, but there is no mistaking the woman in the baggy black sweat suit is Sera. It's been a little while since I last saw her, but I still remember every detail about our last meeting. I remember everything from the braids in her hair to the pale gold polish she'd been wearing on her nails. I silently watch her walk past the nurse's station, seemingly oblivious to the people around her.

I'd be lying, if I said I wasn't a little curious about her hospital visit. Was someone sick? Could it be one of her parents? It's probably wrong of me, but I follow her down the hall to the exit. She doesn't see me, but I see her stop at the revolving door, almost as if she doesn't really want to leave. I walk toward her, as she stands in the doorway, making a small obstacle for the steady flow of people trying to walk past her. I touch her shoulder. She jumps.

"I didn't mean to scare you." My hands on her shoulders steady her.

She looks pathetic. I don't mean to be harsh, but this is not the woman who stood in front of me a few months ago and told me that she was marrying another man. She stares at me blankly, and for a moment I wonder if she even knows who I am. There is no makeup on her face, no curls in her hair, no pep in her step, not even a trace of a spark in those pretty, brown eyes. Everything I remember about her has vanished. I'm shocked.

"Are you okay?" I ask the question when the answer is staring me in the face.

Her lovely face is ashen, and for a moment I think she might faint. I slowly hold out my hand, and to my surprise, she doesn't shrink away from me. She doesn't exactly walk towards me either. So, I inch a little closer, and put my arm around her slumped shoulders, slowly leading her away from the door. I ignore the nurses' curious stares, as I lead Sera past the circular desk and down the corridor to my office.

"Thirsty?" I ask, closing the door behind us. It's after five and my day is done. I have plenty of time to spend with her, if she'll allow it. I pour a glass of water, without waiting for her answer. "Sit down," I order. She'd rather stand. I hand her the glass of water, and she cradles it in both hands, as if she's afraid she'll drop it. I've been on my feet all day, so I sit on the edge of my desk facing her. Her eyes wander around my office.

"What are you doing here?" I ask, and her eyes finally zero in on me.

"I had an appointment with Dr. Tracey."

"Oh, that time of the year again, huh?" I ask, remembering that she usually has her annual exam around her birthday, which was tomorrow.

"You remember that?"

"I remember everything," I chuckle. I grab a peanut butter cup out of my candy dish and hand it to her, "Happy birthday."

"I guess you do remember everything." She hands me her glass of untouched water and opens the candy, taking little bird bites. I notice her engagement ring still resides on her left hand but there is no wedding band beneath it.

"When are you getting married?" I ask.

She stops eating and stares off into space. "Why would you ask me that?"

I'm taken aback. "I was just won--"

She cuts me off with a quick, "I don't know."

Do I smell trouble in paradise? I stand up, and look down at her, taking in the slump of her shoulders, the lazy ponytail, and gray sweats that are hiding her fantastic shape. It's the uniform of depression, and it doesn't look good on her.

"Sera are you okay?" .

"Why?"

"You look like shit." It hurts me to say it but it's the truth and she needs to know.

"Do I?" She laughs nervously. "Tell me, what are you doing in this area of the hospital? Last time I saw you, you were an ER doctor."

It wasn't the least bit subtle, but against my better judgment, I let her change the subject. I explained to her that I'd been offered a paid internship with a pediatric doctor. It meant better hours and more pay in the future. I told her how a little boy with asthma had almost died in the ER because his illness had been misdiagnosed. The experience had influenced my decision to go into pediatrics.

"Pediatrics, huh?" The fake laughter leaves her voice suddenly.

She notices a picture of Jerica on my desk and picks it up, tracing the outline of the baby's face with a broken fingernail.

"Is this Jacob's little girl?"

"Yeah, that's Jerica," I say with a smile.

"She's pretty." She gently places the picture back on my desk, but can't seem to tear her eyes away from the baby's face.

"What's wrong?" I ask, putting a little bass in my voice, attempting to disguise the pleading. "We didn't exactly part as friends, Sera, but I do care."

"I shouldn't even be here." She tries to leave, but I grab her hand and gently pull her towards me. "Why did you bring me here?"

"Because you look like you could use a friend."

Emotions I don't understand flash in her eyes, and for a moment, I wonder if I should just let her go. She looks away, but not before I see the tears in her eyes. I don't know what to do, so I just kind of hold her, trying to keep our bodies from touching too intimately. I can feel my heart breaking. Of all the times I've made her cry in the past, I don't ever remember feeling anything but contempt for her tears. Now, she's in my arms, crying tears that I didn't cause, and my stomach is tied up in knots. So, I hug her the right way. Her face buried in my lab coat, my hands stroke her back, and I feel what I couldn't see through her baggy clothes. She's tiny, as fragile as a china doll.

"You don't have to talk about it," I whisper into her hair, feeling drunk from the berry scent of her shampoo. She's trembling. I take off my lab coat, and wrap it around her shoulders.

"Jeremy, I'm pregnant." She says it so softly, I wonder if she even meant for me to hear.

"Pregnant?" I stutter. My heart breaks a little more, as I force cheerfulness into my voice. "That's great news!"

"Is it?" She asks.

"Babies are always good news."

"I guess it depends on how you look at it."

"So, tell me how you're looking at it. Why are you so depressed? Why are you walking through this hospital looking like you've just lost your best friend?"

She gives me a puzzled look, and in that instant I realize that there is something she's not telling me. Something that maybe she feels I should already know. "You don't know." It's not a question, so I don't feel obligated to answer her. "Khalil is here."

"Who is Khalil?"

"My fiancé."

"He's here?" I look around nervously because the last thing I need is a jealous boyfriend bursting into my office with a death wish. "Look Sera, I'm not trying to come into the middle of anything, but if he's mistreating you--"

"He's in room 1283," she interrupts.

The twelfth floor houses patients who are paralyzed or comatose. When she tells me that her fiancé is there, I let go of her and sit down on my desk.

"What happened?"

"I don't know. He was on his way to the wedding, and some drunk hit him head on."

"On your wedding day?" I'm stunned.

"I couldn't write a better movie plot, if I tried."

"Damn." I pat the empty space next to me, and she sits. I hand her a tissue. "Sera, that's terrible." She gives me one of those "Negro please" looks, and my feelings are instantly hurt. I feel like that little boy who cried, "wolf" too many damn times. All of my play-acting where her feelings were concerned had her doubting me now, when I truly felt sad for her.

"How long ago?"

"Three months."

"You should tell him about the baby. It will give him something to focus on, and take his mind off of his paralysis."

"He's not paralyzed. At least, they don't think so."

I slide my hand over hers. I don't want to say it out loud. Neither does she. So, we sit in my office, holding hands silently. I can't begin to fathom how she is coping with everything that is going on in her life. She's pregnant, and her fiancé is in a coma. That's something people pay to see at the movies, but it's actually happening to her. I feel so guilty, remembering all the times I've wished that man harm. All of the times I've fantasized about him dying, leaving Sera all alone with no one to turn to but me. Damn…I feel like a complete asshole.

"I never thought I'd be sitting here with you, crying over another man." The irony in her words knocks the wind out of me.

"How far along are you?"

"About four months, give or take a few days."

"You haven't been taking care of yourself."

"No."

"Do you want this baby?"

"I don't know." She looks me in the eye. "That's terrible isn't it?"

"It depends on how you look at it." I hand her one of my cards. "I'm here if you need me."

"I have to go."

In an instant, she's gone. Leaving nothing but the aroma of her shampoo behind, as her footsteps fade. My mind tells me to leave her alone.  My heart grudgingly agrees.

## Chapter 25

### Ayzha Nicole Darwin

I stretched lazily, inhaling the smell of bacon and eggs that floated upstairs to my bedroom. Naked beneath the covers, hair in my eyes, sweetly funky, and wickedly exhausted, I felt divinely invigorated. Not bothering to cover myself, I walked across the room into the bathroom to brush my teeth, gargle a quick swig of mouthwash, and slide back into bed without being seen.

Tyree walked in, moments later, carrying a breakfast tray and wearing his famous smile. Of course, I pretended to be asleep; but he wasn't fooled. He proved this by dripping orange juice on my shoulder, then licking it off.

"You're bad," I giggled.

"Not as bad as you."

"I'd argue your point, but you might just be right." I dipped my finger in the whipped cream he'd placed on my waffles, and slowly licked the sweet substance from my nail. "Where did you find whipped cream?"

"I ran to the store."

"How nice of you."

"Not really. I had ulterior motives."

"Oh yeah?"

Tyree slid into bed next to me, and started nibbling my neck.

"Ordinarily, that would work, but I'm starving." I pushed him away and searched the tray for a knife and fork. Tyree stared at me, but I ignored him, instead deciding to concentrate on the feast of waffles, bacon, and eggs he'd prepared for me. I ate with relish, not thinking to offer him any, until I was licking the last of the syrup from my fingers.

"Damn, a brotha would have liked a bite."

"I'm sorry, baby. I'm starving."

"Present tense?"

"Yeah."

Tyree stared at me. It wasn't a look of love or passion, more like a look of curiosity. I stared back, wondering what he was looking for. He broke eye contact, long enough to look around my bedroom.

"When's the last time he was in this bed?"

"Who?"

"Your husband." Tyree caught my eye again, this time not letting go.

I didn't like discussing the intimacies of my marriage with Tyree, and he knew that. So, why in the hell was he asking me these questions? He hadn't been concerned last night, when he'd been all over my husband's bed, all over my husband's wife, all up in the fridge eating and drinking; but I didn't dare speak those words out loud. I wanted to see where the conversation was headed.

"Why?"

"I want to know. When was the last time he touched you?"

"I don't know, Tyree. It's been a while."

"At least a month?"

"At least two or three, and why do you care?"

"Because I saw your calendar."

"What calendar?"

"The one on your dresser. I didn't see any little red dots for this month."

I snatched the covers off and ran to my dresser. Sure enough, my daily planner had been tampered with, and he was correct. There were no little red dots on the calendar, to indicate the start and finish of my period because there hadn't been a period yet. I hadn't even realized...

"Oh shit." By my calculations, my period had to be at least two weeks late. "Oh shit."

"What does that mean?" Tyree questioned.

"It doesn't mean anything. It's only been a couple of weeks. It's probably just stress." I ran past him into the bathroom and turned the shower on full blast, hoping to avoid further conversation with him, but he followed, speaking to me through the curtain.

"Have you been to the doctor?"

"Hello? I just realized it was missing."

"I thought you were taking pills!"

"I am!" I yelled, not liking the tone he was taking with me.

The room fell silent. I angrily turned the shower off, and snatched a towel I'd left hanging on the rod. Tyree barely looked at me, as I walked past him. "You should go," I spat out angrily.

"Maybe I should."

"Lock the door behind you."

Without another word, Tyree left me sitting on my husband's bed, with the possibility of another man's child in my womb. He didn't want to believe it. He'd spoken to me as if I'd missed my period on purpose. Pregnancy was the last thing I needed. After the last miscarriage, I'd vowed never to try again. It was for that reason my marriage had begun its slow deterioration. Riley only wanted to procreate, no matter how much pain the losses caused me.

My temples began pulsating, as memories of long nights and secret rendezvous with Tyree flooded my mind. After a year of fooling around, the subject of me leaving Riley hadn't passed his lips...not since the first time we'd made love and I, being so caught up in the situation, had been too blind to see that he didn't really want that, until now

I stared down at the mess we'd made of my marriage bed, and buried my face in my hands, waiting for tears that, for some unknown reason, wouldn't or perhaps couldn't fall. I stripped the sheets from my bed, got dressed, and threw the sheets into the washer but in my mind I knew those sheets would never be as clean as they were before Tyree's naked body had lain across them. What had seemed like a wickedly sexy idea last night now weighed on my mind like a heavy brick with the word "GUILTY" engraved into the coarse stone.

In the back of my mind, I wondered how Riley's business trip was going, and if in fact, it actually was business that kept him away so much. I needed to find another fault in him. It was the only thing that kept me from feeling sick from the guilt resting in my womb.

\*\*\*

Aleesha and I met for lunch at the park across the street from our mutual gynecologist, Dr. Tracey. We'd been here before, except the last time we met here to talk in the freezing cold, Sera and Stacie had been with us. Somehow, I didn't feel comfortable calling Sera with my problems. She had so many problems of her own. When I'd called, I'd only told her how much I loved and missed seeing her. She'd been preoccupied, but I'd automatically assumed she was thinking about Khalil. I promised myself I'd stop by later to check on her.

Aleesha arrived a few minutes after me, carrying a Styrofoam coffee cup, and complaining about the chill in the air. She stopped short, when she saw me sitting alone on the park bench, hugging myself and shivering, despite the fact that I was dressed in layers and wearing my new Isotoner gloves. Aleesha handed me her coffee cup, and I declined, although the scent of her vanilla cappuccino definitely tempted my taste buds.

"You don't want any French vanilla?" She sat down next to me and took a long and, judging by the way she closed her eyes as she swallowed, satisfying sip.

"It has caffeine."

"So. You drink caffeine all the damn time. And why the hell are we meeting outside in the cold of winter, when there is a perfectly warm coffee shop a block away?" She involuntarily shivered.

"It's not that cold, and caffeine isn't good for the baby," I mumbled.

"What? Whose baby?"

"Mine." I exhaled noisily, and took another swig of the water I'd been sipping on all day.

"Ayzha, you're pregnant?" Aleesha's smile was highly contagious. I felt the corner's of my mouth twitch. "Oh my God!" She hugged me tightly, stuttering about how happy Riley would be when I told him, and that she was glad Riley and I had obviously been doing more communicating.

I started laughing. I laughed so hard that I could see my breath coming out of my mouth in little puffy clouds.

"I can't wait to tell him."

"What do you think he'll say?"

"Oh, he'll probably say, 'Get out of my house and take your bastard child with you!' " I gave Aleesha a moment to absorb the information.

"What?"

"It's not Riley's baby."

"What do you mean, 'It's not Riley's baby?' Ayzha, what did you do?"

"I think the proper question is *who* did I do…"

"I don't want to know," she said slowly. The coffee fell from her hands, leaving a light brown stain on the cold sidewalk. "I don't want to know," she said again. "You never stopped seeing him. Did you?"

"I did. I stopped seeing him for a while, but one day I talked to him, and the next thing I knew we'd graduated to sleeping together and now I don't know what to do, Aleesha." This time the tears actually did come, but Aleesha didn't hold me. She handed me a tissue, and cupped my face in her hands while she gave me a reality check.

"Remember when I told you to leave Tyree alone? Remember when I told you I'd been where you were, and that it wasn't worth it?"

"Yes."

"Ayzha, I meant that literally. I used to mess around with Tyree, and I'm telling you he's nothing but a dog. Does he call you *lady*? Does he always brag about wanting to eat you for lunch? Does he--"

"Shut up!"

"No! I didn't tell you this before because I didn't want to hurt you, but you need to know what you're dealing with. I never went further than a kiss with Tyree. Jason and I were having marital problems, and Tyree was right there waiting to pick up the pieces. There's another woman in our office, a white chick who's about to leave her damn husband for Tyree, Ayzha. They've been messing around for over two years. Since before he met you, Ayzha." I tried to pull away from her, but Aleesha, in her desperation to make me understand, would not let me go.

"Sweetie, he makes a habit of messing around with married women. He knows how unhappy you are at home. He befriends you, and then he goes in for the kill. Hell, just last week on our business trip, he got one of the new girls drunk, and spent the night in her hotel room." My mind immediately flashed to the three times I'd called him last week, only to get voice mail. He'd been too busy with his conference to talk to me for more than a quick minute.

"Why?" I was talking more to myself than Aleesha. "Why?" I said again, weaker this time. Why would he tell me he loved me, if he didn't? Why would he ask me to leave my home, my family, if he really didn't want it? Why would he lie to me about the other women in his life? "Because I let him."

The pit of my stomach caved in, and I had the sudden urge to throw up. I wanted to vomit and get rid of everything within me that loved Tyree. I wanted to throw up, until his baby spilled out of my mouth and ran down the sidewalk with my self-hatred and self-respect not far behind.

"Are you okay?" Aleesha asked, but I couldn't speak. I could only cry from the pain pounding at my head, slicing through my heart and penetrating my very soul. I truly wanted to lie down on the cold pavement and cry until hypothermia set in, numbing me from the hurt, and killing me gently. I didn't want to believe Aleesha, but the pained look in her eyes told me she'd never hurt me intentionally.

"Ayzha, talk to me. I didn't tell you this before because I thought things were over between the two of you. I would never hurt you like this."

I knew, but couldn't vocalize it. I tried desperately to separate my anger from my pain, but failed miserably. I could have blamed myself but it wasn't entirely my fault. Tyree knew my situation from the start. I'd always been honest with him about my feelings, about my marriage... I'd asked the same of him, and he'd failed me. He'd pursued me knowing, in his heart, he didn't really want me; and I couldn't get over it. I couldn't fathom how a man could say, "I love you" and not mean it.

"He said he loved me, Aleesha." It came out choked and desperate, I was grasping at straws, wanting so much to believe in him without calling Aleesha the liar that she wasn't. "I'm pregnant."

"What are you going to do?"

"I don't know. If I try to carry this baby, I'll most likely lose it like I lost the other ones. If I get an abortion, I'll spend the rest of my life wondering if I could have had this baby. What if this is my only chance to be a mother? What if I miscarry? I don't want to go through that again. I swore I'd never put myself through that again, but as soon as Dr. Tracey told me I was pregnant..."

I couldn't describe my feelings with words. I'd been happily devastated. I hadn't known if my tears were from joy or disappointment. I didn't want to be pregnant, but the reality of the pregnancy was confusingly thrilling. At least for the moment, life grew within my body. There was no denying the miracle of that. I took my pills every morning, after brushing my teeth. Despite it all, one of my eggs had forced its way from my fallopian tube, and mingled with the strongest of Tyree's sperm, creating a permanent bond of chromosomes and DNA. How could something that fascinating be a mistake, despite the present situation?

"If you pray, God will give you the answer."

"I think he just did."

Aleesha hugged me then, and I knew she wouldn't leave my side, no matter what Tyree did if and when I decided to tell him. I didn't know when I'd be able to speak with him again without feeling weak and falling for his lies. So it was best that I just not speak to him at all.

## Chapter 26

### <u>Serafina Danielle Jordan</u>

Life has a demented sense of humor. I mean, Dr. Tracey had to be the greatest comedian of all time. When that heffa told me I was pregnant... I chuckled just thinking about it. I mean, she said it like it was the most wonderful news in the world. She said it a few times too, as if I hadn't heard her the first time. I guess my blank stare threw her off because she just kind of looked away from me as if she didn't know what else to say.

"This is the part where you jump up and say, 'SIKE'. " I told her.

" 'Sike'?"

"Yeah, you know, 'Sike', it's something we used to say back in high school, when we were joking with someone. Like when I told my mama that I failed my biology quiz. Just when she was about to yell at me, I said 'SIKE'!"

Dr. Tracey just stared at me.

"Ahh, forget it. I guess they didn't say that, when you were growing up, huh?" I got up to leave. "I guess, I'll see you same time next year."

"Sera, it's not a joke."

"Yes it is," I said sharply.

"You're pregnant."

"No, I'm not."

"Sera I know that things are hard right now, but you have to look at this as--"

"As what?" I interjected, "A miracle? You think having a baby is going to bring me closer to Khalil and un-break my heart? Well it won't. So, you might as well run that test again, and call me when you have better results."

I couldn't remember what was said after that. I just remember wandering aimlessly through the corridors of that hospital, not really knowing where to go or what to believe. I didn't know how to feel about what she'd told me. A baby? Was she crazy? I couldn't have a baby, could I?

Then, there was Jeremy. What had possessed me to let him in on my secret? After all he'd done to me in the past, how could I have let him hug me and talk to me as if we were friends? He didn't know me. He'd never known me.

"I'm pregnant," I said aloud, staring at my emaciated frame in the bathroom mirror. "I'm pregnant," I said again, forcing a smile, and trying to bring joy into my voice. I stopped saying it, stopped staring at my reflection, stopped wondering what Jeremy must have thought, seeing me walk around looking nothing like the woman I used to be.

I slid my fingers through my hair, and watched helplessly as several strands floated around me, landing softly in the sink. This couldn't possibly be real. I didn't want it to be real. So, I chose to deal with it the only way I knew how. I didn't deal with it at all. It was just another segment of the nightmare I'd been plagued with since Khalil's accident.

I was due to wake up at any time.

I was due to wake up at any time.

I was due to wake up at anytime.

Anytime now.

Of course, there were times when I wanted to deal with it. I needed to deal with it. I wanted to talk about it; but who could I talk to? I'd shut so many people out of my life that I didn't know how to invite them back in. If my parents knew, they would force me to move in with them, so they could fawn over me. Max would become even more overbearing, forcing himself into my space.

Stacie? Stacie didn't know what to say to me. So sometimes, she didn't say anything at all. She talked to me, as if everything were normal. She ignored it, the way I wished I could. And then there was Ayzha. My best friend, the one person I so desperately wanted to be able to scoop up my problems and place them in her lap and say 'This is what's going on. What do I do now?"

But I couldn't.

How could I dump my problems on her, when she'd just told me that she's pregnant with Tyree's baby? She didn't know whether to be happy or sad, excited or cautious, glad or mad, and I didn't know what to tell her. I just knew that I couldn't tell her about my situation, without making her worry. So I kept it to myself. I hadn't told anyone. Well, except for that lapse in judgment when I'd told Jeremy, but I was sure he wouldn't say anything. I mean, wasn't he bound by some hypocrites' oath or something?

Yep. I was due to wake up, at anytime now.

***

The first sign of blood appeared three days before Christmas, staining my grey sweatpants, and ruining my silky panties; but I was too excited to be upset. My period had finally come, confirming that the whole pregnancy thing had been a hoax.

"SIKE!" I said giddily, hopping into the shower, and smiling for the first time in days.

I welcomed the blood and  I welcomed the cramps that went along with it. I ate ibuprofen like candy, telling myself that the cramps were only severe because my period was making up for lost time. I could barely walk, and for the first time since the accident, I couldn't make it to the hospital to see Khalil.

I finally "woke up" on Christmas morning.

I knew. As I looked around and realized I was lying on the bathroom floor, I knew. Had I fainted before or after I saw  the blood, the clumps, the thing that I'd tried to deny? I wanted to believe it had all been a dream, but reality slapped me hard in the face, forcing me to wake up.

## Chapter 27

### <u>Jeremy Trent Sanders</u>

My cell phone rings right in the middle of Christmas dinner. This annoys the hell out of my mother; so I send the caller to voice mail, without bothering to see who it is.

"Shouldn't you answer that?" Miss Kendra, Jacob's mother asks me.

"No, he shouldn't. It's Christmas day, and he's not on call; so it's not the hospital," Mama says. "It's probably just one of those pissy-tailed gals he messes around with."

This is how it starts, the conversation that Miss Kendra and Mama love to have in my presence. It's called the *when are you gonna settle down and have us some grandbabies* conversation. Miss Kendra and Mama have formed a bond that outsiders would find strange, but I love the fact that they became friends and allowed Jacob and me to grow up together. Most of the time, I feel like I have two mothers.

"Yall need to mind your business," I chuckle. "You're too nosey for your own good."

"Leave him alone," Jacob says, reaching over me instead of just asking me to pass him the green bean casserole. "Jeremy just hasn't found the right woman."

"That's right." I smile at Mama and Miss Kendra. "I can't settle down, until I find a woman who can compare to the two of you." My cell phone rings again.

"Well whoever it is, she's persistent," Michelle says matter-of-factly, cutting a piece of turkey into bite-sized pieces for Jerica, who has managed to put more food on the floor than in her mouth. "You might as well answer it."

"You might as well answer it," I mimic good-naturedly, as I once again, let the call go to voice mail. The phone rings again, and Jacob snatches it from me, before I can turn it off.

"555-6736," he reads aloud from the caller I.D.

"What?" I snatch the phone from him, but it stops ringing before I have a chance to answer.

"Who is it?" Mama wants to know.

"It's Sera," I say, puzzled.

The table falls silent, but I know what they're thinking. They think I should call her back and see what she wants. I want to call her back, but can't even begin to know why she would want to talk to me.

"Are you going to call her back?" Michelle asks. "Weren't you just telling me--?"

I gave her a look, and she stopped talking. I'd made the mistake of telling Michelle about my visit with Sera, a couple of weeks ago. She was the only one who had any idea how confused I was about my feelings.

"Jeremy, call her back," Michelle says softly.

"Am I missing something?" Jacob asks.

"Yeah," Michelle told him. "He claims that he's not, but I think that he's still in love with her."

"I was never in love with her," I say. "I cared, but it wasn't enough to keep her with me."

"It wasn't enough because you were too busy chasing tail to see what you had right in front of you," Mama scolded.

"What is this? Gang Up On Jeremy Day?" I ask, holding the phone in my hand, wanting to call Sera back, but not in front of my family. I leave the table and go into the kitchen. As I lean against the counter with my phone in my hand I have a sudden sense of dread traveling through my veins and settling in the pit of my stomach like icy water. She answers on the first ring.

"Sera?" I ask cautiously.

"Jeremy?"

"Yes. It's me. Is everything ok?"

"Jeremy, I'm sorry but I didn't know who else to call." She's obviously hysterical, talking so fast I can barely understand her.

"Sera, slow down and tell me what's wrong."

"I'm bleeding."

"Bleeding? What happened? Did you fall?"

"I don't know what happened. I've been feeling kind of funny, and I started spotting a few days ago, but now it's really bad." Her voice is very weak. "I think I passed out. I woke up on the bathroom floor."

I'm not supposed to feel any emotion, as I speak with her, but she hasn't called me as a patient Sera has cast me in the role of the friend you call when you have no one else to turn to. You know...the one you don't think about until something drastic happens in your life.

"Where are you?"

"Home. It's the same place."

I still have a key. I'd found it in a dresser drawer, and couldn't bear to throw it away. I'd kept it as a symbol, but it looked like I was going to have to use it.

"I'm on my way."

***

The sound of her tears greets me, as I open her front door. The apartment is completely dark, but even after two years, I'm able to maneuver through her home like a cat burglar. I step into her bathroom and turn on the light. One look tells me that Sera's baby is no more. It takes thirty minutes to clean the mess and preserve the evidence I'll need to show Dr. Tracey when I take Sera to the hospital for a DNC. The bathroom is now pine fresh, but I wonder if Sera will still see clumps of blood whenever she looks at the sparkling floor.

I finally get the nerve to enter her bedroom. Silently, I walk over to sit on the edge of her bed. Her tears are the result of both mental and physical pain, and I have nothing to offer her but words that will do nothing to change what's happened. I say them anyway.

"I'm sorry," I whisper, not daring to touch her.

"I didn't know," I hear her say softly. "I didn't know how much I wanted it until it was…"

She doesn't finish her thought, but I know what she's trying to say. She didn't know how much she wanted her baby, until it was too late. The cracks in her voice are more than I can bear. Against my better judgment, I climb into bed next to her, sliding my arms around her waist, holding her close to me. As I tenderly place my hands on her stomach, I can feel her uterine walls contracting, causing her to tense up with each painful spasm. She declines the painkillers I offer, opting to punish herself for neglecting her body to the point of miscarriage. I hold her as tight as I dare, silently willing her pain to somehow transfer to me through osmosis, wishing the fingers massaging her sore stomach muscles were magical needles that had the power to perform a pain transfusion, a grief transfusion, a guilt transfusion, anything to keep her from torturing herself this way.

"Why me?" I ask without explaining my question.

"You're the only one who knew," she murmurs into the darkness. She carefully turns to face me. My arms are still around her. I can't let go. She doesn't ask me to. The light from the bathroom illuminates her swollen face, revealing the agony in her eyes. I want to snatch her tears away, but instead kiss her forehead.

"Promise you'll never tell." Her eyes are begging me to keep her secret.

I pull her closer, resting her cheek against my chest. Her tears stain my shirt. The dampness seeps through my garment, saturating my skin and penetrating my heart. I shouldn't say it but I can't refuse.

"I promise."

## Chapter 28

### <u>Serafina Danielle Jordan</u>

I was asleep, yet awake, suspended somewhere between waking and dreaming. My subconscious wouldn't allow my body to rise from this uncomfortable slumber. Even in dreams, my empty womb haunted me like The Ghost of Christmas Past, scolding me for what once was, while The Ghost of Christmas Future nagged me with "should have been, could have been, would have been". A warm hand rested on my forehead. It wasn't Khalil's touch. I knew this, even in my sleep. I opened my eyes, not wanting to face him, but unable to escape the concern on his face. Jeremy's eyes asked if I were okay. My mouth told him yes, but if he were seeing me, I mean really seeing me; he would know that I was lying.

He smiled one of those fake smiles you give a person, when you know you're being conned. One of those, 'yeah heffa, you can't lie to me' smiles, and it made me uncomfortable.

I sat up slowly, shamefully aware of his presence and painfully aware of how I must look to him. I'd called Jeremy, in a moment of pure desperation. No one else knew about the baby, and I didn't know who else to turn to. Plus, I didn't want to hear any more of that broken record called "Poor Sera". I'd heard it so much, in the past few months that it had gone platinum in my mind. Overplayed, I wanted to scream each time I heard it in someone's voice, or felt it under the scrutiny of a pitying gaze. Poor Sera...she lost her man. Poor Sera...she lost her baby. Poor Sera...she's lost her mind. Hey, remember Sera, the chick who lost her fiancé the day of their wedding, then lost his baby a few months later? "Poor Sera."

Jeremy was sitting on the edge of my bed, like it was the most natural thing in the world. I stared at him in his white wife beater and grey sweat pants. It was a familiar sight, but so out of place, so out of time, so out of the ordinary.

"Your phone has been ringing off the hook," he told me.

"You didn't...?"

"Hell no! I didn't answer your phone." He stood up and paced back and forth in front of my bed. "You should call your parents, before they decide to come over here." He couldn't hide his nervousness.

Jeremy was right. I'd missed Christmas Day with my family. I hadn't even called them. I grabbed the phone Jeremy held out to me, and called my mother. Max answered.

Shit.

"Sera, what the hell? It's Christmas Day, and you don't show up! You don't call! What's wrong with you?" His anger filled my ears, and I could do nothing more than close my eyes and try not to cry.

"I'm sorry," I told him. "I wasn't feeling well. I fell asleep, and when I woke up I realized I'd missed dinner." I forced the lie out, choking on every word.

"Why won't you let us help you, Sera? You should be with your family."

"Max, please don't. Not today."

"Whatever. Your mama wants to talk to you." He was angry. He didn't even want to talk to me anymore. I took a deep breath, as he handed the phone to my mother, and braced myself for her voice. I assured her that I was okay, then elaborated on the lie I'd told Max. I told her that I thought I had a touch of the flu. She immediately offered to come over, but I made her promise to stay away.

"I don't want you to catch what I have," I told her. "I'll call you, if I need you."

"I love you baby," she told me. "I know that things are devastating right now. You're going through a lot, but God loves you, Sera. God loves you, and so does your family. Max is just worried about you. We all are." The emotion in her voice almost made me confess.

"I love you too." I hung up, before the events of the past two days unwillingly spilled out of my mouth.

***

She scraped my uterus, until there was no trace of the thing that once lived there. The thing that could have been but would never be. I couldn't stop trembling, even when Dr. Tracey told me to lay completely still. The tremors worsened, until she had to stop and give me a moment to calm down, before continuing. My body cried the tears my eyes could no longer muster. My grief had been internalized. Tears now fell inside of my heart, trickling down to my lungs, and drowning me. Even through closed lids, I could still see Khalil's seed lying in a red trash bag labeled "Biohazard". I wondered how such a thing could be considered waste, and asked Dr. Tracey what would happen to it. She didn't answer. I couldn't bring myself to think of it as him or her because then I would have to imagine what it might have looked liked, or worse...given it a name. I asked again what would become of it, the fetus, the child, the little person, the baby, my baby.

"Almost done," she said, instead.

"Good," I said dryly.

"It's not your fault," she told me, and I could tell it was rehearsed. She'd given the speech many times in the past, as countless women had lain before her, legs wide, exposed, in pain, and filled with grief.

"How come it's not?" I asked.

"Sera, it just wasn't meant to be."

"Whatever," I mumbled, closing my eyes again, welcoming the punishing cramps that tortured my torso. She pulled whatever it was she'd shoved up my birth canal out slowly, and I held my breath, not daring to open my eyes until the intruder was gone. I was bleeding. I couldn't see it, but I could feel it and I desperately wanted to take a scalding, hot shower. I needed to cleanse myself, and scrub all traces of this ordeal off of my body.

Dr. Tracey left the room, giving me the privacy I needed to dress. I did so quickly, shifting uncomfortably in the magnum-sized maxi pad she'd provided. A tear managed to bypass my heart and slide down my sunken cheek. The thing I didn't want, the thing I pretended didn't exist had been real. Now it was too late.

Jeremy took me home, carrying me up the stairs like a sickly bride, unceremoniously stepping over my threshold and into my bedroom. I wanted a shower but the bed seemed more welcoming and less strenuous. I stared at Jeremy, as he played the role of the man I'd needed him to be a few years ago. It almost felt like a joke, but it wasn't the least bit funny.

"You ok?" He asked me.

I shrugged, "I guess."

"Do you need anything?"

"Are you leaving?" There was panic in my voice, but it was too late for me to change my tone. The words had already left my mouth.

"Do you want me to leave?"

I shook my head vigorously, reaching out for him, pulling him close to me, needing to feel his arms wrapped around me. I needed protection, and Jeremy's arms were familiar in a way that didn't have to be explained. There was nothing sexual about the way he eased me back down beneath the covers, and slid his arms around my waist. Nothing sensual about the way he slid one leg over mine, and rested his head on my shoulder, unknowingly tickling my cheek with his long eyelashes.

"Jeremy?" I whispered into the darkness.

"Yes?"

"Thank you."

"Go to sleep, Sera," his voice was deep and comforting.

I closed my eyes and, for the first time in months, fell into a restful, almost peaceful sleep.

## Chapter 29

### Jeremy Trent Sanders

This is the last place in the world I want to be: laid up on Sera's itty-bitty couch, while she's in the next room asleep in her king-sized bed. It's three o'clock in the morning, and I can't sleep because I'm constantly waking up, straining to hear her breathing in the quiet darkness of her apartment. Every now and then, I hear her crying in her sleep, and I want nothing more than to climb into bed and hold her until she stops. But I resist. She's vulnerable, and she's becoming clingy. That's a deadly combination, when you're dealing with a man who is using every ounce of strength in his body to resist the urge to take this situation and run with it. There is a decent man buried deep down inside of me who knows that what Sera needs, more than anything, is a friend. I am determined to be that friend, even if it causes me to go up in smoke, a victim of spontaneous combustion.

I care. I don't want to care, but I do. I've been with her for two days. In these two days, I have cancelled two dates with three different women. I'd actually been looking forward to dallying with those twins from Texas, until I saw Sera curled up in her bed, crying over the loss of a child she wasn't even sure she wanted.

I don't want to care. It was easy to deny my feelings for her as long as she was out of sight. I had plenty of other women to distract me from the not so obvious but the moment I'd seen her walking through the halls of the hospital that day I suddenly remembered everything thing I missed about her.

I miss the same things about her that she probably misses about a man I can't even bring myself to mention. I miss her touch. I miss her cooking. I miss hearing her voice in the middle of a busy day. I try my best to shake these thoughts off, but there is absolutely no denying how perfect this situation could be, if I were bold enough to try and win her back under these tragic circumstances. But I can't do that to her. Why? Because I care.

"Damn," I say aloud, adjusting my pillow, trying to find a comfortable position and failing miserably. I'm on call tonight, and I'm almost praying for an excuse to leave Sera's place and go back to the hospital. So far, it's been a quiet night. Thankfully, none of my young patients has had an emergency. I feel bad for even letting the thought cross my mind, but in a few hours I will have to get up and go into Sera's room to tell her goodbye. I have a job and a life to get back to, and no matter how much I care, I can't let what's happened to her alter my life in a way that would lead me to make the wrong decisions. It's better for both of us.

The ringing phone jolts me out of my thoughts. It stops after the second ring, and I know that Sera has awakened to answer it. I go into her room and sit on the edge of her bed, not liking her tone as she tells whoever is on the other end to turn around and go home.

"Max, I'm fine. It's three in the morning, and I don't need you coming over here playing big brother right now. Just leave me alone. Ayzha is with you? Are you crazy? She's pregnant, and you have her out this early in the morning? Do you even care how this is going to look to her husband?" She slams the phone down, terrified, and looks up at me. "They're down stairs."

"Are you kidding me?" Max is the last person I need to run into at Sera's house, when I'm dressed in nothing but boxer shorts and a t-shirt; but I know it's too late, when I hear the persistent ringing of the doorbell. "What do you want to do?" I ask.

"I guess I should let them in," she sighs, sitting up slowly.

"No." I grab her hand, stopping her from trying to move any further. "I'll do it."

"But Max…"

"I'm not scared of Max. I just don't feel like hearing his shit. I'll be ok. I don't want you moving around until tomorrow." I take a deep breath, go into the living room, and open the front door to find Max and Ayzha standing on the stoop.

"What the hell are you doing here?" Max makes a move towards me, but thinks better of resorting to violence, when he sees the look on my face. "Where's Sera?"

"She's in her room; and as you can see, I've been sleeping on the couch."

"Why?" Ayzha steps from behind Max, and walks into the apartment, "Why are you here?"

"I'm here as a friend."

"Since when are you Sera's friend?" Max sneers suspiciously, then yells his sister's name loudly, as he storms toward her bedroom. I throw my hands up in the air and stand back, letting the scene unfold in front of me. "Overbearing" is hardly an adequate enough word to use, when I think about how Max treats Sera. Hell, her parents aren't as protective as this bastard is.

Ayzha stays in the living room with me. Her expression is more surprised than suspicious, but I don't bother trying to explain myself. To do so will reveal the one thing Sera made me promise not to tell, and I'm not about break to my word, not this time.

"Jeremy will you tell me what's going on?"

"I already told you, Ayzha. I'm here as a friend. I slept on the couch. I'm leaving now. I have to work in the morning." I walk past her and grab a pair of sweats out of my duffel bag, not caring how she may possibly feel about seeing me getting dressed in Sera's living room. Then, I remember what Sera told me about Ayzha. I try to change my attitude .

"She's going to be ok, Ayzha. You shouldn't have come. What about your baby?" I clear off a space next to me on the couch, so that she can sit down. "Traipsing around in your pajamas in December?" I shake my head at her. "You shouldn't let Max drag you around on his egotistical rampages."

"I didn't know what else to do. I was afraid of what he would do, if I weren't here to diffuse the situation," she sighs.

Sera's bedroom door slams, and Max comes storming into the living room. "She won't tell me."

"Max, let's go." Ayzha stands.

"Not until he tells me what's going on!" Max snaps.

"You need to calm down," I say calmly. "You don't need to raise your voice to Ayzha. You don't need to raise your voice to me, and you definitely don't need to be yelling at Sera. She's gone through enough, without you coming over here and treating her like a damn child!"

I wonder what he sees, when he looks in the mirror. He's no different from me. That's why he hates me so much. He sees himself in me, and doesn't want anyone remotely like himself around his sister. I could feel sorry for him, if he weren't such a hypocrite. Sera calls my name, and I look at Max, daring him to stop me from going to her. I don't want to leave, but I know that Max and I can't be in the same house. The sooner I get out of his way, the better it will be for all of us.

"Hey you," I sit on the edge of her bed and lightly brush her cheek with my knuckles. Tears moisten my hand, and I bring my knuckles to my lips, kissing her salty tears. "That's your brother," I sigh, glancing at the clock. It's been four hours since her last Ibuprofen, and she's probably due for another. "Hurting?"

"A little," she mumbles. "Is it supposed to feel like this?"

"It will be better tomorrow," I tell her. "You should start moving around. Get out of the house. I have to go back to work tomorrow."

"I know. I'm sorry," she says softly.

"For what? Sera, I'm glad you called me. I'm the one who should be apologizing to you. I should have done it a long time ago, but my pride wouldn't let me."

"So, I guess we're even." She allows herself a slight chuckle, and I smile.

"This isn't nearly enough to make us even, but I know better than to argue with a pretty lady. You can call me whenever you need me, Sera. I mean that."

"Well…"

"It's time for me to go," I whisper. I try easing myself off her bed, but she grabs my arm.

"Wait." She pulls me toward her, and I feel her arms sliding around me, hugging me tightly. "I'll never forget this," she whispers. Her breath is warm on my ear, and I pull away before the urge to kiss her manifests.

"Anytime, cutie pie," I murmur, the old nickname naturally sliding from my heart and out of my mouth, before I can seal my lips. I kiss her on the forehead, and she reluctantly lets go of me, as Max walks into the room. I quickly leave before I change my mind.

## Chapter 30

### Serafina Danielle Jordan

Max lay on the floor beside my bed, tossing and turning as his mind tried to cope with the fact that I'd called Jeremy instead of him. I understood his concern. I understood his frustration. I also understood that he could never, ever understand what I was going through. He didn't understand why I kept the baby a secret; but how could I tell him, when I couldn't even admit it to myself? That baby wasn't real to me, until it was gone. It. Him. Her. Them. I'll never, ever know.

Ayzha was a piece of work, coming to my house in the middle of the night, in her condition. What a dear, dear woman. What a great friend. What an idiot. Putting her pregnancy at risk to try to save me. Didn't she know that no one could save me?

No one can save me. I'm lost. Lost like a sock in the laundry, tumbling over and over in the dryer, searching for its mate. No one can save me. My heart is breaking. With each beat, a small fragment of my cardiac muscle falls away and lands in the pit of my stomach, weighing me down, and filling me with despair.

So, I lay there with my eyes closed, pretending to be asleep. I listened as Max and Ayzha discussed me, as if I weren't even in the room. Ayzha was lying next to me, leaning over the side of the bed, whispering things about me. Trying to calm Max. Trying to make him understand where I was coming from. After all, she'd been there six times before.

"You didn't shut your family and friends out," Max argued. "You didn't keep it a secret."

"I didn't have a fiancée lying in a coma either," Ayzha told him. "We can't pretend to know what she's going through. We can pity her. We can pray for her. We can sympathize, but we will never understand."

Then, the conversation turned to Jeremy. Why had I called him, after everything he'd done to me in the past? What was in it for him? What was he after?

"I'm not asleep," I said loudly, feeling the need to defend Jeremy. No matter what had happened in the past, I couldn't overlook what he'd done for me. I opened my eyes, staring up at the ceiling, and listening as Max went on another one of his Captain Save A Ho tirades. It was his favorite theory, and the term he used to describe many men, including his former self.

"Max, Jeremy had no reason to help me, but he did. He went above and beyond," I sighed.

"Don't," he said sharply. "Don't see Jeremy as your knight in shining armor. Have you forgotten what he did to you?"

"Max, let it go," I said quietly.

"You're my sister."

"I'm a grown woman."

"Guys, stop," Ayzha interrupted. She'd heard this argument enough times to know that it was going nowhere. I stopped talking, but Max would not be silenced. He had to have the last word. He had to tell me how selfish I'd been, how worried I'd made my parents, how my mother had cried, when I hadn't shown up for Christmas dinner.

"Remember when you carried me out of the hospital?" I asked quietly. "Remember how you held me, and let me cry on your shoulder for hours without saying a word? That's the big brother I need right now. You're always so busy trying to bully me into doing things your way that you forget how to just stand back and love me no matter what." The tears started again, stinging my eyes, altering my voice, choking me. "You don't think I feel horrible enough, Max? You don't think I thought about Mama and Daddy, while I was lying on a table getting a placenta sucked out of me? How much it would have hurt them?" I closed my eyes and tried to harden my voice. "Don't add to this, by telling me how much I've hurt everybody. I hurt enough for all of us."

I felt Ayzha's arms around me, holding me like a sister, smoothing my hair, whispering that everything was going to be ok.

"I miss him," I cried. "I miss him every single day. I was so caught up in missing him that I couldn't even take care of his baby. He always wanted a baby, and I killed the only piece of him I may ever have."

Max went into big brother mode, leaving his place on the floor, getting under the covers with me, and putting his arms around me so that I was surrounded by love. The three of us held each other, as they let me cry every tear in my seemingly never-ending reserve.

## Chapter 31

### Jeremy Trent Sanders

I'm desperately craving the sound of her voice. I haven't seen or heard from Sera in two weeks. I haven't spoken to her, since the night I left her in her brother's capable hands. I keep telling myself that she only called me out of desperation. I want to believe that she knows that she can trust me now, as a friend, if anything. I need to know how she's doing. Is she okay? Her body will heal itself, but her heart must still be aching. I don't know if she ever wants to see or hear from me again. I don't know if she regrets calling me for help. I call her anyway, taking a chance that she'll be willing to talk to me, just to tell me that she's ok.

"Hey Cutie Pie," I say, once again forgetting my proper place, as her voice comes across the phone line.

"Hey Jeremy." She sounds reserved, as if she doesn't quite know what to say to me.

"Are you okay? I just wanted to check on you. You're not having any complications, are you? No bleeding? No cramping?"

"I'm fine, thanks to you." She sounds so lonely, so dejected, "I wanted to call but...I just didn't know what to say to you. I put you in an awkward position, and I'm sorry for that. I had no right."

"What did I tell you about apologizing to me? I wouldn't have had it any other way," I assure her. "You're sure you're okay?"

"Don't worry about me," she says and then hastily adds, "I have to go."

She hangs up without saying goodbye. For the sake of courtesy should leave it at that. I should allow Sera to keep to herself, and wallow in the deep depression she's fallen into. It's not my problem. She has a family who loves her. She has friends. She has a solid support system. I should just leave her alone. I want to call her back, but end up calling my mother instead.

"Hey, Mama."

"Hey, Baby, what's going on?"

"Nothing, just calling."

"Yeah, right. What's really on your mind?" She asks knowingly.

"I don't know, Mama. I just talked to Sera," I confide. "I know that she's ok; but I can tell that she really needs someone, right now. I just don't know if that person should be me." Mama's end of the line goes silent momentarily, and I wonder if we've been disconnected. "Mama?"

"I'm still here, Jeremy." She exhales softly. "Baby, are you trying to be her friend? Or are you trying to be more?"

"I want to be her friend."

"Then, be her friend, but understand that it can't be more than that. This is just so unlike you. I don't want you to set yourself up to be hurt. Many times, when we love someone, we use friendship as an excuse to be close to that person and it always backfires."

"I don't understand."

"Baby, when you try to be friends with someone you love, it complicates things. It gives you false hope that there could possibly be more in the future. Sera can't love you because she loves someone else."

"I'm not in love with her, Mama."

"Then why are you calling me trying to figure out if it's ok to talk to her?" I have no idea how to answer that question, so I remain silent.

"Leave her alone, Jeremy," Mama says softly. "Let her go her own way. It's too late to try and salvage anything with her now, even if it is just friendship. Let it go."

But I can't let it go, and the moment I hang up with Mama, I dial Sera's number again. She picks up the phone, but doesn't speak. I let her silence set the tone. As I sit there listening to her stillness, I'm gripping my cell phone so tightly it's bound to shatter, if I don't loosen my grasp. I'm wary of speaking. I don't want to scare her into hanging up, not when I'm content to just sit there, knowing that she's breathing into my ear.

I guess it sounds a bit insane. Maybe I am a little crazy to even contemplate walking back into her life, after all I put her through in the past...especially with what she's dealing with now. I don't really understand what has come over me. Maybe, I just want to show her that I can be the man she needed me to be way back then. I want her to know how much I've learned from losing her. I want her to know that, contrary to popular belief, I *can* be a friend to her without expecting anything else in return. I just want to be there for her, in a way that exhibits my feelings without overwhelming her. I don't want to take advantage of the situation, and I don't want to fill my head with silly fantasies. I just want to be whatever she needs, whenever she needs it.

She needs me now. I know this without asking, and this knowledge scares me because I don't know how I've come to this conclusion. It's as if she's speaking to me through mental telepathy, calling out to me with her mind because her lips won't allow it. She hangs up suddenly, and I know there's nothing left to do but go to her and pray my interpretation of her silence isn't wrong.

When I arrive at Sera's apartment, I'm relieved to see her car parked in its usual spot. Her comment of being on her way out the door was obviously a lie and as I get out of my car and walk up the stairs I take long deep breaths, preparing myself for whatever reaction she may have to my being there.

She's in my arms in an instant, no tears, no words, just slow, steady breaths, and long, quiet sighs. I am floating on her scent, willing to suffocate and cease breathing, dying in the aroma of the woman in my arms.

"You came," she whispers.

"You asked me to."

"No, I didn't."

"You didn't say it, but I felt it."

"I don't understand why I need you right now."

"You don't need me. You just need this." I hug her closer, kissing the top of her forehead. "Have you eaten?" She shakes her head, and I pull away to stare down at her. She's dressed casually, in a pair of jeans and a tan sweater that flatters her complexion. With no make-up, she looks younger than her twenty-eight years and her eyes shine with the vulnerability of a shy teenager. Her hair is pulled back into a simple ponytail adorned with a leather clip, and I smooth her freshly permed edges with my fingertips. "Get your purse."

She doesn't even ask where we're going. She simply grabs her purse and locks her door behind us, holding my hand as I lead her down the stairs.

## Chapter 32

### <u>Serafina Danielle Jordan</u>

I salivated, like a hostage at a buffet. I honestly didn't realize how hungry I was, until our waiter presented me with a plate piled high with catfish fillets, beer-battered shrimp, red beans and rice, and hush puppies. Conversation was nonexistent as I made up for all of the meals I'd missed in the last few months. Jeremy leaned back in his chair and smiled, obviously enjoying my appetite. I was suddenly self-conscious. I gently placed my fork on the table, and took a tiny sip of my lemonade.

"I look like a pig, don't I?"

"You look hungry." Jeremy smiled at me, "I want a piece of your shrimp, but I'm afraid you'll stab me."

"Ha ha," I smiled. "Have some shrimp."

I picked one up by the tail, and held it out to him. Jeremy reached out reluctantly, as if he were afraid to grab it. I couldn't help laughing. It actually felt good to be laughing. I laughed, as if I didn't have a care in the world. I laughed, as if I hadn't lost anything remotely precious to me. I laughed, as if Khalil weren't lying in a hospital bed, a shell of his former self. I stopped laughing. I stabbed a piece of fish with my fork and slowly began to chew, no longer tasting the flavor I'd fallen in love with on my first bite. I may as well have been chewing a piece of wood. The mood at our corner table suddenly became very solemn.

"I don't think he'd mind if you laughed every once in a while," Jeremy said, trying to catch my eye. "Sera." He placed his hand over mine, stopping my fork before I could take another unwanted bite. "Sera...look at me." I dropped my fork, and snatched my hand away. "Tell me about him."

"What?" I asked, not sure if I'd heard him right.

"Tell me about Khalil."

"Why?"

I was suspicious. It didn't seem right for him to ask about Khalil, let alone say his name. Everyone else avoided saying his name, as if it would somehow make me forget my misery. They talked around the subject or changed the course of conversation, whenever his name left my lips. Maybe, they thought that avoiding his name would somehow make me feel better. Maybe it just made them feel better.

"What's he like?" Jeremy asked.

"He's beautiful.." I pictured Khalil's face in my mind, and smiled longingly. I could almost smell the sweetly scented oil he used to keep his locs shiny and healthy. "Some men are pretty, some men are handsome, some are cute, but Khalil is beautiful. Not just physically, but spiritually. He touches me, and nothing else matters. I never knew a man could love me that way."

"What way is that?"

"Completely, unconditionally, with everything in him. It's like he was born to love me, and I was born to love him."

Jeremy listened, laughing in all the right places, as I told him about the day Khalil and I met. Oddly enough, I didn't break down when I described our conversation in the parking lot that day. Instead, once again, I felt myself laughing and smiling at the memory. The more I talked, the better I felt. So, I continued. I told Jeremy about seeing Khalil's face in the crowd, as I performed my poetry.

"I was there that night," Jeremy remembered. "I tried to find you, but you'd disappeared."

"I was with Khalil," I reminisced aloud, remembering our first kiss, the ride back to his place, making love in the car, locking ourselves in his condo for the entire weekend, as if the rest of the world didn't exist.

"You look like you're remembering something that's none of my business."

I smiled. "None of your business." I agreed. I smiled again. I'd regained my appetite. I began to taste my food again.

"You really love him." Jeremy stared at me across the table. I put my fork down.

"I do. I was so content to be with him that I never even prepared myself for the possibility that I'd ever have to be without him."

"You should talk about him more often, Sera."

"It hurts."

"It helps. You should see yourself. Your whole face lights up, when you're talking about him. You look beautiful."

I leaned forward and asked Jeremy the question that my friends and family were afraid to answer, "Will he ever wake up?"

He stared at me.

"Please? I don't want you to treat me like everyone else does. I need you to be honest with me. Just tell me what you think."

He studied me for a moment. I slid my hand across the table, and he grasped it tightly, encouragingly.

"Honestly, I've seen it happen, but I've also seen people who have been in comas for years. Most of them live in nursing homes. Some people die without ever waking up. Some people wake up with the mind of a child."

"You don't think he'll wake up," I said dully.

"It doesn't look good, Sera."

I shook my head. "Everyone thinks I'm crazy."

"Why?"

"Because I'm going to wait for him, even if it takes the rest of my life." He squeezed my hand tighter.

"You think I'm crazy too, don't you?" I asked.

"I think that Khalil is lucky to have you in his corner."

"But am I being realistic?" I pressed him for an answer.

"Baby, I can't answer that for you. Have I seen miracles? Yes, but as a doctor, I can tell you that the possibility is slim."

"And as a man?"

"As a man who knows what it's like to see someone that you love dearly, and not be able to communicate that love...I can tell you that hope is eternal."

Something about the way he looked at me when he said it made me stare down at my plate. I wasn't uncomfortable, but I didn't want to speculate about whom he was referring to. I looked up at him again.

"You can trust me," he said softly. "I promise."

Somehow I believed him, even if no one else ever would.

## Chapter 33

### <u>Ayzha Nicole Darwin</u>

How do you tell your husband you want a divorce and "Oh, by the way, I'm pregnant with another man's child"? Better yet, how do you tell your husband you're moving in with your best friend because you're not speaking to the father of your unborn child? "I'm leaving you for a man who was never as serious about me as I was about him. I let the lack of positive attention in our marriage, and the fact that you never touch me anymore allow another man's advances to overwhelm me." But of course that would be blaming Riley, instead of placing the blame where it belonged. No matter how horribly I felt about my marriage, I should never have been unfaithful. I should have just left. Cheating on Riley wasn't the answer. Cheating was actually the cause of my present predicament.

Ten weeks along, and I don't have the strength to worry about Tyree's absence. It's taking all of my energy to try to hold this baby in longer than its miscarried siblings. I've been pregnant six times, and my gestational world record is a phenomenal seventeen weeks. I think the fifth baby had been the hardest. We knew we had a boy. We gave him a name. The miscarriage was like giving birth, knowing that the baby was already dead. That was when I decided I never wanted to be pregnant again. I started taking birth control, against Riley's wishes, and the marriage deteriorated. I couldn't give him what he wanted, and he couldn't give me the support I needed.

Tyree can't give me the support I need, right now. Never mind the overwhelming evidence that he not only tried to screw my cousin, but that I'm not the only woman in his life. That bastard accused me of being pregnant, then never called to find out if his suspicions were true. So, how do you break the news to your husband? You blurt it out, like I just did.

"Riley, I'm pregnant." I walked into the den where he was watching ESPN, and stood in front of the television. His face showed no reaction, but the beer he held was being squeezed so tightly that the foamy contents were spilling over, running down his hand and staining the carpet. He closed his eyes briefly. When he opened them again, I took a small step backwards, suddenly afraid, as I realized he was squeezing that can to keep from strangling me.

"It's not mine." We both knew it was true. There was no point in answering him.

"So whose it? Is it Max? You spend a lot of time at that club. More time than necessary." Riley was way too calm.

"It's not Max, but it doesn't matter. It's none of your business." I tried not to let my voice falter.

"So let me get this straight. You didn't want to try to have another baby for me, your husband, but you can lay up with another man and get knocked up?" He stared at me, hatred and fury shooting from his eyes like toxic death rays. "You always were a pitiful excuse for a wife."

"What's pitiful is that your wife tells you that she's pregnant, and you automatically know it can't be yours because you haven't touched her in months!" I shot back.

The beer came flying in my direction, and I had to duck to avoid the blow that was obviously aimed at my face. I barely heard all of the bitches and whores I'd suddenly become. The calm gave way to the storm.

I grabbed the closest thing to me, one of our wedding photos, and threw it at him. The glass frame shattered against the wall behind him.

"You won't get a dime of my money!" He yelled. He stood up and walked towards me. His face was so close to mine I could smell the pepperoni pizza he'd eaten. I wanted to vomit, as he yelled obscenities at me.

I almost laughed, but thought better of it. If he knew I'd already taken half the money from our joint savings and checking accounts, I'd be the next thing flying across the room. I was no dummy. Riley has "secret" accounts and property all over town. Besides, I'd read Waiting To Exhale enough times to know I needed my own private stash. I've been saving for this day, for the past five years.

"I don't care about your money or this stupid house." I tried to walk away but he grabbed my arm, squeezing tightly enough to cut off my circulation.

"I'm not done with you!"

"Let me go!"

"Do you think I'm going to let you just walk up out of here, with another man's baby inside of you?" I looked around for something, anything within reach that I could hit him with, but there was nothing.

"Riley, please let me go." I looked him in the eyes, unable to hide my fear.

He raised his hand as if he wanted to hit me, but let go before his instincts had a chance to kick in. He paced back and forth in front of me, clenching and unclenching his fists.

"Why, Ayzha? Why?" He yelled. "Do you know what I could do to you right now? I could just--!" He reached out to grab me again, but again stopped himself. "You need to get out of here, before I hurt you."

He stepped aside, and I took a few shaky steps away from him. I was almost out of the room before I heard him say, "This marriage is over."

"Riley, this marriage was over a long time ago," I said shakily. "I'm wrong. I know I'm wrong for this, but you can't lay all of the blame on me. You did your share of dirt."

"You have no proof."

"Of course, I do, but it's not even worth discussing at this point. I've already moved my things. I've already filed for divorce. I just need you to sign the papers, Riley."

"You're not getting anything from me."

"I don't want anything! I just want to be free!"

"Then get the fuck out!" He said, the calmness returning to his voice. "Get out, and don't look back."

I left quickly. I got into my car, half expecting him to chase after me somehow knowing that he wouldn't. I was halfway to Sera's house, when my cell phone rang. It was a special ring, one I hadn't heard in weeks. I froze, unsure of whether or not to answer. The phone stopped ringing, and immediately rang again. I picked it up, but didn't say anything.

"Ayzha?" The sound of Tyree's voice filled me with rage.

"What the hell do you want?"

"I just wanted to see how you were doing." He spoke as if we were old high school acquaintances catching up on old times. I wanted to throw the phone.

"I'm pregnant, you selfish son of a bitch." I hung up the phone, before he could react to the news, then turned the phone completely off. Let him marinate on that, for a while.

\*\*\*

I walked into Sera's apartment and sniffed the air. It smelled like baked chicken. I walked into the kitchen and stopped dead in my tracks.

Sera was sitting on the counter while Jeremy, of all people, poured himself a glass of milk.

"What's wrong with this picture?" I asked warily.

"It's the middle of January, and you're not wearing a jacket," Jeremy told me. He poured me a glass of milk and I turned up my nose. "Does milk make you queasy?"

"The last time I drank milk, not only did it come up in chunks, but it came out of my nose." He made a face, and quickly pulled the milk out of my reach.

"I've had enough gross-outs today," he told me. "I'll leave you two alone."

"No, don't leave on my account. I'm tired anyway." I was being a bitch but I couldn't help it. I needed to feel sorry for myself, and I couldn't cry on Sera's shoulder with Jeremy in the room. I left them alone in the kitchen, and went into Sera's spare bedroom. It used to be her computer room, but she'd immediately put a bed in, when I told her I needed a place to stay for a while. I flung myself across my bed, and buried my face in my pillow.

"Ayzha, are you okay?" Sera came in and closed the door behind her.

"Where's Jeremy?" I asked, without looking at her.

"Our friendship still bothers you?"

"Well, he only dogged you out for two years."

"Well, I've let go of the past, and I suggest you do the same." Sera's serious tone told me there was no room for discussion.

"Whatever," I mumbled. "Is he gone?"

"He went to get you some ginger ale."

"I don't need him to do anything for me."

"Ayzha, please, could you at least pretend to be civil? He's trying."

"Fuck Jeremy."

"Okay, now you're just being a selfish bitch!" Sera's words shocked me, but lots of things about Sera shocked me, lately. "Don't look at me like that, Ayzha. I love you. You're my girl, but this is my home and Jeremy is my friend. I'm not going to let you take your shitty life out on him."

"My shitty life?"

"Yeah. I said it. You're sitting over here stressing about things that you can't change. You're moping around here like you're some kind of victim. All this self-pity will consume you. I'm still trying to dig myself out of that hole, and it's hard." I just stared at her as she continued.

"Ayzha, Khalil may never wake up. If I had stopped feeling sorry for myself long enough to take care of my body, we'd be pregnant together, and I would have a piece of him with me. I have nothing. My baby is gone."

"Sera, I'm sorry," I started, but she held up her hand.

"Let me finish. Ayzha you're my best friend. I won't let you make the same mistakes I did. Now, like it or not, Jeremy is my friend and I'm not turning my back on that; but I'm not turning my back on you either."

I started to cry, and Sera made me laugh, by wiping my tears with the edge of my own shirt. "Sera, I just feel so lost right now."

"I know, but you can't blame the world for what happened. You just have to deal with it. I mean, so what if you're on the verge of divorce, pregnant but your husband isn't the father, and your baby daddy is a manipulative asshole? You've got friends who love you."

I laughed, despite myself, "Was that supposed to cheer me up?"

"Did it work?"

"Hell no."

"But you laughed. That's a start. Sooo…did you tell Riley?"

"Yep."

"What did he say?"

"I think…no, I'm pretty sure that he wanted to kill me." I sighed, "Oh, and he told me that I couldn't have any of his money."

Sera started cracking up. "What's he going to do when he finds out you withdrew all of that money?"

"I'm sure he'll be pissed, but legally, there's really nothing he can do. It was a joint account. I could have withdrawn it all. I really don't think he'll fight the divorce. As it stands, he can just tell his friends that I cheated on him, and he left me. I don't care, as long as this marriage comes to an end, before my baby gets here."

"See? You're already thinking positively."

"Why do you say that?"

"Because, you said *when* the baby gets here instead of *if*."

I changed the subject, "What's taking Jeremy so long with my soda?"

"Ayzha, please be nice to him. He's really been good to me."

"Yeah, but why?"

"Because he grew up, and so should you, heffa."

"I'm going to let that last comment slide." I yawned sleepily, and stretched out on the bed. "Did you see Khalil today?"

"Yep," she answered, draping a soft cotton blanket over me.

"Have you told him about the baby yet?"

"Nope." She stood up and walked towards the door.

"Sera…"

"I can't, Ayzha."

"Why not?"

"It would kill him." She flicked off the light, leaving my next question caught in my throat, as she softly closed the door behind her.

## Chapter 34

### Serafina Danielle Jordan

I wanted to snatch her by her hair, until she had slick bald patches scattered throughout her head. The sight of her with her hands on Khalil's body filled my head with such fury, I didn't even trust myself to speak. I stood in the doorway, watching her, wondering how long she'd been alone with my man.

"What are you doing?" I finally managed to say.

Allison jumped slightly, looking over at me with a white face cloth clenched in her fist, dripping large droplets of water on Khalil's chest.

"I'm bathing him."

"I do that!" I snapped.

"I'm sorry. I didn't know." She dropped the face cloth in a tub of water, and stood up slowly, taking off her latex gloves.

"I don't want you here," I told her.

I didn't want her anywhere near Khalil. I didn't want her near anyone who meant anything to me, or anyone that I considered mine. Khalil was mine, and there was no way I was going to just stand back and watch her touch him the way she'd... I stopped my thoughts there, unwilling to venture where my mind and old grudges wanted me to go.

"Please, just go."

I dumped out her bucket, and refilled it with fresh water. She hadn't even used the right soap on him. I didn't want Khalil bathed with baby wash, the way the other patients were. I didn't want his bath to be as clinical as the rest. He was special, and he deserved special treatment.

I shook all thoughts of Allison out of my head and bathed him the right way, slowly, lovingly, gently, patiently, methodically, and obsessively. I bathed him, until his skin felt silky to the touch and smelled like the strawberry guava body wash he'd always loved to smell on me. I guess, somewhere in the back of my mind, I figured that surrounding him with my smell would make him wake up and ask for me. I buried my face in his neck, and inhaled slowly. This scent had once driven him completely bananas. He'd get a whiff of this, and chase after me like a hound dog in heat. A small smile dared to trespass across my face, but left immediately when a familiar voice interrupted my thoughts.

"Everything okay?" Allison walked back into the room, and I couldn't help glaring at her as she stood in the doorway, contaminating the space with her presence.

"You know what? If I need you, I know how to use the call button," I said crisply.

"Sera, I…I know that this is awkward, but this is my job. I'm just trying to help," she stammered.

"Well, like I said…if I need you, I'll call." My tone was dismissive. Without a word, Allison walked out of the room, softly closing the door behind her. I didn't notice Jeremy standing next to me, until I heard his voice.

"What was that all about?"

I didn't even look at him.

"She's a whore." I said.

"Sera--"

"She's…a…whore," I said it again, slowly, just in case he didn't understand me the first time. "And anyway, what do you want? I thought you were working."

"Damn, why the suspicion?" He looked down at me, and then raised his eyebrow when he saw a pair of clippers in my hand. He gave Khalil a pitying gaze, before snatching the clippers from me. "Would he let you do this, if he were awake?"

"Yes."

"You lie. You lie. You lie." He tsk tsked, shaking his head. He then turned on the clippers and made a move towards Khalil's face.

"Don't touch him," I said harshly. Jeremy stopped short, and stared over at me with a puzzled expression on his face.

"What's wrong?" He reached out to me, but I backed away.

"Don't touch me."

I couldn't even begin to explain to him what was going on. I couldn't even make sense of it for myself. Jeremy was my ex-boyfriend. He meant nothing to me romantically. I'd forgiven him and welcomed him back into my life as a friend, but I could not help the hostility I felt when I saw Allison. I knew, in my gut, that he'd been sleeping with her while we were still together. Having her in my face, touching Khalil, talking to me as if she'd never done anything wrong towards me… it made me want to scream.

"Are you kidding me?" Jeremy asked in amazement, "What did I do?"

"Just leave me alone."

I turned on *Dwele*, Khalil's favorite CD, and sat in the chair next to his bed, eyes closed, rocking back and forth like a little, old woman. I waited for the sound of Jeremy's footsteps leaving and when I never heard them I opened my eyes and glared at him.

"What is wrong with you?" He asked, exasperation all over his voice.

"Why did you do it?"

"What?"

"You know what." I cut my eyes at him. "Do you still talk to your little girlfriend?"

"Oh my God." He stared at me, "You're pissed off about Allison? She was never my girlfriend." Jeremy turned away from me.

"But I was."

"Sera, that was a long time ago."

"Whatever," I waved him away. "It doesn't matter. It's not like it makes a difference now, right?"

I could tell he didn't know what to say to me. I didn't expect him to know what to say; but I damn sure expected him to feel as horribly as I did, when I thought about how heartbroken I'd been before we'd finally broken up. I wanted him to feel bad about what he, Allison, and I don't know how many other women had done to me.

"I'll talk to you later," he sighed, walking out and leaving me alone with my uncertain future and the tortured thoughts of my past.

I wondered if Khalil could sense my frustration, at times. I always put on a happy face for him. I always smiled for him. I always talked cheerfully to him, no matter how terrible I felt. I only cried when I said goodbye.

"I miss you Khalil," I whispered, but not loud enough for him hear. "I'll see you tomorrow, okay?" I placed a lingering kiss on his unmoving lips, and placed my head on his chest, giving him a chance to wrap his arms around me. When I got no reaction, I did the same thing I did every day. I kissed him again and then left without looking back.

Jeremy was waiting for me in the hallway, trying to pretend that he hadn't been speaking to Allison. I shook my head, and walked past the two of them, without a word. Jeremy caught up to me and tried to put his arm around my shoulder, but I shrugged him off. I didn't feel like being bothered with him, and I didn't feel like pretending that I did. He was used to my moodiness, and knew not to follow me, as I slowly walked the long hallway alone.

## Chapter 35

### Jeremy Trent Sanders

"What are you doing, Jeremy?" It's the first non job-related thing Allison has said to me since our messy parting of ways; and I take a deep breath, not wanting to say anything, until I see Sera board the elevator, giving me one last angry glance before the door closes, taking her pretty face from my view.

"What do you mean?" I ask, finally allowing myself to look at her.

"You're playing a dangerous game," she says, looking me in my eyes. "She'll never love you the way she loves him. It's been almost six months, and she's here every single day, sometimes twice." Allison shakes her head in sympathy, and I take a quick look at Khalil's chart, noting the fact that there has been no change since the day he was brought in.

"You weren't here when they brought him in, were you?" I ask, ignoring the accusations hiding behind her words.

"No, but Eva was. She does extra things for Khalil because she knows Sera will be here to check on him. We all do." Allison then began to repeat a story Eva had told her about the day Khalil was brought in.

"Don't tell me any more." I hold up my hand, to let her know how strongly I feel about closing the subject. Hearing that Sera sat next to Khalil's bed for days in her wedding dress made my eyes twitch. So, I looked away for a moment, and tried to compose myself before Allison can see my pain. How terribly hurt she must have been. How terribly helpless she must have felt, waiting for that man to wake up and marry her.

"She hates me," Allison says.

"She doesn't hate you," I lie, when Sera's treatment of Allison has already established the obvious.

"You heard what she said to me." She sounds worried, "She doesn't want me around Khalil. What if she starts complaining about me?"

She starts fiddling with the pens on the counter, something she does when her brain is working overtime. "I can't say that I blame her. I'd hate me too."

"I don't understand why she would still hold that against you, after all this time," I say, trying to get some insight into what Sera may possibly be feeling for me. "Do you think she's jealous?"

"Jealous?　Maybe a little, but mostly I think she's angry. Sometimes it's hard to let go, when someone hurts you."

The way Allison looks at me lets me know that she's still struggling with her anger over the way I left things between us. In hindsight, I guess I had been pretty brutal, but I couldn't bring myself to apologize for telling her the truth. I hadn't asked her to fall in love with me and leave her husband.

"She forgave me," I remind Allison.

"She loved you." She shakes her head, "It's easy to forgive someone, when you love them; but think of what it took for her to even let you back into her life, Jeremy. It took her fiancé lapsing into a coma. If that had never happened…"

"I know, but that doesn't explain why she got so angry with me today."

"I just remind her of a bad time in her life. We women have a way of holding grudges, even when it has nothing to do with what's going on in our lives, now." She studies me thoughtfully. "Maybe, I have ulterior motives, but I really think that you should probably back away from her, Jeremy."

"I can't.　She needs me." This feels like a replay of the conversations I keep having with my mother, brother, and Michelle. Everyone feels like I'm setting myself up for heartbreak. "We're just friends, Allison."

"You're in love with her."

"Let's drop this conversation." I'm facing Allison now, looking at her in a way I haven't in a very long time. She's what my homeboys describe as a redbone, tiny in the waist, pretty in the face, and curves that make a brotha wanna drive all night long. She recently cut her dark brown hair short; and even though I prefer the way it used to hang to her shoulders, there's no denying the sexiness of the new cut. We should have resisted one another, but lust and physical attraction had overruled our sense of morals. Had Allison not fallen in love, there's a strong possibility that we'd still be messing around, now.

"Why did you cut your hair?" I ask, reaching out to touch the short, silky strands.

"Don't do that," she tells me. "Don't come on to me to prove that you're not in love with Sera."

"I'm not.　I just want to know."

"Fine. I cut my hair when Earl filed for divorce."

"Does he know it was me?" I ask pitifully. Now, it's my turn to feel guilty.

"No, but he knows that it was someone. When I realized you and I weren't anything more than a roll in the hay, I tried to go home; but it was too late. He'd already packed my things for me." She shook the memory off, then cleared her throat gently, "Anyway, let's not change the subject here. Have you told Sera?"

"What are you talking about? Have I told Sera what?"

"Have you told her that you're in love with her?"

I can't look away from Allison's suspicious green eyes.

"No."

"Good. Don't ever tell her." Allison warns, but I've heard this before too. If I can't stay away from Sera, I should at least spare her my hidden feelings. "Be her friend, but never tell her you love her."

"Why not?" I ask, already knowing the answer; but maybe if just one more person tells me, it will finally sink in.

"Because she'll break your heart."

"She wouldn't do that."

"Not on purpose," Allison says simply. "She's never going to get over him, whether he wakes up or not, he'll always be first in her heart. I don't think she really has room for the two of you. She'll love you in her own special way but it will never be as intense as what she had with Khalil."

"She used to love me."

"Yeah, and you were messing around with me, and several others, at the same time," Allison snaps.

"I'm not like that anymore."

"Jeremy, don't be stupid. It's too soon."

Of course, she's right. I can't just walk back into Sera's life while she's still trying to contemplate the possibility of spending a lifetime without her man. Hell, she's still trying to get over losing her baby. If it weren't for that, Allison and I wouldn't even be having this conversation.

"I have no false hopes, Allison. I'm content with being her friend."

"Whatever. Watch yourself." She walks away.

"Allison," I call out to her departing back.

"What?" She turns around and eyes me suspiciously.

I slowly walk towards her, and she looks down at the ground, as I approach.

"I'm sorry," I say softly, reaching out to grab her hand. Despite my earlier selfish thoughts, I *am* sorry about what transpired between us. I'm sorry about the pain it has caused her.

"Don't," she says softly, looking around to make sure no one has seen us.

"I just want you to know that I regret what happened, and that I would change it, if I could."

"You can't change the truth, Jeremy.   No matter how you present it, it's still what it is."   She smiled then, lifting a watery gaze to meet mine.   "Be careful with your heart, Jeremy."

She pats my cheek absently, then leaves me standing alone in the hallway, to watch another woman that I've hurt walk out of my sight.

## Chapter 36

### Ayzha Nicole Darwin

"Ayzha, why won't you talk to me?" Tyree's voice came over the answering machine, startling me out of my sleep. I sat straight up in my bed, and stared at the telephone as if it were the enemy.

"What the hell?" I mumbled. "How did he get this number?"

"If you're wondering how I got this number, Riley gave it to me."

At the mention of Riley's name, I grabbed the telephone and switched the answering machine off.

"What the fuck are you doing talking to Riley?" Shit, I told myself I was going to stop cussing. The baby can hear everything I say, and I want it to develop in a peaceful and serene environment. "Damn," I thought, as I listened to the silence on the other line. "Tyree, what do you want?"

"What?" He asked in amazement. "You tell me you're pregnant, then hang up on me? I've been trying to talk to you for weeks. You won't answer your phone."

"I can't talk to you."

"Why?"

"Tyree, who is Casey?" I let the name hang in the air, and waited for him to come up with an answer.

"Casey who?"

"Don't play stupid with me!" Here I go again, saying words I never want my baby to hear from my lips. Hell, it's too late now. Just this one last time, and I promise I'll be good from now on. "You know who the hell Casey is."

"Casey and I are just friends," he finally said.

"Okay, a few minutes ago you didn't even know who the bitch was. Now, she's your friend?"

"Ayzha, I know Aleesha probably told you that Casey and I are messing around, but I promise you it's not true."

"Oh, so now you're calling my cousin a liar?"

"I'm not calling her a liar. I'm just saying she has it mixed up. Casey and I have been friends for years, close friends...and I guess some people have misinterpreted that."

This bastard was a real piece of work. If his ass was so in love with me, why didn't I know about his good friend Casey? Why hadn't he mentioned her name at least once, in all the time he was messing around with me?

"Is this why you won't talk to me? You think I'm messing around with Casey? Why didn't you talk to me? Baby, I could have cleared this mess up, and everything would be fine."

"Everything is not fine!" I yelled so loudly that Sera came flying into my room, eyes glazed over, and her hair all over her head. Her scarf must have come off during the night. I motioned that I was fine and continued. "Everything is fucked up!" I lowered my voice. Sera sat next to me on the bed, and watched me as I spoke. "I've left my husband, and I'm pregnant with your baby."

He breathed a heavy sigh. "So you're still pregnant?"

"What?"

"Riley told me you'd probably lost the baby, by now."

"Well, he was wrong." I wasn't about to let Tyree know how much that statement affected me. I gripped the telephone tightly and took a deep breath. "Why? Were you rooting for a miscarriage? I can't talk to you right now." My voice was starting to crack, and the last thing I wanted to do was cry.

"You're talking crazy. I wasn't rooting for a miscarriage. I just don't know how to feel right now."

"Well, I don't know how to feel either. I'll call you when I do."

"Why can't you talk to me now?"

"Tyree, if you care about me as much as you claim to, you'll give me this time. Maybe, I'll call you in a couple of weeks."

"Ayzha, I still love you," he whispered. I hung up in his face, trying not to let his words affect me.

I lay down and pulled the covers around me tightly. Knowing I didn't want to be comforted, Sera got up and went back to her room without saying a word. For a while, I lay in the dark, contemplating my future. I couldn't allow Riley or Tyree to stress me out right now, not when I was so close to passing my gestational milestone. In just two weeks, I will be more pregnant than I've ever been in my life. Eighteen weeks. If I could just stay in the bed and hold this baby in, I'd be eighteen weeks along. In my heart and mind, eighteen was the magic number. At eighteen weeks, everything would be all right in my womb. I'd prayed constantly, and I knew. I just knew everything would work out, if I just gave myself those two weeks.

    ***

I slept for a while, showered, and left before Sera could ask me about my late night phone call from Tyree. I don't know what possessed me to drive by my former residence, but the moment I saw Riley's car in the driveway, I knew I had to stop. I still had my key, but didn't feel right using it. So, I rang the bell.

He stood in the doorway staring at me, and I could tell he was shocked to see me. I studied his face. He looked so much older than I remembered. He looked tired, as if he'd just lost his best friend.

"It's too cold to stand here." He opened the glass door and stepped aside, so I could walk past him into the house. I looked around. Things hadn't changed much. The house was just a little messier than usual. The kitchen was full of restaurant containers, and it looked like he hadn't touched the stove.

"I got the divorce papers." He motioned for me to sit down on the couch, and I did so cautiously, sitting on the edge of my seat just in case I had to get up in a hurry. "Don't worry, I'm not going to hurt you." He shook his head. "I signed the papers. Your lawyer should have them sometime this afternoon."

"Thanks." I didn't know what else to say. There were so many things we should have said, when we were together, before things got so complicated. "Riley, I never meant for things to happen this way." I stared him in the face. "You must really hate me."

"I don't hate you," he sighed.

"But you don't love me. You haven't for a long time."

"That's where you're wrong. I always loved you."

"Well, you had a jacked up way of showing it."

"I was disappointed. I was angry. I blamed you for everything," he admitted. "I convinced myself that I hated you, and I tried to punish you because you wouldn't try to have another baby. I didn't try to understand how hard it was for you to go through all of those miscarriages. I guess I was selfish."

I couldn't believe he was saying these things to me, now that it was too late. Now, he wanted to provide answers to questions I'd asked a million times, while trying to save our marriage. Now, he was apologizing for pushing me away. He was saying all the things that could have kept me from walking away a long time ago.

"Don't. Not now, when it's too late."

"Trust me. I know it's too late. I have a lot of regrets, Ayzha. I regret what I let happen to our marriage." He paused. "I regret putting my hands on you, when you left."

His words moved me, yet they didn't move me at all. They were things I needed to know a long time ago...things that we probably could have worked through...things that could have been fixed, before the damage became permanent...things that could have kept me out of another man's arms.

"You never deserved the pain I put you through," he continued, when I didn't respond to his words. "I was so busy trying to deal with my own issues, that I didn't even think about how it was affecting you. Ayzha, I'm sorry."

"You don't have to--"

"Yes, I do. I have so much to apologize for; and it took you leaving for me to realize how I pushed you away from me and this marriage." He walked over and sat down next to me on the couch. "Ayzha, I'm sorry."

"I'm sorry too," I said quietly. "What I did was wrong, Riley. I shouldn't have cheated on you. I should have just left."

"But you didn't, and now you're..." His voice trailed off, and an unasked question was reflected in his eyes.

"Yes, I'm still pregnant."

"And how are things?"

"So far so good."

"Are you happy?"

"I don't know." I looked away from him. "I guess you're one of the only people who could ever truly understand that, huh?"

"I signed the papers, but we could always tear them up, Ayzha. We could try to start over."

Disbelief had to be written all over my face, but if it was, Riley was obviously oblivious to it. I was shocked and out of kindness, I decided to stop him, before he said something to make the situation worse.

"Riley, don't." I stood up.

He grabbed my hand. The gesture wasn't forceful, but desperate, and made me extremely uncomfortable. It hurt to know that, although Riley was sincerely trying to apologize and make me feel wanted, I wasn't the true source of his desperation.

"Ayzha, don't leave me."

"Riley, stop it!" I snapped. "You don't want me. You want my baby. If anything were to happen to this pregnancy, we'd be right back where we started, and you know it."

"It should be mine." A tear slid from his left eye, and I snatched my hand away. His sudden emotion was pathetically scary and

I wasn't quite sure how to handle it. It was as if he saw, in my pregnancy, his last chance to carry on his family name. He didn't need me for that; and I didn't need him to make me miserable anymore. I'd done a wonderful of job of that, all by myself.

"It should be yours, Riley," I said softly. "In a perfect world this would be our baby together; but it's not, and we're not, and we're never going to be again."

It was much too late to go back. He knew this as well as I. Dwelling on what should have been could do nothing but stifle our growth as individuals.

"I'm going now."

"Wait," he said, as I turned to leave. "You didn't ask for anything, Ayzha; but if you want the house, it's yours."

"I don't want it."

It was a lie. I loved this house. I'd picked out every tile, curtained every window, and picked the colors for every wall. Leaving had been one of the hardest things I'd ever done. The house had become my baby, when I couldn't have one of my own, but my pride didn't want to accept anything from Riley.

"You can't live with Sera forever," he told me. "And anyway, the house is in your name. It was my gift to you, remember?"

"Where will you live?" See, part of me wanted to say, "No, I can't let you do that…" but my practical side took over. He was right. I couldn't live with Sera forever, and I sure as hell wasn't moving in with Tyree.

"I know you've been poking around my investments. I'll be fine."

I smiled for the first time since walking through the door. He still hadn't mentioned the money I'd taken, and probably never would. It wasn't like he needed it.

"Why are you doing this?"

"I feel like I owe you that much."

"I hurt you," I reminded him.

"We hurt each other. I do understand why you did it. I don't like it. I don't agree with it, but I understand. I just want to start fresh, Ayzha; and I can't do that without your forgiveness."

Deep inside, I knew all the anger I'd been harboring against Riley was nothing but negative energy that needed to be released. I didn't really hate him, not really. I didn't love him anymore either. We'd both made mistakes, and now that our marriage was coming to an end, there was only one thing left to do.  I slid my arms around him, hugged him as tightly as he hugged me, and then I let go.

## Chapter 37

### Ayzha Nicole Darwin

It should have been an opportunity for me to start over, to re-evaluate my life and decide where everyone fit. It should have been an opportunity to give myself the one thing I'd always relied on someone else to give me, but instead I pushed Riley out and allowed Tyree to come back in.

*I want to believe his lies*
*For they provide escape from his truths*
*Willing to accept the unacceptable*
*In the name of solitary love*
*I allow him to force his hands into my gloves*
*While I strain to contain him*
*He's too much for me.*

*I want to believe*
*Even when I'm blamed for things that*
*Begin and end with his actions...*
*Words so smooth he leaves me doubting myself*
*My mental health is in danger*
*The mirror reflects a stranger*
*Somehow he's altered me.*

*The sky is blue*
*But he told me it was black*
*I agreed it was a fact*
*And allowed him to fold me up*
*And place me in his back pocket...*
*In case he needed me later...*

*I love too hard*
*Accept too much*
*And fight too little*

*Because I'd rather believe his lies*
*Than accept his truth.*

*He doesn't love me...*

There is a stranger inside of me. He grunts and groans in the throes of a passion I ceased to feel ten minutes ago. For the moment he entered me, I knew it was all a lie. I don't understand what he wants from me. His baby girl thrives inside of my womb, while my love for him festers in my heart. He's still telling me lies, and I'm still forcing myself to believe him. I haven't met his family. I'm not even his girlfriend. Are we even really together? I mean, did he actually say, "Ayzha, lets be together? Let's raise our child together? I want you to meet my mama?" I don't know any of his friends.

He rolls away from me, sweaty and sticking to my sheets, as I feel the shame of our act oozing from me with uncomfortable certainty. *He doesn't love me.* This night did not turn out the way I intended. We were supposed to get together to talk about plans for our daughter's future. He was supposed to tell me the whole truth and nothing but. Instead, he told me what my pitiful heart thought it wanted to hear, crawled into my bed and preceded to inject me with the one thing I couldn't even claim as my own. What was I thinking? We hadn't even used protection. I know he's fucking "Blondie," and I know he tried to fuck my cousin. I just let him fuck me and think that everything is okay with that. I let him lie to me. I let him use me. I let him make a fool of me.

"I heard you were packing your office," I whispered into the darkness. He pretended not to hear me, but I knew he was still awake.

"Tyree, are you leaving?"

"Yes."

"When were you going to tell me?"

"As soon as you decided you were speaking to me again." He reached out to touch my naked arm, and it sent a cold chill down my spine. "Do you want to come with me?"

What? Was he crazy? He couldn't even tell me the truth about his other women, yet he was asking me if I wanted to move out of state with him.

"Would you be here if I weren't pregnant?" I asked softly.

"I take care of my responsibilities."

"Is that what you see in me? A responsibility? A burden? A loose end that needs to be tied up?" Then, it dawned on me. Tyree hadn't called, after accusing me of being pregnant because he knew my past history. He was expecting me to lose the baby. When I didn't, he realized he was going to have to take care of his little mistake. And then, I asked the question I should have asked before I'd let my emotions get the best of me.

"Did you give her a ring?"

"What are you talking about?"

"You told her it was a secret, but she just had to tell somebody. You gave her a pre-engagement ring, and told her that as soon as her divorce was final you were going to marry her." His silence was enough for me. "So, were the three of us going to live together in Baltimore? Or were you going to keep me in an upstairs apartment?"

"I'm going to break it off with her."

"Oh hell Tyree, if you really loved me there wouldn't be anything to break off."

"You can't deny that you love me, Ayzha."

"Honestly, I don't know what I feel for you, Tyree. It can't be love. It's more like desperation. You don't deserve my love. I don't need this shit in my life anymore."

I got out of the bed, and threw on my robe. I couldn't let him manipulate me with the "L" word again. His mouth was constantly verbalizing love he never bothered to rationalize with an action to adequately summarize his supposed feelings for me. "Get dressed and get out of my house. I'm not playing with you, Tyree."

"What the hell just happened here? We just finished making love."

"No, you just fucked me; and this is the last time, Tyree Mitchell." I started throwing his clothes at him, getting pissed off every time he dodged something aimed for his nose.

"If you let me walk out that door, I'll never come back, Ayzha."

"Get out." I stared him square in the eyes, daring him to make another move toward me.

"Just remember my not being a part of this kid's life was your decision," he finally said. He started pulling on his clothes, without even looking at me. I stood there, arms folded across my swollen chest, watching the father of my child walk out of my life, while she wiggled around inside of me. "You'll be hearing from my lawyer. I don't want anything to do with you or this baby. I'm going to sign away my rights. That way, you won't be able to ask me for a damn thing."

"Do whatever you need to do, Tyree," I yelled at his back, as he walked away from me. "I hope you and that little blond bitch are happy together." I followed him to the front door, and slammed it behind him.

"We don't need him," I whispered, "and I don't love him anymore." I spoke the words, and forced myself to believe them. Love was a circumstance; and any circumstance could be overcome with determination.

## Chapter 38

### Serafina Danielle Jordan
### THE NEXT YEAR

Stacie walked through my apartment as if we'd just seen each other a few days ago. In reality, aside from the occasional phone call, I hadn't seen very much of her in the fifteen months since Khalil's accident.

"Trevor is coming home," she blurted out, before I could even offer her a soda.

"Really? When?" I asked curiously.

"Two weeks," she told me. I stared at her for a moment, and waited for the next big announcement because I knew that there had to be something more to bring her all the way to my house.

"What else?"

"We're getting married," she said softly.

"And you've known this for how long?" I asked. She didn't answer, and I shook my head in disgust. "What is it Stacie? Did you think I couldn't handle it? Is that why you barely call or come to see me?"

"I didn't know what to say."

"Yeah, well..." I let my voice trail off, "I would never have done that to you."

"I know, Sera, and I wish that I could be more like you, but I can't. I'm not good with other people's problems. I didn't know what to say to you. I didn't know how to help you."

She could have helped by merely being there, but I knew that Stacie had no idea how to be there for someone when things were bad. She was the kind of friend you called to share good news with, not bring her natural high down with your problems. I knew that going into the friendship, so her absence from my life shouldn't have been such a big deal...but it was.

"What do you want me to say?"

"I want you to forgive me," she said simply.

"Girl, you haven't even apologized," I reminded her. "Old backwards ass..." I mumbled just loud enough for her to hear.

"Sera, I'm sorry," she said, walking towards me with arms outstretched. "I really am sorry. Please, forgive me for being a terrible friend."

"Of course, I forgive you, but that doesn't mean that my feelings aren't still hurt." I gave Stacie a big hug and smiled, welcoming her back into my world. We sat down on the couch she'd helped me pick out a few years ago. I remembered how she'd flirted with the salesman so much he'd confessed that the couch was due to go on sale within the next week.

"So when is the wedding?  Or do you think I'm too broken up to come?" I asked sarcastically.

"Sera, you forgave me, remember?"

"Am I invited or not?  Cuz I will crash your damn wedding and object, if I'm not."

"Of course you're invited, dummy.  You can even bring Jeremy," she said, eying me suspiciously.  She was being nosey, fishing for information that just wasn't there.  I had to laugh at her audacity.

"There's nothing going on there."

"Yeah right.  You can't tell me Jeremy hasn't tried to get at you."

"He hasn't."

"So that means he's still getting it elsewhere," she stated with finality.

"Well, he's not my man."

"Yeah, and how long has it been since you've had a tune up?" She was the same old Stacie.  I'd forgiven my fair-weather friend, and she was picking up right where we'd left off.

"It has definitely been a while and, bitch, I hate you for bringing it up!" I picked up a throw pillow and hit her in the head with it.  Stacie grabbed the pillow and hit me back with it, then quickly changed the subject before I could attack her again.

I don't know why, but I suddenly found myself telling her about the problems I'd been having at work.  Some of the women in my office, once ridiculously envious of my relationship with Khalil were now secretly thrilled that our relationship was not what it once was.  If I smiled, they wondered how I could possibly be happy in my pathetic situation.  If I seemed down, they wondered why, after over a year, I was still hanging on to Khalil.

*"Most people get over the death of a husband in less time,"* I heard one of my co-workers whispering, just the other day.  Obviously, she didn't realize that I was standing in the doorway because she practically pissed on herself, when I casually walked over to the water cooler and said, *"He's not dead."*

Of course the heffa apologized, but I just smiled and walked away.  She wasn't sorry for thinking or even saying such a thing out loud.  She was just sorry I'd heard her stupid ass comments, but were they really the stupid ones?

Maybe, I was an idiot for believing that Khalil was going to wake up one day and ask me for a kiss and a hug.  Maybe, I was crazy to believe that things could ever be as they once were.  Khalil's father had started touring again, eight months after the accident.  He couldn't bear to see his son lying in the hospital like a vegetable.  So, he'd resumed his career, to take his mind off of his troubles.

*"Life has to go on, Sera," he'd told me the day he left for a concert in*

*London. "You need to start thinking about your future."*

*"I don't want to think about a future without Khalil," I'd told him.*

*"Neither do I, sweetie, but sooner or later we have to face the possibility that he is not going to wake up."*

The hospital had made us at least acknowledge the possibility, by suggesting that Karl move Khalil into a nursing home, or some other facility that could care for him. As a result, I was now visiting Khalil at his grandmother's house because she refused to allow Khalil to be placed in a strange home.

I asked her once if she thought that Khalil would ever wake up and marry me.

*"Just pray, child, but don't stop living," was her answer.*

So I prayed all the time, and I lived everyday…but was I really living? For the first time in the history of our friendship, Stacie listened silently, absorbing every word without interruption.

"Stacie, Karl called me the other day, and asked me to move out of my apartment and into Khalil's place; but I can't stay there without him," I said sadly. "He said that Khalil would have wanted me to have it. He said it, like he was already dead."

"What are you going to do?"

"I can't do that. It wouldn't feel right."

"You wouldn't be able to move on with your life."

"That's not what I'm trying to do. I don't want to move on."

"Yes, you do. You're just afraid to admit it," Stacie said gently. "Sera, you don't have a life. You go to work and take care of Khalil. You spend the rest of your time shut away in this damn apartment."

"You haven't been around enough to know what I do." I was a little defensive.

"I know *you*, Serafina Jordan," she scolded. "Plus, I ran into Jeremy a few days ago. He gave me the third degree about not spending more time with you."

"You saw Jeremy? Where?"

"I saw him at the movies with some girl."

"Oh," I answered indifferently.

"He really cares about you."

"Stacie, Jeremy and I are just friends. He helped me out of a really bad situation, and he's just been there for me, okay? We hang out, nothing more." I stood up and headed towards the kitchen, in desperate need of a soda to wet the sudden dryness in my throat.

"You haven't thought about hooking up with him again? Not even once?" Stacie called after me.

"Do you want a soda?" I called back.

"You need to answer my question," she answered.

I poked my head out of the kitchen, "Stacie, where are you going with this?"

"I'm just saying that no one would blame you, if you decided to start dating again." Stacie sounded like she was trying to choose her words carefully but she wasn't being careful enough.

I set my unopened soda on the counter, and leaned against the wall with my arms folded across my chest. I should have expected this from her, but I was still surprised at how easy she thought it was to just pick up and forget my obligations to the man I loved. Stacie was always the friend who encouraged me to do wrong, instead of trying to steer me in the right direction.

"Another man can't make me happy." I studied my fingernails, picking at the acrylic until it chipped. "Sometimes I do think about it, but in reality, I can't imagine myself with another man. I could never love someone else the way I love Khalil.

"But don't you get--"

"Lonely?" I finished for her. "Hell yeah, I get lonely. I go to bed lonely, and I wake up lonely, but I can't give up on him. I can't believe that God would give me that man just to take him away from me, Stacie."

"How long are you willing to wait? Seriously, Sera, because it's been well over a year."

"I know how long it's been," I said angrily.

"I'm sorry, Sera. I wasn't trying to hurt you. I just don't want you to be miserable for the rest of your life."

"It won't be like this forever," I said with my voice full of confidence but in reality, I was really trying to convince myself.

## Chapter 39

### Jeremy Trent Sanders

Mistletoe used to be my friend, but today that innocent looking sprig of sin is hanging directly above Sera's head and I can't stop thinking about how delicious it would be to lick the strawberry-scented lip-gloss from her healthy lips. I smelled it on her, the moment she slid into the passenger seat of my car. Now, as she sits across from me at a booth in my favorite restaurant, I wish the memory of that scent would stop teasing me.

She looks wonderful. No more baggy sweatpants, she's wearing a pair of jeans that hug her little booty so snugly that I want to reach out and touch. Her red sweater looks like cashmere, which is very distracting, because cashmere is a fabric that begs to be caressed. She looks very much in the Christmas spirit. It's good to see a smile on her pretty face. Sera's smile is addictive and her laugh, something I don't get to hear nearly as often as I should, causes me to start laughing, even though I'm too busy staring at her beauty to actually listen to whatever joke she's just told me.

"You're staring," she comments, sipping her hot chocolate. There is a small bit of whipped cream on her upper lip, and I'm slightly let down when she dabs it away with her napkin instead of licking it.

She's my friend. At least, that is what I keep telling myself and anyone else who tries to expose my feelings for her. As her friend, I've learned more about her than I ever bothered trying to learn when we were together. The things I didn't know about her then are what have me reaching for her in the middle of the night now.

I can tell her anything but the one thing that has been nagging me for months. I can't tell her that I've fallen in love with her. I can't tell her that my last date, two weeks ago, ended badly because I kept calling my date by the wrong name, when her name didn't even remotely sound like Sera.

"Jeremy," she says, looking at me strangely.

"What?"

"You're staring at me."

"You shouldn't look so cute," I tell her, then pull myself out of my thoughts, and give her my ears as well as my eyes.

"Are you still up to going to Ayzha's Christmas party next week?"

"Probably," I tell her. "Why is she having it so early?"

"You know my parents are going to New York for Christmas this year. She wanted to make sure we all got together, before they left."

"Oh yeah. Well, I'll tell you one thing. Life is a lot easier, now that your people don't hate me."

"You ain't neva lied!" Sera laughs again, "Even Max has gotten used to you."

"I don't want to talk about your brother." I place a small turquoise box in front of her. She slowly lowers her gaze to the box, then looks at me questioningly. "Happy Birthday." I push the box toward her. "Don't be scared. It doesn't bite."

She hesitantly reaches for the box, hesitantly, as if she is afraid to open it; but once she sees what is inside, tears immediately spring to her eyes. "You bought this for me?" She whispers.

"Do you like it?"

"It's beautiful." A tear slides down her cheek, and I'm worried. I never expected a charm bracelet to cause so much emotion, but I'd never taken into account the fact that the gift would cause her to think about the one she couldn't be with. I move around to her side of the table and cup her face in my hands, apologizing profusely for upsetting her with my gift.

"No, Jeremy, it's a wonderful gift," she whispers. "I love it. I guess, I've just missed having someone to do special things for me."

Call me crazy, but that little sprig of sin is hanging directly above our heads heads and the sight of her tears along with her words has me overcome with a desire to give her the comfort that's been missing from her life. Without considering the consequences, I kiss her softly, quickly. Birds start singing, and my head is filled with a song, "*kissing you is all that I've been thinking of...kissing you is ooh...ooh...*"

"You just kissed me."

The record in my mind starts skipping, as I fumble for an excuse for this temporary lapse in judgment. "I can't believe you just did that." She's mumbling now, not looking at me, but I do see her glance up at the mistletoe a few times. "Mistletoe," I hear her whisper. "Oh my God, I'd forgotten."

"Forgotten what?"

"What it feels like." She's staring at me now, so intently that the force of her gaze threatens to propel me toward her again. "What it feels like to be kissed."

The record starts to play again, "*kissing you is all that I've been thinking of...kissing you is ooh...ooh...*"

She's afraid. I can see it in her eyes. I can see it in the tears that are threatening to spill again. I can feel it in the air surrounding us. I should move back into my own seat, but I don't. There's something about the way she's looking at me that keeps me rooted in place.

"I'm not hungry anymore." She tells me.

"Do you want to leave?"

"Alone," she whispers. "I need to be alone."

I must have gotten up, although I don't remember moving, because the next thing I remember is the sight of Sera hurrying through the crowded restaurant.

## Chapter 40

### Serafina Danielle Jordan

I saw her standing across the street, staring at me as I wordlessly got out of Jeremy's car. I pretended not to notice, as she swayed back and forth as if she were dancing to music that only she could hear. Her red dress blew in the wind, lifting dangerously high at the hem, threatening to expose parts of her that nobody needed to see.

"You are a figment of my imagination," I mused, standing still in front of my stairway. I closed my eyes. "Go away," I whispered. "I can't do this with you today." She always appeared when I was confused, frightened, or just so depressed that I didn't know what to do. It scared me.

"Sera?" Jeremy walked up behind me and placed his hand on my shoulder. I slowly opened my eyes. She was gone. I breathed a small sigh of relief, before allowing myself to look Jeremy in the eye.

"Please talk to me," he pleaded.

"I-I can't talk to you right now," I stammered. I fumbled around in my purse, until my shaking fingers made contact with my keys. "Jeremy, I have to go."

Jeremy stood with a bewildered expression on his face, but didn't try to stop me, as I hurriedly walked up the stairs and let myself inside. It was typical of me, lately: running away from my issues instead of confronting them. It was the one thing I'd mastered, since Khalil's accident. Instead of acknowledging my fears and disappointments I'd developed the debilitating habit of walking through life pretending to be strong, when in reality I was *oh so* weak.

If people saw that weakness, if they saw me falter in any way, they didn't acknowledge it, at least not to my face, for fear of upsetting me. They allowed me to continue pretending. Every now and then, someone would make a small suggestion or indirectly hint that I should move on; but talk like that was met with hostility. Most people had decided long ago to keep their eye on me, while staying just outside of the bubble of denial I'd surrounded myself with.

Jeremy was the only one who'd entered the bubble and forced me to look at things as they were, not as I wanted them to be…but even he held back sometimes, when I became too moody to deal with.

He kissed me. I could wash my face a thousand times and I could take sandpaper and rake it across my lips; but it wouldn't change the fact that Jeremy had kissed me, and I had felt something. It had been familiar and different, at the same time. It had stirred feelings in me that I thought were dead. I picked up the phone and dialed Khalil's grandmother.

"Hey, Grandmamma, I just wanted to make sure you were there. I'm going to come and sit with Khalil for a while."

"Baby, you were just here this morning," she said gently. "He's fine."

"I know, but I really need to see him." I couldn't believe I was practically begging to see my own fiancé.

"What's wrong?"

"Nothing."

"Sera, don't lie to me."

I took a deep breath, and said it before I could lose my nerve, "I'm scared." I could hear her television suddenly lose volume as she asked me to repeat myself.

"I feel like I'm losing control," I admitted.

"Can I ask you a question, Sera?"

"Yes."

"Do you spend so much time with Khalil because you love him? Or because you think its what we expect of you?"

I was dumfounded. No, actually I was pissed. I was pissed off and offended and angry and…ashamed. I was ashamed because for the first time since the accident, I actually had to think about her question, before answering. There was no doubt in my mind that I loved Khalil. My love for him was stronger than my love of self; and I couldn't understand why I couldn't just say, "I do it because I love him. End of story."

"I do love him."

"I know that you do, baby," she said gently. "We all love him. We all want him to wake up, but it's been over a year."

"I'm not going to give up on him. I can't."

"I'm not asking you to give up on him. I'm asking you to live. I think you're scared to live. Isn't that it? Isn't that was you're afraid of?"

I didn't know what she meant by 'Live'. What exactly did it mean to live? Did it mean carrying on with my life, as if Khalil were dead? Did it mean moving on and forgetting about what we had together? If that's what living was, I wasn't sure if I could do that. I knew that I couldn't do that.

"What if he wakes up?" My question hung in the air, until the gravitational force of Grandmamma's answer caused it to land on the ground with an unceremonious thud.

"What if he doesn't?"

I felt as if the air had been sucked from my lungs.

"Sera, listen to me," she said gently, "Your visiting here doesn't bother me, baby; but I'm not going to let you come over here again today. I won't let you torture yourself. I love to see you. I love to hear your voice, and I love the fact that you love my grandson so much, but I hate to see you dying inside, the way that you are."

"But I'm better," I argued.

"Oh, you've cleaned up on the outside, but inside..." Her voice trailed off for a moment. "Inside you're wilting, when you should be blossoming."

I stared at the picture of Khalil sitting on my nightstand, and although my eyes stung horribly, I couldn't cry. I looked away from the picture. I couldn't bear to see his face.

"A man kissed me today," I whispered as if Khalil's picture could hear me.

"A man?"

"Jeremy," I confessed.

"And this Jeremy, have you spent a lot of time with him? You never told me about him, before."

"I was afraid you'd disapprove. He's been a good friend to me."

"Has he ever kissed you before?"

"A long time ago. Before I met Khalil." I admitted.

"Ahh, an ex-boyfriend," she exclaimed. "Let me guess. He's familiar. He's there for you, when Khalil can't be. He's a different person than he was when you knew him before. He's probably handsome. He's held your hand, when you felt you couldn't turn to anyone else. What did you do?"

"I ran away."

"You feel guilty." she commented.

"Shouldn't I?"

"I'm the wrong person to ask. It hurts to think that one day you might give up on Khalil, but it hurts to think of you going through life miserable and alone." She sighed. "I pray everyday that my baby will wake up. It's been over a year, and truth be told, even if he does wake up he may never be the way we remember him. Have you thought about that, Serafina?" I had given it a lot of thought. What if he woke up with the mind of a child? What if he didn't know me? What if? What if? What if?

"What if I did start spending time with another man? What if I went on with my life, and then Khalil woke up?"

"What if you sat next to his bed, until you were old and gray?"

"Why does everyone think that I should move on?"

"I just want you to make sure you see all of your options, while you're still young. I don't want you to wake up one day and realize that your life has passed you by. I don't want you to hate him."

"I could never hate him," I assured her, but inside I did hate him...just a little.

## Chapter 41

### <u>Ayzha Nicole Darwin</u>

She has his eyes, dark, deep, penetrating. Sometimes, I wonder what she's thinking about when she stares at me as she nurses, right before she falls asleep in my arms. It amazes me that a man could walk away from such a gift, but Tyree isn't an ordinary man. He's extraordinarily selfish. So selfish, in fact, that he'd been true to his word. He never contacted me again, not even when his daughter was born three months ago. He's never seen her chocolate face, never heard her soft coos, never smelled her sweet baby scent; and he doesn't want to. He proved it last week, when my lawyer called to inform me that Tyree was attempting to sign away his parental rights. Ironically, the judge had been so disgusted that he'd kindly advised Tyree that he could, in fact, relinquish his parental rights, but that he would still be required to pay child support until she was eighteen. Tyree is still mulling that one over.

I don't want his money. I don't want his presence in our lives. I have all that I need, now that she's in my world. Life now has new meaning, and things that used to bother me in the past no longer cross my mind. If I never accomplish anything else in this life, I rest assured that I was born for the sole purpose of loving this child, Chyna Danielle. She's turned my world upside down and yet, without her, my world would be turned upside down. It's funny how a child can teach you the true meaning of love, with just one look, one kiss. When she wraps her little fingers around mine, she may as well be squeezing my heart.

It's crazy. Stacie faints at the sight of blood. Sera couldn't handle watching me go through childbirth so Max had actually volunteered to go through Lamaze classes and coach me through my delivery. I've begun to see him as more than Sera's older brother, and he's begun to see Chyna as more than just his goddaughter. Sometimes, he acts as if his blood flows through her veins, which is a bit scary because, in my wildest dreams I wish it were. Perhaps I'm just getting too used to his presence. He's always there, helping me before I can even ask. When I need a break, all I have to do is call, and he literally drops whatever he's doing.

I truly think he wishes Chyna were his daughter. It's in the way he looks at her. It's in the way he sometimes falls asleep on the couch with my baby on his chest. It's in the way he looks at me, when he thinks I'm not looking. It's strange. Not *strange* strange, but strange because, sometimes when he isn't looking, I study his profile and wonder how different my life would be if Max actually was Chyna's daddy. What if I had never started up with Tyree? Would Riley and I still be miserably married? Or would I have had the strength to leave him on my own, with no outside influences?

Who knows? What was the point in dwelling on that? I had started up with Tyree. If I hadn't, maybe I'd still be with Riley. Maybe I wouldn't. I definitely wouldn't have my Chyna Danielle, if it weren't for my indiscretions. So, it had all happened for a reason.

I can hear Chyna stirring in her cradle and I strain my ears to make sure she's still asleep. We're having company over for Christmas Eve, and I want to make sure she sleeps long enough for me to finish cooking dinner. I've probably gone too far, but this is her first Christmas. In celebration of this milestone, I've loaded the tree with dozens of gifts that she can neither unwrap herself, nor fully appreciate at such a young age.

The doorbell rang, and my thoughts immediately switched gears. I ran to the door and opened it, without bothering to look through the peephole. I knew that it was probably Max. He had a habit of showing up early. I was right, of course. Max stood in my doorway, handsome in a bulky red sweater and a pair of baggy jeans. He stared at me as if he'd never seen me before.

"What's wrong with you?" I asked.

"How did that get there?" He nodded his head upwards, and my eyes followed until they rested on the sprig of mistletoe hanging over my door. I folded my arms across my chest and curled my lips upward, giving him one of those "you can't fool me" looks.

"Cute," I said, shaking my head.

"What? You don't want to kiss me under the mistletoe?" He joked.

Hell yes, I wanted to kiss him under the mistletoe; but I was afraid that my version of the kiss wasn't the same thing he had in mind. Max was sending out vibes, but I couldn't read them. Sometimes, I thought he wanted me. Other times, I thought he was just flattering me to be nice. I didn't want to make a fool of myself, by assuming too much. I changed the subject.

"Sera isn't here yet." I told him.

Max followed me into the house, and followed my lead, pretending the mistletoe conversation never took place.

"Is she with Jeremy?" He frowned slightly.

"I don't know, but Max, it's been a year; and he hasn't laid a hand on her. We may as well give the brotha a chance."

"I'm trying. I guess he's ok. Did you invite him over?"

"Yes, and please be nice. This Christmas will be hard enough on her, ok?"

"You look nice," Max said, instead of agreeing with me.

"What?" I stuttered.

"I'm just saying that you look very nice. You can't even tell you had a baby three months ago. Well, except for those." He nodded towards my breasts, which were swollen to twice their normal size. "When is the last time you nursed Chyna?"

What was he doing looking at my breasts? I mean, I wanted him to look, but whenever he did I got flustered. I don't know where his head is. I don't know where my head is. My track record is pretty horrible, and I don't want to make the mistake of misinterpreting Max's feelings toward me.

"I'm going to wake the baby," I said, walking past him quickly and practically running up the stairs. I had to get away from Max and his watchful gaze.

"Max is off limits," I told myself. "No matter how fine he is, he's still a man…and I'm still a woman with needs, and he is really good with Chyna, and he's always looked out for me and…" I stopped my thoughts, before they could go any further. Whatever my heart or body thought it needed, my mind did not need the headache.

## Chapter 42

### <u>Jeremy Trent Sanders</u>

Crossing the line is so passé. I mean…I definitely would not call what I did with Sera "crossing any kind of line". Hell, I jumped over the line, did the Running Man, and ended in a split combination that would make James Brown proud.

I'm not really sure what kind of stupidity took over my brain that day, but between the mistletoe and the smell of her lip gloss swirling around my head…the rise and fall of her breasts beneath that red sweater…my undying love for her…my complete and total insanity. What the hell was I thinking? It's been a week, but it feels like a year. I don't know how much longer I can deal with the silence between us.

I need her. I feel like a bumbling idiot, without her in my life. My mind is unbalanced. Work is the only thing that keeps her off my mind, but as soon as I have an idle moment…

I miss her. I miss her smile. I miss her laugh. I miss the way she used to eat my peanut butter cups and not even save me one. I miss the way she would point out pretty women in crowds, in an attempt to hook me up, not knowing that all I needed was the woman standing next to me. I miss our conversations. I miss listening to her read her poetry to me. I miss my friend.

I want that friendship back; and I'm willing to do anything to make things the way they used to be, before I messed everything up with that damn kiss. As brief as the contact was, I can still taste the small traces of hot cocoa mixed in with her shiny lip-gloss. I still hear the tiny crack in her voice, as she thanked me for buying the bracelet.

I'm so in love with her, I can't think straight; and I have no one to blame but myself. I should have listened, when my mama told me to let her go. She told me to stay away from her, before I got hurt…but hey, I'm a man, and I'm hardheaded. I know that I should just leave her alone and not try contacting her until she decides to make a move. It all sounds so rational in my mind. Just leave the woman alone. Give her space. Let her decide whether or not she wants to continue the friendship.

I should do these things, but I'm not strong enough. I'm not wise enough. Or, maybe I just don't love her enough. My selfishness consumes me. It makes me want something from her that she can't possibly give me, and that makes me want it even more. I am ashamed because, as terrible as it sounds, I would love for Sera to give up on Khalil and run directly into my arms. I want to lay her down and love all traces of that man from her mind.

But that's not reality. Reality is Sera loving that man with her heart and soul, standing by that man for better or worse, not giving up on something she truly believes in. I don't think I could even love her, if she weren't this way.

If I could take it back I would. I'd build a time machine and go back to her wedding day, before the moment of impact. I'd snatch Khalil out of harm's way and place him beside Sera in front of the minister. I'd watch as he pronounced them man and wife. I would watch her kiss him with the lips I desire and then smile at him in a way she never could have smiled at me...the smile of pure joy I see in every picture of the two of them together...the smile that claims her face whenever she says that man's name.

But I'm not H.G. Wells. I don't have a time machine, and I can't change the past. I can only pray that she can accept my friendship, and place my mistake in the garbage with the rest of my past mistakes. I can't leave her alone. I admit it. I'm selfish, and that selfishness leads me directly to her door.

## Chapter 43

### <u>Serafina Danielle Jordan</u>

I was putting the finishing touches on my make-up, when the doorbell rang. I was already running late for Ayzha's party, and didn't want to hear it from Max. In my opinion, lately he spent more time at Ayzha's house than he did at his own...but that was definitely none of my business.

"I'm coming," I called out, hopping on one foot as I tried to pull on my black boots. I peered out of the peephole, and sighed loudly.

"No," I thought, while contemplating whether or not I should answer the door. "What is he doing here?"

He rang the bell again, and I had no choice but to open the door and face what had been tormenting me for a week. I'm not going to lie to myself anymore. I'm attracted to Jeremy. I'd thought of kissing him several times, but it wasn't something I'd have ever done on my own.

Hell no. No, no, no!

My lips belong to Khalil. It doesn't matter that he can't kiss me back. My heart belongs to Khalil. It doesn't matter that he can't feel it. It doesn't matter that he can't touch me. It doesn't matter that he can't talk to me, hold me, or be there for me when I really need a shoulder to lean on. It doesn't matter. It shouldn't matter. It shouldn't matter. Should it?

Jeremy holds me when I'm sad. Jeremy makes me laugh, when I want to cry. Jeremy holds my hand, during the scary part of the movie. Jeremy sleeps on the couch, when I'm afraid to be alone in my apartment.

Jeremy makes me feel guilty.

When he kissed me, part of me wanted to kiss him back. That part of me is terrified about what could happen, if he ever kissed me again. It has been way too long since I've felt the intimacy of a lover's embrace, felt the tip of a tongue on mine, had a hand on my breast, felt warmth between my...

"What are you doing here?" I said harshly. The hostility in my voice stemmed from my frustration; I was suddenly sorry I'd opened the door.

"Did you forget? We're going to Ayzha's party together," he told me, then pulled a bouquet of yellow roses from behind his back, and smiled at me in that unsettling way of his, as he handed them to me.

I stared down at the roses in my hand. Yellow roses, friendship roses, "please forgive me" roses. He was trying to go on as if the kiss had never happened, as if we hadn't gone though this past week without seeing or speaking to one another. Didn't he realize what he'd done?

That kiss had created tension between us. I could still feel it; and I wasn't stupid enough to think that he couldn't feel it too.

I used to masturbate every once in a while as a means of relaxation. It helped me write. It helped to relieve the tension of a long, stressful day. And let's face it; an orgasm is the world's best sleeping pill. Lately, since Jeremy kissed me, I've been pretty much doing it every day, sometimes twice. It's become an addiction and it's no longer relaxing or peaceful. It's necessary. It's become my routine: wake up, brush my teeth, masturbate in the shower, get dressed and go to work, come home, eat, brush my teeth, masturbate in the shower, go to bed and fall into a restless sleep.

I dream vivid, x-rated dreams, so real that I sometimes wake up in the middle of the night sweating and squeezing my pillow between my knees. The man in my dreams used to have a beautiful caramel face and long sandy dreadlocks that I could almost feel through my imagination. Lately, I can't see his face. I can't hear his voice. I can't feel his hair. I can't open my eyes because I'm afraid of who I'll see grinding on top of me, so I dream with my eyes wide shut.

"Are you for real?" I asked in disbelief. He seemed taken aback, but I didn't care. I wasn't going to let him pretend that everything was normal. That was something the old Jeremy would do, not the Jeremy I've come to know.

"We just talked about the party," he reminded me.

"Oh my God." I stared at him in amazement. "Jeremy, we talked about the party a week ago. I'm not going to let you walk in here and pretend that the last week didn't happen. That's how you used to handle things with us, remember? I don't fall for that shit anymore." I shoved the roses back at him, catching him off guard, and they tumbled to the concrete beneath his feet. He looked down at the mess of yellow roses, then at me with a pitiful expression on his face.

"I deserve more from you," I told him. "I'm not going anywhere with you, until you tell me why you're really here because I know that you could care less about that damn party." He must have seen it in my eyes...the determination...the anger...the fear, and curiosity.

"Can we start over?" He asked me. I nodded.

"I want to talk to you, but I don't know where to start."

"Start at the beginning." I replied.

"Will you come sit with me?"

"Outside."

"Outside?"

"Yeah." I didn't want him in my house. I didn't trust myself alone with him. He turned, walked halfway down the steps, and took a seat. I slowly followed, gingerly stepping over the scattered roses, and took the step directly below him. I was thankful I'd opted to wear an ankle length skirt because otherwise any passerby would have gotten an eyeful. The evening was chilly, but my seat was suspiciously warm and I had to wonder if the heat were coming from him or from me. He opened his legs and stretched them out on either side of me. I leaned back into him without thinking about how that would affect him.

"Were you ever going to call?" He asked.

"Were you?" I countered.

"I was afraid to call you."

"So instead, you came over here and tried to charm me into forgetting. That is so...playa, Jeremy." Jeremy took a deep breath.

"I saw my pops today," he said softly. "You know I haven't spoken to him since Jacob and I took Michelle and Jerica away. I used to try so hard to be just like him, Sera; and even when I realized what a bastard he was, I still wanted to prove to him that I was man enough to be called his son." He paused for a moment, and I could tell that it was still hard for him to talk about his father.

"When I saw him today...do you know that all of those feelings came back? For a minute, I wanted to run up to him and tell him about all my hoes and feel him slap me on the back and say, 'My Nigga, you're a pimp, just like your Pops'." He took a deep breath, "Sera I was almost ready to beg his forgiveness and ask him to love me again, when that man never really loved me in the first place...not the way a father should truly love his son."

"Did you speak to him?" I asked curiously. I never liked Jeremy's father. He'd hit on me several times, but I'd never told Jeremy. His dad had been his hero and role model.

"I spoke. I said hello, and asked how he was doing."

"And?"

"And he looked right through me. Told me that I was dead to him."

"I'm sorry," I whispered, afraid to look at him. I wasn't used to the vulnerability I heard in Jeremy's voice. I lay my head on his knee and hugged his leg tightly. "You're nothing like him, Jeremy."

"Sera, I'm sorry. You're right. You deserve better than that. You deserve honesty. I was trying to be cool about it, when I've really been broken up all week over this thing. I crossed the line."

"Ya think?"

"I miss you, Sera." I could sense the presence of his hand just over my hair, as if he wanted to touch me but was afraid to.

"I miss you too." There was no sense in lying about it.

"I'm sorry."

"Are you really? Sorry, I mean."

"I said it, didn't I?"

"Yeah, but do you really mean it?" I turned to face him, resting my elbows on his thighs. "Are you sorry that you kissed me? Or are you sorry that I ran away?"

He tried to look away from me, but my eyes willed him to stay focused on me. I don't understand what's going on with me, but for some reason I need to hear everything going on inside of his head. I need to get everything out in the open. I need to know what drives him to be so good to me. What drove him to kiss me, and why oh why was I sitting here with him like this, when it would be so easy to lean in and wait for him to kiss me again?

"Well?" I questioned.

"Can I plead the fifth?" he asked.

"Nope."

"Can I think about it, before I answer?"

"I want to know the first thing that pops into your mind."

"I wanted to know if they still felt the same." He actually did touch me then…on the cheek. I felt as if he'd scorched my skin. Now, I was the one who couldn't look away.

"If what still felt the same?" I asked, knowing full well what he meant.

"Your lips." He stared at my lips hungrily, like a kitty cat with a bowl of milk. I instinctively licked them, tasting the faint vanilla flavor of the shake I'd sipped on the way home from work. Did he lean down toward me? Or did I lean my face closer to his? Better yet, was this actually happening? Or was it another one of my dreams? I decided to go with the dream theory, and as his lips settled over mine, I allowed myself to brand his mouth with the marks of a woman who hadn't been thoroughly kissed in what felt like an eternity.

It was intense; too intense even for Jeremy because he pulled away first, leaving me trembling and gasping for air. The dream theory wasn't working anymore. Only reality could cause a woman to sweat in thirty-degree weather. Only a truly bewitching kiss could ever render that same woman speechless. What I couldn't verbalize overpowered my mind, and I fought to regain control over my disobedient body.

"That wasn't supposed to happen," he said finally.

"Oh yeah? What was supposed to happen?"

"We were supposed to go back to the way things used to be."

"Do you really think we can?"

I turned away quickly and stared straight ahead. I didn't dare lean back into him again; for fear that the result of our kiss would stab me in the back. He never answered the question, and I didn't ask again. I just sat there, between his legs, looking straight ahead, as if I were playing a game of stare-down with my neighbor's front door.

"Sera, I don't know if I can do this."

"Me neither."

"I tried, but I can't pretend that I don't feel the tension between us. Can you?"

"I don't think you understand what I'm going through. I don't even understand it."

"I think I understand more than you could ever know."

The urgency in his voice compelled me to stand. He stood with me, letting me know that I couldn't run away this time. He towered over me, but neither his size nor strength intimidated me. The force that threatened to pull us together intimidated me. I knew that if I spent more than five more minutes alone in his presence, that force would surely take over. Jeremy was no stranger. He was a man with whom I'd shared a considerable portion of my life, but somehow, he wasn't the same man. This man was my friend. We hadn't been intimate in years. Yet, his body standing so close to mine was suddenly so personal that I took a step backwards and almost lost my footing on the steps. Jeremy steadied me, and I tried not to react to the fact that his hand now encircled my upper arm with a gentle, yet firm grip.

"You're hurting me." I told him.

He let go of me, but it didn't stop the pain. My injury wasn't physical. My heart was hurting. I didn't understand how I could love one man, and still feel so attracted to another. It had to be more than just my body needing physical release. I'd always prided myself on being much more complicated than that.

"Can you feel even a smidgen of what I'm feeling right now?" He murmured.

"I don't know what you feel," I answered. "I'm still trying to figure out what I feel."

"I feel like I'm going insane."

"Can I borrow your straight jacket?" I asked, trying pitifully to inject a little humor into the moment.

"You can have anything I've got, girl. I must be crazy to feel like this, knowing that he'll always be standing between us." He looked as if he wanted to say more, but suddenly shook his head. "I changed my mind. I don't even want to have this conversation with you."

"Jeremy, I love him."

"I know. Let's just leave it at that."

And I should have. I should have left it there, ended the conversation and gone back inside, alone, but I couldn't. Something inside of me just couldn't leave it alone.

"How do you feel about me, Jeremy?" I asked him.

"Don't do this to me." His voice was steady. His gaze was level, but something in his eyes begged me to shut-up. I didn't.

"Don't do this to you? Shit, Jeremy, look at what you did to me! You kissed me! How could you do that? Now, I'm so twisted I don't know what I'm doing anymore! I think I deserve to know why you would just totally…why you would just…ohhhhh!" I couldn't even find the right words anymore, "You've totally fucked me up!"

"I love you." He just blurted it out and when I say he blurted it out I mean that I could almost see the word just spring forth from his lips like a damn skit on *Sesame Street*. L-O-V-E. It just hung in the air between us and once it was out, there was absolutely no way we could avoid it.

"You love me," I said quietly. "Wow!"

"Wow? That's all you have to say?"

"What the hell do you want me to say, Jeremy? I mean really, why love me now? Why couldn't you love me when I needed you to love me?"

"I was a different man then."

"Well, I'm a different woman now!"

His words had me on the defensive, fighting to regain control of my emotions. I was so upset that I didn't know what to do. I was angry with Jeremy for loving me, and angry with myself for pushing him into revealing that love. I was angry with myself for even allowing myself to get to know Jeremy again. I was angry with Khalil, for being absent when I needed him the most. I was angry with him, for allowing another man to tell me the things that I so desperately needed to hear from him.

I was sick of being lonely, longing for his kiss, his smile, his touch, his voice in my ear, his presence. I was sick of sleeping alone every night and waking up alone every morning. I was sick of being depressed and crying myself to sleep every night. But most of all, I was sick of feeling guilty every single time I felt like laughing or smiling, or sometimes giving up. I still loved Khalil, would always love him, even if he never woke up. I felt as if my love for him would forever consume me, forever haunt me, and hinder me from having even the smallest hint of a normal life. My love for Khalil wouldn't allow me to admit love for another.

"I'm going inside," I told Jeremy.

"Go." He was hurt. I could hear it in his voice, and it hurt me that I couldn't be what he needed me to be. Not now, when I was so confused. I walked past him up the stairs, but he made no move to leave. He just stood, as if his life was coming to a tragic end.

I put my hand on the doorknob, but couldn't turn it. My hands trembled. My feet felt like they weighed a ton; and I stood, staring down at them, trying to ignore the fact that Jeremy hadn't moved.

"Are you just going to stand there?" I asked brokenly.

"I let you walk away from me, once. It was the worst mistake of my life." He stared up at me. "I don't know what to do Sera. Tell me what to do." Once again I turned away, but this time I could hear him climbing the stairs towards me. I froze. "Tell me what to do because I don't want to lose you. I'll take you any way I can get you, Sera. You want to be friends? Let's be friends. You want more? Let's be more. I need to know what you're feeling right now. I need to know if you feel the same thing I'm feeling." I closed my eyes, as he stood behind me. He was close enough to touch me, but the only thing I felt was his warm breath on the nape of my neck.

"I can't." I opened the door and turned to face him, so that he couldn't follow me in. I started to close the door in his face, but the look in his eyes stopped me from closing it all the way. I couldn't close the door on those eyes of his. "Don't look at me like that," I pleaded.

"Don't shut me out."

"I'm not good for you." I tried to stabilize my voice.

"How could you possibly determine what's good for me?"

I frowned at him, but my mind was leaning towards one more kiss. I should have closed that door. He should have walked away. Special showers and self-serving bubble baths had ceased working a long time ago. Only the good Lord knew what would happen, if I allowed Jeremy to come inside, let alone touch me. The kiss we'd shared on the stairs, the one that *he'd* been the one to break, still had me feeling as if I'd just drank a fifth of tequila. Damn, what could one more kiss hurt? I could do it. I could kiss him one good time, rid myself of this nagging need, and then leave him alone forever. Couldn't I?

"What's going through your head right now?" he asked.

"Kissing you."

"Kissing me goodbye forever?"

"You don't have to say it like that," I told him. The words sounded harsher, when they were spoken aloud. I was shaking. I didn't really want to say goodbye. I felt something for Jeremy that went well beyond my physical needs. I felt a love that I couldn't bring myself to speak because doing so would dishonor Khalil. The house phone rang, and I knew it must be Ayzha, wondering where I was. When I failed to answer, my cell phone rang in my purse.

"Are you going to get that?" Jeremy asked.

"Did you mean it?" I whispered, ignoring the phone and continuing to focus on Jeremy. My hand slid from the door, the only barrier between us, and I reached through the gap to touch his hand. I wanted to hear him say it again. I wanted to hear him say that he loved me. I blocked the memories of the last time those words had been spoken to me. I didn't want to deal with the past, and I definitely didn't want to deal with the future. I just wanted to deal with the present and that was standing right in front of me. My hand was shaking, and not even his strong grasp could calm my tremors. I let go of his hand and took a step backwards, but he made no move to walk toward me. So, I opened the door a little wider.

"What are you doing?" He asked.

"I don't know." I reached for him again, grabbing him by his shirt, pulling him inside, and closing the door behind him. "Did you mean what you said, Jeremy?" I stared at his chest. One of the buttons on his shirt seemed loose and I figured I'd done it with the intensity of my grasp because all of the cloth around the button was wrinkled in the shape of a gathered circle. Jeremy placed his hand underneath my chin, coaxing me to look at his face.

"I love you, Sera," he said intently. "I've never felt like this before. You know that I've never said those words to any woman besides my mother."

He was right. He'd never told me that he loved me, the whole time we were together. The first time I'd spoken the words to him, he'd smiled and hugged me, but hadn't returned the sentiment. After several occasions of my words not being reciprocated, I'd stopped voicing my emotions.

"I feel like a fool," he told me. "I love you, and want to be with you; but I know that Khalil will always stand between us."

"Don't." I placed my fingers to his lips, silencing him. "Don't say his name."

"Sera--"

"Shhhh..." I whispered slowly, sliding my hands over his chest. "Shhhh..."

It took an instant to close the distance between us; but it felt like an eternity, before his lips locked with mine in a desperate battle of emotions. His hands pulled me closer and whispered a gentle greeting to the waist they encircled. His tongue asked mine to dance, and mine responded with a waltz. One two three, one two three, dance with me, dance with me. Walk with me. Walk with me into my bedroom, and do whatever you want to do to me because I've been craving this kind of intimacy for longer than any woman should.

The telephone rang again, but I was too busy pulling Jeremy's shirt open, scattering buttons all over my bedroom floor, tugging his t-shirt out of his pants, pushing and pulling at him until we clumsily fell onto my bed. His hand slid up my leg, and the moment his fingers made contact with my skin I melted into a puddle of desire.

"Sera."

He whispered my name over and over, as he caressed places that screamed to be touched and stroked and kissed and... ohhhh I could feel his love pressing into my core and I just wanted to feel him inside of me. I slid my hands between us and unbuckled his belt, sliding it out of the loops before locating the buttons on his jeans and pushing them down around his hips. I found my treasure quickly, encircling it in my hands, marveling at the length, the width, the smoothness of the thing I'd had so many times, so long ago.

He inhaled sharply and grabbed my hands, holding them tightly as his kisses traveled further down my body, licking me like a lollypop, until my candy center exploded. He kissed me deeply, muffling my passionate cries, and gently wiping the tears from my eyes. Then he stopped. He buried his face in my neck, and paused. I could feel him trembling, holding his breath as if he were trying to regain control of his body. I held him tighter, sliding my legs around his waist, trying to draw him into me; but he held himself back, not moving until I could do nothing but relax my grip.

"Jeremy?"

"Shhhhh…" Now it was his turn to silence me. He placed a small kiss on the side of my neck, before groaning in obvious frustration. After a moment, he pulled away and looked deep into my eyes. "I can't do this to you."

"What? What are you talking about? Yes you can!" I whispered breathlessly.

"Baby, I love you."

"Then show me!"

"I *am* showing you," he whispered, his voice strained from the hardness I could still feel pressed against my thigh. He rolled off of me and lay on his back, staring up at the ceiling.

I stared at his profile in the dim light. I was trapped somewhere between passion and confusion, and I couldn't begin to know what was going through his head, but my body felt so uncomfortably empty, and my heart suddenly felt as if it were loaded down with bricks.

I needed him. I needed to feel as light, and as wanted, and as free as I felt when he was touching me, when he was kissing me, when he was licking me. I snuggled into him, nibbling at his earlobe, sliding my hands down his torso, holding him in my hand, caressing the solid proof of his desire for me. He couldn't just stop. I wasn't going to let him.

"Sera, don't." His whisper was strained. His hands moved to stop me, but I quickly straddled him, staring down at him, forcing him to look at what he'd done to me.

"I don't want you to stop." I leaned down, and the hair that had managed to escape my tight ponytail brushed his cheek I kissed him, sliding my tongue alongside his. It was the way he loved to be kissed. I remembered it the moment his lips touched mine again. No longer resistant, he slid his arms around my back, holding me tightly, and grinding his body beneath mine. He sat up, and without breaking contact with my lips, flipped me over onto my back. My legs rose, coaxing him closer. I wanted him buried so deep inside of me that if I took a deep enough breath, he'd be able to tap my brain and beat all of my past sorrows from my mind. I was lost in his eyes boring into mine, in his hands on my body, in his lips, in his tongue, in his breath, warm against my neck as he murmured things I couldn't hear.

"I need you inside of me," I whispered into his ear. I closed my eyes and allowed the feeling to envelope my entire body. "Now."

He cupped my face in his hands. I could feel him staring down at me, so I opened my eyes and stared deep into his.

"I love you," I said softly. A tear fell from the corner of my eye and slid over into my ear.

"Oh my God," I heard him mumble. Over and over again, he said it, "Oh my God." This time, when he rolled away from me, he sat up, swung his legs over the side of the bed, and sat with his face buried in his hands. He rocked back and forth; and I knew, in that moment, that this just wasn't going to happen. He was trying to calm himself down.

"Jeremy, why?" I scrambled up, slipped my arms around his waist, and tried to pull him back in with me. I didn't want to be in that place alone. In that deep, dark abyss of longing, I wanted him to dive in with me because I was drowning in my need for him.

"Serafina, stop!" He stood quickly, sending me tumbling back into the bed. I watched as he snatched up his boxers, and picked up his pants from the floor beside the bed. He'd called me by my full name, something he never used to do unless he was angry or frustrated with me.

"What's wrong with you!" I yelled. I stood on my knees in the bed, with the sheets gathered around my body. "Why are you doing this to me?"

"Why are you?" He asked. "Serafina, I love you. I never thought I could love you enough to leave you alone, but I do. We can't go on like this. You don't love me."

"I do!"

"You don't love me the way that you love him," Jeremy sighed. "I know that's where you really want to be. I could make love to you tonight, pour all of my love into you, and in the morning when you wake up, you'll still love him. You'll hate yourself for what we did, and you'll hate me for doing it to you."

"I already hate you." I meant it. I hated him for awakening the feelings I thought I'd lost forever. I hated him for finally being the levelheaded, reasonable one. I hated him for claiming to love me, then leaving when I needed him the most. "I hate you." I said it again, directing my anger toward him, when deep down I hated myself just as intently.

"Sera…" He stood there, staring at me with a hurt expression. "Baby, I can't go on like this. I can't be around you. There's too much tension, and I don't know if I can stop myself again. I don't know how I stopped myself this time."

"I didn't want you to stop!"

"And I don't want you sleeping in my arms and dreaming about Khalil!" He may as well have slapped my face. The truth in his words hit me so hard that tears sprang to my eyes and spilled over before I could even attempt stop them.

"I want to be what you need, Sera, but not for the wrong reasons. I won't let myself take advantage of you, and I'm not going to let you take advantage of me."

"Get out." I was shaking.

"Sera--"

"Get out!" I yelled. I grabbed the closest thing to me and threw it at him, missing him and sending it crashing into the wall, glass shattering into dozens of pieces.

Without a word, Jeremy turned and slowly walked out of my room, leaving me crying in the middle of my bed.

It wasn't until I woke up the next morning hugging my pillow amidst crumpled sheets, that I saw my favorite picture of Khalil lying in the doorway...the crystal frame, shattered beyond repair, and his photograph covered in scratches.

## Chapter 44

### <u>Ayzha Nicole Darwin</u>

Max walked into my office and sat down on the edge of my desk. Chyna slept soundly in the cradle Max had set up in my office when I came back to work. I could tell, by the look on his face, that he was in one of his joking moods.

"How are you?" He asked.

"I'm fine."

"I asked how you were doing, not how you look." He smiled at me, and I smiled back.

"You need to give that line back to the old man who let you borrow it," I laughed.

He laughed quietly to himself. "Yeah, well you do look good. I like your hair like that, pulled back from your face."

"Max, what do you want? I'm trying to reconcile the books." He was starting to irritate me with all of this flirting because I couldn't tell if he was being serious, or if he was just joking around. To misinterpret could be a grave mistake.

"Dinner. Let's go get something to eat."

"Max, I need to get home. Chyna has been kind of fussy, and I have a few more things to calculate." I stood, pushed my chair back, and gathered up my books. "As a matter of fact, I'm going to finish this at home."

"That doesn't have to be done tonight."

He took the books out of my hand and placed them back on my desk.

"Max, why are you here? I thought you were going out," I sighed.

"I am. With you."

"Chyna doesn't need to be out with a bunch of strange people and their germs."

"I know. Sera said she'd keep her." Max smiled at me again, and I could swear I saw a twinkle in his eyes.

"You spoke to Sera?"

"Yeah, this morning. You know she's not seeing Jeremy anymore, so she needs a diversion." He poked around in my candy jar until he found a chocolate kiss and slowly unwrapped the foil. I watched, as he licked the candy before popping it into his mouth.

I made a face at him and rolled my eyes, "Are you happy, now?"

"No, I'm not happy. She's miserable. I wanted to kick Jeremy's ass, until Sera told me the story. That girl told me stuff I never want to know again; but I do have a lot more respect for the cat now. Anyway, my sister really needs to have a little fun, and Chyna can make anyone smile."

"Chyna is cranky; and a cranky baby can't make anyone but her mama smile, okay?"

"What about *my* mama?"

"What?"

"My mama could watch her. You know how much she loves Chyna."

"Max--"

"Has he called?"

"Who?"

"Taiwan." Max just loved mispronouncing Tyree's name. It used to aggravate me, but now it just made me laugh.

"No, Tyree hasn't called."

"Then who is on your mind? Cuz you act like you're thinking about somebody."

I stared at him. I wasn't acting any differently than normal; and I sure as hell wasn't walking around humming to myself and singing off key like Max was lately. If anyone was acting strangely it was *him*. Chyna stirred in her cradle, and I glanced over at her, praying that she would stay asleep for a little longer.

"Do you think you really loved him?" Max asked abruptly.

It was a question that deserved more than a little thought. Had I loved Tyree? I had, but when I look back on it, I see that it was more like desperation that led me to him. I was addicted to the way he made me feel. The sex had been incredible; but emotionally, he hadn't been there for me in the way that I needed him to be. I'd been too blind to see it then. Hindsight was 20/20, but had I seen him for who he really was in the beginning, I wouldn't have Chyna.

"He's not worth the breath you wasted asking me that question." I told Max.

"He hurt you. Probably ruined you for any other man huh? Between him and Riley, a brotha will never have a chance."

"A brotha... or you?"

"Anybody." He winked at me.

I wanted to slap him. I couldn't stand the games men thought they needed to play, in order to get a woman's attention. If Max wanted to see me outside of work, aside from the time he spent with his goddaughter, all he had to do was say the word. I liked being around him, and loved how much he loved my child. I loved him for loving my child. I loved him for being there for me. I'd always held a certain attraction for Max, but being Sera's brother made it awkward.

"Max, I'll talk to you tomorrow." I put the books in my backpack, and started packing up Chyna's diaper bag.

"Don't worry about the books tonight," Max told me. "Get some sleep. We can do the books together tomorrow."

"Yeah," I said absently.

"Hey." He grabbed me by the shoulders and made me look at him, "I know it's hard, being alone, taking care of Chyna by yourself, coming to work everyday and dealing with me."

"Max, I'm not exactly alone. I mean, you help out a lot and your parents are always checking in on me…and Sera, bless her heart, she tries."

"Where is Stacie?"

"That heffa?" I started laughing. "Chyna spit up on her, the last time I saw her. Plus, she's busy planning her wedding and picking out terrible dresses for Sera and I to wear. At least, at Sera's wedding, we had dresses that we could wear again."

"Yeah," Max mused, "as I recall, you looked amazing."

"Oh yeah? And what do you recall?" I watched as he picked Chyna up, and carefully dressed her in her little snowsuit.

"Well," he held her close to him, kissing her forehead and smiling down at her before continuing. "I recall that you had an orchid in your hair."

"What color was it?"

"Orange," he reminisced, "and your hair was piled on top of your head in like a million curls. I remember thinking that Riley must be crazy as hell to treat you the way that he did. I also remember thinking about how much I hated Tyree and the bull he was feeding you." I smiled, remembering how many times Max had warned me to stay away from Tyree, and how I thought he was just trying to act like a big brother.

"You're smiling." He handed me the baby, and then grabbed my bags. "I'm going to go warm up your car, give me about ten minutes, ok?"

I nodded and watched as he walked out of the room. It was strange how he remembered the orchid in my hair as if it were yesterday…as if he'd been watching and waiting for his chance. It was a chance I'd have gladly given him then, before Riley, before Tyree; but now, I felt tainted. There was no way he could possibly want me, not really. He was just being nice.

"Did Sera really volunteer to watch the baby?" I asked, as I met him at my car, ten minutes later.

"Yeah, Mama is using Daddy's fishing trip as an excuse to spend the night with Sera. So, if you want to take her up on the offer, she won't be alone with the baby."

"It's not that I don't trust Sera, Max."

"I know, but you worry about leaving her with someone who knows nothing about babies. I understand, Ayzha." I put Chyna in her car seat, and closed the door, blocking her from the chill.

"So where did you want to go?" I asked him.

"We can go wherever you want." He leaned up against his car, which was parked next to mine, and smiled over at me.

"I really need to finish these figures," I stalled.

"I'll tell you what. We'll order a pizza, go to my house, and go over the numbers together. You can sleep in the guest room."

"What about..." I searched for a name of any woman who could object to me spending the night alone at Max's house, but I couldn't remember him seeing anyone on a regular basis in a long time.

"She'll be ok," he assured me.

"Who?"

"Chyna. Mama had two kids with colic. She knows what she's doing."

"Oh...yeah," I stammered, glad he couldn't tell that, for once, my nervousness had nothing to do with my baby.

"I put extra diapers and some clothes in your car," he told me. "I washed and just kept them, the last time she stayed with me." His thoughtfulness touched my heart.

"Pepperoni." I told him.

"Huh?"

"Pizza. I want pepperoni." I opened my door and slid into my car. "I'll meet you at your house."

## Chapter 45

### Ayzha Nicole Darwin

*Mind Blowing*
*Boy you not knowing*
*The effects you have on my psych.*

*You give me blissful hangovers*
*My cup runneth over*
*With this carnal whisky*
*You're pouring into me.*

*I could smoke an ounce*
*And still not feel*
*As high as I do*
*Right now*
*At this moment*
*In this room*
*On this bed*
*Trembling*
*Weak from the aftershocks*
*Of this intellect altering*
*Hallucinogenic drug you call*
*Love.*
*I'll be having flashbacks for the rest of my days*
*I'll be having flashbacks for the rest of my days*
*I'll be having flashbacks*
*For*
*The*
*Rest*
*Of*
*My*
*Days*
*You don't hear me...*

His lips are so soft. Oh God, kissing him is like floating on a cloud during a warm spring breeze. I feel light as a feather in his arms; and I don't even want to close my eyes, as our tongues play hide and seek. I want to watch him as he kisses me. Any reservations I had about getting something started with him disappeared, the moment his lips were on my lips on his lips all over me, ooohhh weeee! Either it's been a long time, or this man is a tenured professor in this craft. Every time he touches me, I learn something new about my body. I'm about to graduate 'suma cum loudly', and I'm so glad that Sera has Chyna because it would be a crime to have to leave this bed, if I woke her up. I can barely speak, as another wave clutches my body. I'm trembling so much that I can hardly stand to be touched.

"Oooh…Max, we shouldn't be doing this."

"Want me to stop?" He asked, dragging his tongue from the valley between my breasts to navel.

"Kiss me," I answered breathlessly.

"Where?"

"Everywhere." I gently nudged his face down, until he was kissing me right where I needed it the most. I don't even know how we ended up in his bed. One minute, we were going over the books and eating pizza. The next thing I knew, we were naked. Who cares? I need this man inside of me, and I need him now. He knows this and accommodates me so powerfully that I unconsciously dig my nails into his back, in an attempt to hold on. I don't want to be loved gently. I want him to pound me through the mattress.

I'll be damned if he didn't try. Afterwards, Max slid his arms around me, and I rested my weary head on his sweaty chest. His heart beat loudly in my ears, and I snuggled closer to him, unsure of how to feel after what my body had just gone through. Legs intertwined, we lay together in silence. I didn't want to interrupt the moment with unnecessary conversation. I closed my eyes and planted a small kiss on his chest. One of his hands smoothed the hair at my temples, and I closed my eyes, willing to lose myself in the memory of what had just transpired between two friends.

"We did a bad, bad thing," I whispered.

"But it felt so damn good." He slid a hand up and down my bare back, and I trembled. "Are you cold?" He pulled the blankets over us and rolled over so that we were facing one another. Noses barely touching, we stared at each other, looking for the one thing that made this present vision different from the past.

"What are we gonna do about this?" I asked him.

"We're going to let destiny take over." Max slid his hand in mine and laced our fingers together. "I could do this forever." He kissed my fingertips one by one.

"Do you really think so?"

"I know." He stared as if he were trying to memorize my every feature. "If I tell you something, do you promise not to laugh?"

"I'll try," I giggled.

"I feel something."

"What do you feel?" I asked him.

"I feel you." He placed my hand on his heart, and held it there for a brief moment. "I feel you right here." Time froze, and suddenly the room felt very cold. Deep down, I knew Max wouldn't joke about something so serious, but I also knew his past. I'd seen the consequences of loving Max Jordan. Hadn't he always tried to shield Sera and me from men like himself? I trusted Max. There was no denying that. But did I trust him enough to allow this moment to lay the foundation for the rest of our relationship? He could be honest with me, as long as I was just an employee, his little sister's best friend, but now that we'd slipped and fallen into the bed together...

"Do you feel anything for me Ayzha?" He let go of my hand, and I reluctantly dragged it away from his heart.

"You're so beautiful," I breathed slowly. I smoothed his thick, black eyebrows with my fingertip, and studied his familiar face as if his features were new to me. His hazel eyes never blinked, as I traced the outline of his face like a blind woman trying to see. "Kiss me, Max."

"Where?"

I closed the small gap separating our faces and kissed him gently on the lips. "I can't do this with you," I said softly.

"I need a reason."

"Look at my life, Max. I'm divorced. I have a baby with a man who wants nothing to do with us, and now I'm in the bed with you. This all happened in the span of a year, what kind of woman does that make me?"

"Do you believe that everything happens for a reason?" I nodded. "You married Riley and couldn't have a baby. Why?"

"I guess he wasn't the one."

"You got with Tyree, and he wants nothing to do with his child," he continued, "but he gave you Chyna. So perhaps, in some crazy way, he served his purpose."

"And you?"

"I'm the man you need, for all the right reasons. Riley married you because you were pregnant. You hooked up with Tyree, out of desperation."

"And maybe we're here because I needed some sex. It *has* been a while."

"You felt me deep, Ayzha. You felt it in your mind, baby. When I kissed your eyes I tasted your tears. Horniness doesn't cause that. Love causes that."

"You and I?"

"Can you think of a better combination?" He smiled at me, and then lowered his voice, "Let me have you, Ayzha." He kissed me slowly. "Please, can I have you?" There was something in the way he said it,

'Please, can I have you?' over and over again until my mind was so full of his question that I could think of nothing else.

"How do you want me?" I made him stop kissing me and look me in the eye.

"In every way," Max answered steadily. "I want you and everything that comes with you."

"Chyna?"

"As far as I'm concerned, she's mine."

"Yes."

"Let that bastard sign his rights away. I'll adopt her."

"You can't do that."

"I can, if you marry me." He said it as if it were the simplest thing in the world. "Let's get married, Ayzha."

"You're serious?"

"I've never been so serious in my life."

"I should think about this."

"You should go with your gut." He directed, "I'll say it again and you say the first thing that pops into your head."

"Okay." I sat up and pulled the sheets up around me.

"Are you ready?" Max asked. He sat up as well, scooting away so there was at least an arm's length between us. He took my hand in his, and gazed deeply into my eyes. "Ayzha, will you marry me?"

"When?"

"We'll go get Chyna and fly to Vegas tonight."

"You're crazy." I shook my head, and stared at him in disbelief. "Just like that?"

"Just like that." He moved closer, kissing my bare shoulder. "I love you."

"You really do," I whispered.

"Come on girl, what's the first thing that comes to mind?"

"I love you too." I started to laugh.

"Okay, that's what I was hoping, but not quite the answer I was looking for," he chuckled.

"Ask me again."

"You're driving me crazy!" He flipped me over onto my back and pressed his body into mine. Nose to nose, lip to lip, he asked me again, "Are you gonna marry me or what?"

"Yeah."

"Yeah?" He kissed me.

"Yes." I kissed him back.

"Tonight?"

"Tonight."

"What time is it?" I turned my head and glanced at the clock on his bedside table.

"That clock says two-fifteen."

"Okay. We'll get showered and dressed, pack, get Chyna, and then catch the next flight."

"After." I told him.

"After what?" He asked as if he didn't already know.

"Kiss me."

"Where?"

"Everywhere…"

\*\*\*

There's something special about waking up next to Max. Well, not exactly next to Max because Chyna wouldn't stay asleep long enough for us to actually consummate our marriage. We finally gave up, and lay her little spoiled butt between us in the bed, trying to tire her out but only managing to put ourselves asleep. I stretched languidly and admired the simple platinum band adorning the ring finger on my left hand.

"I say I'se married now," I whispered, thinking about a scene from *The Color Purple*. I started giggling and put my hand over my mouth, before I could wake them.

"Crazy girl," Max mumbled. I looked over at him and smiled. I hadn't meant to wake him, but since he was up…

"Put Chyna in her play pen."

"She doesn't like it."

"If you let her sleep with us every time she cries, you'll never see this coochie again," I warned him. "She's already spoiled enough."

He looked from me to the baby, and without another word, carried her across the room, gently putting her in the playpen before sliding back into bed with me.

"Meanie," he whispered.

"You'll thank me later." I told him, and to prove my point, I slid my hand underneath the sheets and grabbed him. "See? You're already thanking me."

"You're bad."

"You like it."

And he does, all night long, until we both fall into a deep sleep that can only be disturbed by the cries of a four-month-old child with the lungs of an opera singer. Max already knows the drill. Since I haven't showered yet, he goes to the mini fridge, grabs a bottle and warms it up. I use this opportunity to jump into the shower. I let the water damn near scald me, as I stand there with my eyes closed, inhaling the remnants of our consummations as they are slowly rinsed from my body.

"Can we come in?" Max calls over the shower door.

"Let me turn the temperature down." I switch the water temp to warm, and watch as Max climbs in with Chyna in his arms. She never reaches for me, when she's with him. It used to annoy the hell out of me, but now I'm realizing she's just a daddy's girl. I wouldn't have it any other way. "Come on spoiled butt, Daddy needs to get clean too." I took her from his arms, and she acted like she was going to cry until she felt the warm water hit her little back.

"I like the way that sounds," Max said softly. And I'll be doggone, this big dude is soaping up in the shower with a big ol' tear sliding down his cheek. "You called me 'Daddy'."

"Ohhh, baby." I hugged him tightly, with Chyna between us trying to wipe the soap from his chin. "You're the only Daddy she's ever known."

"Are you happy, Ayzha?"

"Look at this. I have everything I need right here in my arms. I have you. I have Chyna. This has to be the greatest thing in the world."

And it was. We were...and I prayed that we always would be.

\*\*\*

Running away and marrying Max was the easiest thing I've ever done in my life. Telling our friends? Well, that was a bit tricky. While I wanted Serafina to be happy for me, I didn't want her to get too depressed thinking about her own wedding day. I knew that Stacie would always agree with whatever I did in the name of love, but Aleesha would probably think I'd lost my damn mind.

As we step off the plane and take the shuttle to our car, I suddenly realize that we also have to tell Max's parents that, not only am I their new daughter-in-law, but that they are now instant grandparents.

"We should tell Serafina first," Max said, as we climbed into the car. "May as well get that over with."

"Yeah," I agreed. "Do you think she'll be okay?"

"She'll be happy for us. She's been throwing little hints about us getting together."

"Yeah, but will she be okay?"

"We have to stop worrying so much about how Sera will take things. She's my sister. I'd never hurt her, but she's a grown woman. She'll be ok. I promise."

I decided to trust Max, and closed my eyes for a little catnap before we got to Sera's place. It didn't look like she had company; but we had to ring the bell three times, before she answered looking as if she'd slept in her clothes.

"Well, look who's here." She eyed us both suspiciously, before taking the baby from me. "Come on Chyna. Come with me while I freshen up." She disappeared into her bedroom, and Max and I both exchanged "what the hell?" faces. She came back a little while later wearing a blue jogging suit and smelling like lotion and toothpaste. She sat on one end of the couch with Chyna on her lap, and then motioned for Max and me to sit as well. We sat next to each other, barely touching, wondering just what the hell was going on in Sera's mind.

"Soooo...." She stared at us, as if she wanted to ask a serious question.

"Soooo...." Max repeated slowly.

"Soooooooo..." Chyna cooed.

"Hmmmm, Chyna. If I didn't know any better, I'd say that Max and Mommy were F-U-C-K-I-N-G." Sera spelled it out in order to prevent any damage to my daughter's delicate ears.

I half expected Max to chastise her, but instead he just started laughing. Pretty soon, we were all laughing; but Sera stopped abruptly, as if to let us know that we still hadn't answered the question.

"So...where did you go? Mama and I were sleeping good until the two of you came over here snatching this baby up. Then, you both just up and disappear for two days? What's really going on?" She asked and then lowered her voice, "Are you two doing that nasty stuff?"

"We're married," Max said simply.

Sera covered Chyna's little ears with her hands. "Shut the hell up! Say you promise!"

"I promise." Max held up my left hand, to show Sera the ring.

"Daaaamn!" She stared at me with a look that could be mistaken for awe. "Was it THAT good? Wait!" She held up her hand. "Don't tell me. That's kind of gross."

I had to laugh at that, "Guess what else."

"There's more? What could be better than my two favorite people getting married?"

"Max is adopting Chyna. It should go smoothly, unless Tyree decides to fight it."

"What if he does?" Sera asked me.

"Sera cover Chyna's ears," Max told her. Sera obliged, and by the time Max stopped talking, even I'd learned some new cuss words. "So what's up with you?" Max asked his sister. "What was up with that "slept in" look you answered the door with?"

"Long boring story," she told us. "I had a long night, that's all."

"Have you seen Jeremy?" Max asked.

"Nope," she said simply.

"Have you called him?"

"Nope," she answered again.

"Has he called you?"

"No, No, and NO."

I noticed an empty bottle of wine on the kitchen table. It looked like one of the special bottles Khalil had ordered for the wedding reception. She noticed me looking.

"Max, you guys should go see Mama. This will thrill her. The other night, she was pretending that Chyna was her granddaughter." Sera laughed, but I could see the stress in her eyes.

"Do we need to talk?" I asked her, as Max took Chyna to the kitchen in search of cookies.

"Nope," she lied.

"You don't want to talk about it?"

"Nope."

"Will you tell me about it later?"

"It's nothing, really." She leaned in and whispered, "So you got a piece of my brother, and couldn't let go huh?"

I let her change the subject, happy to give her something else to think about, and prayed that my joy would break through her pain, and let a little sun shine in her life.

## Chapter 46

### <u>Serafina Danielle Jordan</u>

The love we had, or the love we had the potential to have, lingers on my mind like dew on a rose. It just sits there, magnifying the place where it has chosen to rest and making that part of the rose the most beautiful sight in the world. It always evaporates, as I go about my day, but each morning, when I wake up, there is a new drop of dew on the rose I call my mind and the cycle continues.

It's early. I should be asleep but sleep has proved to be my enemy. Dreams have proved to be my enemy. I have proved myself to be my own enemy. He's all up in my head. Smiling that smile, laughing that laugh, whispering 'I love you' so distinctively that I sometimes fool myself into thinking he's actually standing next to me, telling me everything I want to hear. He has a face now. It's a face that used to belong to the only man in my heart. Now that face belongs to Jeremy and the shame associated with that face and with those dreams, those thoughts, makes me physically ill.

I feel terrible. For so long I've belonged to Khalil...mind, body, and soul...but even now, as I sit next to Khalil's bed, holding Khalil's hand in mine, it's Jeremy Sanders who occupies my thoughts. I am slowly falling into a pit of despair. Although my heart wants Khalil, my body craves the touch of another man. My ears crave the words that make me smile. My eyes crave the sight of the man I love walking towards me. I crave a sure thing, a man who is guaranteed to be able to make me feel like a woman. Khalil can't do that, lying in this bed, eating through these tubes, and pissing through this catheter. As bad as it may sound, I am starting to resent the hell out of him.

It's not fair. It's not fair to him and it's not fair to me. How long am I supposed to wait? How much love could anyone expect me to have for a man who can't do anything but cause sadness in my heart? I feel so guilty for feeling this way...for wanting the comfort of a human touch other than my own. This guilt sometimes keeps me away from Khalil. I can't bear to be in the same room with him, while thoughts of another man wreak havoc on my brain. This guilt has put a big dent in my visits.

I used to visit Khalil every single day, sometimes twice. Now, he's lucky if I see him twice a week. I've run out of excuses. Khalil's grandmother has been expecting my visits to become sporadic. I see it in her eyes, when she greets me at the door. It's as if she wants to say, "Stop frontin', Serafina. You don't want to be here; and I don't want you here if you can't be honest about your feelings."

The truth is, I don't even know what I'm feeling. Jeremy has been true to his word. He's stopped calling. He's stopped coming by. I haven't seen him in over a month; and my pride won't allow me to call his number. I couldn't see it then, but I see it now. I see everything he'd been trying to tell me that night. He'd stopped himself from taking everything I was throwing at him. He loved me. He'd tried to protect me, and I'd reacted horribly, yelling at him, and throwing things.

The dreams have become worse. I wake up, in the middle of the night, with an ache in the very core of my being. It's more significant than sex. I love him...not with the same intensity that I love Khalil, but I do care about him...a lot. There is only one thing in this world that could make this situation easier, but to speak it aloud would be the most horrible offense someone who claimed to love could ever utter.

I let go of Khalil's hand, and stared at his face. My tears refused to fall, but burned my eyes with an intensity that made my head pound relentlessly. For the first time ever, I left Khalil's room without bothering to say goodbye.

***

I arrived at work bright and early, hoping to be the first to arrive, giving myself a chance to prepare for the long day ahead of me. My hopes were dashed, when I saw Shayla Jones, one of the writers walking out of the break room with a pink mug in her hand.

"Hey Sera." She walked towards me with a cheerful smile on her face. "Looks like I'm not the only one who decided to come in early."

"I was hoping to--"

"Beat the nosey heffas we work with?" She interrupted, "Me too." I chuckled. I knew that there were many people in our office who hated the fact that she'd gone from being the publisher's assistant to a contributing writer with her own column, but there was no denying the woman's talent.

"They just wish they had an NBA star visiting them," I said, referring to her friendship with Keith Robinson, a former LA Laker. An interview she'd done with him had gained her a promotion.

"Yeah, well." Her smile faded for a moment, and then returned with a vengeance. "How are you, Sera?"

"I'm okay."

"How is Khalil?"

"The same." I was touched that she would take the time to ask. I was just the receptionist, but Shayla had always treated me as an equal. She never gave me orders, but asked me to do things as if I were just doing her a small favor. "I should go and start the coffee."

"I already did," she said kindly. "Come on. We have at least an hour, before everyone starts dragging in. Do you mind if I bounce a few ideas off of you?"

She didn't wait for an answer. Instead, she grabbed my hand and pulled me toward an empty conference room. There were folders laid across the far end of the table; and three places were set, each with a pink mug and enough donuts and muffins to ruin anyone's diet.

"What's this?"

"A meeting," she told me. "Have a seat. I didn't know if you liked coffee or tea, so I made both."

I didn't sit. "What is this?" I asked nervously, "Some newer, friendlier way of downsizing?"

She looked at me and laughed so hard, I thought she'd explode. "Girl, please." She motioned for me to sit. "Coffee or tea?"

"Tea," I said softly, trying to figure out just what in the hell Shayla was so giddy about. I sat in the chair she offered, and started spreading butter on the blueberry muffin before me.

"Don't worry," she assured me. "Everything is fine. You've been through a lot, and you're still here everyday on time and ready to work. I admire your strength." She sat in the chair across from mine, and dunked a donut in her cup of coffee. "I think they put crack in these Krispy Kremes." She took a bite and closed her eyes, as if she was getting her morning fix.

"Maybe we could do an exposé," I joked, "because I've been known to eat a dozen, all by myself."

"Oh good, you're both here."

Shayla and I both looked up, as Jennifer Collins walked into the office wearing a red suit that oozed power. She was supermodel beautiful, with business savvy that you either admired or feared. Khalil once told me that his father had a crush on Jennifer, but was too stubborn to admit it. He'd rather hold on to the memory of his deceased wife, his safe place, rather than venture out into the unknown with a new woman.

"Hello, Miss Sera." She placed her hand on my shoulder, as she walked past me and took a seat at the head of the table. "Shayla, I see you made sure to buy these damn Krispy Kremes, when you know that I'm supposed to be on a diet."

"One won't kill you, Jennifer." Shayla rolled her eyes. "If it makes you feel better, there are some oat bran muffins on that tray, as well."

"No, it doesn't make me feel better," she said, snatching up a donut, and taking a huge bite.

I watched the camaraderie between the two of them, as I ate my muffin and took tiny sips of my tea, the whole time wondering just what in the hell I was doing there. As if she could read my mind, Shayla slid a folder towards me. My heart stopped. It was a folder I'd misplaced days ago. It contained extremely private stories and poetry I'd written, in the time since Khalil's accident. It was something no one else was supposed to ever see. I could tell, by the looks on their faces, that they'd read them.

"Don't be upset," Jennifer said gently. "You accidentally gave this to Shayla with a group of reports. Once I'd read one, I couldn't stop."

"I don't know what to say." My muffin felt like wood chips sliding down my throat. No matter how much tea I drank, I couldn't get it to go down.

"How long have you worked here, Sera?" Shayla asked.

"Four years."

"In your interview, you told us how much you loved to write, and that you hoped to one day become a contributing writer with this magazine. Isn't that why you accepted the receptionist position? To get your foot in the door? What happened?" Khalil's accident happened. When I lost him, I lost the will to move forward. I looked at them both, not knowing what to say or how to say it.

"Have you even looked at the wall of opportunity?" Jennifer asked, referring to a bulletin board in the break room where article ideas and opportunities for advancement were advertised to the staff.

"No," I admitted.

"I was just about to give this assignment to someone else, until I read your poetry."

"What assignment?"

"We need someone to go out into the world of poetry, attend open mics, and write an article on it. We're trying to introduce a new monthly column featuring poets and underground artists. It would be nice, if we could get an actual poet to do it." Jennifer placed her hand over mine, "You would be perfect."

"We're going to test a few issues. If the public responds well, you could very well have your own column in SHANI Magazine. It could lead to other things," Shayla added.

"I don't know," I said. "I don't know if I'm the one you're looking for."

"What the hell do you mean? Let me tell you something, Serafina Jordan. Too many women downplay their talents because they don't want to sound conceited or boastful. God gave you that talent, and he wants you to celebrate it, not hide it. If you can't rejoice in what he gave you, then what can you rejoice in?" Jennifer scolded. "Here. Read this one for me."

She pointed out the last poem I'd written in the folder. I'd written it, during one of many episodes of emotional confusion.  It was something I'd never expected to share with anyone other than God.  I most certainly didn't want to share it with Shayla and Jennifer.  It didn't matter that they had already read it.

"Not this one," I said quietly.

"Fine.  I'll read it."  Jennifer began to recite, and I froze, not quite knowing how to feel, hearing my words coming out of someone else's mouth.

*'I'm drowning in dark pools of chocolate*
*That used to be eyes*
*But are now just the vessels used by you*
*To see through me*
*My heart*
*My soul*
*My emotions are naked behind my mask.*
*There is no more whiskey in the cosmic flask*
*Of my denial.*
*I must go through this trial*
*With no help,*
*With no crutch.*
*I should be alone*
*Yet I am sinking deeper,*
*Arms flailing wildly as I begin to lose myself*
*In the sweet sticky brown that is you*
*My savior*
*My wanna be guardian angel*
*My way out*
*My hindrance.*
*YOU who seem to love me*
*Yet more than content to have me by default.*
*YOU who must surely lead the league in boards*
*For you caught me on the*
*Rebound.*
*I'm astounded*
*Dumbfounded*
*Surrounded in this chocolate pool with no shore in sight*
*I am unable to tread*
*And so I sink deeper.*
*I try to scream*
*But only manage to fill my mouth*
*My lungs*
*My arteries are clogged with your desperate love.*

*Your reassurances course through my veins like the blood of life*
*Creating palpitations*
*Irregularities in a heart that beats for another*
*Yet, clings to you.*
*I'm confused.*
*I could let you go*
*But then I'd be*
*Alone.*
*Which is where I need to be*
*But somehow*
*Your arms have become home.*
*Your kisses, my midnight snack in a cozy kitchen of dreams*
*Where I am still myself but you are HE.*
*He that I want*
*He that I crave*
*He that visits my closed lids as I sleep*
*In your arms.*
*In your bed*
*In my lies.*
*And like an alcoholic I drink of you*
*To ease the pain*
*Of the loss of him."*

After she read the poem, Jennifer just stared at me with her hands folded primly. "Sera, I wonder if you think you're the only woman on this Earth with problems. There are so many people out there who could actually benefit from your experience. You write for yourself, but for every life-altering event in your life, there is a woman out there who needs to know she isn't alone.

Sera you have a gift. If you don't want to do it, I'll understand; but you need to at least think about it. Opportunities of this magnitude are extremely rare. I'm not going to beg you to do this. I have already received ten applications from your co-workers who want to advance their careers or pad their resumes." I heard every word she was saying. I needed to either do something with myself, or be destined to wallow in self-pity for the rest of my life.

"Do you need more time to think about it?" Shayla asked. "Why don't you let me write up a proposition? You can look it over and give me your answer tomorrow, okay?"

"I want to do it," I told her. "I definitely want to do it. I mean, I know that I can do it. I need to do it."

"Good." Jennifer gave my hand a gentle pat and smiled warmly. "Consider it therapy that you're being paid to take."

I smiled.  I couldn't wait to tell Max and Ayzha what had just happened to me.  There were two others I would have loved to tell; but one couldn't hear me, and the other didn't want to.

## Chapter 47

### Jeremy Trent Sanders

She has burgundy tips on her fingernails. It looks like a French manicure gone all the way wrong, and I want to laugh but can't because my mother is giving me 'the look'. I give her 'the look' right back, and then politely excuse myself on the premise that I've left something in my car. I dial Jacob's number, as soon as I get outside.

"Dawg," I say, laughing into the receiver, "This heffa has burgundy tips on her fingernails."

"Her nails are burgundy?" Jacob asks.

"Naw, dawg, the tips! You know how Michelle is always getting that French manicure? The one with the white tips?"

"Man, shut up!!" Jacob yells, finally realizing what I'm trying to explain to him. "Where the hell did your mother find her?"

"She's one of her church members' daughter. I'm assuming that Mama never saw her before today because she knows damn well that ain't my style."

"Yeah, we all know your style, don't we? How long has it been?"

"Fool, I don't want to talk about that," I cut him off, not wanting him to start in on me about Sera again. I know that I did the right thing, where she is concerned. "Look, I gotta go before Mama comes looking for me. Kiss Jerica and Michelle for me." I hang up before he can answer me, walk back into the house, and try once again to sit through this uncomfortable dinner my mother has planned with a woman I don't care to know anything else about.

"So your mother tells me you're a doctor." Burgundy Tips says, as I take my place at the head of the table. She holds her teacup delicately, her burgundy-tipped pinky sticking out from the handle like a tacky reminder of my mother's pitiful matchmaking skills.

"Wow," I think, "her braids are the same color as her tips."

"He's a pediatrician," Sister Jessie Mae, one of mama's church members, answers for me when she sees how preoccupied I am with her daughter's appearance.

I can't believe I'm sitting here in my mama's dining room, eating off of the good dishes, and being sized up by Sister Jessie Mae and her daughter Jaquita. I feel like a field hand being invited into the big house, so Missy's friends can get a good look at me. Don't get me wrong. Jaquita is cute, in an around the way girl sort of way; but I can't help comparing her to Sera. This girl's style is loud, where Sera's simple yet sexy style announces itself quietly, whispers sexiness with every word she speaks and every step she takes.

Mama ain't fooling me. She's playing matchmaker again; and for the seventh time in as many weeks, it isn't working. It's been almost three months, since I've seen or spoken to Sera; but no girl with a ghetto manicure and tri-colored braids is going to erase her from my mind. My cell phone rings. Mama is daring me to answer it. I suddenly have flashbacks of Christmas Eve, Sera's phone call, the panic I felt as I drove to her house.

"Who is it?" Mama asks. I glance down at the display.

"It's the hospital."

"I thought you weren't on call."

"I'm not."

"Well, answer it then," she sighs.

Happy for a possible excuse to leave this uncomfortable situation, I answer; but the moment I realize who is on the other end of the line, I have to stand up and walk to the other side of the room.

"Allison," I say, trying to keep Mama from hearing her name. "What's going on? I'm not on call."

"They just brought Khalil in," she whispers.

"What? What happened?"

"I don't know all of the details yet, but it does not look good. He has some kind of infection. Jeremy, I heard his Grandmother on the phone with Sera. Sera won't come. I took the phone and tried to talk to her, but she just kept saying that it was her fault, and she didn't want to have to see what she'd done to him." Allison was still whispering, and it was hard to hear her. "Jeremy you have to bring her here."

"I can't."

"Why the hell not? I thought you were her friend. I thought that you had her best interests at heart. I guess I was wrong." Allison slammed the phone down so hard I jumped.

"Excuse us." Mama nods towards Jaquita and Sister Jessie Mae, before grabbing my hand and pulling me into the kitchen. She leans against the fridge and stares at me, her eyes full of worry.

"Who was that?" She asks, "Was it Sera?"

"No. It was Allison. She said that they just brought Khalil in, and that Sera won't come to the hospital."

"What does she want you to do?"

"She wants me to go and get Sera, then bring her to the hospital."

"Are you going to?"

"No."

Mama sighed loudly, "Baby, you know that I have always loved

Sera."

"I know."

"You never loved her the way I thought you should have, Jeremy; but now that you do… Baby, I just don't want you to set yourself up for pain."

"I know, Mama," I sigh. "I don't know what to do."

"Call her. Call her and find out what's going on. I have a feeling she's been trying to keep her distance from you, the same way you're trying to keep your distance from her. Maybe, she needs you right now, but doesn't know how to ask for your help. Did you think of that?"

"No," I admit.

"Jeremy, do what you need to do." It's all that she tells me, before leaving me alone in the kitchen. Reluctantly, I dial Sera's number. She answers the phone, and I can tell that she's been crying.

"Jeremy?" Her tone threatens to pull me back into her world.

"Are you okay?" I ask, knowing full well that she isn't. "Allison called me."

"Well, I didn't ask her to."

"I know, baby. Just tell me what's wrong. Why won't you go to the hospital?"

"I can't."

"What do you mean 'you can't'?"

"He's going to die," she whispers. "I don't want to see him die."

"You don't know that," I say cautiously, not really wanting to comment without knowing the full prognosis. "Listen Sera, please go to the hospital? I'll meet you there. I shouldn't have to go over there and drag you to see him. If I were lying there, possibly dying, I would want you there by my side. Khalil needs you with him, no matter what. Now, I want you to get yourself together, right now. Your brother is going to pick you up."

"You've talked to Max?"

"No, but I'm getting ready to call him." I hang up, not really knowing what else to say to her, but knowing that if anyone can get her to the hospital, it's Max…because it shouldn't be me.

***

"It looks bad, Jeremy." Allison's voice is filled with compassion, but she says it so matter-of-factly that I have to remind myself that she's a nurse. She sees people die everyday; and unlike me, Allison has learned to completely disassociate herself from it. Still, I think that Khalil's case has touched her in a way that no other case has. It's been two days since they brought Khalil in. Although I've been at the hospital, I've done my best to avoid Sera because I just don't know what else to do or say.

Dejected, I lean against the counter and focus on the black Stacey Adams Mama loves to see me wearing. They look good with my suit, but somehow seem out of place, in this area of the hospital. I briefly recall strolling up and down these halls in sneakers, looking for a place to sleep or do other things, when I was working the graveyard shift as a resident. I shake my head at the memories.

"Are you ok?" Allison asks softly.

"I'm fine. Have you seen him?"

"I went up to ICU on my break. I told myself I was going to check on him, but actually...I went to check on Sera. She's a mess, but I guess you already know that, huh?"

"I haven't talked to her since I had Max bring her here. Was she mean to you?"

"No," Allison assures me. "I think she's too worried about Khalil to be concerned with me. Plus, that fine ass brother of hers is with her."

"He's married."

"I can still look." Allison sticks out her tongue, something that used to drive me crazy.

"Stop it," I tell her.

I know what she's trying to do, and it isn't working. She's trying to take my mind off of Sera and Khalil. She's trying to make me joke around with her the way I used to, but I can't. I'm too wrapped up in Sera to even joke about the past.

"Jeremy, we're not friends, and we probably never will be, but do you value my advice?"

"Depends on the advice."

"I'm going to say this one time, and then I'll never speak on it again," she says. "Sometimes, we have to do what's in our hearts, in order to set things right."

"I don't understand," I sigh. "I can't begin to know what you're talking about, Allison."

"You will, Jeremy." She rubs my arm reassuringly. "Trust me, when the time comes, you'll know exactly what I'm talking about, and you'll know exactly what to do."

\*\*\*

Allison's words haunt me, as I get on the elevator. How can I do what's in my heart, when I'm not sure what's really there? I only know that, regardless of how long it has been since we last spoke, Sera needs me. The ICU is full of activity. As I approach Khalil's room, I see Max standing with his hands stuffed in his pockets. He smiles half-heartedly when he sees me, and extends his hand.

"Hey man," I say, grasping his hand and giving him a brief hug. "How is she?"

"She blames herself," Max sighs.

"What? How can she blame herself?"

"She thinks she's being punished for something." Max gives me a knowing look, and then shrugs. "I can't talk to her. She doesn't want to listen."

Max and I had long ago agreed to co-exist and not aggravate each other. I give him a brotherly pat on the shoulder, and then go into Khalil's room without fully knowing what to expect. Her back is to me as she stands next to the window, her cheek pressed against the glass, eyes closed, breath fogging up the glass near her lips. She's so still, I wonder if she's even heard me walk into the room. I approach, and she turns to look at me. Her eyes are dull and empty. Her face is ashen. Without speaking, I go to her, pull her into my arms, and rest her head on my chest. I smooth her hair, until she goes limp in my arms. I hold her, and the past three months wash away, as if they never happened.

"I wished him dead," she whispers guiltily.

"Shhh…"

"I did, Jeremy. I dreamt he was dead, and when I woke up I felt so free. When realized it was just a dream…" Her voice trails off. "Jeremy, look at what I've done to him."

I pull away from her, holding her at arms length and forcing her to look at me. "Sera you did *not* do this. You don't have that kind of power. None of us do. Your feelings are natural. It doesn't make you a monster."

"But I felt so unburdened. What kind of woman am I?"

"You're human. You have wants and needs, and you're frustrated right now; but you'll get through this…and so will Khalil."

"I don't want him to die. I really do love him. You have to believe me." Her tears were always more than I could take. I pull her into my arms again, and hold her until her trembling stops.

"I know, baby."

"I'm sorry," she mumbled into my shirt. "I'm sorry for everything. You were right. I never meant to use you."

"No, don't do that. It's okay, Sera. Look at me. I want you to go get something to eat."

"But--"

"I'll stay with him," I whisper. "I'll watch over him. You need to eat, and get some rest. If you don't, I'll have you banned from his room."

She's heard this threat before. So, she doesn't argue with me, just grabs her purse and leaves, as if she has something important to do. There is a chair next to Khalil's bed. I flop down into it and yawn. If I'm going to stay here all night, I'm going to need some caffeine. I really don't know why I volunteered, but Sera was in no shape to be with him; but I knew she wouldn't leave unless Khalil were with someone she trusted.

"She trusts me *dawg*," I say, as I watch the equipment monitoring his oxygen and heart rate. I don't expect him to answer, and of course he doesn't. So, I sit and think of the irony of this moment. Here I am, nursing Sera's man. I'm actually taking care of the man who has claimed her heart. My Sera, my passion, my love… He has all of that, and can't do a damn thing with it. Yet, I sit and stare at him as if my constant eye to closed lid contact will somehow revitalize him.

My emotions are mixed. I don't wish this man harm. Really, I don't. I just wish the situation were different. I wish he didn't exist. I wish he'd never come into Sera's life, and stripped her of her love for me. I don't want to admit that, had it not been him, it may have been someone else. Sera can only take so much. Once she's through, she's through. Circumstances brought us together again, and I suppose I have good ol' Khalil here to thank for that.

"Thanks, *dawg*." I give him a pound on his limp hand, and lean forward, close to his ear. "You should see her, man. I bet she's even more beautiful than you can possibly remember. She smiles, and the whole room feels warmer. When she's sad, the atmosphere is so cold you think it will snow anytime. As warm as it is right now, it's snowing when she's around. You make her sad." I tap him on the forehead. "Is any of this getting through to you *dawg*? She's sad. She needs things you can't give her. I can give those things to her. Maaaan…you don't know how close we came to…but you don't wanna hear that do you? You don't want to hear about how soft her lips felt on mine, and how sweet her tongue tasted."

I look up at the monitor, and what the hell? His blood pressure rose has risen…just a little. Is it the infection or my words that cause the blood to pump through his body with such intensity? I push a little harder, wanting to see if Khalil will react to my words.

"You hear me," I say simply. "Good. Hear this." I lean even closer to him. "I love Sera. I love her so much that I could easily rip one of these plugs out and just kill you. I mean, she'd be sad; but I'd be there to comfort her. Eventually she'd forget all about you, and start a brand new life with me."

His pressure goes up a little more. So, I decide to back off a little. "Don't worry *dawg*. I would never do no shit like that. Number one: I'm no murderer. And number two: I love Sera too much to ever hurt her, even if that hurt will eventually lead to love for me. So, this is what I'm gonna do. I'm gon' pray for you. I'm going to get down on my knees and pray to God that you wake up and live a healthy normal life because the next time she comes to me, I'm going to take her so far away from you it will make your damn head spin.

I love her, Khalil. I love her, but she loves you. So, I'm doing everything I can to make her happy…even if it means helping you. She needs you, man. She needs you; and you need to wake yo ass up, before she either goes insane or ends up with another man, simply because she can't be with the one she loves. I don't think I love her enough to willingly be your substitute, Khalil. I don't want her to see your face, every time she looks at me. She told me that you were her destiny. You don't look like much destiny lying here like a vegetable!" I push the chair away from his bed. "Wake up, man. Somebody loves you; but she can only take so much. I learned that the hard way."

True to my word, I'm on my knees next to his bed with my eyes closed, praying to my God. I'm praying for Sera's happiness, no matter the outcome of Khalil's illness. I'm praying for the guilt to leave her mind, and for her joy to return ten-fold. I'm praying for myself. I pray for forgiveness. The sins of my past are many, and I've left a seemingly endless trail of broken hearts along my journey. I've fornicated with married women. I've hurt people who would have done anything to please me. I hurt Sera, the only woman I can ever say I've truly loved.

I haven't been to church in years. I pray for the strength and will to do right by my Lord and myself. I pray for my father. I pray that one day he'll wake up and realize that it doesn't take a heavy hand or a stable full of women to make him a man.  But most of all, I pray for a miracle.  I pray that Khalil opens his eyes and looks at Sera with that smile she's always talking about. I want him to get up out of this bed, free of infection, and of sound mind and body. I want doctors to look at him and say, "I can't explain it other than to say God must have reached down from heaven and laid his hands on this man. This is medically unexplainable. People, I think we just witnessed a miracle."

I'm on my knees now, doing the only thing I know to do when all hope is lost. When I finally open my eyes, I feel drained. I'm shocked to feel tears coursing down my cheeks. I haven't cried since I was a child. The day my father walked out on my mother, he'd looked at me tears and said *"Never let them see you cry, son. Crying is for sissies."* I'd taken his words to heart; but now I see how cleansing tears can be. I feel as if my slate has been washed clean. Suddenly, I understand what Allison meant when she told me to do what was in my heart. I'm doing what's best for the woman I love. Amen.

## Chapter 48

### Serafina Danielle Jordan

He's going to die; and when it happens, as it surely will, it will be because I gave up hope and allowed myself the luxury of fantasizing about life without him. I let my mind pretend that I was free of the burden, free of the worry, free of the sadness, and free of Khalil. This could actually be the end of damn near two years of waiting for Khalil to wake up. Waiting for Khalil to open his eyes, move his fingers, wiggle his toes. Waiting for Khalil to do…something…anything.

Where did things go wrong? When did my visits with him become a chore? When did I start dreading my time with him? I can't even pretend to use Jeremy as an excuse anymore. Yes, Jeremy is convenient, and he's been a better friend to me than I've been to him; but his role in my uncertainty is smaller than the mustard seed containing the miracles I'd stopped believing in so long ago. I have to face the reality of my situation, and the reasoning behind my wavering.

I'm just not that strong. I'm not the pillar of strength that people believe me to be. I'm not strong enough to live with the uncertainty of my future. I'd been prepared to live an eternity with him, but had been forced to consider a lifetime without him. I'd been willing to live with the memory of him and forsake all others, but somehow, Jeremy had given me a small taste of what I'd been missing. Things just couldn't be that simple. I couldn't allow loneliness to determine my loyalty to the man I loved; I also couldn't get away from the truth.

I'd wished him dead. It wasn't deliberate. I didn't open my mouth and say, "I wish Khalil would just die, so I can get on with my life." I'd dreamt it…and aren't dreams just the reality of your subconscious? In the dream, I'd felt free. Freer than a bird gliding through the air with the ability to land anywhere it chose. I landed on Jeremy. I've been there before. So, it wouldn't be totally weird to go there again, but it's not fair. And isn't that why he left in the first place?

What am I supposed to do? I was supposed to be able to make this decision on my own. Khalil isn't supposed to leave me with no other choice but to move on. I'm supposed to go to him, and whisper in his ear how much I love him; tell him that I can't handle living without him anymore. I can't handle his half-life, and I can't handle the guilt I feel every time I smile, every time I laugh, every time I remember that I haven't thought of him in the past few seconds, minutes, or hours.

What am I supposed to do, if he dies? I want to be wherever he is. I'd rather be dead than live without him. As long as he's asleep, there's a chance. There's no chance, if he's dead. I can't help the feelings of selfishness overtaking me. Somehow, I'm allowing myself to believe that death might be the best thing for him. In Heaven, he'd be free to write poetry and play his piano, to laugh, smile, and sing. He'd be with his mother, and who better to watch over him than she? He wouldn't be trapped in the endless sleep that has taken over his life. I don't know if he can hear me. I don't know if he's aware of my presence. Can he even dream about me?

What if he did wake up? Would he still be my Khalil? Or would he be a stranger? Would he be a man with a child's mind, or a man with no recollection of me? Would he be normal? I drove in the direction of the hospital, but had no true sense of where I was going. I didn't want to see him. I didn't want to look at what I'd done to him, but I knew that to abandon him now would be the worst thing I could possibly do.

I was halfway to the hospital, sitting at a stoplight, when I heard it. It was very faint, and I had to turn my radio down and strain my ears, for a moment. As the sound got louder, there was absolutely no mistaking the voice. I'd heard it before. I closed my eyes, unwilling to turn my head; afraid of who I might see standing next to my car.

"Why aren't you smiling?"

I hit the automatic locks, and turned the stereo up. Not even Maria Carey's high notes could drown out the voice of the woman I'd been avoiding for longer than I cared to remember.

"Go away," I whispered, unable to stop the sudden flow of tears. "Please go away."

"Why aren't you smiling?" Now was not the time to be having these crazy hallucinations. Now was not the time. Now was not the damn time.

"I can't deal with this, right now," I whispered, my eyes still squeezed shut. "Now is not the time to deal with this crazy bitch."

"When is the right time, Serafina?"

I opened my eyes. How in the hell had she heard me? Better yet, how in the hell did she know my name? Was I really as crazy as I'd always suspected? I slowly turned to my right, and found myself face to face with the owner of the voice that seemed to haunt me at my lowest moments. It was definitely her. She was wearing the same dirty red dress, and her face was still covered in that crazy make-up. She tapped softly on the glass.

"Why aren't you smiling?" She asked again, louder this time.

"Get the fuck away from my car!" I yelled over my music, over the sound of traffic, and over the sound of her voice asking the same damn question over and over again.

"Serafina, I have something to tell you," she told me.

There it was again, my name on the tongue of a stranger who had no rights to it. I must have been truly crazy, to even think of listening to anything she had to say; but something told me that I would never be rid of her, until I heard her out. I stared at her through the glass and inhaled slowly, not quite sure of what I was doing, but somehow willing to deal with whatever came from this meeting. I turned down my music and unlocked the doors, without comment.

I watched her, as she walked around to the passenger side of my car and opened the door, wordlessly sliding in next to me. Her gaze was too intent, too knowing. I had to look away from her. She softly closed the door, behind her and my head was suddenly filled with the light, breezy scent of citrus. It was a far cry from the smell I'd been expecting, and I exhaled gratefully.

"I've been waiting a long time for this moment." She told me.

"You have? Because I've been avoiding it."

"I know," she laughed. She smiled and her dazzling white teeth lit her features, giving her face an unexpected glow. "I suppose I do look rather, horrid."

"You look...fine," I stammered, not wanting to offend this stranger who knew my name and stared at me as if she were reading my mind. "Do I know you?"

"Under different circumstances, we probably would have known each other very well." She held out her hand, and when I hesitated she withdrew and folded her hands in her lap primly. "I would have loved you very much, as I do now, but I would have been more able to show you." For the first time, I noticed that although she didn't look like a lady, this woman carried herself with the confidence of an African Queen.

"You're afraid of me; and yet you opened the door for me. Why?"

"I don't know," I admitted. "I don't know anything anymore."

"You know more than you think." She cocked her head to the side, and smiled at me again.

"I don't know why you're following me." I put the car into park, and faced her. "How do you know me?"

"I've known you for a very long time."

"But how? I mean, what could you possibly know about me?"

"Serafina, I know more than you could ever imagine," she revealed mysteriously. "I'm here to tell you that everything is going to be alright."

"Is that what you had to tell me? Is this the profound statement that will forever change my life?" I asked her. "Who are you; and why do I keep seeing you? What the hell could you possibly know about me that I don't know about myself?" I was repeating myself, but I could think of nothing better to say to her. I felt like a deranged lunatic, trying to grasp reality with slippery hands. "I'm crazy aren't I? This dementia has finally caught up with me!" In my mind, I was yelling and screaming; but from my mouth the words sounded hoarse, barely above a whisper.

"Careful with the tears, dear. You'll ruin your makeup." She took a clean, white, handkerchief from her pocket, and gently dabbed at my eyes. It took a moment for me to appreciate the irony of her concern.

"Who are you?" I asked again.

"Khalil needs you, Serafina." She ignored my question and reached out to dab my eyes again. The sound of Khalil's name on her lips rendered me speechless. She continued in a soft steady voice, "He needs you now, more than ever; but you have to make a choice. Are you willing to go the distance? Or do you want to move on, perhaps with your gentleman friend?" She didn't give me a chance to answer. "If you want him back, you can have him."

"What?" I grabbed her hand, before she could wipe another tear from my face.

"You can have Khalil back if he's really the one you want."

"Don't say his name." My hand squeezed hers, but the strength in my grip didn't seem to faze her.

"Khalil needs you to save him." Her eyes never left mine.

"Why are you torturing me like this? I can't just wake him up!" I yelled tearfully.

"You can, if you really want it."

"If I really want it? You don't think I really want it? You tell me what I can do that I haven't already done! That the doctors haven't done! That his friends and family haven't done! What am I supposed to do?" I asked her. "You tell me what I'm supposed to do!"

"You already know."

"No, I don't!"

"Yes." She touched me with her free hand, slid her hand across my cheek, and pushed a loose strand of hair from my face. "You know what you have to do. You're just afraid." Her touch was warm, motherly and I could feel my tears slowly drying. "Tell him the truth, child. Stop pretending like everything is okay. Tell him how horrible you feel. Tell him about the other man." She paused for a moment. "Tell him about the baby."

I let go of her hand.

"The baby?"

"Yes. Don't you see? You spend so much time trying to keep him from worrying about you, he doesn't think you need him."

"But I do need him."

"Then tell him. Tell him everything. Make him get up, Serafina." She leaned in close and whispered into my ear, "Tell him about his son."

My heart stopped. I wrapped my arms around myself, shivering despite the warmth inside of my car. I recalled how much denial had flowed through my veins, as Khalil's baby had tried and failed to thrive within me. I hadn't known how to respond to its presence. *His* presence. "His son? How could you possibly...? Who are you?" "How do you know so much about Khalil and me? About our...about our baby..." I never knew whether our child had been a boy or a girl but the word *son* coming from this stranger's mouth felt too real to be false.

"Sometimes, the form we are given varies drastically from the form we first left this place in," she said simply.

"I don't understand," I whispered.

"You will." She cupped my face in her hands and leaned forward, kissing me the way my mama kisses me whenever we say goodbye. "Smile, baby."

I managed a weak smile for her and then, as if that was all she'd been waiting for since day one, she opened the car door and slowly climbed out, leaving me to wonder if she'd actually been there. I looked around, but she'd disappeared from sight, despite the lack of a crowd to envelope her. The car behind me started honking, and it took me a moment to realize the light had changed to green. Finally, disgusted with my lack of movement, the driver behind me swung out and drove around me. I didn't care. I was still trying to understand what had just happened. She'd been real...hadn't she?

I could still feel her hands on my face; still smell the faint, citrus scent she'd been wearing. I could still hear her voice, soft and reassuring, giving me permission to smile without guilt. I glanced down at the passenger seat, and noticed the white handkerchief she'd used to wipe my eyes. Slowly, I reached out to pick it up, wondering if the delicate cloth might evaporate the moment my fingers made contact. Amazingly, it kept its form. I unfolded it, turning it over in my hands and watched as the cloth suddenly transformed before my eyes. No longer lily white, the handkerchief took on an older, more antique appearance. As I stared at it, I could make out three initials that were delicately hand-stitched in the corner. "CMR"

"Oh my God," I whispered, holding the handkerchief to my nose and inhaling the scent of, "orange oil," I whispered, suddenly remembering a conversation I'd had with Karl after Khalil proposed to me.

*"I met Celeste in the frozen food section. She walked past me and her beauty intrigued me, but pretty girls were a dime a dozen. What got me was that blast of wind that followed her. It mesmerized me...I had to get closer. I had to inhale her again. She smelled like the juiciest, sweetest orange just waiting to be picked from the vine. I knew right then that she would be my wife."*

"Sometimes, the form we are given varies drastically from the form we first left this place in," I said quietly, reciting word for word the answer the woman in red had given when I'd asked who she was. "CMR," I whispered. "Celeste Marie Roberts."

"Oh my God," I said again. I put my car into gear. I now knew what needed to be done.

　　　　\*\*\*

I don't even remember driving to the hospital. It was like I'd fallen asleep at the wheel; and when I'd awakened, I was walking down the hallway towards Khalil's room. The sight that greeted me gave me a momentary pause. Jeremy was asleep on a cot next to Khalil's bed. His cell phone lay on his chest, in case some emergency sent him downstairs on his day off. He must have felt me watching because he opened his eyes suddenly and quickly wiped the drool from his mouth.

"You stayed." I walked over and licked my thumb, cleaning the crust from his cheek the way a mother would do a child.

"You sound surprised."

"I am.".

"I told you that I would."

"You didn't have to."

"I know that." He stood up slowly and stretched. "I'm going to get some coffee. Do you want any?"

I shook my head no, trying not to let Jeremy's formality hurt my feelings. "Jeremy," I said, as he opened the door to leave. He stopped but didn't turn around to look at me. "Thank you," I called out to him.

He glanced at me over his shoulder and smiled, before leaving. The door slowly closed behind him, and I was suddenly alone with Khalil. I slipped my hand into my jacket pocket and closed my fingers around the handkerchief, drawing some of my strength from the knowledge that Celeste was watching over me and had entrusted her only son to me.

I didn't know where or how to start. So, I just started talking, until my syllables became words, those words became sentences, and those sentences slowly began to weave a tale of a woman abandoned and alone at the alter, of a child that couldn't survive the grief of the mother, of lonely days and lonelier nights, and the arms of a man who had the power to take that loneliness away…if only for a little while. I spoke frankly and freely. I spilled more than my guts. I spilled my soul. I begged him to wake up. I begged him to hear my words and come home because I didn't know how much longer I could put my life on hold.

"Khalil, I love you, but I need to feel your love too. I'm so sick and tired of living on memories. I want to hear your voice. I want you to hold me. I need you just as much as you need me, right now. I pray for you every day. Can't you feel me willing you to wake up and be the man that you were?" I rubbed my damp cheek against his, not caring if his stubble chafed my skin. I wanted him to feel my tears, to know how miserable my life was without him.

"Can't you feel me?" I asked him. "Because I can't feel you, Khalil, I don't feel your energy anymore; and I am so fed up with making sacrifices for a man who isn't even coherent enough to appreciate it. You said you would never leave me. You lied!"

All of the anger, all of the frustration, all of the bitterness, loneliness, and feelings of betrayal that my subconscious had buried deep inside of me suddenly bubbled up and spilled over as my body verbally regurgitated all of the emotions I'd been forcing myself to swallow in his presence.

"I should have known that it was too good to be true. I should have known that you would leave me! I needed you Khalil! I needed you, and where were you? You were asleep, while my entire world was falling apart!"

"Sera, what are you doing?" Jeremy stood in the doorway with two cups of coffee in his hands.

I ignored Jeremy and turned back to Khalil. "I hate you!" I yelled, "I hate you; and if you don't wake up, you might as well be dead because I can't do this anymore!"

"Serafina, NO!" He dropped the coffee, sending it crashing to the floor and spilling out in several directions, as he grabbed me by my arm and swung me around to face him.

"Jeremy, he lied to me!"

"Sera, don't talk to him like that!" Jeremy said sharply, "He can hear you!"

"Good! I want him to hear me! I want him to know! I can't do this shit anymore!" I pulled away from Jeremy and ran over to Khalil, "Do you hear me Khalil? I can't do this anymore!"

Jeremy wrapped his arms around my waist and pulled me, kicking and screaming away from Khalil's bed. "Baby, calm down or they will put you out of here."

"So! Let them put me out! Maybe they should! He doesn't love me! If he did, he would get up and be with me!"

One of the nurses came running into the room. "What's going on?"

"Watch your step, I spilled coffee!" Jeremy yelled, just as her sneakers were about to make contact with the slippery mess he'd made.

She stopped short and stared at me, struggling against Jeremy's grasp and trying to bite the hand he'd placed over my mouth.

"Everything's fine," Jeremy told her. "Just please, get me some towels so I can clean this mess? I'll take care of it." He pushed me up against the wall, but didn't take his hand away from my mouth. "Sera, it's very important that you calm down," he said quietly. "Khalil can hear you, and so can all of the other patients. You can't do this here. You've got to be strong." I vigorously shook my head, no. I couldn't be strong anymore. I just couldn't do it.

"Sera, if I take my hand away do you promise to stay calm?" I nodded and he cautiously let me go. "See?" He put his arms around me. "Everything is going to be okay."

"Everything is *not* going to be okay," I told him. And now, I feel as if I really am going insane because I just want to open my mouth and scream as loud as I possibly can. My skin is burning. My scalp is itching uncontrollably, and I can feel myself beginning to sweat profusely. "Everything is not okay," I mumbled. I began wringing my hands so hard I thought my bones would shatter from the pressure.

The nurse looked over at Jeremy. "You need to get her out of here before she does something crazy." She tried to whisper but I heard her.

"Crazy?" I asked. "You think I'm crazy?" I yelled, "Khalil, wake up! I need you; and I swear to God if I leave now, I'm never coming back! Get up!"

"She's hysterical. You need to take her out of here, before I have to call security," I heard her tell him, but I was one step ahead of them. They didn't need to kick me out. I was already on my way, and the sound of Jeremy yelling my name did absolutely nothing to slow my pace. In fact, it caused me to run as far away from Khalil as I could.

## Chapter 49

### Jeremy Trent Sanders

She had finally lost her mind. I watched her run from the room, and my initial reaction was to go after her; but the sound of the nurse's voice stopped me dead in my tracks.

"Dr.Sanders..." Her voice was shaking, and when I turned my head in her direction, I froze. We stared at each other for a moment, and then slowly turned our attention back to Khalil. I moved closer to his bed and yelled for the nurse to snap out of it and go get help. His heart rate and blood pressure were sky high and his right arm was outstretched, stiffly defying gravity, reaching for something...or someone. I reached out to touch his arm. I wrapped my hand around his, but he wouldn't react, just kept reaching.

"Khalil, can you hear me?" I asked loudly. "Khalil, squeeze my hand, if you can hear me."

Three nurses and what seemed like every available doctor on the floor came rushing into his room, practically knocking me over in their haste to get to Khalil. The nurse who was in the room when Sera had her breakdown stood next to me and took Khalil's hand. When he still didn't respond she said softly, "He wants her."

"He's going into cardiac arrest!" I heard a voice say.

"He needs her," I mumbled. "He's reaching out for her."

"Well, whoever she is, go and get her!" One of the doctors yelled.

I was gone in an instant, running through the halls, screaming Sera's name. My stethoscope jumped up and down on my chest, and the white tails of my lab coat trailed behind me, as I dodged trays and gurneys in my attempt to get to Sera before she reached the elevators. The moment she saw me running towards her, she started pushing the down button frantically. When the elevator doors didn't open fast enough, she darted into the stairwell, descending the steps two at a time, with me directly on her heels.

"Sera, wait!"

"Leave me alone!" She stumbled and had to grab the railing to steady herself. "I'm not going back in there!" She was winded and her words came out in short, stacatto breaths.

"You have to!"

"I don't have to do a damn thing!" She stopped descending the stairs, but refused to turn around and look at me.

"He's trying to wake up!" I yelled so loudly that my voice echoed in the empty stairwell. "If you don't go back in there, he could die!"

"What are you talking about?"

"Girl, I don't have time to explain!" I took her hand and practically dragged her up the stairs. "He heard everything you said to him, Sera!" I looked back at her face, and noticed that she looked as if she were going to faint. "Get it together! He needs you now!"

"Oh my God, " she said, panic flooding her voice, "I've killed him!"

"NO! You made him react." I shook her harder than I meant to, but I needed Sera to snap out of whatever had come over her. "Sera, he's reaching out for you!"

"What?"

"He's reaching out for you, literally. His hand is in the air." I said it slowly, making sure she understood what I was trying to tell her. "He needs you."

"Oh my God!"

She pulled away and ran past me up the stairs, as if she'd suddenly been handed a second wind. I could have used a small dose of the adrenaline fueling her small frame because it took a large amount of effort to keep up with her. Somehow, chasing her back to the room didn't take quite as long as it took for me to run after her in the first place. By the time we got back to the room, there were doctors and nurses everywhere.

"What is that?" Sera yelled, as they wheeled a crash cart into the room. She pushed past the doctors and nurses, and made her way to Khalil, whose arm remained outstretched as if he were straining to touch something just beyond his reach. Ignoring the doctor telling her to leave the room, Sera grabbed Khalil's hand; and the room was suddenly filled with a shocked silence, as Khalil grasped her hand tightly, as if his life depended on it. Within seconds of Sera making contact with Khalil, his blood pressure and heart rate gradually decreased, falling to near-normal levels, as everyone in the room watched in trance-like disbelief.

"I think he's trying to talk," I heard Dr. Donell Rodgers mumble in amazement, "Someone get this tube out of his throat."

At that moment, thinking that she was in the way, Sera let go of Khalil's hand. His blood pressure and heart rate started rising again. "Don't let go of his hand!" Dr. Rodgers was so excited that he could hardly contain himself. Sera, still in shock, hadn't actually said anything to Khalil or anyone else in the room.

"Can he breathe on his own?" I asked cautiously.

Dr. Rodgers turned off the respirator, and we watched as Khalil's chest rose and fell in a steady rhythm. Without asking permission, I quickly removed the tube from his throat. He was definitely trying to speak. Sera leaned in close. Her hands cupped his face, as she tried to hear and understand what he was trying to say. Khalil could only manage one word. He was painfully hoarse, but there was absolutely no mistaking his first post-comatose word...or the loaded meaning.

"Don't." Tears fell from the corners of his closed eyelids, as he said it again, "Don't."

"I won't, baby. I promise." Sera finally found the words lodged in her throat. She covered his face in kisses, wiping his tears away and replacing them with her own. "I'm not going to leave you. I'll never leave you again."

The silence of the awestruck spectators was finally broken, when Khalil's nurse took a shaky step forward, and put her hand on Dr. Rodger's shoulder. "What just happened here? We all saw it. This man was going to die!"

Dr. Rodgers just shook his head slowly. His hand had been over his mouth, for the past few minutes. When he finally removed it, I experienced an eerie sense of déjà vu as he softly said, "I can't explain it other than to say God must have reached down from heaven and lay his hands on this man. This is medically unexplainable. People, I think we just witnessed a miracle."

The room was suddenly filled with applause. Medical personnel, and even family members of some of the other ICU patients rejoiced in the awakening of a man who had, until that moment, been in a coma for over eighteen months. Surely, if God could lay hands on Khalil, everyone on this floor had a chance of surviving whatever ailed them. I looked around at all of the smiling faces, and then gazed down at Sera, holding Khalil, kissing him, and whispering that everything was going to be ok. I couldn't speak for anyone else in the room, but I definitely planned on going to church Sunday morning.

## Chapter 50

## <u>Khalil Jamal Roberts</u>

*The pleated hem of her yellow sundress floated on the clear blue water, making small ripples as she kneeled at the pool's edge, arms outstretched, smiling proudly as a toddler kicked, splashed, and laughed high pitched squeals. A mass of sandy curls covered the child's head, and I could tell from the gentle yet masculine features of the tiny face that he was a little boy. He noticed me watching them, and pointed with chubby fingers attached to even chubbier hands.*

*"Daddy."*

*The woman turned to see what the child was pointing at. My knees buckled. I stumbled, catching hold of a park bench and sat quickly, denying my body the chance to fall to the ground. My heart beat rapidly, almost violently, and I felt breathless, as if someone or something were sucking the very life from me. She gathered the baby, he couldn't have been any older than eighteen months old, and stood, staring at me with a serene smile on her face.*

*"You shouldn't be here," she said softly.*

*A gentle breeze washed over her. The child shivered, but the woman seemed unfazed, even with the wet edges of her dress fluttering around her legs. I inhaled deeply, as the scent of oranges caught in her wind and blew her beautiful spirit in my direction. The color of toasted almonds, her hair hung to her shoulders in thin locs, adorned here and there with shells and wooden beads.*

*I was afraid to whisper the word on my lips. So, I opened my mind and began to think that which I was too scared to say aloud.*

*"Daddy!" The little boy said again, wriggling from her grasp, and running toward me as fast as his little wobbly legs would carry him. I scooped him up and held him at arms length, studying his little face, which was strange to me and yet so familiar. I'd seen his eyes before...in another face...in another time.*

*"Come, Amiri. You will meet him again." She took the baby and stared down at me, as she balanced him on her hip. She motioned for me to scoot over and I obeyed.*

*"Mama," I cleared my throat as she sat next to me on the bench. I reached out to touch her hair, so long, so beautiful, so different from...*

*"In Heaven, things are as they should be," she whispered.*

*"I still have your hair," I whispered, finally able to look her in the eye. I remembered helping her cut her locs before the chemotherapy could take them from her. "I still have it. It's in a velvet lined box on my mantle." I didn't realize I was crying until the baby, Amiri, reached out to wipe my eyes with his little hand. I held his hand in mine, kissing the tiny fingers, wondering why I felt such a strong kinship to this child.*

*"Who is he?" I asked her.*

*"You have to go back."* She placed her hand on my cheek and smiled, ignoring my question.

*"He called me Daddy."*

*"He did."* She acknowledged.

*"Is he...?"* I couldn't bring myself to say 'dead'.

*"He's waiting for another chance,"* she told me. *"You have to go back, baby. You don't belong here with us."*

*"I can't,"* I whispered, welcoming the arms that slid around me. She held me tightly, in the way that only a mother could hold her son. *"Serafina is gone. She hates me."*

*"Serafina loves you."*

*"She said a lot of things I don't understand."* I stared at the baby again.

Mama held me tighter, as if she didn't want to let go of me. *"You'll see Amiri again, but you have to go back."* She pushed me away from her and stood up, staring down at me with an expression that was both happy and sad. *"I love you Khalil. I'll always love you; but you've got to wake up, baby. Wake up and reach out for her. She'll be there."* She walked away, holding Amiri's hand as they slowly made their way back to the pool.

*"Mama, don't go,"* I called out weakly. I tried to stand up and follow them, but a strange force kept me rooted to my seat. *"Mama!"* I called out again, but she wouldn't turn around.

Amiri, however, let go of Mama's hand and turned to look at me. *"Bye, Daddy,"* he said, waving again before turning and running back to the pool.

I couldn't open my eyes. An excruciating pain shot through my arm; but something inside of me would not allow me to calm myself, until I felt her touch and heard her voice. There were voices swimming throughout my head, but none belonged to the one person I yearned for. Strangers grabbed my hand, begging me to squeeze, but my muscles would not allow me to acknowledge the presence of another. I needed Serafina, and I couldn't rest until I found her...even if it killed me, which I feared it would.

Tears slid from the corners of my closed eyes, as the one I sought finally took my hand, squeezing my hand as tightly as I squeezed hers. There was so much I wanted to say, but my weakness would only allow me to speak one word.

"Don't," I whispered hoarsely. *Please don't go. Please don't leave me. I'll die without you.*

"I won't, baby. I promise," she whispered tearfully.

It was all that I needed to hear. I slipped into a fitful sleep, afraid to drift too far away from her. I was afraid I wouldn't be able to wake up again.

Her beautiful face loomed above me. Worry invaded her features, but a smile broke through her worry, bathing my rainy season with more sunshine than I could handle. There was no church. There was no minister, and Serafina wasn't standing by my side wearing the top-secret wedding dress she'd spent months hiding from me.

I stared at Serafina in her blue jeans and frilly white top. She looked like a beautiful gypsy. Every time she moved, the wooden bracelets on her arms gently bumped into one another creating a melodic sound for my greedy ears. I couldn't get enough of her face, her voice, her hands touching me, her lips kissing me, her tears mingling with mine every time she placed her cheek against my cheek.

"What do you remember?" She asked.

"Darkness."

But I remember so much more, or at least I think I do. I remembered my last conversation with Serafina. I remembered the orange moon. I remembered falling asleep that night with a smile on my face, and slipping into a nightmarish sleep a short while later. I remembered a man threatening to take Serafina away from me. Perhaps, they were dreams.

In these dreams, I begged her to come back; but my vocal chords were ripped, emitting no sound. I'm not sure if I want to know how much reality was contained in those dreams. I only want to know that she is still here, touching me constantly, as if she is afraid of what will happen if she lets go.

"I love you." She whispered it over and over again. Each time she said it, there was a tiny catch in her voice.

The doctor said it would be a few days before the raspy edge in my voice left and my throat felt normal again. Serafina kept telling me not to talk, but I had to tell her what happened to me in the moments before I felt her soft hand grasping mine.

"I saw her," I whispered, each word laced with an uncomfortable soreness.

"Who?"

"Mama."

"What did she say?"

I didn't have the strength to describe how I'd clung to her, crying from the pain that seemed to rip my heart apart when I heard Serafina say she was leaving me forever. Just like when I was a child, my mother had stroked, held, and told me that everything would be okay.

"She told me how much she loved me. Then, she told me to wake up," I shared. "She said that if I just reached out, you would be there."

"I thought I'd lost you forever."

"No."

"I love you."

"There was a little baby there," I said softly. "He kept calling me Daddy." I tried to look into her eyes, but she kept averting her gaze.

"Shhh… Stop trying to talk so much." She tried to silence me with a gentle kiss, but I shook my head.

"Serafina, she had a little boy with her," I said urgently. "I heard you say something about a baby."

"Remember? I told you that Ayzha had a baby. She had a little girl." She gave me a shaky smile. "You need to get some rest."

I've been resting for eighteen months. I don't want to sleep. I'm afraid of the darkness. I'm afraid that if I close my eyes on her face, I'll never see this vision again. So, I focus on her and make her talk to me. I need her to tell me what happened while I was away from her.

"My mother called him Amiri."

Serafina's smile faltered, and she smoothed the edges of my blanket before standing up and taking a few steps away from me. I saw her reach into the front pocket of her jeans and pull out, what I thought was a folded piece of paper.

"What is that?"

"She gave this to me." She held out her hand, and I slowly reached out to take what she offered.

I saw the initials first. "CMR" hand-stitched in the far right corner of the handkerchief. I'd threaded the needle she'd used to stitch those letters. I brought the handkerchief to my nose, and allowed myself to remember how it had felt to be wrapped in her arms and surrounded by her smell.

"We buried her with this handkerchief." I looked up at Serafina, "How did you? Where? You saw her?"

Serafina sat down on the edge of my bed with her back to me. I could tell by the droop in her shoulders that she was crying. I gripped my mother's handkerchief tightly, for the moment, unable to comfort Sera in the way that she probably needed me to.

"I didn't know it was a boy," she said finally, sniffling between each word. "I didn't want to believe that it was true. I didn't know how much I wanted that baby, until it was gone…until *he* was gone." She sighed, "You saw him?"

"We'll see him again," I said, repeating my mothers words, but unable to stop the pain that ravaged my heart. I should have been there, but I wasn't. There was nothing that I could do to replace all of the heartache and pain she'd suffered while I was asleep.

"It won't be the same baby."

"Serafina, I saw him. It will be him. He's just waiting for his second chance." I placed my hand over hers and squeezed her fingers. "I promise."

"I love you."

"I love you too." One hand grasps my mother's handkerchief. The other I keep on Serafina. She's been without me for far too long; and it doesn't take a rocket scientist to know how close I came to losing her completely. I can see it in her eyes...the guilt, the relief, the way she jumps every time the door opens, almost like she's expecting an unwanted visitor.

He visited me as I slept; and every time he spoke, I felt angry. I wanted to fight. I wanted to kill him. I felt like he was trying to steal the one thing that kept my heart beating. I want to know. Then again, I don't want to know if he really touched her, kissed her... I can't imagine another man exploring the body she's pledged to me. I can't envision another man kissing the tender lips I've always considered mine.

"You really should rest." Her sweet voice cut into my thoughts.

"Stay." I gripped her hand a little tighter. I knew that she was exhausted, but I wasn't ready to let go of her yet.

"Always." She kissed my knuckles, and climbed into bed with me, being mindful of the I.V. my doctor says I probably won't need in a few days.

With her head on my shoulder and her arms around me, holding me beneath the thin blankets, I felt a familiar warmth envelope my body. I finally allowed myself to relax and close my eyes. I slowly inhaled the scent of the woman breathing softly on my neck. She'd already fallen asleep. The doctors keep telling me how lucky I am, but I know that luck has nothing to do with it. I am divinely blessed.

## Chapter 51

### Ayzha Nicole Darwin-Jordan

The site of Sera and Khalil snuggled in his narrow hospital bed, both asleep, made Max and I pause in the doorway, just watching them. To wake them would have been a crime so we just kind of stood there, waiting for the right moment to enter the room and see for ourselves that Khalil would actually open his eyes and focus on us.

The nurses had put a sign on Khalil's door that read, "The Living Miracle". Everyone was talking about the man who'd awakened from a coma, and by all appearances, seemed to be of sound mind and body.

The television stations had already gotten wind of the story and were crowding downstairs, trying to get a glimpse of Karl as he arrived. The lobby had been so crowded that the police had to be called to remove most of the press. The son of a famous musician suddenly coming out of a coma was great news for a nation overwrought with depressing headlines.

"Can you believe this?" Max asked me. "Look at her. I haven't seen that look on her face in so long."

I saw it too, that look of pure serenity. Her facial features were totally relaxed. Her eyes weren't jumping behind her closed lids the way they normally did, as if every nap contained a nightmare. A stirring from the bed caught our attention. Khalil was waking up. I held my breath as he opened his eyes. Tears sprang to my eyes and I hastily wiped them away. It was really true. He was really awake. It wasn't a figment of imagination or a cruel joke. Khalil was staring at us with Sera in his arms and from his smile I knew he recognized us.

"What's up, *Rip Van Winkle*"! Max stood at the foot of the bed grinning like he'd just won the lottery.

"Hey," Khalil whispered.

"Don't talk. I know your throat hurts," I told him. "I'm so happy for you Khalil. We really missed you."

"My throat is starting to feel better," he told us.

"You want some water or something?" Max poured a glass of water, and held a straw to Khalil's lips as he took tiny sips.

"Thanks, Man." Khalil's voice already sounded a little better. "Is my Daddy here yet?"

"Not yet," I told him. "His plane lands in about 30 minutes though. The press is all over this, so Max is going to go pick him up. There's a limo parked in front of the airport, and everyone assumes it's for Karl."

"He's so sneaky," Khalil chuckled.

"As a matter fact, I'm leaving now." Max gave Khalil's hand a gentle pat, and then gave me a brief kiss before leaving.

The room was quiet. Khalil just stared at me with a knowing grin on his face. "You and Max huh? I've definitely been asleep way too long."

"It caught me by surprise. One minute we were going over plans for the club, and the next minute we were married." I left out a small detail, but I wasn't fooling Khalil. I could tell by his smirk. "She's really missed you." I leaned in and placed a small kiss on his forehead, and then kissed Sera who was still sound asleep. "There were times when I didn't know if she was strong enough to survive all of this."

He looked over at her sleeping face on his shoulder and smiled. "I want to ask you a question, Ayzha."

"Okay."

"In my dreams, I heard Jeremy's name. He spoke to me. I remember being angry." He spoke slowly, as if he wasn't sure if he really wanted an answer.

"He was here watching over you, when they brought you back in."

"At first I thought he hated me, but then I thought I heard him praying." He looked to me for validation.

"He loves Sera," I said simply, remembering the solemn phone call I'd received from Jeremy after he'd prayed for Khalil to wake up. I felt, in my soul, that Jeremy's prayers had caught God's attention. I told Khalil. I told him that Jeremy had taken care of Serafina as a friend, and that he loved her enough to know she could only be happy with the man of her dreams. "You're that man, Khalil. I never liked Jeremy in the past, but he's a totally different man now. He never took advantage of her vulnerability. He always made sure she had what she needed."

"Did he help her with...?" His voice trailed off, as if it pained him to finish. "Did he help her with the...with the baby?"

I nodded, and he looked away from me for a moment. Sera was starting to wake up, so I knew our conversation was over. If Khalil was still the same man I knew before the accident...and I had a strong feeling he was because Jeremy had prayed for total recovery; and God is good. If he was the same man, then he would release any jealousy, and thank God that Jeremy had been there when her chosen partner couldn't be.

"Where's my little Chyna doll?" Sera asked groggily. She sat up slowly, trying not to disturb Khalil's IV.

"Well hello to you, too," I said with mock sarcasm. "She's with your mother."

I watched the two of them together, and couldn't help the smiles that must have radiated from my entire body. I wasn't sure how long the doctors would keep Khalil in the hospital. According to Jeremy, Khalil's diagnosis was so good that the doctor's were almost afraid to verbalize it. As far as any of them were concerned, he only needed physical therapy to help him get used to using his limbs again. It was, indeed a miracle. I didn't want to question it. I was just thankful that God had finally answered our prayers.

## Chapter 52

### <u>Jeremy Trent Sanders</u>

It's Sunday morning and as I pull into my mother's driveway, she's locking her front door. She's so petite and pretty in black Chanel suit I bought her with my first paycheck as a doctor. I can see her little white gloves peeking out of her small black Coach bag; and for the millionth time, I wonder how any man could walk away from a woman as kind and beautiful as my mother. I quietly walk up on her and grab her around the waist, planting a sloppy kiss on her cheek. She turns around with her fist drawn back, and I laugh hysterically.

"Boy, you almost made me lose my religion." She lands a stinging slap on my arm, and eyes me suspiciously. "What are you doing up so early on a Sunday morning...besides scaring your mother?"

"Well, I thought I'd drive you to church; and then maybe I can come back here and help you cook dinner."

"Well son, I don't need you to drop me off at church. You know I like to leave when I'm good and ready. I don't like to wait."

Either I've said it wrong, or she's just misunderstood me. Didn't she notice I wasn't wearing my usual Sunday attire? I'd left my jeans and sneakers at home, and put on a pair of khaki slacks and a beige linen shirt. I even have on my shiny tan shoes.

"Mama, I meant that we could go to church together, and then come back here and cook," I say, trying to make my meaning a bit clearer.

"You want to go to church with me? What day is it? Have I lost my mind and forgotten it was Christmas, Mothers Day, or Easter?" She opens her bag and pulls out her calendar.

"Mama," I take the calendar from her and stare at her. "Come on. Stop playing. I want to go to church with you."

"What's wrong baby?"

"Nothing's wrong. I just know that things will never be right, unless I get God on my side."

"Baby, he's always been on your side. He just doesn't interfere, unless you ask him to. That's all." Suddenly her hand is on my arm and she is steering me towards my BMW. "How is Serafina?"

"She's doing fine."

"That young man of hers finally woke up, huh?"

"I was going to tell you. I've just been doing a lot of thinking." I open the door for her, and help her in. She reserves comment, until we are sitting in a pew at her large Holiness church.

"The news says everything is okay with him. God was definitely looking out for that man," she whispers softly during praise and worship.

"Yeah," I answer, keeping my eyes focused on my Bible. "Mama, if I tell you something, will you promise not to think I'm crazy?"

"Boy, you know I can't control my thoughts."

"Just try." I want to stick my tongue out at her; but she's still my mother, and she has one mean backhand. "I got a sign from God."

"What kind of sign?" I can feel her gazing intently at me.

"I prayed for Khalil to wake up the same man he was when he had his accident."

"Okay…"

"I prayed for the doctors to say something specific about his recovery."

"Did they?"

"They said exactly what I prayed for." I glance at her. She is still staring at me, her mouth wide open. "Word for word, Mama," I add quietly. "It's like He was listening to me, and wanted me to know He really does exist. I mean, I always knew He existed; but I guess I never actually thought He gave a damn about me."

For once she doesn't tell me to watch my mouth on the Lord's Day. I feel her hand on my arm, and I am comforted in her presence. The sermon speaks to me, as if the minister has peeked inside of my life and has taken notes. I feel as if he wrote the sermon specifically for me; but I'm not spooked, I'm intrigued. Church used to take forever; but although I've been sitting here for about two hours, I feel as if I just arrived. I'm filling out an offering envelope, when I hear the alter call. My body stiffens, and a chill overcomes me. I want to get up, but I can't move my legs. A thin layer of sweat forms on my brow, and my mother takes a handkerchief out of her purse, gently dabbing it away.

"He can only do so much for you, baby. There comes a time when you have to trust him completely and let him take over. Are you ready for that?"

I nod slowly.

"You know the devil is going to be knocking your door down, baby. He's probably sitting beside you right now, holding you down in that chair. Tell him to go away, Jeremy. God has your back and even if you fall, he'll lift you up again. Once you give him your life, he will never leave you."

I nod again. For the second time in a week, I feel the urge to cry. I push my father's words to the back of my mind, and stand slowly. There is comfort in knowing I am not the only person approaching the altar. I'm not alone. Even if I were the only man standing there, I am still not alone. He is with me; and He doesn't see any weakness in tears. He only sees a man who wants to make the right changes and I am that man.

## Chapter 53

### <u>Serafina Danielle Roberts</u>

He is…the breath of fresh air you receive after being submerged in stale water for an obscene amount of time. He is…the cool breeze that blows over my body during a heat wave. He is…the man who makes me smile, the man who makes me laugh, the man who makes me feel as if I am not only the most important woman in the world…I am the *only* woman in the world. He is…my husband and I am Serafina Danielle Roberts. No need for hyphenation, I am his…completely, totally, there is no me, only *we*.

Six months ago, I was staring at the closed lids of a man I thought I'd never kiss again. Today I'm staring into his eyes, leaning forward to meet the kiss that awaits me, as our limo pulls away from our wedding reception. I feel lighter than white rose petals floating in the wind…he loves me, he love me not, he loves me…he loves me…he loves me… And I love him so much it would take a new thesaurus to describe this feeling being pumped through my heart.

"Have you ever made love in a limo?" His voice melted into my ear, as he gently nibbled my tender lobe.

"No, but I have done it in a Mustang," I confided, as if he didn't already know.

I could feel him smiling into my gossamer veil; and I leaned into him, thankful for the strong arms that held me closer than skin. "Are you really here?"

"I don't know; but if this is a dream I never want to wake up," he told me. "I don't think I've ever been this happy."

"Then it can only get better." I kissed him tenderly.

From the corner of my eye, I saw a figure in red waving at me from the curb. The raggedy dress I was used to seeing had been replaced with a sleek, form-fitting gown. Her long locs were piled regally atop her head. She was beautiful, as she'd been in life; and I was happy to see that her mission on Earth had finally been fulfilled.

"He is your destiny," I heard a familiar voice say.

"You are my destiny," I repeated.

"God sent her back to bring us together," Khalil told me.

"She led me back to you. She told me how to wake you up."

"And you did."

"Yeah," I whispered. "I did."

I rolled down the window, and made eye contact with Celeste Marie Roberts. She stood still where she was, her face full of pride.

"Thank you," I mouthed silently, placing a hand over my heart.

She placed a hand over her own heart, made a smiling motion with her index fingers, turned, and then slowly walked away, disappearing into the crowd as if she'd never been there.

"Let's bring Amiri back." It was the first time I'd ever spoken his name aloud; and I knew, without a doubt, that I was ready to welcome my little boy back into my life.

"When?"

"As soon as possible."

"Are you sure?"

"I'm sure that I love you," I said simply, "and I don't want to waste anymore time.

It was all that needed to be said; and when my husband, my destiny, pulled me into his arms and held me…I knew. I knew in my heart…in my soul…this man would bring me smiles for the rest of my days. I smiled. He smiled. We smiled.

**THE END.**

---

## SEQUEL TO "SLOW BURN"

# ORCHID'S NECTAR

### Orchid Maya Ishmael

The harmonious sounds of Jodeci echo throughout the den and for the first time in a long time I actually want to thank my brother, Giovanni, for buying me those expensive surround sound speakers. The bass vibrates my heart as the music plays and just like the song, I'm feelin' for more of Jeremy's thick lips all over mine, his hands all over my bare arms because I'm suddenly without my sweatshirt and thank goodness I'm wearing a t-shirt underneath. This feels like high school. On the verge of naughty while still being innocent, I feel like that virgin I used to be, grinding with my little high school boyfriend, wondering if I should let him put his hands underneath my shirt, but content to just roll around and kiss until we just have to stop.

Jeremy is kissing me just like that. He isn't trying to feel me up or coax me out of my panties. He's just kissing me, and the sensation of his lips on my lips, his body stretched out on top of mine, proof of his obvious desire for me rubbing up against my obvious desire for him as I sink deeper and deeper into my tan leather couch is so delicious I'm craving more and more. I could very well gorge myself on this beautiful man. Curiosity is the reason I'm lying beneath Jeremy and my late mother's advice is beginning to ring true.

"Curiosity killed the cat, Orchid", She used to say, shaking her head and smiling at the same time.

Well, if I'm not careful, mutual curiosity will have Jeremy killing this kitty before I have a chance to say "condom".

"Let's watch TV." I whisper, turning my head so he can't hypnotize me with those eyes of his.

"Good idea." His voice is strained. His sweats are strained. My bra is strained. We have so much in common at the moment. His brow is wet. My panties are less than dry. I should ask him to leave but of course I don't because I want to sit here, on the couch with him, watching television with no sound because I still haven't quite figured out my new remote control. The stereo is still playing Jodeci but the television is showing an old episode of Kojak.

"I've never seen a coroner so involved in his work." Jeremy is staring intently at the television and to my surprise; we proceed to watch the entire show with no sound. Instead, we start making up our own dialogue and cracking jokes about the storyline.

"This is fun." I say softly. And I truly mean it. This is fun. I feel as if I've known Jeremy forever and sitting next to him, holding hands on my sofa, watching television with no dialogue and listening to music feels as natural as freshly fallen snow.

"Yes." He gives me a satisfied smile before directing his attention back to my big screen.

His hand tightens around mine and my arm begins to tingle as if the circulation has been killed. I'm nervous because I've never felt such serenity in a room filled with so much sexual tension. Overwhelmed, I stand and walk over to my fireplace on a fake mission to stoke the fire. My back is to him but I can feel him coming towards me, slowly, quietly. I turn my head, expecting to see him standing behind me. I nearly jump out of my skin when I see him crawling towards me with the stealth of a black panther stalking his prey. Instinctively, my eyes close as he slides his body around my legs like a kitty cat begging for attention. He's taking my breath away, releasing me of all control and taking over my psyche with his animalistic behavior. I'm hot and it's not because I'm standing near a roaring fire.

"You make me wanna do strange things." He mumbles, reaching for my hand and pulling me down to the floor beside him.

"Like?" I ask. My eyes are still closed. His tongue is drawing circles on the back of my neck.

"Like this."

Oh my...I can't speak, only feel his hands sliding down my legs and snatching off my ballet slippers. Thank God for fresh pedicures and paraffin wax because the moment my toes slide inside of his mouth I know I'll never look at a pair of shoes the same way again.

"You're nasty." I tell him.

"You don't know the half of it."

"What are you going to do to me?" I ask him.

"Whatever you want me to do."

Why did he tell me that? I want him to do to my body the same thing he's doing to my toes. Licking and sucking as if he's eating the best damn ribs he's ever tasted. I want him to strip me to the bone and sop up my juices with a piece of white bread.

"I don't know if I should tell you what I want." I gently pull my feet away from him and wiggle my toes, trying to rid myself of the tingly feeling.

"I bet I can guess." He kisses me again.

"I bet you can." I laugh.

"So if you want what I think you want, and I want what you think I want, what's keeping us from doing what we think we want to do?"

"Because I don't want to do it tonight."

"You're such a liar." Jeremy grabs my feet and threatens to tickle them.

"Don't you dare." I snatch my feet away and jump up, practically running for the front door. "You have to leave." I yell from the foyer.

"So soon?" He yells back.

"Get out of my house." I'm trying to sound serious but laughter is erupting from me, making any threat I make sound like a pitiful joke.

He walks into the foyer with the confident swagger of a man who has just accomplished his mission.

"Are you sure?" He asks tracing the outline of my jaw with his index finger.

I have to fight to keep my eyes open as he leans in to try kissing me again.

"You've gotta go." I slip from his embrace and open the front door, practically pushing him out.

He turns around to speak, possibly to say goodbye, but I slam the door in his face, unsure of how much longer I can resist him.

"Just call me tomorrow, ok?" I call through the door.

"No." He says back.

No the hell he didn't just tell me 'no'. I fling the door open only to find myself staring into his smiling face.

"Gotcha." He pulls me into his arms for a kiss that has enough heat to burn my panties off without leaving one charred stitch.

Weakly, I watch him walk off of my porch and down the sidewalk humming to himself while I can barely stand without leaning against the doorframe. I slam the door...hard. Of course, I want to open the door again as soon as it slams close. I want to open that door and invite him in. I want to invite him back into my home, onto my staircase, into my bed, into my...

"Damn it all to hell." I slide my hand away from the knob and instead, engage the deadbolt before setting the security system. There is still, at least, one tiny part of me that has some semblance of control.

I need to regroup. I need to get a firm hold on this situation before I forget who the hell I am. I need to talk to myself. I need to slap myself in the face and give me a proper scolding but I'll be damned if I'm not as speechless as an atheist having an orgasm, not quite sure who to call out to. How in the hell did this happen? How in the hell could I have allowed it to happen? I'm Orchid Maya Ishmael, dammit! I'm the woman who gives advice to the confused and lonely hearted. I'm the feisty diva who doesn't need a man to complete her. I'm the woman who can flirt with the best of them and throw attitude like no other so what is it about this man that makes me so...weak? And he knows it. He knows what he's doing to me and he's doing it on purpose. He's challenging my authority. He's challenging my psyche. He's challenging everything that makes me...me. It's a challenge I can't help but accept.

"Congratulations, Jeremy." I think as I walk up the stairs into my bedroom. "You just made my to-do list."

# Orchid's Nectar
## Book in Stores Fall 2008
## www.EbonyFarashuu.com

## Acknowledgements

First and foremost I want to thank my Lord and Savior JESUS CHRIST for I can do ALL things through CHRIST who strengthens me (Philippians 4:13).

I want to thank my mother and father, Albert Nash and Patsy Nash for loving me, raising me, and always believing in me...even when I didn't always believe in myself.

My husband, soul mate, lover, and best friend, Darrell Raye Taylor Jr. – What can I say? Not even a divorce could keep our hearts from re-connecting. (smile) I love you more today than I did yesterday and I'll love you more tomorrow than I do today! You are truly my King and you will always be my baby...be my baby...be my baby.

My children- Kannon Karon Taylor and Darrell Raye Taylor III. Everything I do, I do for you!

My sisters Kiona Tyler and Diona Drew, you used to annoy me but as we grew up I learned that not only do I love you as sisters, but I also love you as friends!

My sister-cousin Karon Kay Cain - I love you so much I named my daughter after you!

Willetta Terry – God truly blessed me when he placed you in my life. So many people complain about their Mother-In- Law...but I simply consider you my 2nd mother! I love you!

Barbara Taylor – Thank you for being there to pray, to listen, and to encourage!

Leonard Hancock– You've always been there for me and I will always love you!

Sisters Sippin' Tea Literary Group! Thank you for embracing and supporting me throughout the years! I would especially like to thank our founder Wilhelmenia Williams. I would like to give an extra special thanks to the Tulsa Chapter of Sister's Sippin Tea – Sharon Haynes, Saundra McGee, Terri Williams, June Brown, Mary Walker, LaTricia Rose, Rhonda Thomas, Maryam Ali, Yvette Phillips-Theard, Alicia Latimer, and Deborah Boykins. I would also like to thank Cathy Bausley. You are my mothers, my friends, my editors, and my confidants, but above all, you are my sisters!

My best friend, Kelli Little of Keligraphy Studios! You are like a little sister to me and I cherish our friendship!

S. James Guitard, thanks for all of your encouragement, motivation, and words of wisdom!

My agent, Jeremy Braggs of Braggs Literary Agency. Thanks for believing in me!

Cedric Mixon and the staff of Kobalt Books! You gave me a chance when no one else would! I will never, ever forget that!

My brother, Derrick Taylor Sr. a*k*a DEETEE... You are a shining star and I am proud to know you! "ALREADY!"

Darrell Taylor Sr., Sylvester Terry, Denise Jones, Aunt Buffy and Aunt Sylvia, Aunt Gerry, Pa Pa Willie Cornelious, Tannika and Travor, My nieces and nephews, Kierra, Derrick Taylor Jr., Ryan, Shane, Kullan, Knyiah, Lauren Danielle, Alex Jr., Aubrey, Durien, Gabriel, Noah, Travor Jr., and Kalel. The Nash Family, especially my aunts and uncles: Delores Smith, Sylvia Wilson, Evelyn Marks, Nathaniel Nash Jr, Eddie Nash, Delbert Nash, Ella Redricks, Daryl Nash, and Nadine McQuarters! My cousins Michelle Nash and Tiffany Nash-Robinson: THE best familial publicity a cousin could ask for! The Williams Family, especially my Uncle Larry Williams, Grandmother Dorothy Williams, Uncle Dewayne Williams, and Aunt Phyllis Smith, Aunt Ora Williams, and Sonita Williams! Christal Jordan- Mims: My partner in crime! Travis Hunter: Thanks for all of the great advice! Terry Williams: we only met once but your words touched and encouraged me! Karen E. Quinones Miller: Thanks for being there! Omar Tyree: Thanks for the motivation and granting the interview that officially got me started on my journalistic path! J.D. Mason, you're an honorary member of Tulsa SST! Marlive Harris, Thanks for the inspiration and opportunities! My SOUL CITY AUTHOR FAMILY: Gena L. Garrison, Ronald Hanna, Cheril N. Clarke, Corey Whitsett, Nyne Elementz, and Richard A. Parks Jr. My SOUL CITY FAM: Kevin Mills, Eric and Maggie Brown, Janita Diggins, My future son-in-law Noah Shelton (smile), Sandra Poole, James and Yolanda Andrus, Lynn Womble, Napualokelani Wiley, James J. Johnson, George Mattison, Neahle Jones. Jamile Grandison, Derrick Cotton, Ralphlia Whitsett, Kandyss, Rufus Ayeni, and Keenan: I promise not to tell anyone that you're a nice guy! Syncere, thanks for keeping me laughing! My good friends Lorenzo and Connie Holmes and family, Brenda George and family, Brian Pointer, Shayeon Senters, Grace Howard, Marsha Johnson who read the very first draft of this novel! CoCo Jones, Aaron Bernard of KJMS 105.3, Reggie (Jay Jay)... thanks for putting my poetry on the radio! TaNisha Webb of the KC Girlfriends Book Club...THANK YOU for your honesty and for your insight! Special thanks to Maya Azucena and LuQuantumLeap, the gorgeous models who grace the cover of this book! Greenwood Cultural Center! Charlie Redd of The Full Flava Kings, thanks for putting me on stage! To my Spoken Word Family, Miko, Angelique, Brother Ivan, Tony, and anyone who ever graced the stage at WORD on Greenwood! I know that I have probably forgotten someone...If so...please pencil your name in here_____! Charge it to my head and not to my heart!

Last but not least...I would like to thank someone whom I have never met, but your music played a major role in my decision to be a writer. I am sure this will get a few snickers from those who truly know me...(smile) but I couldn't have written this book without the inspiration I received years ago from Al B. Sure! Hey Christal...remember the days of camping out in each other's rooms listening to New Edition and Al B. Sure! And writing until our fingers hurt? Let's trade notebooks!

To anyone who has ever bought one of my books, told someone about my work, attended an open mic, or encouraged me to pursue my dream...I thank you from the bottom of my heart!

**E.F.**